THE
DEATHSNIFFER'S
ASSISTANT

BY KATE McINTYRE

A Division of **Whampa, LLC**
P.O. Box 2160
Reston, VA 20195
Tel/Fax: 800-998-2509
http://curiosityquills.com

ISBN 978-1-62007-908-9 (ebook)
ISBN 978-1-62007-909-6 (paperback)
ISBN 978-1-62007-910-2 (hardcover)

To Elzie
Who I love more than anything
Who is always there for me
Who magically knows just what I need
Who has changed my life more than she'd ever believe
And who is going to kill me for writing this

TABLE OF CONTENTS

PROLOGUE

I f you listen to certain voices in this city, we're all about to die,"
Michael Buckley declared.

The gathered crowd laughed in delight.

Michael raised his hand, calling for quiet. "Now, now," he
soothed. His voice projected out to the whole of the grand
ballroom. "It *could* happen!" He put a bit of mock consternation
into his voice.

Another titter of laughter went through the upper crust of
Darrington City society, all dressed in silks and satin and studded
with diamonds and pearls.

"The reformists want to be right so badly they could lose their
minds! They could pour through those doors, armed to the teeth,
howling about hubris! Firing their pistols and freeing elementals!"

Jewels glinted as heads tilted in merriment, and Michael Buckley
chuckled. "Of course, I highly doubt they'd have the courage, after
how soundly we've sent them all running with their tails between
their legs."

Five hundred of the most important men and women in Tarland
burst into wild applause. Beside Michael, his wife, Julia, reached up
and gripped his elbow.

Michael half-turned, indicating the bubbling champagne
fountain on the table behind him. That sparkling crowd fell into
silence once again, following him with their eyes. The fountain was
as tall as a man, and it glowed with an unearthly, azure light.

Turquoise sparks fell in bursts, and when Michael turned his attention to it, he felt the tiny tug of its reluctant inhabitant in the back of his mind. A cascade of those glowing motes sparked off the fountain at the exact moment he felt her try and break free of her bonds.

Imprisoned elementals were rarely complacent companions.

Oh, calm yourself. He directed the thought at that bundle of furious awareness as he took two empty champagne flutes from the table. One, he handed to his wife, and the other, he held up to the crowd with a flourish. "Tonight," he said, letting his voice carry, "we celebrate the finest moment in Tarland's history since two centuries ago, when Richard Lowry taught us all that *magic* is an outdated notion from an antiquated time. It isn't *magic* that has made tonight and all its wonders possible! It's hard-working, bright Tarls who never believed for a moment our way of life could fail us."

They hung on his every word, and why not? He'd seen Darrington's best and brightest all crowded around the windows, looking down and *oohing* and *aahing*. This ballroom with its marble floors, vaulted ceilings, sparkling chandeliers and grand staircases drifted effortlessly above the city. To the people both above and below, it seemed as though a shimmering cloud supported their flight. The tiny lights of Darrington winked and twinkled below, a world away. Who could blame these people for their wonder? Nothing like this had ever been done before.

He smiled.

"So many of you made tonight possible," he continued. "The seeshifters and your glamours to turn dust to gold! The gearsetters and your clever minds, designing all the mechanisms! And even the ironcutters, those manual labourers! That's the society we advocate, the society the reformists have no respect for. One where everyone has value." He paused for a moment, not wanting to undermine the words he'd just said, feeling pride swell in his chest. "But," he continued, "of course, the real champions of this night are the spiritbinders and their amazing creation, a network of sylphs bound as one! I may not be one of the pioneers who made this wonder possible, but though my contributions were small, I am proud to share my categorization with brilliant progressives like them! Someday, my own lovely daughter will join those ranks. Listen not to the doomsaying of the reformists. Our future will be bright and glorious!"

At that, he turned and dipped his flute into the burbling moat at the base of the champagne fountain he had created. "Thank you, little water princess," he murmured to the undine trapped within.

The cerulean nimbus pulsed dangerously, and Michael chuckled.

When he straightened and turned back to the crowd, he held the glass aloft and raised his voice in an exultant cry. "Ladies and gentlemen of Darrington! Join me in raising your glasses as we celebrate our greatest modern accomplishment—the Floating Castle!"

Five hundred glasses rose in unison, and Michael turned to clink his against Julia's…and stopped.

The liquid within his crystal flute was trembling.

He stared, brow furrowing. The Floating Castle was built to be as steady as a building with a concrete foundation. The liquid should be still as a quiet lake at morning.

A murmur went through the crowd. His wife looked up at him, her eyes wide. "Michael?" she whispered. "Is something—"

The floor moved.

The musicians stopped playing their soft, triumphant tune and lowered their instruments. Wives took a step closer to their husbands. Julia gasped, hugging his elbow tighter.

In that corner of his mind, the undine danced.

The floor shifted again, hard enough half the guests stumbled. Julia gave a startled cry and Michael darted forward to catch her in his arms. Sounds of alarm rose around the room. His gaze flew up to the crowd, all staring at him, waiting.

"Ahh," he said.

Julia clung to him so tightly he couldn't turn away from her to give them his full attention.

"Everyone," he continued, trying to sound confident and fearless despite the way his stomach had dropped, "if you could all just wait a moment, I'm sure this is—"

Then the floor heaved and everyone screamed. Over the sound of growing panic, a voice bellowed, shocking Michael cold. He raised his eyes to see Edward Edison, the leader of the Floating Castle Project, waving his arms from atop the grand staircase.

"The net is compromised!" he howled. "The sylphs are breaking loose! Everybody out, everybody get out! Get out *now!*"

And then, pandemonium.

The panicked guests tore off in all directions like a spooked herd. Women tripped over their skirts and were trampled by the men accompanying them. Everyone was screaming, shouting, crying.

Michael seized Julia, struggling to keep terror at bay. "Stay close," he commanded.

He felt her nod against his chest. Her body was rigid as steel.

His eyes scanned the room. People scattered and only Edison's *"It's collapsing! Everybody, now!"* could be heard above the stampede.

"Michael..." Julia keened, shuddering against him. "Michael, we—"

"Quiet," he commanded and she went silent. He caught sight of one of the service exits, concealed behind an intricate ice sculpture glowing with the silver light of a bound fiaran. "There," he said, and grabbed Julia's hand tightly in his. He dropped his flute to the ground and it shattered, golden liquid splattering against marble. "We go there."

The undine's mental laughter followed after him as he fled.

They threaded through the swarm. The floor heaved once again, sending them staggering, but they regained their footing. While others bolted in all directions and crushed one another to reach the main doors, Michael and Julia moved with purpose toward the hidden exit. When the floor lurched again, Julia stumbled and fell, but Michael pulled her to her feet.

"Stay with me, Jewels," he ordered. "Stay with me."

Her face was streaked with tears, cosmetics running everywhere, but she nodded.

They reached the door and Michael braced himself to push the ice sculpture aside. It was heavier than expected, and so cold his fingers stuck to its surface. Pain burned through his fingertips and he panicked.

He shoved the damn thing.

It hit the ground with a *crack* and frozen shards scattered across the marble floor. Michael watched in horror as its silver glow flickered and then went out. A tiny figure, sheer and ghostly white, appeared with a puff of crystal snow and a sound like shattering ice. Michael held Julia close, but the fiaran had no interest in her dubious saviours. She streaked off into the crowd, a white trail following her like misted breath on a winter morning, and her cruel laughter sounded like tinkling icicles. She sent a blast of freezing air after a fleeing man, who didn't even have time to scream before he hit the floor and shattered like glass.

Julia shrieked and gagged, averting her eyes. Michael only wished he could. He'd caused that. If he hadn't lost control of himself—

The Castle gave a sick lurch. One of the bannisters on the great staircase cracked. He snapped out of his horror. The Floating Castle was falling, and they had to get out.

He turned away from the ruins of the shattered man and tore open the door, yanking the stupefied Julia after him. Five sets of stairs to get down to the base level, and then a mechanical staircase that could be lowered to the ground. He started down the white, stark service stairwell, pulling Julia behind him.

The Castle careened sharply to one side and they tumbled down the steep staircase like toys, balls of limbs and hair.

Everything went black.

Michael came back to himself at the landing. His head pounded and when he raised a shaking hand to it, it came away bloody. He stared at the dark smear on his fingers. What had happened? Where was he?

"Michael!" Julia stared down at him, framed by sterile white walls.

It all rushed back. The Castle. The Castle was falling. He sat up straight, fully alert, and she pulled him to his feet, sobbing all the while.

The floor quaked and pitched as they clung to bannisters and flew down the stairs. One flight. Two. Three. Michael allowed himself to hope. The salvation of that simple mechanical ladder hovered before him like a holy symbol. They could make it out. They could walk away from this. They were so close.

"Julia," Michael panted. "We're going to make it. I swear to you, we are going to go home and hold Chris and Rosemary in our arms."

"Michael," Julia said, but whatever words she'd prepared would never fall on living ears.

The Floating Castle shuddered then, trembling like a terrified child. He heard the singing of the sylphs even through the walls, the glorious scream of the wind in a tornado, wild and beautiful.

They broke free of their prison, swirled into the starry sky, and the Castle fell.

The last thing Michael Buckley knew before they hit the ground was the exultant, echoing song of the bound undine in the back of his mind. *Free*, she sang, *free*.

CHAPTER ONE

Christopher Buckley heard the song when he reached the last stair, and his heart stopped.

Somewhere nearby, water was bubbling, ceramic and silverware were clattering, and loudest of all, two female voices were joined together in song. One of the voices was girlish and innocent, the other, experienced and throaty. They curled together like braided locks of hair. It was an ancient song, a binding song, and none of its words were recognizable as any more than an arcane incantation.

"Dammit," Chris breathed. He pushed the door to the dining room open with a trembling hand, breaking into a run as he headed towards the kitchen. "*Rosemary?*" he cried, throwing open the door to the kitchen.

Rosemary stood by the washtub scrubbing at a pot, face lowered close to the turquoise undine sitting on the edge of the tub. Chris's petrified rebuke died on his lips, his hand went limp on the latch of the door, and he found he could only watch, caught up in the spell of the song as though he were an elemental himself.

The undine's indigo hair moved as though she were still underwater, curling up into the air and waving in time with the music. Her azure skin glowed and it shone wetly in the light. Her dainty feet dangled over the side of the bin and her arms cradled the small jar she held in her hands—the tiny, eternal source her water sprang from. She smiled: a warm, kind, seductive sort of smile, and that observation was enough for Chris to shake his head and snap out of his trance.

"Rosemary!"

He regretted speaking at once. Rosemary jumped and whirled to face him, but so did the undine. Rosemary was more capable than he gave her credit for, however. She never missed a single note. She held up a finger, flashing him a pointed glare before turning back to her little blue captive. Her song changed and the undine shrank away, her face growing sullen and angry. Rosemary's voice swirled upwards and upwards and the undine's expression grew darker and darker. When the song hit a crescendo, the spirit burst into a shower of raindrops. The wash bin pulsed and then blinked into a glow the same turquoise of the undine's skin, and the water within it bubbled merrily.

"Rosemary," he repeated, only this time it was a sigh of relief.

"I was fine," Rosemary pronounced. Even after all these years, he was amazed she hadn't even put down the plate she washed. She set it aside and a jet of warm air erupted from the spinning crystal above the drying rack, blasting away the water.

"Is she secure?" Chris asked, shooting a nervous glance at the glowing wash bin.

"Of course she's secure!" Rosemary sniffed, her brows pulling down over her nose. "I'm not stupid!"

He managed a weak smile. "Of course not. If you were stupid, you wouldn't be able to unbind an elemental just to have a little visit. *Reckless*, though…" He tried to make himself relax. His heart hammered in his throat, but at least they were no longer at risk of drowning in their own kitchen.

She sighed, reaching down into the bubbling bin for another soiled dish. "I had it under control, Chris." Her expression went distant, a sad curve touching the line of her mouth. "They just get so tired of being chained to sinks and pipes and tubs, you know.

Sometimes…they just want to come out and sing for a minute. Wouldn't you?"

"And when one gets loose and sets half of the city on fire?"

"It was an undine. They don't *burn* anything," she retorted.

He took in her flashing blue eyes, flushed cheeks, and wet forearms, her hands still scrubbing away. Her long, jet-black ringlets were all pulled stylishly up away from her pretty doll's face, but her blue dress was twice as threadbare as his own clothes, and almost as desperately out of fashion. He walked over to lay a hand on her shoulder and felt her melt beneath his touch.

He reached up to touch her hair. "Remember what Father used to say?"

Her shrug was only halfhearted, but he knew she did, and after a moment she answered him.

"No matter how smart you are, the rules still apply to you."

"Just be careful."

"I'm always careful!"

If you're doing it in the first place, you're not being careful enough. There was no point saying it out loud. What could he do? He was her brother, not her father. It wouldn't solve anything to make himself the enemy.

She pulled away from him eventually, setting yet another dish into the bin where the chained sylph hit it with another blast of air. She shot him a look over her shoulder. "You look nice," she said, sizing him up with a quick glance and a shy smile.

He didn't. It had been five years since he'd had something new tailored. Considering he had been fourteen at the time, it might as well have been twice that long. It would take a perhaps impolitely intent eye to notice his coat was a little threadbare around the elbows, or that the weathered seams of his trousers had been mended by an inexperienced hand in a mismatched thread, but the flaws were there. Even so, the part of him that used to have four wardrobes full of the latest fashions couldn't help but bask in the empty compliment. He grinned, bashful.

"Well," he murmured. "I did my best with what I had."

"Oh, he's going to be *so* impressed with you, Chris! You're going to do so well. I'm *sure* he'll request your services permanently."

She was lying for his sake again. How could she possibly know what the mysterious *O. Faraday, Deathsniffer* wanted from an employee? But his jangled nerves eased. Rather silly, how the uninformed comments of a thirteen-year-old could make him feel better about anything, much less something so serious as an interview for employment after a long string of rejections.

"We'll see." He patted her on the shoulders. "I thought, perhaps—" He heard a door close from a few rooms over, and the bell in the hall begin to chime. "Oh. That must be her," Chris said. He leaned down to press a kiss into Rosemary's hair.

His sister twisted her head around to catch his eyes with her own before he could go to greet their guest.

"Don't you think I'm too *old* for a nanny?" she asked plaintively.

He half-smiled and touched her nose. "You're thirteen and I just caught you singing down an undine in the sink."

Even she had to smile, though she turned back to the sink to try to hide it from him. "Well," she said, voice dripping with feigned indignation. "Good luck, I suppose."

"I'll be home before you know it." He left her at the tub.

The tutor in question was a tall, slender woman with a prim brown bun pulled up behind her head. He noticed she was dressed respectably—if unspectacularly—in a simple grey gown. It had not been tailored to her dimensions and it was twenty years out of fashion. She was poor or oblivious to her image, then. She was also considerably younger than he had expected. This was hardly an experienced matron, well-versed in the many pitfalls of child-rearing.

Chris fought down a wince. The agency he'd contacted to employ her services was a meager one. Fernand had insisted Chris couldn't afford to give Rosemary the best available, and, after being shown a report of the Buckley family finances, he'd reluctantly been forced to agree. He tried to smile.

She gave a tight nod and did not smile back. "Good morning. Mister Buckley, I'd assume?"

"Yes. A very good morning to you, as well." Chris widened his smile, but it felt very silly in the face of her cold composure, and so he wiped it off his.

"And where is *Miss* Buckley this morning?"

Chris turned and pointed in the direction of the bubbling water and clattering plates. "She's in the kitchen. You'll find she's a good girl, and I think...I need to go." The last part came out ruder than he'd intended, but he'd glanced up at the twisted hands of the grandfather clock halfway through the statement and had to swallow a moan at the time. He turned back to the governess, trying to hide his distress. He tried to be minutes early for every appointment, but would be lucky to arrive ten minutes *late* for Mister Faraday.

The governess didn't seem to notice his curtness. "I see, of course." She stretched a hand toward him. "Rachel Albany, by the way. It's a pleasure to do business."

"Yes, charmed, Miss Albany." Chris took her hand. She had a good, firm grip and he found himself more willing to trust her. "She...*can* be difficult." He felt the sudden need to warn her. "She really can, I'm afraid, but...once you start to get a sense for how she is..."

Miss Albany gave a small, tight smile, the first hint of one he'd seen. Despite the lack of generosity in the gesture, he felt it was sincere. "As I said, Mister Buckley. I'm not worried. I have a way with people, you'll find. I wouldn't be doing this if I didn't."

Really. Well. If her way with all people was as charming as it was with him, he feared for everyone who crossed her path. "No, I suppose you wouldn't." He released her hand, stepping away from her. "Well...good day, then."

"Good day, Mister Buckley," she said, and swept past him without a glance back, her attention fully focused on the girl she had yet to meet.

He desperately wanted to linger and see if Rosemary was well in hand with this tightly laced woman and her horrible shoes, but another quick glance at the clock was enough for him to abandon the notion. He scurried out the door and started down the walk.

A soft flutter of wind touched his face and hair, telling him he'd passed through the soundshield. A moment later, a cacophony of noise blasted him. Voices called, animals brayed, bells rang. A winged carriage soared close to the gate of their yard, carefully avoiding the borders of the soundshield; its great, swan-like wings flapped lazily as the car glided smoothly through the cloudless sky. People passed by on the sidewalk before him: an elegant woman riding sidesaddle on a snowy white horse, with a large black feather bouncing above her hat; a father hurrying along with a glower on his face, his tie and bowler hat askew, two shouting children hanging from his arms. A gold-trimmed black carriage rattled by, pulled by a majestic pair of turquoise and orange hippogryphs, their wings bound so as not to rip their harnesses—or worse, lift off the ground and try to fly, leaving the passengers to tumble about as the carriage dangled helplessly below.

If the papers were to be believed, the city's dark corners, ripe with unpleasantness, were spreading. Employment was difficult to come by, hard workers were dismissed daily, and poverty grew and grew in the face of national crisis. But he saw none of that here. In the past ten years, the land that had once belonged to the Buckleys had become one of the cleanest, most respectable neighbourhoods in Darrington. Despite how he was inclined to gaze longingly at paintings from when his ancestral home had been an idyllic country estate, the chaos filled him with a strange sort of pride. Perhaps it was because he thought his father would have been pleased. *Progress.* That had been what mattered most to Michael Buckley.

Chris pushed open the iron gate and stepped into the busy street. He flagged a taxicab pulled by a twin pair of well-bred grey palfreys, their steps light and elegant.

The driver tipped his hat down at Chris. "Where to, sir?"

He didn't remember. Chris fumbled in his pocket, holding up one finger to request the man wait. There had been an enclosed business card in the response he'd received by mail, inviting him to this interview. He found it now, pulling it out. *O. Faraday, Deathsniffer*, it read, and then, beneath that...

"Corner of Tenth and Regency Street," he parroted off the shimmering writing.

"Something in the way of ten royals, that."

Chris slipped the card back into his pocket and pulled out the wad of notes from inside his waistcoat. He held them up to the driver, showing he could pay. "When we arrive," he said politely. He'd been scammed before.

The driver jerked a thumb back towards the car with an easy grin. Chris liked him. "All right, pretty boy, get up and get in then."

It seemed like barely an instant before the hackey rolled to a halt and the driver was calling back at him.

"Ten royals, then! Don't dally!"

They were in a quieter part of the city now, though sound still assailed his ears. He handed the notes to the driver, his attention mostly taken up by the modest building they were parked in front of. A well-tended sign in front declared this was the *Office of O. Faraday, Deathsniffer*. The structure itself was austere in design and presentation...except for the grey fog hanging artfully around it, clinging to every corner, curling up around it like a nest of wispy grey snakes. An illusion spun by a seeshifter, obviously, but the question in Chris's mind wasn't how, but *why*? There was enough of a bad air around the title *Deathsniffer* as it was. The way Mister Faraday seemed to embrace rather than shy away from the label was remarkable in itself.

What was the point in making the office even more ominous?

The driver squirmed as he took the notes, licking his lips and regarding Chris as if he were a dog, equally likely to wag its tail playfully or bite his hand off. Gone was the easy smile, replaced by a reverent sort of distaste. Chris darted his gaze from the cabbie to the sign, and then let out an uneasy chuckle.

"Oh, no no, it's—it's not me," Chris explained in a rush. He pushed up his spectacles and straightened his threadbare coat, trying to make himself look more...respectable. *Normal.* "Christopher Buckley. I'm...I'm just a wordweaver."

"Huh." The driver folded the notes, slipping them into a pocket. "Someone you know meet a sad end, sir?"

No more teasing "pretty boy," for him, then. "N-no, it's nothing like that." Chris smiled briefly, but the driver didn't return it. "It's...I just...hope to be in his employ, that's all. We all take work wherever we can find it in this day and age, don't we?"

The driver was clearly unsure of what to think of that response. He nodded once, tight and uncomfortable.

"If I do...ah, maybe we'll be driving this way together again?"

"Maybe so." The man slid his gaze away from Chris's. He flicked the reins over the backs of the horses and the carriage lurched into movement again, starting off down the cobbled street.

Chris watched after him with a twist of worry in his gut. Would he find that cool sort of reception from everyone if he were offered this position?

But then, he couldn't forget the rejections from a dozen other offices that couldn't afford to pay the wage he needed, and seemed incredulous he would even ask. Mister Faraday had advertised an exorbitant sum for a simple clerical worker in his newspaper advertisement. Chris's lips twisted. Stigma or no, he was on the cusp of graduating down from a pauper to a beggar, and beggars couldn't be choosers. Better to relish whatever flimsy illusion of choice he had left.

He sighed, then turned up the stone-tiled walk.

CHAPTER TWO

I nside the lair of the Deathsniffer, it was dark.

There were no windows. Most of the illumination came from flickering, old-fashioned candles scattered around the room. Their unpredictable light sent shadows dancing across every surface. A door in the far wall led off further into the building. There was a desk pushed against the same wall and several armchairs set up like a waiting room, but there was no one doing any waiting today. The room was empty of all life, and he couldn't hear so much as a flutter of sound from deeper inside.

He walked over to one of the chairs, experimentally prodding one of the arms. It was soft, and well-upholstered with a luxurious velvet covering. Mister Faraday didn't cut corners on details, then, not even when money was on the line. Chris stood for a moment, wondering what to do, and then he slid into the chair. This, too, was followed by an awkward period of waiting, but no one appeared.

He reached for the newspaper on the small, elegant tea table beside him.

SHORTAGE OF HIGH LEVEL SPIRITBINDERS LEADS TO RISING PRICES IN DARRINGTON, the headline shouted in bold black print, and then, smaller, in a forgotten corner of the page, *Dr. Francis Livingstone's Alternative Technologies Meet With Heavy Resistance.*

Chris swept his eyes over the words, and then turned to the Society section, but the words jumped around on the page and he found himself staring blankly down at the writing while his thoughts roamed. He painted the cozy sitting room of their home in his mind, putting a fire in the hearth, adding in his family. His father would have agreed with the Assembly—and its inevitable support by the formidable and powerful Lowry Academy of Proficiency Categorization. He would have told his children that proponents of "alternative technologies" were just Doctor Livingstone's cadre of damned reformists, quick to make assumptions about the future. His mother would have quietly stated, apologetic but firm, that they were only being wise and no one should ever gain too much reliance on any one thing. Rosemary would have sided with father, and together they would have shouted gentle Julia down.

And Chris…Chris would have stayed quiet, like he always did, and his father would have been as angry about it as ever.

Rosemary still went on about "those damned reformists," Father's words in her mouth, while Chris just tried not to think about any of it. It always brought back the taste of vomit in his mouth and the sound of screeching steel and shattering glass.

He heard footsteps. A door opening. He sat straighter, looking up from the paper.

A woman emerged. She was small in stature, miniature looking. It made her stylish, well-made gown look like it belonged to a doll or a child. Her long, unbound, ruler-straight blonde hair swayed like a curtain of water as she took a step towards him, hand falling off the latch. She blinked at him curiously, clasping her hands behind her. "I *thought* I heard someone come in," she said. Her voice was sing-song. "Are you waiting?"

Chris set aside the paper, climbing to his feet with as little urgency as he could manage. He wanted to look composed. Responsible. Adult. "Ah, yes, I'm here for the appointment."

The woman's brow furrowed. "Is that so?"

"Yes. You…" He frowned. "Do you work here?"

"Hmm?" She blinked, then laughed and flicked her wrist. "Oh!

Yes, I do." She narrowed her eyes, looking him boldly up and down. "I'm sorry, just what is the appointment for?"

Chris licked his lips, feeling quite exposed under her piercing, ice-blue eyes. "...I'm a wordweaver? I...I responded by mail to an advertisement in the paper a week ago, like the ad said, and was told to come today, at this time. Am I...mistaken?"

"Oh," the woman said, and then, "*Oh!* Yes, yes, that's *right*, the wordweaver! I'd completely forgotten that was today."

"Should I come in, then?"

She laughed merrily. "Hold your unicorns, handsome!"

He took a deep breath, calming his nerves. It wouldn't do to make a bad impression. This woman was representing his prospective employer. A bad report from her could ruin everything for him.

"Meaning no offense, miss, I've been waiting on you. I think I'm owed that much courtesy, at least."

She stepped to one side and gestured for him. "Fine, fine. Come along."

"Is Mister Faraday not in?"

She folded her arms, frowning slightly at the question. "No, actually, he's not. He's out working on a case. I'm his...assistant, I suppose you could call me. Olivia. I handle interviews and the like, so if you don't mind, please come inside."

There was nothing to argue; he did as she requested.

The hallway beyond was lined with doors and was even darker than the main room, lit only by a single lamp hanging on the wall. An impossibly tiny salamander with a sullen red glow crawled along the inside of the glass. It fixed them with a baleful eye as they passed. Rosemary would have opened it up and let the thing play in her hands while she sang it down. He had to admit, the spirits around their home never seemed quite so resentful as this one did.

"I thank you very much for your time, Miss Olivia," he heard himself saying, going through the practiced motions of courtesy.

"Just Olivia, if you don't mind!" she chirped. "And what was your name again? Christopher something, I think. Butler? Bennett?"

"Buckley."

"Yes, that's right, I remember now! I have a memory like a sieve when it comes to names. And what do you prefer, exactly? Chris? Kit? Chrissy? Oh, that sounds a little girlish, doesn't it? I've heard some use *Topher*, which sounds silly to *me*, but—"

"Buckley is fine," he interjected. "Mister Buckley."

She sighed dramatically. When he turned to look at her, she shot him an amused glance. There it was again, that thinly veiled mockery.

"Now," she said. "I don't care for that at all. I give you a perfectly good opportunity to put aside the tiresome formalities, and yet you immediately grab them back and wrap them around you like a blanket."

Chris struggled not to be stung. He searched for a decent reply, and fell back on what he'd been quoting at Rosemary for almost six years. "My father used to say that rules are what separates men from elementals. That we can only bind them because our order can overpower their chaos. And *I* believe that courtesy is just another layer of rules…and that it's always better to have too many than too few."

"Hmm," Olivia mused.

He thought he'd made an impression. Then she barked a harsh laugh. "What a bunch of poppycock." Before he could react, she brushed past him and pushed another door open.

It revealed a cozy-looking study. Unlike the rest of the building, it was brightly illuminated by light streaming in from grand windows that filled the entire back wall. A large, oaken desk sat in the centre, a rich-looking carpet on the floor, and all the walls were filled top to bottom with books. Everything smelled of leather and paper and ink.

Olivia breezed past him, maneuvering around the desk and plopping herself into the seat behind it. She fumbled with some papers, eyes shrewdly scanning lines of words, and all the while Chris stood just outside the door, waiting helplessly for an invitation to enter.

It seemed as though an hour crawled by before Olivia glanced up, frowned at him, and jabbed a finger at the unoccupied chair in the corner. "Well, don't just stand there like an idiot."

He obeyed, his face heating.

She barely looked up from her pages. "Tell me about your past experience."

Not a good start. "I...don't have any."

Her eyebrow climbed her forehead. "You haven't worked before?"

"No."

"*Never?*"

"...n-no."

"Well, *that's* unfortunate."

"I've only been categorized very recently," he hurried to explain. "I just moved out of mandatory training three months ago."

"Yes, *Mister* Buckley, I can tell. You have the face of a particularly pretty baby."

He felt about a foot tall, and she still wasn't even looking at him. He made a show of straightening to his full height, puffing out his chest indignantly. "I'm nineteen! That isn't so young."

She smirked at her papers. "So say all people too young to know any better."

He bit his tongue down against his protests. He should attempt to foster a feeling of companionship between them. Build a rapport. "My parents died six years ago," he said. "In the Floating Castle Incident. Michael Buckley was my father. You may have heard of him. He was tied to the project?"

She gave no indication of having heard. He pushed on.

"I'm from a long line of talented spiritbinders. Very wealthy. Or rather...well, we used to be. Thing weren't looking so wonderful even before they died, and since then we've been living off savings." He offered a small smile. "It's...been tight, from time to time."

"Mister Faraday isn't interested in your personal history, and neither am I." She dismissed his words with a wave of her hand.

He felt as competent as a fish flopping about on a dock, and just as stupid looking. None of his other interviewers had told him not to talk about himself. Was that why they hadn't offered him a fair wage? Had they all been internally reacting like this woman?

In the time he took to try and pull his face back together, she barely paused, merely kept speaking. "What Mister Faraday *is* interested in is someone who can keep records for him. Can you keep records, Mister Buckley?"

He had a moment of confusion through his mortification. "Isn't that something *you* would do?"

She looked up to flash him a humorless, toothy smile. "I'm not talking about keeping the books, filling out forms, writing official letters—though that will be a part of it. No, what Mister Faraday *really* wants is someone who can transcribe what he's thinking as quickly as he can voice it. He needs someone who can record what's happening *as* it happens, as exhaustively as humanly possible. He can sometimes forget details and he wants to be able to check things accurately later. I'm not a wordweaver. I can't do that."

Chris turned up his chin. "Well. *I* can."

"How fast are you?"

"Fast," he said with some pride. Of all the proficiencies one could be categorized as, wordweaving was one of the basest. The Academy's official stance was that all were equal, but they hadn't even tried to conceal their sympathetic looks when they'd printed his categorization card. Authorized for little more than low level clerical work or rubbing shoulders with rough tradesmen in engraving, it was as menial as one could get. Some wordweavers performed well enough as fiction writers, but it was at the bottom of the authorized profession list—and tended to pay abysmally when it paid at all. Not that it mattered. Chris's creative abilities were nonexistent.

His situation was far from ideal. Michael Buckley would have been ashamed to see his only son categorized as a wordweaver, especially when he'd failed interview after interview for the simplest scribing positions. But if there was nothing else, at least he could say he was *good* at it. He could have one hundred words on a page while others were still on their fifth.

"I'm going to need to see a demonstration." Olivia picked up a pen from the desk and dipped it in ink. It scratched along the paper as she scribbled something down. He hoped it was something flattering. If it was about him at all. "What about your stomach?"

"My stomach?"

"Are you *queasy*?"

Chris frowned. "Not…at the moment?"

Olivia sighed dramatically, laying the pen aside and fixing him with a long-suffering stare. "Mister Faraday works exclusively with *murders*. Brutal and bloody killings. He sees very unpleasant things in his line of work. A strong stomach is absolutely necessary." She arched an eyebrow, smiling. "Do you faint at the sight of blood, Mister Buckley?"

"*No*," Chris insisted, more forcefully than he'd intended. But her voice, that pitch of teasing suggestion…it was like she'd implied he was a swooning lady. He set his jaw. "My stomach is strong enough for whatever Mister Faraday wants me to look at, I assure you."

She smiled devilishly, leaning back in the chair. "I'll just have to take your word for it. Those are really the two most important things, I suppose. Can you handle what you see? Can you work very fast? There are other things that help. Patience with long periods of boredom, being constantly on call, having half a brain to bounce ideas off. But…well, Mister Faraday isn't picky in hiring. He can't really afford to be. This happens *every* time he needs to replace his secretary. Did you know, Christopher? You're the only person to reply to his advertisement at all."

"Mister Buckley, if you please. And, well, that's—" Chris began, and then quickly silenced himself. He gave her a smile to smooth his error down and apologize for his quick words. It felt shaky on his lips.

Olivia tilted her head to one side, sending her hair sliding off her shoulder like a sheet of ice. "That's *what?*" she demanded.

"...That's...well, that's...because he's a Deathsniffer," Chris said hesitantly. "Not just a truthsniffer. He seeks out murders. Only murdrers. Because he wants to, no other reason. And...and if that weren't bad enough—and it is, there aren't many who're going to leap into an arrangement with one of those. Naturally. But...well, but Mister Faraday isn't even shy about *announcing* it. Printed right on his card, in his advertisement, on his sign. 'Deathsniffer,' bold as anything. It makes people *curious*, but"—he shrugged one shoulder awkwardly—"it makes them nervous."

She pursed her lips thoughtfully. "And what about you? Does it make *you* nervous?"

"I'm people, aren't I?"

She beamed like a little girl given cotton candy. "Oh, now, but here you are, standing in this office! How *fascinating!*"

"I need the work," he admitted. "I'm living on a limited supply of money, and supporting my sister, as well. It *will* run out. It's *already* running out. My financial adviser insists I find employment, and fast, or we'll need to sell our family home." He paused, searching for the right words. Olivia watched him intently. "I...I can't say that Mister Faraday's frankness about all of this doesn't make me uncomfortable. It does. Very much. I'm sure you can understand that, Miss Olivia. But I can admire...some bluntness, when it's not just a cloak for being rude. There are plenty of Deathsniffers in Darrington, but they all try to deny it. Pretend they're just normal truthsniffers who just happen to specialize.

Maybe the only one willing to just call himself that is the best." He cleared his throat uncomfortably. "Maybe."

Olivia twirled her pen thoughtfully. "Do you hold Mister Faraday in *contempt?*"

"I think it's an important job that few people really want to do."

Her smile was thin. "Just like...cleaning latrines!" There was a joyous tune to her words, but they were clearly delivered as a challenge.

His nerves clattered and he tried to collect himself. "Not like that. I don't look *down* on it, not at all. After all." He smiled ruefully. "It's a more noble calling than what *I'm* going to be doing."

"But you do realize there's a stigma by association? Every time you're seen with Mister Faraday, every time you walk into this building, every time someone sees you dogging his heels faithfully, they'll all say the same thing. Oh, there he goes. The Deathsniffer's little assistant. You take that stigma onto *yourself*. Don't think you're exempt from it just because you aren't him."

He laughed weakly. "You would know, wouldn't you?" He ducked his head, ashamed. "Miss Olivia, I...I *need* the work. As I said. The rest doesn't really matter, does it? With the state of Tarlish affairs, I can't afford to be picky."

She stared for a very long time. A bead of sweat crawled between his shoulder blades. He was certain she was reading him like only his mother ever could, seeing deep and drawing it all out. He shivered.

Abruptly, she stood up from her chair, grabbing a small, black, leather-bound book. She stepped out from behind the desk and crossed the room. Handed him the book. "Show me how fast you go," she said.

He swallowed the feeling of exposure. "...what do I write?" he asked, flipping open the first page. It was clean and white and empty.

"Anything. Describe the room. Describe me! Or just transcribe your thoughts. To be honest, I absolutely do not care. Just show me you can go as fast as you say you can."

He licked his lips, staring down at the page, and tried to gather his thoughts into order. That was the difficult part, he'd found. He went *so* fast there was barely time to organize or separate what was pouring onto the page, so in the midst of a list of things he needed to get from the market, there was always a wisp of himself stirred in. *Tomatoes, Eggs, Threadwonderifthegirlwill, Milkbethere.* He decided to describe himself, instead of any of her suggestions. It was least likely to contain traces of *just what in the three hells is her problem* or *Gods, why the fog in front?* He built the image of himself up from his reflection as he'd studied it that morning, and then he sharpened the edge of his thought, took a deep breath, and focused it down on the page.

slender blond fairly attractive at least I'm usually called so I think they're probably right always wear spectacles can't see anything far away part my hair down the middle wear it combed down but mother's curls are always getting loose and

always strive for sense of style though clothes are old I present a sense of togetherness to the world or at least I'd like to think I do

dressed in dark trousers dark coat light blue waistcoat white shirt black shoes hats are in style now but don't suit shape of my face only wear occasionally

The words poured out of his head and onto the page in scarcely more than the time it took to blink.

have Rosemary's eyes blue deep both got them from Mother

got most of my looks from Mother, hair color face fine wavy hair eyes and Gods I mi

It was harder than he thought it would be to put together a fair, comprehensive description of himself without delving into thoughts and pouring out feelings. It was all too close to old hurts and personal observations. He sharpened the edge, cut it down to just the image. Just the image in the mirror.

cleanshaven high cheekbones barelyvisible adam's apple slender build short side of average high collar hair cut short combed down look always striving for the right image. nice coats nice pants nice shoes I always try to have nice shoes ohGods in the heavens thenannys shoeswere so awful I thoughtid

He broke away from the page, a flush spreading across his cheeks. Olivia was hunched over his shoulder, staring with interest down at the words. She turned her eyes over to him when she realized he was done, raising her eyebrows slightly. Their faces were very close together. "All done?" she asked.

"Yes," he murmured.

"Now that *is* a crying shame," she said, and drew back from him, plucking the book from his hands as she did so. "I was *so* curious where you were going with that."

His ears burned.

She slid the book onto the surface of the desk and closed it after another moment of study. The whole transcription had taken less than ten seconds, and he'd completely filled a page. *That* had to have impressed her. Her hand lay flat on the cover, then her fingers steepled so it looked like a spider crouched there. She had lovely fingers, like a flutist or a pianist.

"It's a full time position," she said finally, seeming to forget the book. "Be here at this time *every* weekday. You'll be home for dinner, usually, but it could be later. No complaining." She continued to move as she spoke, going back around the desk, dropping into the chair. "Some days, you'll be behind a desk. You'll welcome guests to the office, receive the post, collect the paper, do piles and piles of boring paperwork. That's between cases. But when one comes...well. This *isn't* a job that leaves you in the office. Oh, you should be so lucky." The pen was in her hands again, but she wasn't writing. Instead she was spinning it about with two fingers, juggling it like a fool at a circus. "You'll be following a Deathsniffer around, smelling more death than you can handle and getting every detail of every horrible, horrible thing you see down on paper. You understand all of that...don't you?"

"Yes," he said quickly.

She focused her attention fully on him, then, the pen stilling. "You're *sure?*" she asked severely. "It's something you might want to take a minute to think about, instead of just jumping into." Her expression went mocking. "After all...you're climbing into bed with death, Mister Buckley."

He wondered if this woman had been bright and cheerful and innocent before coming to work for O. Faraday, Deathsniffer, instead of this twisted, arch, difficult to touch creature who didn't seem to notice the strange environment she spent her days in. He wondered if he would be like her in a year, maybe two. Would his smile set people on edge? Would every word be a strange barb? He wondered if he could really afford to bring that home to Rosemary.

And then he had to bottle up a hysterical bout of laughter. Could he really afford not to? The money *was* running out. It was an exhaustible source, and it would be exhausted very, very soon. Fernand had been perfectly clear, and he'd never been wrong before. Their grace period was coming to an end, hard times were ahead, and Chris needed this job.

He had no choice.

"I'm sure," he agreed.

Olivia sat back in her chair and let out a deep breath of satisfaction. She looked as though she'd just finished a grand meal. "All right," she said. "You're hired."

He coughed politely. "Don't you mean to say you'll recommend me to Mister Faraday?"

She laughed. "No," she said. Then sighed and shook her head. A smile spread across her lips. "You see, Mister Buckley, you seem a little naive, so I'm not going to hold it against you. But really, you shouldn't have made such assumptions, and you *should* have put it together as soon as you heard my name. Olivia. O. Faraday." She leaned over the desk to hold out her hand in a pleasant greeting, and the smile widened, feral and cheerful and horrible all at the same time. "Deathsniffer."

CHAPTER THREE

The encounter was still fresh in Chris's mind when he stumbled, dazed, up the front steps of his home. He closed the front door and leaned back against it.

Employment. Finally, at long last, employment.

Employment under a woman who appeared to be mad. Employment with a Deathsniffer who wore the name like a badge of honour. Employment earned in an interview where he had humiliated himself to depths he had hitherto not known he was capable of.

But it was employment.

He closed his eyes. *Be in at 8 o'clock tomorrow, Mister Buckley,* the Deathsniffer had told him, teeth gleaming through her smile. *No later. I'll run you through the ropes, and soon enough you're going to be right at home here.*

The thought was far more unnerving than it was comforting.

He didn't hear the sound of approaching footsteps. In fact, he didn't notice anyone else was in the room at all until he heard a tentative clearing of a throat, and then a tight, professional voice saying, "Mister Buckley. I see you are home."

Chris's eyelids flickered open. The room swam in tones of too-blue and too-white. He blinked and focused his gaze on the horribly dressed woman standing in the alcove off the staircase. The governess, yes. He'd forgotten about her in the face of Olivia Faraday's...everything. He straightened, brushed what may have been a piece of lint off his topcoat, and gave the woman a polite nod. "Miss Albany, yes, of course." She still didn't smile. "You'll be pleased to know I have been offered the job I interviewed for today. Assuming you want it, your position here at the estate can be permanent."

"Ah. Yes," the woman said. "Of course." Her prim nod came a moment too late, and she reached up to push a few loose strands of hair back behind her ears.

For the first time, Chris noticed how pale she was, how her hand trembled ever so slightly as she lowered it back to her side. It seemed quite out of character that her tight bun was anything but immaculately maintained. He frowned. Something had spooked her.

His thoughts immediately leaped to the worst of all possible conclusions. He scanned the foyer, panic rising in his throat. "Where is Rosemary?" he asked. It wasn't like her to not be right at the door the moment he returned from an errand. After all of his previous interviews, he'd had to fend her off with two hands, hiding his disappointment as well as he could. Where was she now? If something had happened to her...

But Miss Albany shook her head. "She is fine," she assured him. "In the kitchen, just where I found her." Her eyes flickered in that direction and Chris saw something pass beneath her carefully maintained expression. Fear...but awe, as well.

That was when he knew what she'd seen.

"...she's not as powerful as she appears," he said. He shifted into the practiced lines with ease. He'd been repeating these lies for nearly six years, after all. *Gods, Rosemary, again?* "Really, it's just minor wizardry. Very minor. She likes to show it off, but her control is mostly an illusion. She has a naturally beautiful voice, is all."

Miss Albany started. She looked away from him. One of her hands reached up to grip the bannister of the staircase towering over them. "I just didn't expect," she said in a small voice. "One never expects to meet a wizard of any sort, but a binding wizard…" She looked back at him and composed herself. "It was just a surprise, that is all. I expected a normal girl."

"She is a normal girl," Chris stressed. He tried as hard as he could to make himself seem dismissive. Flippant. Like someone being gifted with a proficiency before having it awakened in Categorization was a daily occurrence. "She's hardly the first wizard in history, and she won't be the last." When the governess did not immediately reply, Chris peered at her. She stood straight and appeared coolly professional. He swallowed "It's…" he fumbled. She knew now. The last thing he wanted was to make her any sort of enemy. If she told the wrong person…Visions of Hector Combs's lackeys at Lowry flooding into his home to seize his sister flashed across his mind. He struggled not to show his distress. "If this makes you uncomfortable, you can feel more than free to decline the offer and—"

Miss Albany's eyes widened slightly. "*No*," she exclaimed, and then her cheeks flushed red hot. She did not blush prettily. "No," she repeated, with more restraint. "No, Mister Buckley, I would be glad to accept this position. I find myself fond of the girl. She is difficult, but I appreciate a challenge. And times being what they are, she could be a demon from the hells and still be worthy of the risk. Royals are royals."

"Good, I'm glad." Thank all the Gods. He had no attachment to this severe, grey woman, but her response implied she had no intention of making life difficult for the Buckleys. And he hated the thought of sending her back to her agency like an undercooked chicken. "Tomorrow then? Eight o'clock?"

"Eight o'clock," Miss Albany confirmed with another tight nod, and then dipped a shallow curtsey before pushing past him on her way to the door. She wore neither hat nor wrap, but it was a warm spring day, and she would doubtless be fine. Christopher watched

35

her go until the door shut behind her, and then he went in search of Rosemary.

"It was just a dryad," she snapped, her angry footsteps on the stairs like rolling thunder.

"There is no such thing as *just* when you're 'binding in front of people who we can't trust!" Chris yelled after her. He clenched his fists at his sides. "This isn't about what will happen if it gets free, that is an entirely different issue and I have explained this to you a hundred times!"

"That governess you made me have is going to be here every day, you know! I can't just never bind again!"

"It's eight bloody hours a day, Rosemary, even *you* can manage that much restraint!" Chris growled and started up the stairs after her. "Don't walk away from me, young lady! I've explained this to you before! If the wrong person finds out about you, all they need to do is go right to Hector or Avery Combs and they'll have you 'binding for them until you're completely—"

She whirled on him, black ringlets flying. Her blue eyes flashed with fury, and her full lips were folded into a thin, angry line. "*Good!*" she screamed down at him, and they were so close a drop of spittle hit his face. "I hope they *do!*"

And no amount of yelling after her would slow her, not until she slammed her bedroom door behind her and he heard the *click* of the lock.

Exactly a week after he had started working for Olivia Faraday, she came into the office singing.

He'd gotten there first, as he tended to, and he looked up from his desk when he heard the door open. She fluttered into the room dressed in a sunny yellow dress with ruffles and bustle and delicate cloth roses. The colour muted the silver and highlighted the gold in her long hair, which was curled and half-piled atop her head, stray loops cascading around her shoulders. She looked like a virgin princess from a storybook, and right away he saw her mood was verging on euphoric. "Good morning," he greeted.

"Good morning to you, as well, *Mister* Buckley!" she chirped, saluting him. She threw the daily paper onto his desk and then breezed into the back hallway. The door of her office slammed shut loud enough to make the candlesticks rattle and the flames dance. Shaking his head, he turned his attention to the paper she'd flung at him. *FIARAN BREAKS LOOSE, KILLS 3!* the headline read. He quickly turned to the Society section.

Olivia was back in the waiting room only moments later, dancing about from one spot to the next, gathering books and papers, putting some candles out, lighting some others. He couldn't help but clear his throat and raise his voice. "You seem pleased. Did something happen?"

"Yes!" she sang. She didn't turn to look at him, just continued about her business, steps as light as air. "I finished my case, and now I'm ready to start a new one. It's a bright and brilliant new day, Mister Buckley! The sun is shining! The birds are singing! The spirits are flittering about!"

Chris was quite sure the sullen salamander in the hallway wasn't doing any flittering. "I take it you found out who did it."

She made a dismissive gesture, still barely paying attention to him. "Oh, I knew weeks ago. At least. I knew from the moment I saw the body, in fact, but I had to be sure. I always do, unfortunately. It was a good case. A little easy, thought. It really *was* obvious."

Isn't that a good thing? he wanted to ask, but he didn't.

She continued. "Since I ordered the arrest, I've been working on the paperwork. So much paperwork! It's the worst part. I hate it! I'd pay someone else to do it for me, if it weren't illegal. Maris always checks, too. Awful!" Chris didn't have the first idea who Maris was, but he said nothing. Olivia finally straightened, arms full of paper and leather, hair spread all about her shoulders like a lady's fan unfurled. "But now it's done!" she declared. She finally looked him right in the eye. "Oh, happy day."

"Well," he said, "congratulations."

"Thank you," she said sweetly, dipping a shallow curtsey to him. The stack of books wavered, but before he was half out of his chair to help, she had it together. "I'm fine," she said, and turned towards the door. "…hmm, but I may need your help *here*."

"Of course," he agreed. He got the rest of the way out of the chair and moved to the door, grasping the latch in his hand and pushing it open.

"Obviously, if someone comes, let them in, won't you?" she asked, and disappeared again.

He shouldn't have been surprised when he heard the front door open less than an hour later, while he was drinking his morning tea and reading theatre criticism in the paper. Olivia was ready to take a client, so obviously, one came through the door.

The woman who swept into the room looked about with eyes that judged everything she saw the moment it crossed her vision. There were two types of people who did that: those who had ideas above their station, and those who *were* above those they looked down on. Even if this woman had been naked, he would have been able to tell she was in the latter category. The way she held herself, tall and proud, with high nose and rounded shoulders, the way she'd piled her chestnut hair atop her head, the regal beauty of her smooth, elegant features—it was a potent combination. Her elaborate velvet gown was rich burgundy, off the shoulder, trimmed with gold and black, and tastefully bustled at the back. It was all the very pinnacle of style, and it had certainly cost enough to buy a small house. She wore delicate, lace black gloves, a jaunted black hat trimmed with burgundy cloth roses, and held a small black handbag. He'd only just read about lace gloves coming into fashion this morning. Impressive.

"Hello," she greeted him. Her voice was icy and the subtle tones of her accent were quite posh. "How does the day find you?"

"Well enough." He climbed to his feet and dipped a small bow. If his hunch was right about her station, that was the least respect she deserved. "And you?"

"Less so, I'm afraid. I'm looking for O. Faraday. The Deathsniffer. Is he present?"

"Yes—er, *she's* in the back. Shall I get her?"

There was no reaction to the correction. "Please do."

"And what should I tell her you're here for?" Chris opened his notebook and focused down on the page to record her reply.

A moment of silence. Chris looked up to see the fine lady gathering herself. "My name is Duchess Evelyn val Daren, and my husband has been murdered," she said finally, with an edge of steel proclaiming any sympathy would be the highest of offences. "I'd like to know who to blame."

It was moments like this where he was glad for his polished geniality. It allowed him to do nothing more or less than nod once, smile graciously, and say, "I'll see what I can do. If you could take a seat, it will be only a moment."

The salamander flicked a long, forked tongue at him as he passed, a threat or a warning.

"Interesting," Olivia murmured pleasantly around a mouthful of hairpins, barely looking up from her page. Her dauntless white-blonde hair, arranged so nicely an hour before, was now flowing all around her shoulders again. "A noble, you say? Brilliant! I love working with the upper class, they kill each other for the most needlessly dramatic reasons."

She was cheerful, pleased as punch. Murders were for her entertainment, scripted in advance, and she might have been a noble herself, a delighted patron in a box seat, hands clasped in curiosity. He forced himself to continue smiling. "She's waiting in the front."

"Right, yes, I know! I'll be out in just a moment. Let me finish this." Olivia waved him off as if he were a pesky fly.

It wasn't as if he could protest, and so he left, shuffling back to the waiting room. "She'll be with you in a moment," he told the woman, who nodded briskly. She'd taken her gloves off and was studying them closely. For ticks in the lace, which were common to come by and could easily ruin them. He felt sorry for Darrington's ladies with this new fashion.

He slid into the chair at his desk, studying her discreetly out of the corner of his eye. Her meticulously applied cosmetics, the way not a wisp of hair escaped her arrangement, how her skin appeared so smooth as to be ageless...she was flawless. A noble. From the Old Blood, who never had their children categorized, who lived off ridiculous old fortunes, who rarely interacted with common society, and who sat in the best box seats at the best theatres, swathed by black velvet to shield them from view.

He knew the wealthy. Upper society was comprised mostly of families who produced especially powerful spiritbinders. They were immeasurably valuable to Tarland and their bloodlines were treated as sacred as long as they remained so. There was a time when those high, respected names had been Buckley peers. He'd nearly been one himself, and might one day be one in truth, when Rosemary was an adult and could use her abilities without being abused for them.

But the Old Blood were not merely wealthy, not merely high society. They were something else, something so much greater. They were a living relic of a time before Richard Lowry, before the Assembly, before categorization laws. They were Tarland's oldest surviving piece of history aside from the Monarchy itself.

The door banged against the wall. Chris didn't jump. He'd

expected it. "Good morning, prospective client!" Olivia chirped, and he sensed her breeze into the room. "I'm *so* sorry I kept you waiting. *Very* important business. I'm sure my assistant told you."

Duchess val Daren sized Olivia up with one glance, but it was impossible to tell what she saw there from her expression. "Well," she pronounced with deliberate care, "you arrived eventually. I can forgive the first offence."

Olivia swept across the room. She laid a gentle hand on the Duchess's shoulder as she moved past her. The gesture could have been presumptuous and disrespectful considering their gap in station, but Olivia managed to make it welcoming. She dropped into the closest chair. Chris watched, mesmerized by the silent exchange. It was, he realized, the first time he'd seen Olivia interact with someone other than himself, and there was a change about her, a flimsy mask of empathy and *correctness* she had never bothered to maintain with him. He didn't know whether to be offended or flattered.

"Duchess val Daren," the Duchess introduced herself without pomp.

"Olivia Faraday," Olivia said. "I hear there's been a death in the family. My condolences."

"It's been a very…trying day," the Duchess replied. There was barely a hint of emotion in her voice. Chris admired her restraint. "I only just found him. He and I have tea together with our daughter every morning at the same time, and when Viktor didn't—"

Olivia held up a finger at the Duchess and turned her gaze to Chris. "I hope you're getting this down," she said, her gaze accusing. As if it weren't obvious he wasn't.

Quickly, he grabbed his book, flipping it open to the first empty page. He weaved.

tea every morning with daughter wasn't there wife found him

"Please, continue," Olivia said, and then, conspiratorially. "He's new."

41

Chris's ears burned.

"He's never missed a morning before. Not ever," the Duchess continued. "Until then, I'd assumed he was busy in his study, doing *whatever* it is he does, but it was then I knew something must be wrong. Of course, I never expected..."

"No one does," Olivia supplied helpfully.

...found in study never expected...

"He was dead when I went in," the Duchess said with a sad flourish of her voice. "For some time, I believe, because he was quite cold. I quickly consulted a listing and the fact that you were so frank about your unique specialization...well, it gave me hope you could afford that sort of audacity. I've personally found the incompetent don't try to call attention to themselves."

Chris looked up, waiting for Olivia's reaction. She smiled her cheerful, wicked smile and tossed her loose coils of hair over one shoulder. "That's one way of looking at it."

If the Duchess noticed anything strange about the response, she was as good at politely saying nothing as Chris was. She nodded once and dragged the black lace gloves back onto her hands, one dainty finger at a time. "I made haste here immediately, pausing for nothing. As I've never required the services of an investigative truthsniffer before," she continued, as collected as if she were ordering breakfast, "you may instruct me on how to proceed from here."

One corner of Olivia's mouth pulled up slightly at being given permission, as though it were the most audacious thing she'd ever heard, as though this wasn't a member of the Old Blood. "We both sign a contract and then I poke around in your life until I discover who killed him. The contract promises you can't go get a new 'sniffer unless you lodge a formal complaint with the police. It'll be investigated by my supervisor who'll assign you a new 'sniffer. As for me, well, *I* can't throw my hands in the air and be done with you!" She laid an elegant hand on the Duchess's wrist. "Not that I would, of course, I'm sure we're going to be birds of a feather."

The Duchess nodded, considering in silence. "I don't like the idea of you involving yourself in my personal business," she murmured. "There are, of course, private matters of some delicacy in my family, none of which have to do with why Viktor was murdered. I would rather you not—"

"I'm sorry," Olivia cut in. "I understand the sentiment, really I do! Cross my fluttering heart! But you have to agree to let me involve myself as deeply as I personally see fit. I'm not just going to go around being nosy, obviously. There's a method to all the madness! Murderers can be hiding in the most peculiar of places, and drama breeds them like nothing else. I'm sure you can find someone who wouldn't pry. But, well. They wouldn't find your killer. I will."

Duchess val Daren took another quiet moment. While she did, Olivia turned and met his eyes, gesturing with her chin towards the shelves at the other side of the room. Chris understood. He climbed up from his chair quietly, walking over, opening the drawer, searching all the files stacked with paper for the contracts in question. Olivia couldn't organize to save her life, he groaned to himself as he pawed through it all. He should have spent his idle week putting the place together correctly.

"I suppose I can see your point, Miss Faraday," the Duchess concluded, sounding half disgusted, half resigned. Chris flipped through a collection of rental renewal contracts and baffled at the idea of Olivia having a landlord. "But if I believe your interest has tipped towards the 'nosy,' as you say, that *will* be cause for a complaint. My family's affairs are not on display."

"That goes without saying," Olivia said. "And, hmm, just one more thing, Duchess, before we make things official. You may find I won't always bow over to kiss your hand and scrape around your feet. It's just my way, sorry. I think it's better to warn you in advance. I know you're used to that, but, well."

How could she be so…

The Duchess gave another sigh. She was beginning to sound irritated, and Chris did not blame her. "If that is your *way*, Miss Faraday, then I can accept it for the short time we're working together. Please keep in mind, however, any direct disrespect will—"

"—only be used when I think it benefits our business relationship and the discovery of the Duke's killer!" Olivia cut in. "I *do* know how to do my job."

And there it was. *Contractual Business Agreement.* He carefully pulled it from the file, being sure not to bend it.

"…yes, I suppose." A cluck of the tongue. "Very well. I will sign your contract."

"Excellent!" As Chris turned around, he saw Olivia clap her hands together before her, eager as a child served up a bowl of iced cream. "Then lead the way to the corpse, Duchess."

CHAPTER FOUR

Great winged carriages were available only to the most privileged and wealthy. It was a status symbol to even rent one, and Duchess val Daren's own private version was grander than any flying taxi Chris had ever seen. When he looked out the window, he could see the majestic, feathered goose wings beating slowly, then gliding, beating and gliding. They were soaring in and out and up and down and around corners and were barely jostled in the confines of the car. Whenever Chris managed to pull his attention away from the scenery and focus, they would slip past a tower or turn a corner in a wide arc, and his eyes would slide away and back to the wonders gliding past.

He didn't, however, look directly down.

"...nothing," the Duchess was saying dismissively as Chris tried to turn his attention back to his job. "Our family is in excellent standing, you should know. We're invited to every Old Blood affair, our finances are impeccable, our friends are many. We have no enemies."

"Not even the jealous? It seems to me that with you being so grand and excellent, you'd have all sorts of people wanting to add a little misery to your happy life. It's the nature of people."

The Duchess sniffed and judiciously studied her fingertips. "Of course, that's always a possibility when one lives as well as my husband and I, but I sincerely doubt it's the case. Certainly we have our share of envious admirers, but none so delusional as to honestly risk *murder*. Killers tend to get caught, after all, and when they do, it's something of a social suicide."

Olivia tilted her head and leaned back in her chair. She looked like a cat stretching. "Your answer doesn't make sense. You claim someone killed him and then turn around and tell me nobody had any desire to kill him? You can't have it both ways."

"It was a murder," the Duchess said firmly, with stone-hard certainty. "It…" And she faltered slightly, turning to look out her own window. Chris used the excuse to follow her gaze, his heart swelling with wonder as a bird swooped right by them. And then the Duchess sighed, shaking her head and straightening her chin. "It isn't a death he could have made for himself."

"Then someone killed him," Olivia reiterated.

"Yes," the Duchess agreed, "but I can't possibly imagine who."

Olivia shrugged, visibly letting it flutter away. *duchess has no suspects olivia seems to allow that*, Chris transcribed. "Then how was it done?" Olivia asked.

"Excuse me?" the Duchess asked.

"You're so certain he couldn't have killed himself. I find that intriguing! Along with how you still haven't told me how he died or what you saw when you went to his study, I'm fairly sure it's worth hearing!"

The Duchess smoothed folds in her skirts and reached up to straighten her black hat. "I'd really rather not say," she said finally, prim as a well-sewn button.

Olivia snorted, loudly and obscenely. Chris wanted to put his face in his hands.

Clearly, the Duchess agreed with him. Her features went very tight and her jaw bulged. "Is there a *problem*, Miss Faraday?" she challenged.

Olivia chose to ignore the question. "Are you just not going to say? I'm going to see when we get there, you know. It'll be best if I have some context before we start."

"I've had a very trying day, Miss Faraday," the Duchess ground out. Her chin jutted so far forward that her face looked like a crag. "Please have a moment of sympathy. I've lost my husband. My heart is broken."

"I'm sure—" Chris began against his better judgement, but Olivia silenced him with a sharp glance and turned back to the Duchess.

"But you haven't cried," she said. It was an accusation.

"…excuse me?" the Duchess asked, taken aback. Her shock melted into rage in less than an instant and her eyes flashed dangerously. "How do you *dare* to presume whether or not I've—"

"Oh, please!" Olivia interrupted, and continued before the Duchess could regain footing in the conversation. "Here's what I know. Your husband didn't show up for breakfast. You went to his study, you found him, and then you came to see me. Now, I can tell from what sort of woman you are that you wouldn't have gone to breakfast without being fully combed and prepared for the day ahead. I also know your sort eats a little later, so you came to see me immediately after you found the body, judging by what time you arrived at my office. Not to mention your own insistence that you hurried to me as soon as you possibly could. It all tells me one simple fact: you haven't shed a single tear."

"And why is that?"

"Because your cosmetics are perfectly intact."

The Duchess raised a hand to her face instinctively, touching one of her flawless cheeks. Then, "I reapplied."

"Of course you didn't. You expect me to believe it doesn't take you half an hour—at *least*—to do your paints? I know your type, Duchess val Daren."

"Why does it *matter* if I've cried or not? I'm a lady. I don't express that sort of thing. It's utterly inappropriate."

"Normally, I'd agree," Olivia sighed. Her tone was so unbelievably *conversational.* Chris stared down at his page, not sure what to write. *olivia accusing duchess of SOMETHING.* "Tears are so

47

over dramatic. I've never met anyone who cries often I've liked. Histrionics, so ridiculous. But your husband did die, and you did find his body in some condition so horrible you don't want to tell your Deathsniffer about it. If anything warrants a few tears…"

"*What* exactly are you accusing me of?" the Duchess demanded waspishly.

"At the moment? Not crying. We'll revisit the implications of that when I know more."

The Duchess's face went very dark. She looked down to where her fingers were plucking at her skirts, her expression stormy. She said nothing; none of them did. And then, finally, "There have been some difficulties, between Viktor and me."

"Oh, and here it is!" Olivia clapped her hands like Duchess val Daren had just declared they were going to a faire.

"Every marriage has them," the Duchess continued, jutting her nose up into the air.

"So I've come to see," Olivia agreed amiably, "but I'm not certain a lack of tears at your other half's *murder* is all just status quo. Now tell me, exactly what sort of *difficulties* have there been? Don't worry about ruining my opinion of you. There isn't much to tarnish."

The Duchess turned away, petulant, to look out the window. Chris remained focused on his page, *seems to sulk*. The only sound was the great swooshing sound of the carriage's wings pushing through the open air. Then Olivia began tapping her feet.

"Viktor is a devoted patron of the arts," the Duchess said finally. The petulance was gone from her countenance, and now she seemed distant, quiet. Her eyes were looking out the window, but unfocused, staring at something that didn't exist. She stroked her collarbone thoughtfully. "*Very* devoted. He wasn't when we were first married, no, but he had an…awakening, as he grew older, I suppose. At first, it was something I appreciated. Suddenly he had this sensitivity he'd never possessed before. He would find the most talented young persons, those who were just bursting with creativity, and use his means to bring them into the light, immortalize them. I found it all admirable. I thought he'd become the person he'd always been meant to be." She shook her head. Her eyes refocused. She turned away from the window, stared down into her lap, and smoothed out her skirts. "Well, that was a very long time ago, now," she said. "I realized, eventually, that things had changed for good. He could never love me half so much as he loved his up and coming sopranos and actresses and poetesses. It became very difficult to compete, so I stopped trying."

"And came to hate him?"

"I never hated him. I just grew tired of hearing, day after day, about a new painter with the most delicate brush strokes, or a girl with a violin who wasn't even a hymnshaper. A new one every month. They were his life and I was irrelevant."

"Was he sleeping with any of them?"

The Duchess's head snapped up to confront Olivia's only semi-interested and thoroughly unsympathetic face. "That is *horribly* inappropriate and none of your business," she accused, a rough edge in her voice. Chris wondered if she had been about to cry after all.

"It's fully valid."

The Duchess's resistance melted and she pressed an elegant hand to her temple. "I don't think so," she murmured, shaking her head. "I always had my suspicions, what wife wouldn't have? He spent all his time with young, talented, pretty women. But no. He loved their minds, and loved loving their minds. I don't doubt he fell for all of them, but…relations? No, that would have ruined all of the art."

"So you have no reason to think he was?"

"No."

Olivia pursed her lips. "And would any of *them* have reason to hate him?"

49

The Duchess looked genuinely surprised by the question. "...I..." She frowned. "I wouldn't know, to be perfectly honest. I barely ever knew any of them. Though the most recent...well, I suppose I'll leave that for you to decide."

Olivia gave Chris a pointed look and he nodded to her. *duchess doesn't know any of the victim's* He paused in mid sentence, unsure of what to write. *proteges,* he decided eventually, opting for the most tactful of options open to him. *potential killers?* he put underneath, and underlined it.

As they swept under the sprawling blossoms of an apple tree and moved to settle into a carriage house as large as the Buckley estate, Chris tried and failed to take in every detail of the five-story val Daren manor. What he did see set a fire of envy burning deep in the pit of his stomach. The Duchess didn't make a move to leave her seat until the doorman jumped down and opened her side for her. She barely looked at the fellow as she stepped out and alighted on the ground beneath her like a bird on a branch. Olivia followed, and Chris slid across the seat after them.

Duchess val Daren's lovely shoes clicked against the front walk and the Deathsniffer and her assistant tagged along behind almost like dogs dutifully at the heels of their kennel master. Almost. Olivia was far too curious to be a faithful hound. Her gaze snaked about, took in everything and filed it away, and Chris could see the wheels working in her strange head. What was she trying to do, he wondered, solve the case by analyzing the landscaping? He wondered if that was possible. He knew that the abilities of a truthsniffer were about hunches, pattern recognition, subconscious flashes of precognition. Was it as easy as glancing around and just knowing what had happened?

They mounted the stone staircase flanked by two bubbling fountains glowing azure. The Duchess pushed open the oaken front door and they stepped into a sanctum of style.

Chris felt himself dizzy at the level of taste displayed. It was obvious everything there was worth more than his family could have afforded even at their most wealthy, generations ago. But none of it was tacky or extravagant, nothing stood out to say *see how much money changed hands when I came here?* It all blended into mahogany and gold luxury. Chris sighed in utter bliss. He'd have liked nothing more than to lay down in the centre of the floor and fall asleep surrounded by elegance.

"You have a very lovely home," he heard himself saying to the Duchess, awe in his voice.

She spared him a moment's glance before looking away. "Thank you," she said, and then seemed to forget he was there once again.

"Ana!" the Duchess called. She slipped off her black lace gloves, laying them on a polished mahogany table beneath a large, gold framed magic mirror shimmering like snow on a clear morning. "*Ana*," the Duchess called again, impatience entering her voice. She turned to Olivia. "I trust you'll want to meet her?"

"Who is this?" Olivia asked archly.

The Duchess didn't seem to notice her tone. "Lady Analaea val Daren. Our daughter, and our only child."

"For lack of success or lack of trying?" Olivia murmured. If the Duchess heard her, she made no move to show it, and they stood there, once again in silence, while Chris tried to record things in his book that weren't *flawless floors* and *must be hundreds of gold candles in that chandelier.*

While they waited, he constructed an image of what Evelyn val Daren's daughter would look like. He gave her tightly contained chestnut hair like her mother, and a collected, icy countenance. Well dressed, of course, and demure in a proud way. He didn't even notice he was doing it until the Duchess said, "Ah, there," and he looked up to see the girl descending the stairs.

Analaea val Daren was a tall girl, *unusually* tall, with long, straight, jet black hair hanging unbound around her shoulders—not like Olivia's, straight and sleek, but limp and untouched. She was thin, bordering on skinny, with a simple gown draping her like she were a hanger in a wardrobe. Her face *could* have been beautiful, but was devoid of the cosmetics it would need. Her cheeks were red, her eyes swollen.

"Mother," she murmured when she reached the first landing.

"Come down, Ana," the Duchess said, gesturing. "This is Miss Olivia Faraday, the investigative truthsniffer who will be looking into your father's case. Miss Faraday, this is Lady Analaea val Daren."

Olivia inclined her head with such theatricality, Chris was certain she was making fun of something. Everything, perhaps. "It's a *pleasure*, my lady," she said.

The girl nodded, her eyes barely taking Olivia in before slipping to her mother. "I was just leaving."

Duchess val Daren's eyes narrowed. "Where?"

Analaea hesitated. "…Ethan thought I shouldn't stay in the house, with—"

"*Ethan's* here?" The Duchess's voice was razor sharp.

Analaea flinched. It was to her credit she didn't cower outright. "Yes," she answered. "He's waiting in the stable. He thought we could ride. He said it would clear my head. He's bringing his paints with us…"

"Miss Faraday will want to speak to you. I don't think going out would be a very good idea." The Duchess dismissed the matter with finality.

"No, not right away," Olivia said. "Go riding with this Ethan fellow, Lady. To be perfectly honest, I'd rather not have you underfoot during my investigation. I'll question you later if I think I'll need to. When you get home, perhaps?"

"Oh, thank you," Analaea breathed. She didn't wait for her

mother to confirm Olivia's dismissal, but brushed quickly between them to the door, and then vanished outside.

The Duchess let out an angry stream of breath once it closed. "*Ethan Grey*," she spat, shocking Chris with her tone. She had been cold and haughty from the moment she walked into the office, but this was outright acerbic. "She's enamoured with his little drawings and how he pretends to fawn on her. She's so blinded by it she doesn't see *anything* else about him. An *artist* for her, yes, of course. She certainly *is* her father's daughter." She swept past them up the stairs. "Please, do come up, then." Her tone was once again measured and tight. "Viktor's study is at the end of the hall at the top of these stairs. Feel free to leave your coats on the table, there, the butler will be by shortly to deal with them."

Playful, brightly coloured salamanders frolicked cheerily inside the lanterns lining this hall, flicking their long, fiery tongues as the three of them passed. Chris described them in his book as *scaled with yellow blue and violet beautiful creatures*, though he doubted Olivia would have any need of the information.

The Duchess pulled a large brass key from her pocket as they walked along the lush ivory carpeting. "An antique lock on his door," she said. "It was one of his little things, since he turned to the arts. He romanticized the old world before categorization, the time of true wizards and real magic. He couldn't even accept the present, much less the future."

She stopped before a door, considerably more scratched and older than the others, fitting the key into the antique lock. She turned it and it *clunk*ed twice as the tumblers fell. Upon withdrawing the key, she gave it a tiny, sad smile. "It is quaint," she murmured, barely audible. Then she pushed the door open and they stepped through.

Do you have a strong stomach? Olivia's voice echoed in his memory.

Duke Viktor val Daren had been a handsome man in life. That much, Chris could tell. His hair was faintly silvered black; his face was chiseled and smooth. Chris assumed the eyeglasses discarded on the desk in the corner were the Duke's, and they would have suited him very well in a time before he was hanging from the rafters.

Someone had wrenched his arms back behind him far enough to pull them out of their sockets, back and *up*, and then bound them at the wrist. The rope was tied to the rafters and the Duke was left to hang there by the two barely connected threads that were his arms. The sleeves of his simple white shirt had been removed, revealing a long cut from wrist to armpit on both arms. Those wounds seemed clean compared to the long slash sliced across his neck, ear to ear. Blood had burst forth, soaking through the armless white shirt, his waistcoat, and his trousers, splashing on the floor below in a great crimson river.

Hung like a pig in the window of a butcher shop. Chris reached for the wall to steady himself as a wave of dizziness crashed over him. He gulped and fumbled for his notebook. He needed a clear head to write down the most horrible thing he'd ever seen in full, colourful detail.

The Duchess could barely look, and Chris felt the same, but Olivia seemed unaffected. She stepped forward, peering closely, inspecting the body. She walked a circle around it, hands folded behind her back, looking like a buyer inspecting an animal before making a purchase. *Deathsniffer*, he reminded himself. She must have seen worse, though he couldn't imagine it. He wondered what she smelled.

"This is how I found him," the Duchess said, her voice thick. "I locked the door immediately after. I haven't let Ana see, or the servants. This is *not* how I want Viktor remembered. Whatever faults he may have had, he was my husband, and I loved him."

"Have you touched anything?" Olivia asked.

throat opened, knife wound? so much blood feet dangling above ground how could anyone do this Gods there's somuch blood, Chris weaved.

"Nothing," the Duchess said.

Olivia stopped in front of the hanging meat, leaning in close. "You're sure?"

"...yes," the Duchess said.

"And *no one* else has been in here?"

"I am certain no one has."

Olivia sighed. She turned to the Duchess, her face as pleasant as if they were on a morning walk. "When people lie to me," she chirped, "I tend to assume guilt. I've found I'm usually right! This is the *second* time today you've lied to me, Duchess. It's not looking very good for you."

The Duchess met her piercing gaze, and Olivia broke their eye contact to shrug with exaggerated flippancy. "Well, suit yourself. I don't have all day to waste on a staring contest. I'll spell it out for you." She reached out a hand, and, to Chris's utter shock, placed it on the hanging corpse's groin, fingers splayed out. "You see here, Duchess?"

The Duchess said absolutely nothing, though her face had gone grey.

"The blood here isn't like the rest," Olivia said, as though what she were doing was totally natural. And perhaps it was, under the circumstances. "It didn't hit this side of the fabric." And then, before Chris could register what she could possibly mean, the Deathsniffer was tugging at the button, and then the laces of his trousers, opening them up, ignoring the Duchess's sharp intake of breath. She spread open both sides of the opening, and—

Chris turned his gaze away, focusing on the book, his face burning. He couldn't even tell what he was weaving onto the page; he was sure it wasn't anything useful, but it was better than looking.

"Now why would there be so much blood *here* if this was all snug inside?"

"*Miss* Faraday—" The Duchess's voice was shrill with protest.

"Oh, *honestly*, it may have been awhile, but you do have a child together. The secret is out, you've seen it before. Let's not ignore what's *really* important, here."

Duchess val Daren made a strangled sound.

"Did you tuck him back in, then, Duchess? Or has someone else been in the room after all? And recently, oh yes, this was all moved after the blood had dried. The killer couldn't have done it, not unless they came back hours later."

"I—" The Duchess cut herself off in midsentence. "I didn't think it would make any difference."

"*Really?* Why do you think we want to see the place where the crime was committed? For a lark? The scene tells the story of the murder, Duchess, and *really*, this story becomes much more interesting when your husband's ducal willy is hanging out! Come now. You're not a stupid woman."

The Duchess continued to keep her silence, though her breathing was uneven.

"And didn't you just say you had *no* reason to believe he was sleeping with anyone? This would certainly plead otherwise! I find it—"

Finally, Duchess val Daren found her voice. "This family," she said sharply, "is based on appearances. Our place—*my* place in society is entirely dependent on appearing above the common rabble. It's going to be difficult enough maintaining peerage with my husband strung up in his study, butchered like a cow. If anyone should know he died like *this?* The val Daren name would never recover! I act in the interests of my family. Me, my daughter, even Viktor. As soon as *one* person knows he"—she broke off, gathered herself, plunged on—"he was found like this, a tip goes to a reporter and it's in the papers by tomorrow morning. Surely even commoners like yourselves can understand!"

The air hung weighted and clung to everything in the aftermath of the Duchess's outburst. While propriety demanded Olivia respond to such an impassioned show of honesty from a woman who didn't seem prone to either passion or frankness, she didn't.

56

She paced back and forth before the dangling body, and Chris watched her shoes on the hardwood floor, still not daring to look up at the obscene sight displayed there.

Olivia's steps stilled and she let out a long, thoughtful stream of air. "So what you're saying," she said slowly, "is appearances matters very much to you, and you would go to lengths to protect them." She hummed cheerily and the joyous tone of the song somehow served only to make it all that much more macabre.

They searched through some of the Duke's things while the Duchess left them, presumably to gather up the tattered shreds of her dignity. They found nothing of insight. Olivia studied the corpse at length before reluctantly using the magic mirror to contact her police supervisor about clean-up. Questions were posed to the help—*were you here last night?* and *have you worked here long?* and *did you see or hear anything suspicious?*—all which garnered similar answers: *yes, ma'am* and *yes ma'am* and a shy, apologetic *it's our business not to see or hear much of anything, ma'am.* They tried to question Analaea, but the younger val Daren was off with her artist and neither could be found.

On the leather seat of the val Daren winged carriage, Christopher put voice to the question that had been on his lips all day. "Do you think it was the Duchess?" he asked.

Olivia didn't seem startled by the sudden break in silence. "It certainly seems possible, now doesn't it?" she murmured, staring out the window.

Chris looked down at his notebook.

Duchess? he weaved in clean, deliberate script, and then closed the cover.

CHAPTER FIVE

I wish you'd let me wear cosmetics, Chris!" Rosemary pouted at her reflection in the swirling glass of the magic mirror. "Just some powder and blush! That's all I'm asking!"

Chris was trying to decide how to word a response that would put the matter to rest when the stairs creaked behind him. Surprised and a bit alarmed, he turned to see a familiar grey head shaking in fond exasperation and a cane pointed like an accusing finger at his sister. "Oh, no. We know you too well for that, young miss. Next it'll be just a mascara and just a little colour on your lips and just a little kohl and before we know it, we'll have a little harlot on our hands."

"*Fernand*," Chris muttered.

"Fernand!" Rosemary stamped a foot and planted her fists on her hips. She was grinning, though, and within a moment she sniffed and turned back to the mirror, posing and playing with the brim of her hat.

Chris gave Fernand a look of gratitude, and the old man smiled like a proud uncle. He always knew just how to handle Rosemary, and throwing her a scrap of the scandalous was one of his best tricks. "I didn't know you were here," Chris said. "You know I hate it when you come find work on weekends."

"Oh, but I do so love work!" Fernand beamed and indicated a file he had tucked under his arm. "And to work efficiently, I had to pick up some things from your father's study"

Fernand Spencer was a very old fixture in this house. He had handled Grandfather Buckley's finances and then Michael's. After the Floating Castle, Fernand had moved on to serving Chris. And when he'd advised dismissing the entire staff, Chris had signed his letter of dismissal himself, only to have him refuse to leave. Family stays together, he'd said firmly, and Chris had known better than to point out there was no blood between them. Sometimes, that wasn't what mattered.

"Going somewhere nice on your day off?" the loyal old man asked.

"White Clover!" Rosemary said into the mirror, fussing with one of the curls framing her face, trying to make it bounce right.

Fernand chuckled. The sound was like boulders rolling down a crag. "Ah, the old family tradition. Aren't you two getting a little old for a zoo?"

"It's not a zoo!" Rosemary protested, still not looking over at them. "It's much better. At a zoo, you only *look* at animals, but at White Clover Farms, you can actually do things with them. That makes it better."

"Oh, I see," Fernand nodded knowingly.

Chris indicated Rosemary's fine leather shoes. "You're probably not going to want to wear those. Unicorns may be prettier than horses, but their droppings certainly don't smell any better." Rosemary flushed and quickly set about obeying.

"Chris…" Fernand began. "I know you prefer to let me control your finances without your supervision, but you might want to make an exception this time."

The gravity in his voice straightened Chris. "Why? What's going on?"

"Well…" Fernand looked away as if ashamed. "The fact is, Christopher, I had a look over your finances yesterday, and it's worse than I thought."

Chris's heart sank. "Oh?" he asked, trying to sound casual. "How bad is it, then? Should I be worried?"

"Savings are dry."

The bottom fell out of the floor. Chris reached out to the bannister to steady himself. Whatever he'd expected, it hadn't been that. "…oh," he whispered. He took a step closer, lowering his voice. "…are we…done, then?" He looked around the foyer, struggling with the very idea of selling the Buckley home. Reginald Buckley had been one of Richard Lowry's most trusted assistants on the Awakening Project, as well as one of the first categorized spiritbinders in Tarlish history. This home was a testament to history. Selling it would be…

"Not so bad as that, not yet. That's what these are about," Fernand tapped the file.

"Please tell me that's stuffed with hundred royal notes."

Fernand chuckled. "Not quite. But you aren't so far off the mark." He flipped open one of the files, revealing a document Chris didn't recognize apart from his father's tidy signature set at the bottom. "These are your father's investments. Your income. I had a thought we could sell the shares they represent. You wouldn't get monthly returns from them anymore, but they could be just the buffer your coffers need while this new job of yours settles in. With the figures you quoted me, you'll be all right in the end, and if we sell these, you can keep the house this month."

Chris raised a hand to push up his eyeglasses and pinch the bridge of his nose. "Fernand, Gods, you know you're talking over my head. I'd have lost everything within the first week without you. I trust you. Do what you think is best. I've always trusted you."

"Then trust me enough to take one last piece of advice." Fernand indicated Rosemary with his chin, who was struggling to pull on a rubber boot, making a face at how it ruined her ensemble. "You don't want to hear it, but you spoil her far more than you can afford to. That pretty little dress she's wearing doesn't look home made." He squeezed Chris's shoulder. His grip was surprisingly strong. "It's only for a few years. When

Rosemary is categorized, things are going to change for both of you. She's already better than half the binders powering this city combined. She'll set things aright." He peered at Chris's face. "Are you upset with me?"

Chris started. "Mother Deorwynn, no! Fernand. You do the best you can for us and ask nothing in return. And your best is much more than I'd even dare ask for. Thank you."

"Oh, Chris, as if I've ever done it for your thanks," Fernand murmured kindly. "I hope you know I'll always be here, I—"

The chime of the mirror startled them both.

Rosemary jumped to her feet. "Ooh!" she exclaimed, delighted to find a relief to the boredom of adults talking above her head. "Someone's on the mirror!" She rushed to stand before it, now peering into the clouding depths instead of her own reflection.

The chimes tolled again and again as the gnomes on either end were forced to connect and intertwine their consciousnesses. The reflections in the mirror darkened and then disappeared, and the faint suggestion of a face emerged. Rosemary leaned close, curious who could be calling them so early. The pane shimmered, the brown glow around it surged, and the vague silhouette in the glass sharpened all in a moment.

It was Olivia Faraday.

She stared at Rosemary. Rosemary stared back. "Ugh," said Olivia Faraday, folding her arms. "*Tell* me he gave me the right frequency. Does Christopher Buckley live there?"

"Oh!" Rosemary perked up. "Yes! That's my brother! He's right here!"

"Wonder. Could you please tell your brother to get off his lazy, unreliable arse and get—"

Chris hurried in front of the mirror, nudging Rosemary to one side and shooing her in the direction of Fernand. "That's my sister," he snapped at the mirror. "And she's thirteen, so if you could please watch your language—"

61

"Thirteen, really? And you're still washing her mouth with soap?" Olivia tossed her head. "She hears twice as bad from all her friends, I'll bet. Probably uses twice as bad, herself."

"You don't know anything about my—"

"*Why* aren't you here?"

Chris paused in the tirade he'd been preparing. He stared at Olivia, at her carefully chosen professional dress, her hair braided no-nonsense down her back. And behind her, dim lighting, flickering candles—she was at the mirror in the office. "…isn't it…" He half-turned to look at Fernand and Rosemary, who looked back with helpless expressions. "It's my day off," he finished foolishly.

When he looked back at the mirror, Olivia's face was incredulous.

"What, isn't it?" he demanded, suddenly indignant. "I worked for five days straight. It's Healfday. Tomorrow is Godsday. You said I would have both off from work. Last week—"

Olivia threw her hands into the air. "Did you sleep through yesterday?" She waited for him to realize what she meant, and when he obviously did not, she growled. "You're an imbecile. Someone was *killed*, murdered, and whoever did it is probably working on concealing themselves in plain sight right *now*, and you"—she let out an astonished bark of laughter—"and you want to sleep in? What did you think, we would pick this up on Maerday? Like we hadn't let all the evidence go cold and potential witnesses wander free for two days?"

"I don't know!" Chris snapped. "Shouldn't you have told me instead of just assuming I knew? I've never done this before! You, on the other hand, are quite—"

Olivia pointed a finger at him through the mirror. "Come to work. Right now. And do stop crying about it. Gods, that's irritating." She paused for a moment of thought, and then added with a sneer, "And if have you a problem with any of that, then I'll happily go looking for a new assistant. One who doesn't give me any shit."

"My *sister* is—" he began, but Olivia was turning away from the mirror and the image was going unfocused and cloudy. His own reflection replaced it, and the brown glow became dull and inert once again.

He balled his hand and forced himself not to put his fist right through the mirror. This was ridiculous. How could anybody be expected to *deal* with such a person? One moment, he thought he could grow to respect Olivia. Maybe even like her. And then in the next, she was like a bat out of the three hells and his greatest comfort came in the fantasy of marching into her creepy little office and sacking himself.

Fernand's words came back to him.

He breathed.

The key to any situation was self-control. He had to find his self-control, and then everything would be all right. He turned to Fernand and Rosemary wearing a rueful and apologetic smile. "Well, Rosie," he said, pleased at how composed he sounded. "I suppose we're going to have to postpone White Clover."

Rosemary was, for once, shocked into silence. It was Fernand who replied. "Well, I'm sure the young miss doesn't mind terribly, do you Rosemary?"

"…no," Rosemary said faintly. "Of course not. That's fine, Chris. I can wait."

"Could you contact Rachel Albany for me?" Chris asked Fernand. He hated to put this on the man—he did enough as it was, but he couldn't leave Rosemary alone. "I hope she'll be willing to come in on a Healfday."

Chris turned to look at himself in the magic mirror. He was overdressed for work, but there was certainly no time to change. "I just need to get my notebook," he said to the mirror, as if Olivia could hear him. It would be a fine day, he told himself. Everything would be just fine.

When he was halfway up the stairs, he was stopped by

Rosemary's voice. "Chris!" she called. He stopped and turned. His sister looked up at him with wide blue eyes, something between fear and wonder swimming there. "Was that *her*?"

Not even that brilliant little scene could shake her out of her admiration of the woman. "Yes, Rosemary," Chris droned. "That was Olivia Faraday."

"I thought so." Rosemary cast a glance behind her at the mirror. A furrow appeared between her brows and she twirled one of her artful curls around a finger as she stared. "...she made the gnome laugh when she yelled at you," she murmured, a small smile curling onto her lips like a contented cat. "And he never, ever does."

Christopher arrived up at Olivia's office to find her standing at the curb tapping one foot. The dark professional gown from her image in the mirror had been replaced by a flamboyantly colourful piece, layered extravagantly in a style that hadn't been popular since his mother had been a young debutante. Her hair, gloves, and shoes were all fitted into the same era as her dress, making it look like she had stepped out of a fashion plate from thirty years ago. She rolled her eyes and flagged a taxi as soon as he fell into place beside her. "Finally," she said just loud enough for him to hear.

He kept himself under control. "Good morning, Miss Faraday," he said politely. "I'm very sorry for keeping you waiting."

Olivia growled and flung open the door of the cab. She climbed up inside, folded herself down, and gave him a jerk of her head to indicate the other seat.

Chris nodded cordially to the driver. "The val Daren estate, please."

The cabbie pulled his pipe out of his mouth and took his time prodding around in the bowl. "Long way out of city limits, that place," he drawled.

Olivia made a frustrated sound. "We'll pay."

The driver put his pipe back in his mouth and puffed on it leisurely until even Chris felt a twinge of annoyance. Finally, the man shook his head and extended a hand. "Going to need some upfront, for a run like that."

"Oh, for—" Olivia snapped and bustled out of the hackney with her voluminous skirts flouncing. She reached into her handbag and thrust a handful of notes into the cabbie's hands without counting. "Is that good enough, or should we beg, too?"

The man puffed on his pipe and the corner of his lip curled. "Aye, missy, that'll be enough. Get your arses up in the car."

The trip was considerably farther when they weren't soaring over the city. Chris wished they were in that splendid winged carriage today, not only because of how fine it had made him feel, but because he could have used the vistas as a welcome distraction from the tense air in the cab. He watched the city go by in its most mundane of ways, and thought of witty, unflattering remarks he could throw at his employer.

And saying any of them would have been idiotic. Fernand's dire words this morning couldn't be ignored. He was a pauper, there were another six years ahead of him, and Olivia was paying him an absurd amount of money for clerical work. Apparently, Healfday mornings spent smelling death was part of the reason why.

He pushed up his specs and rubbed the bridge of his nose. She wasn't going away, and whether he wanted to or not, neither was he. There had been moments in the past week where Chris had found himself fond of her. He had to focus on those times and get through these ones.

"It won't happen again," he said, not looking at her.

A long silence followed his statement. They turned from the clothiers' district and down into one of the jewellers' roads. Chris wondered if Olivia had fallen asleep, if she'd even heard his near-apology at all. Gods, that would be too cruel. He wasn't sure he could say the words again.

But after they'd driven down three different streets, top to bottom, Olivia made a neutral sound and murmured, "I know it won't," and then, after a brief pause, "Your sister is lovely."

The view changed from the claustrophobic streets of Darrington's trade district to the rolling hills of its peaceful countryside. Chris turned to look at his employer and found her staring listlessly out her own window. "What are we doing today?" he asked. Encourage communication. Show interest. Six more years.

Olivia jumped, swinging her gaze to his. "I'm sorry, what?"

Chris repeated his question, adding, "I'm sure you have some clever plan. I'm just wondering if I can be let in."

She raised her eyebrows then, and a bit of her usual delighted mischief crept into her expression. "Are you trying to proposition me, Mister Buckley?" she teased, fluttering her lashes. "It's not going to work. I'm impervious to charming, handsome men, you see. And I'm at least ten years older than you."

Any other day, that would have had him blushing and stammering, but he recognized it for what it was: a peace offering. "What a harsh refusal," he replied, playing along.

"Sorry, but I have no choice. I know your type. Brass balls blunt, I have to be, or you never learn." She drummed her fingers on the window ledge. "We need to speak to the daughter. Right now, that's the most important thing."

"Analaea?"

"Was that her name?" Olivia gave a dismissive shrug. "I'm wondering how *she'd* be affected by her father spontaneously becoming a devoted patron of the arts. She looked about your age, which means she was probably old enough to have known him before the change and after. Was she neglected by his sudden interest in young women? Confused by the change? Did their relationship deteriorate? Was she *jealous*, maybe?"

"That's disgusting," Chris said without thinking.

Olivia gave him a suggestive look. "Of the *attention*." Chris looked away, embarrassed. "Or the other way, why not? You'd be shocked at how many daughters have *issues* in that vein."

"Can we not talk about this?" Chris muttered.

Olivia gave a full-throated laugh. "You're so easy to offend, Mister Buckley!" she said when she caught her breath. "Oh, we're going to need to work on that."

"Lady Analaea," Chris persisted, desperate to change the subject. "Is that all you want to learn from her? Her relationship with the Duke?"

Talk about the case sobered Olivia and she took on a thoughtful pose, head cocked, brow furrowed. "No," she said, then went quiet as the gears of her mind worked. "I want to know where her loyalties lie," she said. "There's obviously a rift in the marriage. Is the daughter loyal to the mother or the father? Or is she a free agent? Once we know, then we'll know what we can use her for. And, of course, we'll need to have her alibi for that night."

That caught him off guard. "Do—do you think she might have done it?" It was unthinkable to him. There had been many times when, angry and young, Chris would have sworn on everything he believed that he despised his father and wished he'd die. But actually losing him had made it painfully clear no matter how little they'd gotten along, Chris never would have truly wished harm on him. The thought of anyone willing to do such a thing...

Olivia pursed her lips. "Maybe."

"But—"

She shrugged. "Don't think so much. I don't rule people in, I rule people *out*. She's connected, and that means she might have done it. Nothing personal." She tapped a finger on the inside of her arm and then made a thoughtful sound. "But if I had to call Maris and tell her to arrest someone right now, just from my gut..." A small, toothy smile. "The Duchess."

"She *is* hiding something," he agreed.

Olivia shot him a surprised look. "What makes you say so?"

Suddenly flustered he'd given his unasked and uninformed opinion, Chris turned away from her and looked out the window. He squinted against the bright morning sun and was relieved to see the val Daren estate close enough to make out the flying buttresses. "Oh, look," he deflected. "We're nearly there."

Olivia moved across her seat to join him at his window. He awkwardly tried to move his knees so he didn't bump hers. It all felt terribly ungentlemanly. "So we are," she said, sounding pleased. "Gods, this is a longer drive when you have to use the road, isn't it? I wonder how much it costs for one of those winged carriages."

"A lot," Chris said ruefully, still bruised from his encounter with that particular price tag.

"A shame, that." They turned down the long lane leading to the estate. "Why do you think she's hiding something?"

He'd so hoped she'd forgotten. "I just...something in the way she talked," he fumbled. "It always seemed like..." He shot her a look, his cheeks warm, hoping she would let it go, but her gaze was as intent as a hawk's.

"Keep trying. I like to know what normal people are thinking."

Normal people. How very well said. "She just always seemed to be talking around something. I suppose? Skirting an edge. Using what she was saying..."

"—to hide what she wasn't," Olivia finished, and gave him an appraising look. "Well observed. Maybe you aren't so dumb, after all, Mister Buckley."

He held the door open for Olivia, letting her exit before him. She paid the cabbie, though not without an attempt to haggle and a few choice insults, and she didn't exactly *hand* him the notes so much as throw them at his face. And then they were up the steps, ringing the faintly glowing bell and hearing the ice crystal sound of a singing fiaran. A plainly dressed servant ushered them in, bowed, and disappeared into the manor.

Olivia removed her old-fashioned hat and held it at her side. "Hello?" Olivia called none-too-politely into the empty foyer. "*Hello?*"

"I'm sure that maid went to inform the Duchess that we've..." A handsome young man stepped out of the hall and into view, and Chris trailed off at the sight of him. "Here, you see?"

Olivia marched up to him, holding her feathered hat before her like a dark age iron shield. "I need to talk to the Duchess," she declared. "There's plenty enough to do without wasting time standing here in the entrance way. I can't believe she didn't send me her winged carriage—do you have any idea how long it took us to drive out here in a hackney? Next time, I'm going to take a winged cab and tack that expense onto my fee. And another thing—"

"You're wasting your time, Miss Faraday."

Olivia and Chris both turned to see Duchess val Daren standing above them on the landing. Her gown was midnight blue with frothing white lace spilling from her cuffs and enclosing her long, elegant neck. Her hair was pinned and coiffed becomingly. She wore no hat or gloves, but she was, of course, not dressed for out of doors.

She ignored the both of them and focused her cold gaze on the slender young man. "*Mister Grey* was just leaving. Weren't you?"

The young man's gaze flickered between Chris and Olivia. "Are you the Deathsniffer?" It was difficult to tell which of them the question was directed at. Chris could only hope Olivia took no offense. "You're trying to find what happened to Ana's father, aren't you? If there's anything I can—"

"*Mister Grey*," the Duchess snapped. The young man flinched, and Chris could hardly blame him for it. Her voice was cutting, a warning that would not suffer to be ignored. "Did you hear me?"

"Yes, ma'am," the young man murmured, barely audible. He jostled Olivia as he passed between her and Chris. Chris caught a glimpse of a splotch of green on one of his cheeks, and then he was no more than a retreating back with hunched shoulders. No servant escorted him out as Chris and Olivia had been honoured with the night before. He simply opened the door and closed it quietly behind him.

The Duchess sighed. "Ethan Grey," she pronounced. "My daughter's paramour. I can't seem get rid of that contemptible little parasite no matter how hard I try." She trailed one hand along the banister as she descended the staircase, seeming to float. "Miss Faraday," she greeted. "I must say, I didn't expect to see you today."

"Where is everyone getting that idea?" Olivia said. "Duchess, your husband was *murdered* yesterday. Does everyone think I sit in my solar and drink tea in this situation just because it's a certain day of the week? Please don't think so little of me. It doesn't suit you." The Duchess's eyes flashed, but before Chris could witness another clash of goddesses, Olivia simply turned away. "Now! I want to look around that room again. I presume Maris and her team cleaned it all up and dealt with the leftovers?" She turned back to the Duchess for confirmation at this and received a tight nod for her efforts. "Good, I'll need to talk with her and see if she found anything I didn't after I see the room in its current state. I'd also like to talk to any of the staff who weren't here yesterday, but are today. Yes?"

The Duchess nodded again. "I can arrange that."

"Good, thank you! I'll be down in the parlour to speak to them within the hour," Olivia chirped. She motioned jauntily to Chris and they'd taken five steps when Olivia stopped so suddenly he had to catch himself lest there be a collision. She turned back to Duchess val Daren with a look on her face that seemed to be only idly curious, but Chris knew better. "Oh, and your daughter."

"Ana?"

"Was that her name?" Olivia said again, with an equally convincing shrug as in the carriage. "Well, whatever it was, you have only one daughter, so that one, yes. I'd like to speak to her, as well. Alone."

The Duchess's eyes narrowed. "Why?"

"Because I think she could be useful," Olivia replied, making her way up the stairs before the Duchess could argue.

Not long after, Chris stood in one corner of the room where the Duke had been killed, trying to make himself invisible. Olivia turned circles in the centre, muttering to herself and taking measurements with her long, graceful fingers. Chris held his book open and his mind at the ready, but it was impossible for him to make out anything she said.

The room looked completely different without a butchered corpse hanging from the rafters. Whoever this Maris person was— Olivia's supervisor with the police, Chris hazarded—they'd done a terrific job scrubbing the place clean. A faint brownish stain was still on the floor where the Duke had bled out, but otherwise, the room looked much the same as Chris imagined it had before its inhabitant had been split open. What Olivia hoped to see in the empty, immaculate skeleton of a murder scene, however, Christopher couldn't imagine.

"No weapon," Olivia murmured glumly.

"Maybe Maris found it?" Chris suggested. He began transcribing their conversation.

"Absolutely not. She would have contacted me." Olivia clucked her tongue and then sighed with a thespian's skill. "I so wish there was a weapon. If we get lucky, I can have the culprit fingered in two days or less."

"Were you...hoping to find it in here?"

She snorted. "No, of course not. Why would I? If it were here, I would have seen it yesterday. If I hadn't, Maris would have found it and mirrored me. No hope of finding it today, not unless the killer came back and replaced it like an idiot."

"Then why *are* we here?"

A chair scraped across the floor. "I'm setting the scene."

Chris stopped taking notes and looked up.

She no longer stood in the centre of the room. Instead, she sat before the large bureau on the chair she'd pulled out. She mimed a pen in her hand and an open book. "He would have been sitting here, at his desk," she mused. "At least, we can assume. He might have gotten up to look out the window, or gone to get a book from the case, but best guess was that he was here." She suddenly turned her eyes on Chris, keen as a hawk. "Are you getting this down, because this is what I'm paying you for."

Quickly, he looked down and weaved what he remembered of what she'd said...*gone to get a book from the case but best guess was that...*

"Door opens," Olivia continued. "Viktor turns about to see who it is."...*to see who it is (olivia twisted in chair here to look at the door)...*

Her brow furrowed in thought. "This room has an antique lock, not a modern one. Just brass, tumblers, and old-fashioned keys. Terribly inconvenient things, those old models." She linked her fingers, stretched her arms, and cracked all her knuckles at once. Chris winced. "So," Olivia pronounced. "Was the door locked that night? Check your notes."

Chris flipped through the book to yesterday's initial tour of the room. He'd recorded that the door had an antique lock and there were only two keys, one belonging to the Duke and the other to the Duchess. The Duchess had sworn to her key's location on her person all night. But there was nothing more about the Duke's key, and no mention of whether the door had been locked that night. "I don't think anyone has said."

"Make a note to ask," Olivia commanded. He did. "If it was locked, either someone else had to open it, or...someone had to have called to him to open it, someone he would have trusted."

"Or someone who had the key," Chris put in.

Olivia frowned.

"The Duke's key," Chris elaborated, feeling foolish.

"Hmm. That's a thought." Olivia tapped her chin with one of her long, long fingers. "Just where exactly is the Duke's key? Why don't we know that?"

"Ah," he said, shrinking under her reptilian gaze. His eyes flicked down to the page with its messy, swirling notes, and then back up to her. She raised her eyebrows in a silent enquiry. "...are you...am...am I supposed to be...?"

She dismissed him with an airy wave. "Oh, you're adorable." She giggled and stood up. "Make a note of that key business. I want to know where the thing is. In any case, the Duke gets up and walks to the door, like this. We know he was killed right here." She stopped in the brownish stain. "Because there's no blood anywhere else." She raised one finger to tap at her chin thoughtfully. "So, of course, he had his throat slashed first, then he was hung up, *then* his arms were cut."

Then his arms were—Chris looked up. "How do you know?"

"What, didn't you notice?" Olivia shot him a playful look. "Oh, ordinary people are so slow. Check your notes. Almost no blood came from the cuts down the arms. That means there wasn't much left by the time they were made. Though why they were made, now, that *is* a mystery." She walked in a small circle around the outside of the brownish stain. "Then, heinous deed accomplished, our killer leaves the room. Now. Tell me. What did I miss?" She gave Chris a devilish look.

He blushed and averted his eyes. He had not forgotten the ignoble peculiarity of the Duke's death. "The, ah..."

"When did he get his pillock out?" Olivia teased.

Chris studiously avoided her gaze, focusing on the page and weaving the ridiculous sentence she'd just uttered. "You said," he began, choosing his words like he was picking his way through a cow pasture, "it was before. He died."

"I did." She preened like a pleased bird. "Yes, I did. That's the key to this whole thing, you know. Now, I'll need to talk to Maris before I know for sure, because it's her and her coppers who are going over the body and doing all of that postmortem foolishness. But it looked to me like there wasn't a struggle." She turned slowly around the room. "Do *you* remember seeing things in disarray, Mister Buckley?"

He shook his head.

"Check your notes."

He did as he was told, and then repeated the motion with more certainty.

"I thought not." She tapped two fingers against her chin. "I'd think if someone had tried to open his pants while also trying to kill him, he would have reacted to that, don't you?"

"...probably."

"So." Olivia nodded with satisfaction. "That narrows things down quite a bit. Whoever stabbed him might have been someone he was expecting to *stab*, himself, if you know what I mean."

"Then it's the Duchess." Olivia smirked, and Chris felt a rush of defensiveness. "*What?*"

"Adorable! Christopher, really. Did you hear anything she said yesterday? I think her opening up his pants would have shocked him more than the cook doing it. Women don't kill their husbands when they *are* in bed with them. They kill them when they're *not*." She tapped her chin. "But this doesn't disqualify anyone. He could have already had it out when the door opened. If the door was locked the killer was in possession of a key, he might have been so startled he didn't take the time to make himself presentable before he stood up, took two steps, and got his throat slashed open. But I think it's relevant. It's too interesting not to be."

The certainty in her voice prompted him to voice his curiosity. "Miss Faraday, meaning no offence, but don't you just...know who it is?"

"Wouldn't that be lovely?"

"But you're a truthsniffer."

She shrugged one shoulder. "There are truthsniffers in a lot of different fields. Science and engineering and law enforcement. Don't you think things would get done faster if we could always just go with our first guess? My gut isn't always right. Just more often than everyone else's is." Her eyes swept over the room and she nodded once to herself. "There's still a lot of work left to be done."

CHAPTER SIX

T he parlour was empty but for a slender, dark-haired young woman curled in the window seat. She had her knees drawn up to her chest and was staring out into the countryside. Her gown was simple and her feet were bare. She didn't stir when they came in, but jumped and turned when Olivia cleared her throat.

Chris didn't recognize her, but Olivia did.

"Oh," the Deathsniffer droned. "Is your mother hard of hearing? I asked for her staff *and* her daughter."

Chris blinked. Now that it had been pointed out, he recognized Lady Analaea from the day before, but he couldn't imagine how Olivia had done so. Her hair still hung unbound, but now was glossy and clean. Her face, no longer blotchy and puffy from unashamed tears, was made up with simple but well-chosen cosmetics. Her lips were full and pouty, her eyes soulful and intense. Her gown was austere, and she was still so thin she seemed underfed, but gone was the awkward and plain girl who'd sniffled down at them from the stairs yesterday. In her place was a fragile young blossom, not quite beautiful, not quite ethereal, not quite aristocratic, but something in between all of those, altogether remarkable.

Analaea studied them both, and then lowered her head in an unspoken apology. "Mother didn't want to take them away from their work all at once. She said the estate would have to shut down. She said she'd send them, one after the other, once you spoke to me."

Olivia rolled her eyes. "Of course she did."

Analaea flinched at the venom in Olivia's tone. "Is that a problem, Miss Faraday?"

Chris saw Olivia preparing to launch another of her acerbic barbs and he took a chance, stepping between them. "Lady Analaea val Daren," he said, sweeping his best courtly bow. "I'm Miss Faraday's assistant, Christopher Buckley. We know there's nothing you can do about your mother. From you, we want only a few questions answered."

"Oh..." Analaea whispered. She looked him over and then turned back to the window. "It's just Ana. Only my father ever called me Analaea, and he stopped a long time ago."

Chris glanced at Olivia. He tried to convey a silent apology in his gaze but, to his surprise, she didn't seem bothered by his interruption. "Ana it is, then," she said agreeably. "That might be easier on my overly charming assistant, because I can't even *imagine* how to spell your full name. What a *swamp* of vowels." The girl didn't react. "Mind if we have a seat?"

"Please," Ana murmured.

Olivia folded herself down in the middle of a spacious settee, spreading her layered, old-fashioned skirts out all around her. Chris chose a seat below both Olivia and Ana in quality, an old rocking chair with a padded back. He opened his notebook and turned to the first fresh page.

"Were you close to your father?"

"No."

Chris could hear the raised eyebrows in Olivia's reply. "That's all? 'No?'"

"No, we weren't close. We haven't been for a long time."

"And why is that?"

"If you know about the sort of man my father became, you know why." Ana sighed. "I wasn't one of his sopranos or his painters or his actresses or his ballerinas or his poets or his

77

harpists. I wasn't interesting to him, and he grew tired of trying to make me so."

"But there was a time when you *were* close."

Ana flinched. "...yes," she said. "But as I said, that was a long time ago. Before he changed."

"Do you miss him?"

The girl growled and pressed a shaking hand against her forehead. "Why are you asking me these questions? Of course I miss him! How couldn't I? I was his darling and everything was fine, and then one day he was just sad all the time and there was nothing I could do. The night he agreed to go to the opera with us, I was so happy! I thought things would be better! But he just sat there and stared at nothing. He didn't even acknowledge anything I said! He only looked up when *Kristin* came onstage, and then he lit up like he was hearing Maerwald the bloody Maiden sing!" Her voice had turned to a snarl and her eyes flashed. But when Olivia only stared at her, the anger on the young woman's face melted and then drained away. She slumped. "I thought it had been bad when he didn't care about anything. I thought that was as bad as it could get. I was so wrong. When he cared about them and not us, it was worse."

Olivia relented. *he cared about them and not us*, Chris weaved, and Olivia changed tack.

"Were you here at the estate on the night he died?"

"No. None of us were. Ethan...that's my beau. He's so wonderful, and so talented." She smiled a dreamy little smile. "He's a worldcatcher, and his paintings...they're like you're right there. Sometimes, I swear I can feel wind on my face or hear the sea in the distance. I know that's not supposed to be possible, that's not what worldcatching *does*...but it's not just movement with him. It's so much more."

"I do hope this is coming to a point."

Ana trailed her fingers along the windowpane. "Ethan had some of his paintings accepted to a gallery in the city. It was the first time.

I was *so* proud of him. I even convinced Mother to come along. She *despises* Ethan. She always has, so I thought she wouldn't accept…but she did." She leaned her head against the glass. "We spent the whole night there, surrounded by his admirers, and then we all went for a walk together in Lowry Park." Chris saw her reflection in the window twist into a pained expression. "It was…it was nice."

"How late was that?"

"Oh, very late. It was long past midnight by the time we got back."

"All three of you were there?" Olivia asked. "You're certain?"

"Of course I am. It isn't like I'd remember something like that wrong."

"Is there anyone we could talk to and confirm that?"

"Plenty," Ana said. "Our staff. We took the winged, so there was no driver that night, but the gallery owner can tell you all about Ethan's paintings. The attendants would mention us having been there, too, if you wanted to check with them." Chris was certain to get all of that down.

"What about your father, Ana?" Olivia asked. "Why wasn't he there?"

The girl scoffed. She laid her chin on her knees, curling her arms around her legs. "He didn't care. He liked that I loved an artist, but only because he wanted me to learn something from him. Father doesn't think art is art when it's created by a man. Men aren't pure enough to make true art. There isn't enough innocence or beauty in their souls. That's what he always said."

"He sounds like he was a right bastard," Olivia proclaimed.

Ana started, and then glared. "Who are you to say so?" she demanded.

Olivia raised her hands helplessly. "I'm only echoing what you're not quite saying, darling. Don't *you* think he was?"

Ana hauled her tiny body tight against the window and closed her eyes. "Go away," she murmured. "I've answered your questions. Or do you want to ask if I killed him, too?"

"Did you?" Olivia asked with genuine curiosity.

"*No.*"

A small smile crept over Olivia's thin lips and she drummed her fingers against her elbow. "Well," she pronounced with great care, "forgive me if I don't just take your word for it. If I made it a habit, I'd never manage to sniff out killers like you."

It was a ploy.

It worked.

Ana shot to her feet. She stood on bare toes as she stalked over to Olivia, trembling with anger and grief. "Would you blame me if I had?" she demanded, voice cracking. "My mother's always hated me. All I had was my father, and then Kristin came and stole him away. I thought when she left, I'd have him to myself again, but then it was Jillian and then it was Coral and then it was Gwen and then it was Elizabeth and then it was Vanessa and he never, ever looked at me again!"

She towered over Olivia, fists clenched and tears streaming down her cheeks.

Olivia didn't react. She picked at her skirts, examined her nails, and then, "Vanessa," she said, and rolled the name on her tongue as though she were tasting it.

The name was confirmed by everyone else in the val Daren household. Vanessa Caldwell was a poetess, the Duke's newest project. She'd been a household fixture for months, giving orders to the staff and treating her benefactor's wife and daughter like unwanted guests in their own home. None of the Duke's protégées had ever been so bold—or so hated. The Duchess had been only too glad to give them the address for the woman's flat, full of recriminations. Perhaps the Duke had decided to no longer sponsor her. Perhaps he'd spurned her unwanted, disgusting romantic advances. Or perhaps she'd simply snapped.

Olivia said her fill on the matter as they travelled back into Darrington with the val Daren winged carriage. "If she knew someone capable of killing her husband, and that person was involved in a curious relationship *with* her husband, why didn't she say as much when I asked her if she knew anyone who might have done the deed?"

Chris had no answer, but he was eager to meet the diva who'd turned an entire household against her.

However, no one came to the door of Vanessa Caldwell's flat, no matter how hard Olivia pounded her fist and glared at it.

It was the most depressing building Chris been inside in his entire life. Plaster was coming off the walls in dusty white chunks, showing the old clay brick beneath. Every footstep taken on the scuffed wood floors groaned like an old man shifting in his sleep. The hallway was lit with flickering, jittery lights surrounded by a black haze, a sure sign of alp lamps, the poor man's salamander.

"It doesn't seem like the Duke's patronage has improved her lot very much," Chris mused, leaning against the wall.

Olivia gave up on her pounding and looked over at him. "I'd noticed the same," she said. "This place is an absolute dung heap. A little low-end for someone who lorded over Old Blood nobility, don't you think?" She *hmm*ed. "Is that a reason to kill him? Maybe she thought he left the entire fortune to her. Middle aged men have been promising pretty young women that sort of thing since we all lived in mud huts."

Chris watched the sterile, nervous light of the bound alp. "Where is she now?"

"Maybe she fled the city!" Olivia's eyes gleamed with excitement at the thought. It seemed to ignite new fire in her, and she turned back to the door, laying into it once again. The crumbling walls shuddered.

It wasn't long before they were invaded by a glaring, wrinkled woman holding a candle in one hand and a croquet mallet in the other. She held the former like a shield and the latter like a weapon as she peered at them out of half-blind eyes. The candle flickered as it shook in her palsied hand. "What's all of this bloody racket?" she demanded in a crackling voice. "You're disturbing my tenants!"

Olivia looked pleased. She immediately stopped assaulting the door and extended a hand to the old woman. "Ah, finally, the landlady arrives! Pleased to meet you. I'm Olivia Faraday." She smiled toothily. "Deathsniffer by trade."

The woman recoiled and made the symbol of Three in a warding gesture. "Bloody cursed thing! Get out of my building!"

"Where is this particular tenant?" Olivia asked as if she hadn't heard. She took a step forward, hand still outstretched.

The old woman backed far out of Olivia's reach. Her little eyes were wide and her toothless mouth worked without sound. Finally, she shook her old, wrinkled head. Her grey braid swung. "Vanessa aren't in Darrington. She goes to the capital by and by, days at a time. Usually comes back. Eventually." She jutted her chin forward. "None of your business, either. Get the hells out of here, or I'll call coppers on you. I know all about you 'sniffers! The investigating kind! Police give you a long leash, but when they haul you back, you go with your sad little tails 'twixt your legs."

Olivia tipped her hat to the old woman. "Now, now," she pronounced, voice dripping with feigned innocence. "No need for threats, old bat. If Miss Caldwell isn't here, then neither are we. Come along, Mister Buckley." She started off, beckoning to him as though he were a dog. Obedient as one, he followed.

"And don't come back without a permit!" the old woman shouted after them, shaking her croquet mallet.

Olivia erupted into great peals of laughter the moment they were outside, bending at the waist. "Oh, something from a *story*, that one!" she crowed. "How else could this day have ended? Brilliant, bloody brilliant! Is this ever a case!"

Chris didn't see anything funny and had actually been rather unsettled by the old woman. He stepped away, arm outstretched to hail a cab. Immediately, Olivia seized his wrist and yanked him to her side. "No!" she protested with fierce conviction. "We're two blocks from the office! Let's just walk, shall we? Oh, I love the fresh air!"

He didn't want to walk. He was tired. He'd stayed up too late last night, thinking this would be a relaxing day at White Clover with Rosemary, not a dash around the Tarlish countryside. The rain had held off so far, but it was only a matter of time. He hated being rained on. It did awful things to his hair, and his aged leather shoes couldn't take much more water damage.

But all of a sudden Olivia was in a fine mood. All day, she'd been irritable and surprisingly serious in turns, but now she skipped down the street, pulling him along without waiting for him to agree or disagree. She greeted every person they passed with a jaunty salute, none of whom appeared to recognize her. She chattered at him about absolutely nothing while he watched the lowering clouds with trepidation.

The first drop hit the end of his nose and snapped his thin temper. "Do I at *least* have tomorrow off?"

Her bubbling voice went flat. "Oh, don't be like this. You'll have your day off when we find the killer."

He sighed. "It's *Godsday*, Olivia."

"And naturally, you're fervently religious and will spend all day in a church, repenting your sins before the Three and Three."

The statement caught him off guard. "Well—no."

She shrugged one shoulder. "Then why do you care if it's Godsday?"

"Because any *normal* person would—" Chris cut himself off before he could launch into an ill-considered tirade. Gods, it was like arguing with a child. Abruptly, he realized she wanted this. The conflict, the fun of pinning him into a corner, tackling and wrestling him. She was a bored puppy and he was giving her precisely what she wanted. "All right, then. Fine. First thing in the morning. Though I'm not sure what we're going to do with Vanessa Caldwell not in Darrington."

"There are other things, Christopher."

"If you say. You know more about this than me, Miss Faraday." If she could call him by his first name, he could call her by her last.

She was quiet for a time, and he counted it a victory. "I need to know about the postmortem," she said at last. "And talk to someone else about all of this. And the moment Miss Caldwell steps off the train and shakes cloudling sparks out of her hair, I want to know where she is. I'll need to mirror Maris." Olivia blew out a stream of air. "I wish we could find that weapon."

Chris glanced over at her to see that her expression was glum. Not for the first time, he wished that he'd inherited his mother's proficiency. If he had, perhaps he could even begin to understand Olivia's mercurial moods. "Why do we need the weapon so badly?" he asked, less out of curiosity and more out of mild concern for her. "Isn't it fairly obvious that it's a knife?"

"Of course it's a knife. But if I have the knife in hand, Maris will get me an hour with the timeseer. Oh, what we could learn!"

Chris stopped in his tracks. "A—*timeseer?* Is this a joke?"

Olivia started, then blew out a stream of air. "Oh, dear." She held a finger up to her lips. "Keep that quiet, won't you?" Her voice dropped so low he had to strain to hear it. "Sorry. I forget. I *always* forget. Lowry doesn't like ordinary folks knowing that's a real thing."

Chris himself had always dismissed them as a fable, someone taking legendary magic from an old wizard story and trying to pretend it was something that could be done by real people in the modern world. It was said a timeseer could search deep into the past and witness events that had come and gone, rewriting old histories and turning memories into visions that always told true.

"We use them in law enforcement," Olivia continued, barely seeming to understand what a revelation she'd just made. "One per city, two for the biggest ones when they're available! They're not, at the moment." She laughed. "Not surprising. Is anything, these days? I don't think half the cities in Tarland have one at all, right now. But we do, finally. New one, young thing. Royal pain in the bloody arse, too, thinks he hung the moon, lit the sun, and crowned Queen Gloria himself."

"An actual *timeseer.*" Chris raised a hand to his temple. He felt dizzy, wondering at the possibilities. If there was a man in Darrington who could just simply look into the past and see anything that had gone before, always infallibly true… "Why are investigators even needed, then?"

"Well, they need a spark for the seeing. And then they follow the timeline for the spark. It's said an especially brilliant one can use people or places or even strong emotions to create a spark, but who's that good at anything anymore? No, these days, items are your best shot, and an item that's come into contact with blood? Well. Blood carries memories strong enough to shock you senseless." She shot him a look full of dark suggestion, and Chris found himself intrigued despite the macabre implication. "Of course, even that's not flawless," Olivia continued. "If it's a very old item or one that's changed hands often, the timeline is too long and winding. It's useless. But…" She tapped the side of her nose. "Well, trade secrets, can't say any more. Suffice to say, there aren't enough of them to drag along behind me from crime scene to crime scene. But we have the one, and when we can get an item with a strong enough spark, well. Sometimes William can make the rest easy." Her mouth twisted into something that was only half a grin. "*If* His Majesty is bloody well in the mood." She dropped his arm suddenly and stretched like a sleepy cat. "And here we are!"

The rain started in earnest when they were halfway up the walk, the sky opening like the bottom of a well dropping out. Water rushed down in a pounding deluge. They ran for the office door, but they were still dripping when Olivia shut it behind them. She collapsed back against the door with a *whoop*, panting and flushed, drops of water chasing each other down the strands of her hair and pattering on the floor below. Chris's specs were so spotted he could barely see. All three layers of clothing at his shoulders were soaked completely through.

Olivia was laughing like a drunk.

With a sigh, Chris pulled out his handkerchief. He cleaned his eyeglasses as Olivia moved over to the magic mirror. Still giggling, she banged at the chimes and said something about slow connections in the rain, breathless excitement in her voice. He was slipping his specs back onto his face when he heard a woman's voice, a deep, low alto, coming from the mirror. "*Faraday.*"

"Maris!" Olivia squealed. "I need to talk to you about—"

"For the last time, it's *Officer Dawson!*" the woman snapped. Her voice was hard and commanding, with a thick northern accent. "I've been trying to get you on the mirror all bloody day. Where have you been?"

Olivia planted her hands on her lips. "Up at the val Daren estate, obviously."

"And your assistant?"

Chris slunk out of view of the mirror, not wanting to be seen and remarked upon.

"With me! I don't keep them around to answer the mirror and collect the paper, you know! They assist me. That's why we call them assistants. Listen, Maris, I need to have a word with you about the—"

"Where's my damned paperwork, Faraday?"

"Oh, Maris, please don't—"

"Don't be cute with me. You *always* do this. Listen, you started a new case yesterday. You signed a contract with an *Old Blood noble.*

Mother Deorwynn! You know how this works. You take a case, you go over the initial investigation, and then you have preliminary paperwork to me at the station within a day." A pregnant pause, during which Olivia was, shockingly, silent. "Where's my paperwork, Faraday?"

Olivia folded her arms and continued to say nothing. Chris could see her pouting.

Officer Dawson gave a long-suffering sigh. "I did my part. I took my boys out there and cleaned up that body. I even have an autopsy report and a few other interesting things you might want to know, including the initial report from the heartreader. Apparently, he had some last minute emotions still circling she managed to pick up."

"Oh, good!" Olivia clasped her hands together in front of her like a delighted child. "Can you have that all sent here by tomorrow morning?"

"I'll have them sent there, Faraday," Maris Dawson said firmly, "after I have my paperwork. And—now that I think of it, how about all that backlog you owe me from last month?"

"This is ridiculous!" Olivia protested, her coy act vanishing in an instant. "I don't have time to sit around and pander to the bureaucracy! It's a stupid system! I'm chasing a killer, and I have almost nothing concrete yet, and you want me to fill out forms? And you're going to hold actual substantial evidence *hostage*? Just send me what you have, and—"

"When I get my paperwork."

Olivia went silent. She folded her arms across her chest.

"There, that's better. Will I have it?"

"First thing tomorrow," Olivia grumbled.

"Good. And—Faraday! Don't you just have Constance do it again, because if you think I can't tell the difference between words written and words weaved, you're forgetting the last two times you tried. Are we understood?"

"Understood."

"Good. I'm going home, now. I've spent too much time today trying to get a hold of you, so please at least try—"

"Maris, wait, I need you to do something for me. It's important."

"Is it actually important, or is it Olivia Faraday important?"

"It has to do with the case."

The police officer sighed. "Make it quick."

"A suspect of mine is out of town. Could you put a tag on her? She's apparently in Vernella for some reason, or so says her landlady. She should be coming back in by train, I would think. It's important I know the moment she's back in Darrington."

A silence, some papers rustling, and then, "Send me her identifying information and I'll let you know when she comes back in."

"Oh, *thank* y—"

"As long as I have my paperwork. Good night, Faraday." Even though Chris didn't have a clear view of the pane, he could see the reflection of light on his employer's face, and he saw it dim. The officer hadn't even waited for confirmation before disconnecting.

Olivia turned around and made a face at him. "My supervisor," she said flatly. "Charming woman, isn't she?"

Chris took his time choosing a response. His first impression—that he couldn't have imagined anyone being able to keep Olivia on such a tight leash—was unlikely to be well received. "I certainly wouldn't want to cross her," he said, trying to appear sympathetic and not impressed.

Olivia sighed. She leaned back against the table before the mirror and folded her arms in front of her. "Well," she said. "So much for jumping back into this tomorrow morning." She gave him a half-smile. Even that didn't seem especially sincere. "Tell me, Mister Buckley," she said. "If I give you tomorrow off after all, will you *please* stop whining about it?"

CHAPTER SEVEN

I t was Godsday morning and Rosemary was about to try and free a salamander.

He watched her lean into the ticket booth while he tried to pay their White Clover fare as quickly as possible. It was a grey, dreary, and bitingly cold morning, and at first he'd assumed it was the warmth that had caught her attention. But as the gleam in her eyes turned stubborn and fey, he realized with a snap of crystal panic that it was the *source* of the warmth that concerned her.

"Rosemary," he murmured a warning, but she didn't even turn in his direction.

The attendant looked down at her, smiling like a kindly uncle. "You can't come in, if that's what you're going to ask." His voice lilted pleasantly with a Northern accent. "Though you'd be the fifth today to try. Cuts right through you, this wind, eh?"

"Yes. It's a salamander, isn't it?" Rosemary demanded.

Chris sucked in a breath. "Come on, Rosie," he said the words as gently and as casually as possible. "Let's not bother him." He took her by the wrist, but she twisted out of his grasp and danced a step away, rising on her toes to look inside the booth.

"Where is he? I can feel him."

The attendant's welcoming smile wavered. "A bit young for categorization, aren't you, little one?" he asked with awkward levity.

"He's *angry*, so angry I can hear him even though he's not mine. He's been bound for fifty years. He's so tired he can barely do it anymore. It's hurting him, but he can't stop because the man who bound him told him he couldn't, not even if he was about to die from being worked so hard, and—"

Chris hefted Rosemary up under her arms and set her to one side. She stumbled and half-fell, curls all bouncing, and Chris couldn't spare a moment to see to her. "Please," he begged the man, who was still staring at Rosemary. "Just ignore her, sir. I'm sorry. She likes it pretend she's a 'binder. It's not—"

"We turn it off most days," the attendant interrupted. His expression had gone dark and he didn't seem to see Chris at all.

"Turning it off doesn't help at all," Rosemary insisted, ignoring everything else he said. "Why don't more people know that?"

"Now just what..." The man studied the young girl in her Godsday finery, fourteen at the very oldest and talking about things no child should know. Chris could see the wheels in his mind turning, moving towards the inevitable conclusion. He wanted nothing more than to step between them and shield her from view, as if that would hide their secret. He waited for the questions to come. The silence grew so long the air thrummed with it.

Finally, "Move along, little girl," the attendant said, voice gruff with what he'd chosen not to say. "Or you're going to waste your whole day. That doesn't sound like much fun, now does it?"

Before Rosemary could say another word, Chris *did* move between them, blocking her from view. "I'm so sorry." He all but prostrated himself before the man. "She's—she's very precocious. And very young. And has—a very vivid imagination." Chris turned and seized one of Rosemary's hands in his own, tightly this time. She struggled in his grasp and protested as he ignored her distress. The attendant watched with wary consideration. "We're leaving," Chris said firmly. "Have a nice day. I'm so sorry." He yanked Rosemary after him.

"You're going to be sorry!" Rosemary called over her shoulder at the man, fighting against Chris's grasp every step. "He needs to go back to the plane! It'll be nobody's fault but yours if he breaks free!"

"Stop it," Chris hissed down at her as soon as they were out of the attendant's field of vision.

"What they're doing is dangerous, and you don't know anything about it!" Rosemary dug her heels in, and there was still enough muck from the rain the night before that she got purchase and anchored herself.

Furious, Chris whirled to glare down at her. "You're one to talk about dangerous," he hissed, keeping his voice as quiet as possible. "How many times do we have to have this conversation? All it would take is one person believing you, Rosie, *one*! If Lowry finds out about you..." He stopped, growled, and tried to reign in his temper. A deep breath. Another. He forced a smile, reached out and tucked one of her curls behind her ear. "Rosie," he murmured. "Let's just forget about it and go see the unicorns."

But she rejected his offer of peace and jerked away. Her expression had not a trace of affection or respect. "What do you know?" She glared up with venomous disdain. "Maybe I want them to find out about me. You're someone's secretary. What do you know about *anything*?"

He saw white. Without thinking about the mud or his trousers, he dropped to his knees, seized Rosemary by the shoulders, and yanked her close against his face. "I know you're a child, an insolent little child, and I'm an *adult*," Chris spat. "I know I'm your legal guardian—which isn't a job I *ever* wanted, by the way, and I'd give back in a heartbeat if I had the choice."

The scorn in Rosemary's eyes washed away in a torrent of alarm. "Chris—" she started, but he wasn't done.

"If you have problems taking orders from a mere wordweaver, maybe you'd rather take them from a nun in a children's home. Do you like that idea?" She shook her head. "I didn't think so. So when I say that's enough, it means that's *enough*. Do you understand me?"

Her eyes had gone very wide and they glimmered in the grey, clouded light. Her lower lip protruded slightly. She drew a long, shuddering breath, and cringed away from him.

Guilt washed through him then, flushing out everything he'd felt so strongly only a moment before. As if recalling a fading dream, he replayed the words he'd spoken and wondered, in a daze, where they'd come from. He didn't resent Rosemary. Of course he didn't. He did everything he could for her, so much that Fernand always warned him it was too much. He ached for her, how young she'd been when the Floating Castle had fallen, how little he could do to give her a normal life.

Why had he said any of that? What had summoned it to the surface?

Dizzy with shock and shame, he struggled against his instinct to back pedal and further confuse her. With deliberate care, he changed his expression from angry to stern. "I only want to protect you, Rosie."

"I was just..." she said, and then, to his surprise, she threw herself into his arms. "I'm sorry, Chris. I'm so sorry. I shouldn't have said that to you. You're right."

She buried her face into the crook of his neck. Dazed, he raised his arms and encircled her with them. "Rosie, no. It's fine. I forgive you. Of course I do." He pulled away. He tried to disguise his own feelings with a comforting smile as he straightened her hat and her curls. He pulled out his carefully pressed handkerchief to wipe the tears from her rosy cheeks. "There, now, it's all right," he said. She didn't look convinced. "It's all right," he repeated, and she sniffed. "I know you're sorry. I forgive you. Blast it, I'm sorry, too. I never—can't we just forget all about this and have a nice day? No crying on White Clover days, isn't that a rule?"

She managed a smile. "Well...if it's not a rule, I think it should be."

"It is now." He climbed to his feet and offered Rosemary a

hand. He tried not to notice the curious, disapproving eyes that had turned to watch them, or wonder how much they may have heard.

Sometimes, he felt like he was living in a fishbowl, and it was only a matter of time before someone came at it with a cricket bat.

As they roamed the park, things between them were awkward at first. He'd never lost his temper with her, and the fear in her eyes haunted him. But by the end of the first hour, they had given themselves over to their haven of childhood memories. The ghosts of their parents walked along the trails beside them, but for once, they were a comfort and not a torture. Chris swore he could sense Michael's glowing charisma, feel Mother's soft, small hand on his shoulder. When he glanced down at his sister, she seemed younger than her years, a six-year-old girl once again, happy and carefree. Lost in the winding paths of White Clover, surrounded by the green glow of dryads and creatures both exotic and mundane, they were transported to a simpler time.

By noon the weather had turned mild and Chris was glad he hadn't worn a heavier coat. Rosemary clung to his side, chattering away. She'd heard one of the keepers say they might be getting monkeys from the southern continent. Tales of those wild lands, so far away from Tarland and its neighbours, captured her sense of adventure.

"Miss Albany says their language is completely different from ours," she prattled, "and they've been building amazing tombs and temples and cities since we were still living in mud huts and dingy old castles! I always thought they'd be dreadfully primitive, but Miss Albany says I was wrong! And they did all of that without categorization! They don't even have wizards, here! Isn't that amazing?"

"...actually," he mused, "yes, it is." He'd read a bit about expeditions to the southern continent in the papers, but those publications had always painted the place as savage and dangerous. "That seems an odd topic for Miss Albany's lessons."

"Miss Albany says we can learn a lot from somewhere so far removed from categorization! She says being so close to us has actually made Frelia and Girvane and Denlar develop much slower than they would have! It's interesting! I like her lessons better than any of the other tutors you've hired for me. At first I just thought she was—hey!"

While she'd chattered on, Chris had reached down and pinched her cotton candy between thumb and forefinger, pulling away a knot, dangling threads like angel hair.

"Chris!" Rosemary protested, shooting him a pointed but playful glare. "That's mine!"

"But I bought it for you," he reminded her.

"You should have just bought your own!"

"But then I wouldn't have to steal yours." He popped the candy into his mouth, closing his eyes in pleasure as it melted on his tongue. If he could have afforded the purchase, he *would* have bought his own. Though it was just as well, he thought with a sigh, swallowing the melted sugar with relish. He'd be twice his size and cut a horrible figure if he could afford all the sweets he wanted.

"You are absolutely the worst brother ever!" she declared, but she pressed her face up against his side with a happy murmur, and he felt like not quite the worst brother ever after all.

Rosemary stopped in her tracks. She stared up over the pulsing green glow of the dryad-tended trees and he followed her gaze, up and up until it connected with the massive steel contraption looming over White Clover like the staring eye of the Elder. "Oh, Chris," Rosemary gasped, heart on her sleeve. "Oh, Chris, could I *please* ride the wheel today?"

Chris winced.

The observation wheel had been the main attraction of White Clover when it had first been built. It was a recent idea at the time and eager children crowded to it in a way they never had for the cloud drakes. But now it was one of six wheels in Darrington alone, and most of the others dwarfed it embarrassingly. It was no longer a new idea, but that didn't stop the zoo from charging twenty royals a spin.

"I...I don't know, Rosie..." he said. He could actually see money circling the drain. "It costs more than admission to the whole zoo."

"Oh, *please*, Chris?" She turned to look at him, eyes large and begging, hands clasped before her. "I never ask! And I would only go for one spin, just one! How much can it be, really? Is it more than your taxi to work every day? You could always walk for once and make it up! *Please?*" She seized one of his hands in both of hers on the last word, drawing it out so long he wondered how she had enough breath in her lungs.

She was manipulating him outright. He had learned to tell; she certainly did it often enough. The big eyes and fluttering lashes, the platitude in her voice, the entreaty on her upturned face, the *pained* pinching around her mouth. The performance of a smart little actress and nothing more.

He sighed and reached for his wallet inside his coat. "One spin," he said. "*One.*"

"*Thank* you!" Her face lit up and she darted forward to wrap him in a tight hug before pulling away and skipping off down the path. He hurried after her at an only slightly more sedate pace, knowing from experience she'd find it all too easy to leave him behind and then scold him for tarrying when he caught up.

He was winded by the time they reached the observation wheel, but Rosemary seemed bright-eyed and energized as she gazed up at the towering structure. This close, its size was dizzying. Chris could only glance up before looking away, heart somersaulting in his chest. He'd loved the wheel as a little boy, loved being up at the top and seeing the whole world stretched out before him like a patchwork quilt. He'd been so high, high enough to see all three heavens. It had been thrilling, amazing, absolutely brilliant.

It had also been before the Floating Castle.

The wheel was halfway through the turn it was already taking, and Chris could see three small figures waving down from higher than he wanted to consider. Two men standing together near the fence gave him and Rosemary polite smiles before turning back to their conversation. Fathers and their children.

The attendant tipped his hat. "Got to wait a minute, there, love," he said to Rosemary, voice thick with a West Vernellan accent. "Put you on when the others reach the bottom, eh, and you can do a nice full spin just on your own, how's about that?" He gave Chris a look. "You going along?"

"Ah, no," Chris said quickly. He fished about in his coat pocket for his handkerchief to wipe his forehead.

"Right then, just hold a tick, won't be long," the attendant said. "Twenty roys, it is, if you want to be giving it now. Save time when they come down."

Grateful for the excuse to cover his distress, Chris pulled the notes out of his wallet. Smiles and money were exchanged, and then he and Rosemary walked a bit away.

"You never used to be scared of it." Rosemary looped her arms through two rungs of the fence, leaning back and looking up at him. It was not a ladylike pose, but he didn't scold her.

"Things change," he said, hoping that would be the end of it.

This was Rosemary, however, and so it wasn't. "You're not scared of the winged carriages," she persisted. "Weren't you just telling me about how grand it was to ride in the Duchess's, and how amazing the city looked from the sky?"

"That's...different."

She giggled. "Why?"

"It just is. I can't afford it anyway," he said. He shot another quick look up at the wheel to see the position of the children already on it—and then back down, ignoring the twist in his stomach. The winged carriage *was* different. Falling didn't scare him. The height was not what tightened his chest and shortened his breath. Rather, all he could picture was the wheel breaking free of its steel restraints, rolling about, crushing, screeching and squealing and— "It looks like it's just about your turn, Rosie."

She shot him a sly look. "Are you going to watch me?" The question was stated with practiced innocence, but he knew that glint in her eyes.

"Absolutely not."

She laughed. "Father would say you were being such a baby."

Chris looked away before she could see his face turn stormy. "He certainly would," he muttered, a sour taste on his tongue.

She might have noticed but at that moment the wheel squealed to a halt and the clamour of excited children interrupted them. Two boys and a girl called to their fathers from the seat, demanding another ride, and Chris watched one man laugh and hand the attendant a handful of notes. He felt a stab of envy. Why couldn't things be that simple for him? The men were finely dressed in the newest fashions, no darning or patching. They probably had useful categorizations and were providing tangible benefits to society, with salaries to match.

"Well, lovey, you're up!" the attendant called to Rosemary.

Rosemary rushed past Chris and toward the gate where the attendant stood. "I won't be long!" she called back. The fellow opened the gate for her and escorted her to the waiting seat. Chris watched to ensure that he strapped her in well, but had no complaints. The man was careful and thorough and knew his job.

Life could be worse, Chris reminded himself. People working that sort of job had proficiencies so weak they were authorized only for such menial positions. The money they took home was considerably less than what Chris managed wordweaving for Olivia Faraday. And even they weren't the worst off—some had nothing at all awaken in categorization. *They* were sent to the church and were forced to leave all their worldly possessions behind. What would he have done if he'd been in *that* situation?

He should be more grateful.

The wheel's control pad and levers all shone bright yellow with the light of bound cloudlings. Sparks and waves of energy cascaded off the engine in bursts as the attendant approached it. The cloudlings didn't operate the machinery; they were needed only for the power. Most of the more impressive advances categorization had brought were a result of their electric currents and the things they could fuel with them. Richard Lowry himself had been a wizard stormbinder before he'd developed the categorization initiative. But cloudlings were also the most volatile and dangerous spirits, more so than even salamanders. They had the instability and wildness of striking lightning. The feedback sparks of the spirits fighting their bonds were always more evident with a cloudling.

The wheel creaked and squealed, and then it was off again, beginning its turn. Rosemary waved to him, face glowing, and he returned the gesture. He watched her until she went out of his field of vision, and he didn't tilt his head back to follow her.

He leaned forward against the fence. Tomorrow, it would be back to the office of Olivia Faraday. If Vanessa Caldwell was back from the capital, they would be going to speak to her. That might provide some insight. Idly, he wondered how long it usually took to find a murderer, and whether this feeling of an aimless lack of direction was normal.

His mind wandered. He closed his eyes, drifting, enjoying the feeling of the sun warm on his back.

He didn't realize he'd begun eavesdropping until the conversation became interesting.

"...with the val Gerthins, you know how it is," one of the men was saying to the other with a wince in his voice. "I've been after Duke val Gerthin to pay back his last loan for three months now, but the bastard is always full of excuses and platitudes. Always the same, with the blasted Old Blood."

"Oh, I bloody well know," the other man said with a chuckle. "Old Debts." Old Debts, not old debts. The distinction was plain. "The val Brennans aren't any better. And I've been chasing Duchess val Cander for an update on the books for a week, now. But I have it in hand. The only way to clear up Old Debts is to not let them get away from you. Some of the boys will give that speech about not sending good money after bad, but you can break the rules with Old Debts. They all have money lying around somewhere. You lend, you wait, and then you take it back."

"Sure, when they deign to *give* it back. I swear, old val Gerthin is holding out on me. I sent my best man there last week, and—"

"Push harder. Threaten to escalate it. All Old Debts are the same. Scare them enough, and they'll find the money *and* the interest. Old Debts are new profits." It was said like a proverb, and accompanied by laughter.

"You make it sound so easy."

"Just find the sweet spot, and then it is. None of them have got a single tangible copper, all of them are desperate for our credit, and I've never met one who couldn't liquidate enough to buy the clothes off your back."

Interesting. Better than interesting. Fascinating, in fact. Chris furrowed his brow. *All* Old Blood were the same? What about the val Darens? Olivia might be interested in this. If the Duke's creditor had decided he'd never get his investment back, couldn't he have been killed to send a message? Of course, that didn't explain the one particularly...unique aspect of his corpse, but the way he was strung up and mutilated was certainly consistent with someone trying to say something to fellow debtors.

Chris was so focused on those thoughts he didn't notice what was happening until it was already too late to intervene.

A *crack* and sizzle in the air started him out of his considerations. He came back to himself and glanced about, confused. What was...

The attendant let out a stream of panicked curses, jumping back in alarm, and blue arcs of electricity snapped and crackled around the console.

Where before they had come only in short bursts, now they were shooting sparks and bolts in all directions. The steel frame of the observation wheel arced with the currents, and, most horrifyingly, the bright yellow light that had haloed the machinery so consistently just minutes before was now flickering in and out.

All of Chris's thoughts froze. Headlines flashed across his mind. Elementals breaking loose and wreaking havoc. Entire blocks destroyed. People dying. Families in mourning. 'Binders in demand. Doctor Francis Livingstone advocating alternative technologies.

The Floating Castle.

He shot his gaze up the observation wheel. Rosemary was near the top, he saw, with a sick twist in his chest. Much, much too high to jump and save herself. The very thought of her splattering on the ground below made his stomach heave. The children of the sumfinders were shrieking and waving their arms, and the men had ceased their conversation and were bellowing at the attendant to do something. But the man wasn't a spiritbinder, and he only cursed and spit and ran from the console.

"Get away!" he shouted. "There's nothing I can do, run, get away!"

Chris couldn't run. He couldn't *move*. And neither could the fathers standing beside him. No matter how foolish it was, no matter the certainty that the cloudlings would speed towards the closest humans they saw and fry their bodies to charred sticks, they couldn't leave the children on the wheel. How could they?

"Rosemary!" Chris called up, his voice cracking. His heart raced and pounded. Gods, what was happening? *How* was this happening? At any second, the cloudlings would break loose of their bonds. The wheel would conduct the electricity, turning it into a crackling circle of death. Rosemary would be killed as surely as he would. "*Rosemary*," he called again, feeling a ragged sob in his throat. There was nothing calling to her could do, but he had to do *something*, even if it was the most useless thing imaginable. The wheel had stopped turning, the cloudlings no longer powering it as they struggled against their bonds. There was no way for the children to get down.

He was about to lose his sister.

Gods, he was about to lose his *life*.

A sickening *pop* almost deafened him, and there was a *snap* in the air. All the hair on his body stood up straight. His spine tingled.

And then the cloudlings broke loose.

Ethereal and insubstantial, bursting with barely restrained energy, the formless beings of pure electricity sizzled into being in a blinding cascade of arcs. Lightning bolts flickered within their barely visible bodies, dark and shapeless as the clouds they were named for. They spiralled together, exulting in their freedom, and then, without pause, they shot towards Chris and the other two men with single-minded fury. They were pure rage and no reason, and all they wanted was to punish the humans who had bound them to service.

Chris had only time to take one step back, squeezing his eyes closed and raising his arms in useless defence against his inevitable end.

The first clear notes of Rosemary's song reached his ears.

He cracked open his eyes to see the twin cloudlings sizzling with energy only inches from his face. His body shivered with the electricity, gooseflesh raising and power thrumming along his skin. A sharp, pungent smell hung in the air.

The cloudlings trembled, shuddered, but they did not move forward.

Chris could barely breathe. Slowly, he took one step back, and then another. The cloudlings did not follow. Rosemary's song filled his mind and ears, that ancient song in a dead language that she knew the words and cadences to only by instinct. Chris tried to calm himself, tried to gather his wits, but he could find only snatches of panicked thought. Rosemary was too far away, surely, and the spirits were too wild and too angry and she hadn't been the one to summon them. They had faltered, but they hadn't stopped. They couldn't be stopped. Even as he watched, he could see them struggle and fight against Rosemary's binding song, straining towards Chris, seething with chaotic rage at the knowledge of an enslaver so close...

The children on the wheel still screamed in terror, their fathers called their names in hoarse voices, and Rosemary's song was so difficult to hear. Chris wanted to shout at them to be quiet, to not distract her, to let the song ring clearly. Her focus was the only thing keeping them all alive. He took another step back, another. It would do no good to put such little distance between them if the cloudlings broke free again, but he couldn't help but want to be as far from them as possible.

The cloudlings shuddered and struggled, but, slowly, to Chris's utter disbelief, their positions solidified. They stopped moving but for tiny twitches in the air, and Rosemary's song resonated all around them. It rose in tone, higher and higher and faster and faster. Slowly, the cloudlings floated back to the console, fighting against the compulsion with all their energy. Rosemary's voice entranced them, commanded them, the mathematical rules of music overpowering their anarchy. The very air churned with power, the raw power of the elementals and the ancient power of Rosemary's song. Chris allowed himself to hope, allowed himself to breathe.

The song climaxed, and the cloudlings burst into a blinding shower of sparks that sent spots across Chris's vision.

And when it cleared, the console was glowing bright yellow once again.

"*Gods*," Fernand gasped breathlessly.

Chris looked up, keeping his arm protectively wrapped around his sister. She shook against him, both from shock and exhaustion. His father's financial adviser stood over them, his face haggard and terrified, his body trembling. He'd run here, Chris saw immediately, probably run all the way from the zoo gate, and he had never looked so frail or pained. There was no sight of his cane.

"Fernand." No matter how much he'd gone through to get here, Chris couldn't describe how happy he was to see him. "I'm so glad you were home. We had the emergency workers mirror you as soon as they arrived."

"I came the moment they did." Fernand limped past Chris, feeble and panting, and settled onto the bench on Rosemary's other side. "Rosie. Rosie, dear, are you all right?" he asked, voice trembling.

Rosemary shivered, but nodded. "Fine," she said in a tiny voice. Chris had never seen her so subdued.

The song had drained her. She'd never done anything so intensive or so difficult. Singing down not one, but two cloudlings at once, from so far away, when she hadn't been the one to summon them. The 'binder with the emergency dispatch had been beyond incredulous, even after the story was verified by the three crying children and their terrified, pale-faced fathers. But a quick examination of Rosemary by the lifeknitter had confirmed it. She'd exhausted herself completely, pulled strings of energy from her very life to weave the song and bind the rogue spirits, and she would be drained of all vigour for days.

"Gods, I was terrified. When I heard—you both scared the damned hells out of me," Fernand said. He sounded as if he were letting out a breath he'd been holding for an hour. "I assumed the worst. They gave me platitudes over the mirror, but you know how they can be."

"We really are fine," Chris assured him. Rosemary shuddered weakly against his side, and he amended with a pang in his stomach, "...mostly."

"Gods," Fernand said yet again.

"I wish we could go home," Chris murmured. "The police officers keep coming and asking so many questions. I don't see what else they can learn that they don't already know." He shook his head. "Rosemary is exhausted. She needs rest, not an inquisition." He didn't add that he was near falling asleep, himself. He'd sit by Rosemary's bed tonight; no matter how tired he was, there'd be no rest while he was so worried for her.

It wasn't just the burnout. Far from it. If anything, that was his least concern. While there hadn't been any sign of reporters, yet, that didn't mean this would stay contained. No. He couldn't fool himself into thinking that was a possibility. Too many people had seen this, something so wondrous, so astounding...it was going to spread. It had to. Who could ever keep quiet after having seen what happened here today?

Their years of hiding were over.

He shivered. He tried to keep his mind on the present, but he was so exhausted it was impossible not to find himself drifting. Drifting ahead to the realities of a future now staring blackly at him, very real dangers that would surround his sister like wolves in the night. Drifting back to that night, the clear sky, the cool air on his face, his nightshirt brushing his bare legs.

"I don't see the point," Fernand muttered. "Can't they see the girl needs to be at home with her family?"

Chris said nothing. He stared out into the darkness, trying to clear his thoughts. Now. The present, think about the present. There was enough terror in the future. There was enough pain in the past. He couldn't handle either.

"How did she do it?" Fernand asked. "They said on the mirror there were *two* cloudlings and she was forever away. How is that even possible?"

"I don't know. Even I never knew she was capable of something like that," Chris murmured.

When they looked down at the girl between them, they saw her eyes were closed and she was breathing slow and even. Her face was pillowed up against Chris's arm and the blanket was wrapped tightly around her shoulders. Despite all of it, despite everything crashing down around them, a small, sad smile touched Chris's lips. Rosemary's face was serene. Peaceful. Tightness closed around his heart as he reached out to brush stray curls from her cool cheek. Her breath misted on the back of his hand.

"Well, there's nothing to be done," Fernand said, as if hearing his thoughts. "Everything's changed, now, Chris."

He closed his eyes. "I know."

CHAPTER EIGHT

Chris woke slumped in a chair.

For a moment, he wondered where he was and why his neck was sore and why he was still wearing his eyeglasses. He blinked slowly in the early morning sunlight, trying to piece it all together. He looked around, and saw he was in Rosemary's room, all done up in blue. She slept beside him, her smooth face a picture of peace and rest.

It all flooded back.

White Clover, the observation wheel, the air snapping with the energy of the rogue cloudlings. And Rosemary. Her clear, strong voice singing them down, saving his life and that of five other people.

Gods.

That had actually happened.

He looked down at his sister in dazed wonder. He'd always known even at her young age, her abilities were beyond what most 'binders could achieve in a lifetime. The simple fact of her wizardry, her innate knowledge of the arcane spirit language, was proof enough. Her casual unbinding and rebinding of elementals, her easy affinity with them, her understanding of complex technologies that were beyond even the most experienced 'binders...yes. He'd known she was remarkable, *exceptional*. He'd spent the last six years doing everything he could to hide it.

But he'd never imagined she was capable of what he'd seen yesterday. And he'd never expected it would save his life.

He jumped near out of his skin when the silence was shattered by Rosemary's cuckoo clock bursting into excited chirps, though she didn't stir. He counted the chimes while he watched her face. Was she in pain? Would she recover from this? Or had she pushed herself too close to the edge to come back? Would she—

—with a shock of panic, he counted the chimes again.

He was going to be late.

He was loath to leave Rosemary, but after his tardiness on Healfday, he doubted Olivia Faraday would excuse another lapse. He needed to be at the office on time, or there would be hells to pay. He sprang from the chair, which rocked on its legs, and rushed to his own room.

His reflection was not an inspiring sight, but he didn't have the luxury of time to fix it. With a groan and a muttered curse, he threw on whatever he could find and dismayed at his mismatched clothes, the tousled mess of his hair, and the filmy spots on his specs. No time to fix any of it. He grabbed a bowler and hurried down the stairs.

He was out of breath when he reached the bottom, and he was relieved to see Miss Albany already sitting in the parlour, her back straight as ever, with a cup of tea cradled daintily in her hands. To his surprise, Fernand was also there, and they were locked in conversation so deep they didn't even glance up at his hurried entrance.

"I need to go," he said by way of introduction. They both turned towards him with a start. Miss Albany's cup clattered in its saucer. "I'm going to be late."

Fernand exchanged a look with the governess. "You're going in today?" he asked. He didn't have to actually vocalize his disapproval. It was there in his mouth, his voice, the furrow between his brows.

Chris's lips twisted. "I don't think I have much of a choice."

"I'm very sorry to hear what happened," Miss Albany said. She slid her tea onto the table and her hand shook. "It all must have been…very frightening."

He'd told her all the usual lies, he recalled. That Rosemary seemed more powerful than she was, that it was only her beautiful voice that made her seem so remarkable. "I…" he floundered. Should he respond to the unspoken question? Should he pretend like nothing had happened? He cleared his throat, which felt as if there was a burr lodged in it. "Miss Albany," he hedged. "About what—about the conversation we had on your first day here—"

"It's fine, young master," Fernand said in a quiet voice. "I've already explained the situation to Miss Albany."

"You have done what you could to protect your sister from harm," Miss Albany said, inclining her head. "I consider that more than admirable, and I intend to do my best to aid you in whatever may be coming."

Chris sighed his relief. "Thank you," he told her. He turned to the door, and then remembered, quite suddenly, what he'd overheard at White Clover before the incident. *No time*, he thought, but he found himself pulled back regardless. He may need whatever he could find to make himself valuable to Olivia. "Fernand," he said. "I don't suppose you could do me a favour?"

Fernand gave him a look that made Chris's heart swell. "I'll do anything I can for you, my boy."

"You have connections with the others sumfinders, don't you?" At the old man's nod, Chris continued. "Could you possibly get me a list of names? I'm interested in finding out more about creditors."

Fernand frowned dourly, disapproval clouding his face. "You may think credit will solve your problems, Christopher," he began in his lecturing tone, "but I promise you it's not—"

"It's not for me," Chris cut in. "It's for Olivia." At Fernand puzzled expression, he shook his head again. He was in such a hurry he was forgetting himself. "Miss Faraday. The Deathsniffer. I'm sorry, Fernand, I don't have time to explain, but if you could possibly get me a list of creditors who work with the Old Blood—"

Fernand's cloudy expression only deepened. "Don't go poking around in Old Debts. It's messy business."

"It's not for *me*," Chris repeated impatiently. He took another look at the clock and groaned aloud. "I'm sorry. I really, truly am, but I need to go *now*. Just think about it, Fernand, please. I'm sorry. I need to go." He settled his hat onto this head and, seeing it was once again pouring, grabbed his umbrella from the closet. It was going to be a very close shave.

Olivia was in the waiting room when he arrived. Her eyebrows shot up as he shook out his umbrella and shrank under her gaze. With pointed deliberateness, Olivia turned the face of the pocket watch she held towards him. Its hands pointed to twelve and eight on the nose. When she snapped the cover shut and tucked it into her bodice, there was a wry smile on her lips. "Cutting it a little close, aren't we, Mister Buckley?"

He flushed, raising a hand to pull off his bowler and run his fingers through his already unruly hair. He looked a mess and he knew it. The whipping wind howling through the streets had not helped. His hair was a scraggly mess, his cheeks were probably bright red, and his trousers were soaked up to his calves. "I'm on time," he protested. Barely.

"So you are," she allowed. She turned away with a jaunty flounce. Today, she was dressed all in orange, a lazy peasant girl's gown that was loose in the bodice and gathered in the arms, skirts plain but full. She'd threaded her hair with marigolds, bringing out the orange in her dress. The colour seemed to match her state of mind. He could tell from the way her steps bounced and from the teasing in her voice that she was in one of her good moods. *Thank all the Gods.*

"There was an accident yesterday," he felt compelled to explain. "I was at White Clover Farms with my sister and—"

She turned to look at him, eyebrows in her hairline again. "You were *there?*" she demanded. Without waiting for an answer, she rushed across the room to his desk and picked up the paper, turning to face him with it displayed before her. The headline read, in dark bold letters, *TWIN CLOUDLINGS GO ROGUE AT WHITE CLOVER FARMS, CHILD WIZARDLING REBINDS WITH MASTER'S SKILL.* "I don't suppose you saw this young lady! That sounds *most* impressive."

So the press had found the story after all. It would be all over Darrington by noon. There was never any real hope this could stay quiet, but Chris's heart sank regardless. They may not have discovered Rosemary's identity yet, but they would. He readied the usual lies, clinging to a vain hope that turning one person away could stop the mighty tide sweeping towards him, but there was no point. Olivia would consider an evasion a lie, and she'd find out the truth in the end. She could probably already smell it.

The time for hiding was over.

"Actually," he said, feeling a wave of bone-deep weariness crash through him, "that was Rosemary."

For a moment, he suffered from the sincere worry her eyes would roll out of her head. She regarded him with a new sort of appreciation, and all was quiet as they regarded one another anew in the light of this revelation.

Then, quite suddenly, Olivia Faraday burst into delighted laughter and deposited the paper back on the desk without turning to look. "*Well,*" she declared. "How very, very interesting. I'll keep your little sister in mind, Mister Buckley. A 'binder like *that* could be useful! Now," she said before he could protest, leaving his stomach in messy knots, "today we pay another visit to our dear friend Vanessa Caldwell."

He had no choice but to shelve the rest of it for now. Just do the work, get through the day. He tried to look interested. "She's in Darrington?"

Olivia bobbed her head up and down. "Maris mirrored me this morning! She got off a train four hours ago and is at work as we speak. We'll be going to meet her there, isn't that nice? I do hope she doesn't mind uninvited company."

"You got your paperwork done?"

Olivia's good mood was far too pervasive to be pushed aside by the reminder of her arch-nemesis. "Yes, *finally*! Maris is so unreasonable. Really, we're already behind, and she's forcing me to take a day to do office work? I'm going to blame it all on her when the killer gets away." And then she gave him an arch smile and tittered. "No, no, I'm only joking. The killer isn't going to get away. It's obviously the Duchess. I just need to find a way to prove it. *Now*," she said, changing gears in mid-sentence again, "let's be going! I don't want to leave our friend waiting all morning, do you?"

They were out the door before Chris could even start to dry off. He huddled miserably under the flimsy protection of his umbrella, which did very little to block the wind blowing up rain and lashing against his face. Puddles as deep as his ankles were everywhere, impossible to avoid.

He realized, with a surge of incredulity, that Olivia didn't seem to notice the rain. No—more than that. She seemed to enjoy it. While he struggled to position his umbrella at just the right angle, she turned her face up towards the sky, grinning with wild glee as the freezing water doused her face and drowned the marigolds threaded through her hair.

Chris crawled inside the hackney the moment one stopped, throwing himself down into the seat, folding his umbrella, and huddling miserably against the stained and cracked leather. He hated wet clothes and dry surroundings. It felt unnatural, like he was in two places at once. He tried in vain to push his dripping hair back under his hat. At least people would blame his frazzled appearance on the weather. Small blessings.

Olivia joined him in the car. She folded herself gracefully into the seat across the way and spread her skirts out like a lady's fan. She should have looked absolutely terrible; water ran off her in rivulets, her hair was dripping, and her skirts were soaked. But instead she looked energized, fresh, clean. For the first time, Chris noticed she wore no cosmetics. Her face looked the same after being pelted with rain.

The carriage lurched forward. Chris sat back, listening to the wind and rain lash against the car. He squirmed in his seat to try and find a comfortable position despite the aged leather and his damp clothes, but then surrendered to his misery. In stark contrast, Olivia hummed happily to herself, drumming her fingers on her knee, and it came as no surprise when she bore the silence for barely a minute before seeking diversion in conversation.

"You have to be joking." Her tone was pleasant and casual. "Your sister didn't really bind two cloudlings at once and save the day."

"Yes, she did." Chris sighed. "I don't want to talk about it. It was very hard on her and she's incredibly drained. It doesn't feel right to gossip about it when she's lying in bed at home." Or when she was already in the papers, and Gods knew how far the story had spread.

He wasn't really surprised when Olivia scoffed and heaved her shoulders with girlish petulance. "Oh, pish, I'd say it's best this way!" she sang. "We're appreciative of what she did! She's a wizard, then?"

She was not going to leave it be. "As it were."

"And a very good one at that! So fascinating!" Olivia tapped her finger against her cheek, pursing her lips in thought. "It's a wonder she's just sitting at home. I'd have thought Lowry would have come along and scooped her up for all sorts of uses."

Chris felt his jaw tighten. "Well, they haven't."

"But why?" Olivia leaned forward. "With everything going on in Tarland today, she'd be a beacon of hope for anyone trying to make a point that the old ways will sustain us forever. A 'binder this strong, and a wizard at that? Why, she's proof there's still potency in proficiencies after all! And all the things they could have her do! Why haven't I ever heard of her?"

"Because I've spent my entire life *preventing* it!" Chris snapped. Olivia startled, blinked, and then grinned. Discomfort climbed up Chris's spine at the look on her face. He growled and tried to explain himself. "She's a little girl. And her abilities are…tempting. As you've pointed out yourself, she's exactly what Lowry has been looking for. She could solve so many of their problems. They wouldn't care about ethics. They wouldn't care about Rosemary at all. My father was a Lowry man, I know them. They'd burn through her and throw her away without a second thought if there was even a chance it could hurt the reformists."

"Or help Tarland."

"It doesn't matter. She's a little girl," he repeated. "And it's not just the traditionalists, either! Doctor Livingstone might be some sort of saint, but do you think he'd resist Rosemary's powers if they fell into his lap? It would be a hell of a lot easier to convince people to embrace his alternative technologies if someone like Rosemary could smooth the transition, no matter what it took out of her."

Olivia raised an eyebrow. "You're very passionate about this."

"Obviously," Chris ground out, feeling his defensiveness rise even higher at the amused tone of Olivia's voice. He gripped the edge of the seat. "Is that surprising to you? It's my sister. Our parents are gone. It's my job to protect her."

When he met Olivia's eyes, they were full of a deep consideration. "Interesting," she mused, then shrugged and looked away.

He watched as she pulled aside the curtain and stared out the window at the grey, rain-lashed streets of Darrington passing by. Her lips were pursed in deep thought, and knowing she was sitting there musing about his life and his sister as if it were her business. It lit a fire under him so hot he couldn't let it go. "*What's interesting?*" he snapped.

She dropped the curtain. "Just that I seem to remember you consider yourself desperate for money. You mentioned it in your interview. I would think if you're in such dire straits, your sister's talents would more than plug the gap."

Chris clenched his jaw hard enough that he swore a tooth cracked. "I am not selling my sister," he growled.

"Hardly *selling*," Olivia protested. "If anything, she probably would like to—"

"No," Chris cut in. "It's not up for discussion, from her or from anyone else. Rosemary is thirteen years old. No matter how adult she thinks she is, she can't defend herself against the sort of person Hector Combs or Francis Livingstone would send against her. I'm *not* going to let anyone take advantage of her before she's old enough to understand what she's giving up."

Olivia's smile went wide. It was a half sincere and half arch as she said, with great satisfaction, "I see. Integrity, is it? Interesting." That word again.

He huffed and turned away from her, yanking aside the curtain as she had. He watched Darrington rush by without seeing it. He didn't have any interest in the doused cityscape, only in diverting Olivia's attention and regaining his composure. And whether from his clear dismissal or for her own unfathomable reasons, she pursued it no further. They sat in silence for some time, splashing along the road and soaking the few foolish or poor pedestrians who'd ventured out onto the sidewalks.

"Is she all right?" Olivia asked, her tone softer than before. Chris looked at her without thinking, and saw something that looked like actual concern on her face.

It was wrong on her. "...she's fine," he responded, and then amended. "Hopefully. We think. She's very drained. She wove her own life into the song. That's…not wonderful. Time will tell."

She nodded, and he turned away once more. This time, he actually took note of their surroundings. His stomach dropped. He recognized this quarter very well. Pure white buildings, all displaying the three linked circles of the church, towered above them. Hospitals and clinics may not have been funded and controlled by priests of the Three and Three anymore, but the tradition of using their symbol had not similarly evolved. He breathed deeply, assuming they were only passing through the sector on their way to the arts district, but the carriage slowed and then stopped before one of the ubiquitous white buildings.

"I thought we were going to see Vanessa Caldwell," Chris said weakly, gripping the curtain so tightly the folds bit into his hand.

Olivia gave an amused snort. "We are."

Chris released the curtain, shutting out the white building, and turned to look at her. Unease built in his chest. "I thought she was a poet. She's one of Viktor val Daren's protégées, isn't she?"

"She's an *aspiring* poet," Olivia corrected. "Really, if she had an artistic proficiency, do you think she would have needed a wealthy patron? By evening, she writes silly little ditties and tries to sell them to papers with more interesting things to print. And by day, she's a doctor's assistant. Lifeknitter categorization. Nobody important." She gave him a playful look, tilting her head and smiling sideways. "Like you."

Before he could be offended, she slid off the seat and opened the cab door, and Chris had to scurry to keep up with her.

They emerged into the wild wind and pounding rain. Chris struggled with his umbrella, trying to open it up and use it as a shield while Olivia paid the cabbie. He turned his back against the wind, which put him facing the direction of the hospital they would be entering. It was small, but tidy. The occasional body who exited was dressed in simple clothes, old, practical hats shielding their faces and collars turned up against the wind. He saw one doctor, identified by her white uniform with linked three circles over the heart, hurrying inside, a newspaper held over her head to block the rain.

"All right!" Olivia declared at his side, making him start. "All paid and done with. Shall we go?"

Twenty minutes ago, he would have given his left leg to be inside a warm building, well away from both rain and wind. But now he was already soaked, tousled, freezing...and he'd rather be in any other building than the one they were staring up at.

He'd had no problem with hospitals when he was young, not even after a prolonged stay as a boy, when an attempt to impress his father had ended in a broken arm and serious burns. In fact, he had rather liked them, being reminded of convalescence and healing, of kindly doctors and their even more kindly nurses, of their assistants asking him questions and gifting him with candy when he gave answers they liked. That had changed after the long night he'd spent wandering the sterile white halls of Deorwynn's Heart, surrounded by death and bleeding and sobbing, desperately searching for his mother.

He gritted his teeth. No choice. "Let's go."

Inside, everything smelled clean and was bleached white. Doctors, nurses, and assistants bustled about, all wearing variations of that same white uniform. There were tables filled with strange, unidentifiable instruments, waiting rooms filled with bored or apprehensive looking patients-to-be—or perhaps, the family members of patients-that-already-were. They also passed a great many empty rooms, empty counters, and small offices with wide open doors, interiors all empty and white.

Olivia stopped before a reception counter. The woman sitting behind it looked up from a notebook that was blossoming with print. A wordweaver like him, though her words appeared almost as slowly as handwriting. "Can I help you?" she asked, offering them a professional, welcoming smile.

"I'm an investigative truthsniffer and this is my assistant. We're looking for Miss Vanessa Caldwell. Do you think we could speak to her?" Olivia replied just as sweetly.

"Caldwell..." the wordweaver said, turning away from Chris and Olivia to look over a sheet of paper full of names. She ran her finger across it, clicking her tongue. There were many empty spaces in the page that matched the gaps they'd seen in the hospital. Chris glanced about as she looked. The sterile, blinding white of everything crawled under his skin and writhed there.

"Ah, here we are, Vanessa Caldwell!" the secretary announced. "At the moment, she's doing stock in Doctor Harvey's supply room. If I can see your categorization cards, I'll point you right to where you can find her."

The location the wordweaver gave them turned out to be a closet marked *SUPPLY A-4* with thick black letters woven into the door. It was so small Chris couldn't actually manage to follow Olivia inside when she threw open the door and strolled in. Miss Caldwell had a difficult time turning to gasp at the intruder, and Olivia barely had space to put her hands on her hips and say, with her studied impertinence, "I hope I'm not interrupting?"

Vanessa Caldwell was a beautiful young woman. Her hair was wavy and black as night, her eyes so dark Chris couldn't even tell what colour they were. She was slender and curved like the graceful lines of a harp and her petite frame hugged the contours of her white uniform. She wore as many cosmetics as Olivia did not, and her features were delicate, especially her small button nose. She clasped the small white cloth she held against her chest. "Who are you?" she demanded, voice shrill.

"Olivia Faraday, Deathsniffer," Olivia replied. "And before you start asking why I'm here, I think you know."

Miss Caldwell studied her uninvited guests with wide-eyed, confused innocence. She seemed a sweet thing, a far cry from the imperious brat described by the val Darens and their house staff.

He wondered if she'd even heard about what had happened to the Duke. After all, she'd been out of Darrington, hadn't she? "Oli— Miss Faraday," he murmured. Maybe they should…

"I didn't do it," Miss Caldwell declared, impudence instantaneously replacing her angelic innocence.

"Of course not." Chris could hear the smirk in Olivia's voice. She held Miss Caldwell's gaze in a bold challenge. "Hmm," Olivia said. "Come inside and close the door, Mister Buckley. I doubt Miss Caldwell wants any attention called to herself."

It wasn't an easy task, but somehow Chris managed to squeeze into the tiny closet and shut the door behind him without crushing all three of them. He pushed himself up against the door, trying to create as much space as possible. The air went heavy with their combined breath, and he fought to get his notebook out and record the conversation to come.

"Normally when someone didn't do it, their first reaction isn't to say they didn't do it," Olivia mused.

"And why not? I know why you're here. And I know what that bitch would have said about me."

Chris skipped over the language in his transcription, then he forced himself to go back and add it in. He also noted the venom in Miss Caldwell's voice. Both seemed like things Olivia would want to remember.

"And just who is the bitch in question?"

"You know who I'm talking about. Viktor's charming wife." Vanessa Caldwell's voice dripped with disdain. "She's ever so fond of me."

"I don't blame her," Olivia chirped. "I already adore you!"

The two women stared at one another, and Chris used the momentary lull to describe the room and Miss Caldwell in his book. Boxes upon boxes filled with things he couldn't fathom. Stacks of white cloth: linen, towels, and bandages. A low ceiling, tiled floor, and every bit of it all in white. It was a struggle to keep his thoughts clear enough to transcribe what was happening, and not thread in his memories.

have you seen mymother? i needto find her slipped into his description of Miss Caldwell's uniform, and he gritted his teeth.

"It would help me find out who killed the Duke," Olivia said, "if you could just answer some simple questions for me."

Miss Caldwell thrust her elegant chin into the air and tried to fold her arms, but her elbow hit one of the steel shelves hard and sent it rattling. The cool image she was trying to convey didn't survive the blunder. "Why should I?" she demanded.

"Because I'm investigating his death, and—"

"I don't have to tell you a single thing," Vanessa Caldwell interrupted, defiance gleaming in her eyes. "I know what Evelyn has told you. You came thinking maybe, just maybe, I'm the one who killed Viktor."

"I don't care what the Duchess told me," Olivia replied, "but I never rule out a suspect, especially not before I talk to them. So yes, I do have it in my mind that maybe, just maybe."

"Let me tell you something," Vanessa snapped, her beautiful face pulling into a sneer. "I've been trying to get my poems into a decent publication for seven years. Seven whole *years*! It hasn't been easy when all anyone wants to print about is proficiencies losing their puissance, reformist propaganda, people losing their jobs, and yet another elemental accident." Chris thought of Rosemary at home with a pang. "It's been an uphill battle the whole time, and the few times I've gotten horrible gossip rags to print me, no one cares enough to notice. Not with Darrington falling apart."

"That's a very sad story," Olivia said, in a voice that said she didn't think it was an especially sad story at all.

"It's not finished," the lifeknitter shot back. "Seven years, everything I've done has been about furthering my career, and trying to get out of these little closets. I'm not strong enough to be a doctor. I'm not even strong enough to be a nurse."

"Are you going somewhere with this?"

"Where I am *going* is just this one simple fact: Viktor val Daren and his money were the only things that could possibly have given me all I wanted. He was every possibility of a future I had." Vanessa Caldwell's eyes flashed. "The only thing more stupid than me killing the Duke would be you thinking I did."

"Is that so?"

"I told you. I didn't do it."

"Well, lovely, why don't you let me decide that for myself?" Olivia chuckled and shook her head. "Right. Now, I was wondering where you were on the night of—"

But Vanessa interrupted her by turning away with haughty dignity. She began folding the white cloth she was holding. "I meant what I said, Miss Faraday," she said as she did so. "I don't have to tell you anything. You're not police."

Another silence, which Vanessa filled by lifting another white sheet and folding it, and then another. When Olivia spoke again, her tone was considerably less amused. "It would take me five minutes on the mirror to have an officer here."

"Then do that," Vanessa said, folding yet another sheet.

"You're adding a completely unnecessary step to finding out who *did* kill the Duke with this stubbornness," Olivia pressed. There was a hint of anger in her voice, now. "Do you have any idea how suspicious it is to refuse to talk to a Deathsniffer? At most, you get a day before I come in here with an officer, which is—"

"Long enough for you to realize this is none of my doing and stop wasting our time," Vanessa interjected.

"Even if you didn't kill the Duke, there are things you could tell me that would help the investigation." There was no doubt about it. Olivia no longer found Vanessa's stubbornness funny. "Every second that passes between the moment of his death and the moment I realize who killed him makes it more and more likely that they get away. You need to realize anything you say, no matter how innocuous, can be the one piece of information that tells me who—"

"I can tell you who. I can tell you right now." Vanessa twisted her neck about, and she looked at Olivia with hatred in her flashing, dark eyes and certainty on her beautiful, delicate face. "It was Evelyn. She cut him up herself. Now leave me alone."

CHAPTER NINE

What a *complete* waste of time," Olivia growled across the seat, and Chris couldn't help but agree. "It's a bloody idiotic rule," she continued. "Don't I work for the police? Don't I do most of their work *for* them, even?"

The silence dragged long enough Chris realized she wanted an actual answer. "I don't know?" he hazarded.

"Well, it's foolish. I'll be back with Maris tomorrow morning and she'll have done nothing but ruin my day," Olivia snapped. She turned half about in her seat and beat her fist against the wall of the car. "*Are we nearly there?*" she yelled.

"Ain't makin the horses go any faster!" the driver shouted back, voice muffled.

Olivia huffed, throwing herself back in her seat and crossing her arms. "He's going slow so he can charge us more," she spat.

Most cabbies calculated their fee based on distance, not time, but Chris didn't feel much like telling her that. There was no need for the driver to gouge them; he was going to make plenty enough royals on the flat rate. The val Daren estate was *not* close by.

"I'd like to talk to the Duchess alone," Olivia announced.

Whatever she'd thought of Miss Caldwell's attitude, one thing was for certain: she did love to see someone agree with her initial suspicion.

Chris frowned. "Don't you need me to transcribe?" he hedged.

She waved her hand at him. "No, no. I'll recount everything for you later. Everything I remember, at least. I'm so scattered. That's why I absolutely need a good assistant, you know. I forget everything unless it's written down!" She blinked and shook herself, realizing she'd wandered off. "It's not ideal, but it's necessary. Obviously, the Duchess is a woman who values appearances. That's why she risked evidence tampering by tucking Mister Wiggly back into the Duke's trousers." Chris flushed and avoided her frank, unashamed eyes. "Some people think assistants are invisible, but I don't think she's one. You being there doubles the amount of people who'd see her family—or worse, her*self*— embarrassed by something *scandalous*."

"So you think she'd be more open if I weren't there."

Olivia nodded in satisfaction. "Yes, exactly."

Chris considered it, and concluded it might be wise. He knew all too well about the value of appearances. "So what about me? Do I sit in the foyer and wait?" If that were the case, he would just as well have gone home to be with Rosemary. He wanted to be there when she woke, wanted her to know he was by her side. If their home was going to be stormed by politicians and reporters, he wanted to protect her.

"I don't pay you to sit on your fancy bum," Olivia said. "Obviously, you're going to snoop."

Her pronouncement sent his thoughts of Rosemary scattering. His stomach flopped. "I hope you're not asking me to do anything…"

"Anything *impolite*, Mister Buckley?" She smirked. "Perish the thought."

She was mocking him; his hackles rose. "Anything *illegal*," he snapped. "And you might try being polite. People would tell you more if they liked you."

He regretted the words the moment they left his mouth, but to his surprise, Olivia only sat back in her seat and giggled. "Big words, Mister Buckley," she said, her voice lilting. "A little bit of spine, is it?"

Chris huffed. "I'm not snooping around the val Daren estate. They're Old Blood."

"It's part of your job," Olivia said.

"It's not," Chris retorted. "You didn't mention anything about spying for you."

Olivia shrugged. "Your job is what I say it is," she said flippantly. "You're not my secretary, you're my assistant. You assist."

"This—"

"Stop thinking about things in black and white. There was a murder done in the val Daren house, and murders are never done without evidence. How am I supposed to find that? Do you think the Duchess, image-obsessed Evelyn val Daren, is going to just *let* me search her home?"

"Probably not," Chris allowed, "but I'd still hope—"

"You're sweet! You're pretty! You're very nonthreatening. You're perfect. Snooping is easy. Stop whining." She made a dismissive gesture with one of her slender, long-fingered hands. "I'll have the Duchess occupied, so just do whatever. If you look like you belong, no one is going to question it."

"If it's so easy, you do it." His voice came out very sullen. He sounded like Rosemary losing an argument.

"We've been through this! Sweet! Pretty! Nonthreatening! *I* need to keep the Duchess busy, and you don't know how to question her," Olivia said, irritatingly reasonable. "Also," she continued, "I want to see whether you can follow orders."

Defeated, he sighed. "Fine," he bit off. "What am I looking for?"

Olivia rubbed her hands together, leaning forward in her seat. Childish glee shone in her eyes like evil stars. "Anything interesting," she replied. Chris swallowed. *Is that all...?*

He cleared his throat.

She rolled her eyes. "Look for suspicious things! Is that so difficult? Anything that stands out, pops, piques your attention. The smallest things can make you think about—" She cut herself off, all of a sudden looking almost abashed. "None of this is helping, is it?"

"Not in the slightest," he admitted.

"Gods, you could be looking right at something and no alarms would be going off at all, would they?" She scrunched up her face in thought. "Let me think about this."

Truthsniffing. This was the gift that made Olivia a valuable member of society while he was fit only to keep her records. He tasted jealousy, like he'd bitten down on rusted iron. It hardly seemed fair. A gift so subtle and so intangible she couldn't even describe it, while his was clear, clean-cut, impossible to misinterpret.

"All right," Olivia tried again, "how about this. We need the weapon! I would *love* to get the weapon to William. *That* would be a lead worth following. So, usually...look for fast drops. Cubbies, vases, cupboards, drawers." She nodded to herself. "Yes. Also, blood. Any blood, that's easy enough. Throat wounds are messy. After this long, it's probably cleaned up, but with that much blood, there's bound to be a bit left somewhere. Check the laundry!" she continued. "Blood only comes out in cold water, and only when it's fresh. Look for brownish stains. With luck, the Duchess was wearing white when she slashed him. And it can't *hurt* to poke about and see if anything catches your attention." She looked at him expectantly. "Does any of that help?"

"You would really be more suited to this than me," he murmured.

"Well, if you're *completely* useless, I'll have to see about doing my part. Gods know you might be. But who knows, Mister Buckley." Her sideways smile returned. "You might just surprise both of us."

He didn't know whether to try and exercise stealth, or to stride openly through the halls. In the end, he alternated between the two like an insecure debutante trying to decide between being a delicate flower or a scandalous temptress. He knew he was calling more attention to himself than either extreme would warrant, but his indecisiveness over weighed his good sense.

It was opening things that was the worst. He had no excuse to give if someone asked what he was doing. And the worst of *that* was when a drawer or cabinet was full of papers and he had to rifle through them like he actually was some sort of miscreant. He reminded himself of the cheque he'd receive from the office of O. Faraday, Deathsniffer for this sort of work. He could pay off the reporters that would come sniffing. He could afford to pay Fernand. Gods, he could buy Rosemary *food.*

Staff passed by him routinely. Few paid him mind. Some stopped to offer bows or curtseys, asking if there was anything they could do to help him, to which he mumbled refusals that were blatantly hiding some great shame. But, miraculously, none questioned him, merely nodding and scurrying back to work.

He scanned up and down the hallway every time he went to open a door. He tried to avoid servants seeing *that,* as he could find no good reason, even if he had the Duchess's permission, to be poking about in private rooms. Some were locked—all with sensible, modern locks rather than the old fashioned and clumsy piece on the Duke's study—but most were not. There were sitting rooms, guest bedrooms, small, cramped offices filled with papers Chris didn't understand…

In a small office decorated in brown and forest green, he found a handwritten document half-hidden under a pile of bills for salamander binding renewals. It was adorned with neither crest nor seal nor watermark, and its very plainness caught his eye. As he read it over, a furrow grew between his brows. *Evie,* it read, *we thank you for your continued support and hope to see you at our scheduled meeting next week. The date is soon approaching and there is a great deal of work left to do. I've recently come to believe L has some suspicions, but if we move quickly, as planned, he'll not have the time to react. Nevertheless, I wish to tighten our plans and prevent giving him the chance. Your presence is always welcome and I believe you integral to our successes, past, present, and future.* It concluded with a scribbled *Yours, HC.*

Chris read over the letter twice, and then, more on instinct than any logic, he opened his notebook and transcribed it before sliding it back under the bills, careful to make it appear undisturbed. He wasn't sure the letter was worthwhile, but something about it left a queer taste in his mouth. Hadn't that been all Olivia had asked for? Anything interesting. Anything suspicious.

The rest of his search was less eventful, which was remarkable considering how insubstantial what he'd found actually was. The laundry yielded no results, and he found nothing that could be used as a murder weapon, not even a particularly sharp letter opener. Looking for brown stains proved useless. As he made his way down a hallway lined with doors and every room proved itself as useless as the last, Chris's insecurity mixed in with his nervousness and created a potent draught that left him surly and skittish.

The hall was clear of staff for the moment, so he grabbed the next latch in line and pushed the door open. He entered backwards, peering out to be sure no one suddenly came along, closing it softly behind him.

"...hello?" a voice from behind him asked.

Chris whirled, realizing too late that it made him look like he was guilty of something. He was in another sitting room, well-furnished in dark, sombre colours—navy blues, blacks, and soft seal greys. A beautiful worldcaught painting of the val Daren estate occupied an entire wall, its wafting clouds and swaying grass so lifelike it could have been a window.

On a low couch, sitting close enough to be walking the line of propriety, Lady Analaea val Daren rested in the arms of the beau her mother so venomously disapproved of.

Too late, he swept a courteous bow. When he straightened, he wore his most charming smile with just the slightest tinge of ruefulness. "Ah, my lady," he said, his voice falling into the cadences of genteel propriety. "I'm very sorry to interrupt you. Should I leave?"

Ana looked him over, puzzlement wrinkling between her brows. "Why are you here?" she asked.

He returned her gaze as he searched for an answer. She'd obviously been crying. Her eyes were puffy and her cheeks were streaked. Not only that, but her hair fell in limp strands about her face and her dress was sombre and flattered her slender, willowy frame not at all. Once again, she was the awkward, mousy-looking young woman he'd seen that first day. He marvelled at how easily she switched between ethereal, simple beauty and mere plainness. *Answer*, he reminded himself. The silence was stretching long. He remembered the explanation Olivia had given him and fell back onto it, trusting it to hold his weight. "Miss Faraday sent me," he said, not truly a lie. "She wanted me to ask you some questions."

Ana looked away, but not before he saw a flash of pain in her eyes. One of her hands was linked with Ethan Grey's, fingers threaded together. "More questions," she murmured. "Why do I have to answer more questions?"

"It's all right, Ana," Mister Grey murmured. Chris saw him squeeze her hand, and he swallowed, glancing away. His presence felt like a cruel intrusion. "The Deathsniffer could help find who killed your father."

"I don't care who killed him," Ana replied distantly, a hoarse catch in her voice. "He's dead, and he's never coming back."

"I'm sorry," Chris hurried. He felt terrible. He shouldn't have asked for her assistance. He should have sheepishly explained he'd chosen the wrong door and backed out, no matter how transparent it would have been. "It won't take long, there are just a few things Miss Faraday wanted to know, and she's busy with your mother at the moment, so she sent me to…" He trailed off uncomfortably when she didn't stir at all in response to his rambling words.

It was Mister Grey who turned to meet his eyes. "Is this really necessary?" he asked. His voice was a pleasant, smooth baritone, but there was a ragged edge to it that made Chris realize the painter had been on the verge of tears himself. "She's upset. She just lost her father."

"I know," Chris said. "It won't take long," he said. Realized he'd repeated himself. "I'm sorry." That was repetition again. He ground his teeth helplessly.

"You could come back tomorrow, or—"

"It's fine, Ethan," Ana interrupted him quietly. She buried her face into the back of the couch. "They're not going to go away until they're satisfied. Ask your questions," she said, voice muffled by the upholstery.

Now he needed a question to ask, one important enough to excuse his marching in and tormenting a heartbroken girl. Her relationship with her father had been left unresolved and full of questions and pain, and Chris knew exactly how she felt. It was an ugly thing and he didn't want to exacerbate it. He tried to think of what Olivia Faraday would do, but he knew he couldn't imitate her. What Olivia would do was what *felt* right, what her precious intuition *told* her to say. She'd feel out the situation in a way Chris couldn't.

So he would need to feel it out in a way Olivia Faraday never could.

He put on his best, most empathetic smile. "You said you were at a gallery on the night your father was killed?"

Ana and Mister Grey turned away from him at the same moment and met one another's eyes. The painter reached out to stroke his lady under the chin and give her an encouraging smile. Chris fought the instinct to clear his throat.

"Yes. I was with Ethan," Ana replied eventually. "…and Mother."

"It wasn't *my* gallery," Mister Grey elaborated. "I'm afraid I've not been so lucky with my art as that. But I had an offer for some of my paintings to be hosted by another artist. It was the first opportunity of the sort I've had since categorization."

Chris nodded. "I'd heard about that," he smiled. "Congratulations." He turned his attention back to Ana. Just a few more questions, and he could leave without having drawn suspicion. "You said you were surprised your mother went with you?"

"I shouldn't have been. She did it only to make a point."

"It's not so bad as all that," Ethan said, more to Ana than to Chris. "Really, Ana, I was honoured she came at all."

"It wasn't to support you." The denial was a harsh growl. "You know it wasn't. She doesn't support anyone in anything. She made her little comments about you, and then she just—she does this all the time! She expects everyone to just do what she asks because she wants it. She doesn't even acknowledge what they might be giving up for her."

"Ana…" Ethan soothed. He laid a gentle hand on her shoulder, but she shook him off like an insect.

"All that matters to her is image and appearances. She doesn't care about what I want! What I can *do*!"

She closed her eyes, and then she raised her voice in a familiar song.

She didn't have Rosemary's power, and she stumbled awkwardly over some of the words. The tones were flawed; it was merely a woman singing, no otherworldly and eerie perfection. Where Rosemary spoke to the elementals as if she were one of them, Ana sounded like she was speaking a second language.

But it was still a binding song. Chris took an uneasy step back when the lamp on the table dimmed, brightened, and then flickered wildly, its dark nimbus fading in and out. The alp that materialized did so gradually, as if struggling to manifest, a swirl of dark anti-stars spiralling around its comically chubby and awkward body, a sound like the lowest note of a pianoforte thrumming through the room. Its large black eyes were almost intelligent. It blinked at Ana, and then focused on Ethan, then Chris. A shiver went through him as he glimpsed something wild and unfathomable deep in those dark eyes.

The alp climbed to its feet. Its light illuminated the room far more brightly than the lamp had. Chris knew it *could* flow and swirl through the air like the cloudlings, sylphs, salamanders, and fiarans Rosemary frequently unbound and danced with in her fey way, uncaring of the lurking disaster. But like gnomes and dryads, alps preferred not to. It jumped from foot to foot, fat rolls jiggling, and then, in an ugly, nasal little voice, it joined Ana in her song.

Alps were the least dangerous elementals. They controlled only the powers of light and darkness, and their capacity for harm was therefore limited. While they were known to cause blindness or seizures, they had yet to wreak any chaos on a large scale. Nevertheless, Chris's heart pounded in his throat and his shoulders bunched up rigidly tight as he watched the awkward thing move and sing in tandem with the young woman's faltering voice.

He kept his gaze trained on the alp, frozen in shock and fear, as the song rose to the crescendo. The last note held. And held. And held. Ana's voice cracked and Chris's head jerked in alarm. The alp's fat little cheeks bunched in a devious, evil smile…

…and then he vanished in a swirl of black smoke. The lamp glowed darkly once again.

The room rang with silence. Chris fumbled for his tongue. "I thought Old Blood were exempt from categorization," he said, sounding feeble.

"We are," Ana said. "I've never been categorized."

But—no, that was impossible. If she had never been categorized, than her abilities would need to be innate, not awakened. And if that were true…Chris swallowed a gasp, snapping his gaze to the girl and studying her with renewed interest. Could it really be? No. What were the odds he would meet two wizards in one lifetime? In *this* lifetime, where even categorization wasn't foolproof for finding a proficiency anymore? True, Ana demonstrated none of Rosemary's astounding power—if anything, her proficiency was one of the weakest for 'binding he'd ever seen—but to be able to use *any* proficiency uncategorized was exceedingly rare, much less the most powerful and important of all.

"That's...amazing," he said finally, entirely without guile.

Ana averted her eyes, but her cheeks flushed with what might have been pleasure.

"It is," Mister Grey spoke for her. "Evelyn doesn't think so."

"She says it's shameful that I want to bind," Ana said, seething anger and deep bitterness hovering just beneath the quiet hurt in her voice. "Our exemption from categorization is what sets us apart. It's what puts us *above* people like...like you," she said, faltering and shooting him an apologetic glance. "She doesn't care that I'm a wizard, not categorized. She doesn't care about how much it matters to me. She doesn't even care that it...it..." She visibly searched for the words. "It makes me feel alive," she finally concluded with a flash of confidence that vanished as quick as it had appeared.

Chris tried turning the conversation back to realms less intimate. "What time did you leave the gallery?"

"...I don't know," Ana said. "It was very late. Most had already left when we..." And then she sighed, closing her eyes. "When we fought."

Chris furrowed his brow, momentarily distracted from his distress. That was new, was it? Yes. Yesterday, Ana had spoken of what a lovely night the three of them had spent. He remembered weaving it into his transcription. He fought to keep his voice neutral as he asked. "You and the Duchess?"

To his continued surprise, Ana shook her head. "All three of us. But Ethan and me, especially."

"It was over something so silly," Ethan said. He reached out and brushed hair back from Ana's face. "I'm sorry it ever happened. When she mirrored me the next morning and told me about...about Viktor, I was here within the hour. It wasn't something to hold against each other, not when it was so idiotic to begin with."

"We shouldn't have started," Ana amended. "But Mother loved that we did, and she just pushed it as far as she could."

"I left the gallery," Ethan admitted sheepishly. "My own opening, my first one. I was so angry over absolutely nothing, but I just needed to clear my head. I walked along the road, feeling stupider by the moment. But I was too proud to go back and apologize."

"I stayed. Mother and I both," Ana concluded. "Until very, very late. We were the last to leave. She kept trying to talk to me about how proud she was that I'd stood up to Ethan, that I'd 'finally seen him for what he really was.' I didn't want to hear it, but she's so *tireless*."

"I know you didn't believe a word of it," Ethan hurriedly told her, and she gave him a tremulous smile. Once again, Chris felt the intruder. He could leave, but Ana's story had changed, and that was something he felt Olivia would surely want to know.

"And then, when you returned home..." Chris trailed off. *Was the Duke still alive?* He didn't want to ask.

He could have fallen onto his knees in gratitude when Ana spared him having to. "I didn't see him," she murmured. And then, all at once, her face crumpled and she gasped for air as though she were dying. "Oh, Gods," she gulped, and the sheer pain in her voice was enough to rend Chris's heart in two. "Oh, Maiden Maerwald, I wish I could see him just one more *time*."

And then the dam broke, and words surged out of him. "I'm sure he loved you very much!" he exclaimed. "I'm sure if he'd have known what was going to happen, he'd have told you!" Ana turned slowly to stare at him through wide, dark eyes, and he was still talking. "I know it must be hard to think you'll never be able to ask him if he cared, if you just weren't good enough, if—" He shook his head. Mister Grey had turned to stare as well, and his shoulders had gone tight as he leaned into a protective position, but Chris just couldn't seem to stop *talking*. "But you have to know he can't have just not cared. You were his daughter. You—"

"Who do you think you *are?*" Ana cut in. Her voice was shrill and she stared up at him with eyes full of tears.

"I—" Chris crashed back into himself, and there weren't any more words.

"You don't know me!" Ana buried her face in Mister Grey's shoulder, and her shoulders shuddered. "You don't know anything *about* me. I don't even know your name!"

"I...Christopher Buckley. I'm—"

"—the Deathsniffer's assistant, yes, I *know*." Ana's voice was muffled against her beau's shoulder. Mister Grey glared at Chris fiercely enough that he took a step back and reached blindly for the latch. "I don't want sympathy from anyone who would work for someone like her," Ana continued, and the sob that had barely been held back suddenly wracked her body. She collapsed, weeping, against Mister Grey.

"Get out," the painter commanded.

Chris didn't need the direction. Already, he was half-turned and fumbling with the latch. His heart pounded and his stomach twisted. The door fell open and Chris tumbled into the hallway. He hadn't noticed he'd been leaning all his weight forward, and he was so confused he had to catch his feet and still almost sprawled onto the hardwood floors. "I'm sorry," he blurted. "I'm so sorry. I—"

He cut himself off, closing the door in his own face. He sank to the floor, pressing his back up against the door and putting his face in his hands.

"Dammit," he murmured, and then, when he realized absolutely no one would hear him, and even if they did, things could not possibly get worse, "*Horseshit*."

Would they tell the Duchess he'd been snooping about? What would Olivia think of that? Why had he been such an utter idiot? The last question was especially compelling. The words had just fallen out of him like unrestrained cargo. What had he been thinking?

He growled. Nothing to be done for it. He braced his legs under him and started to push up…

…and stopped.

He squinted down between his feet. The hand that had been rubbing the back of his neck slowed, then stopped. He blinked, peering closer. Was that…?

He let himself fall back down, twisting uncomfortably to get a better look at it. There in the cedar, of a grain so fine it could only be the result of an attentive dryad's cultivation, there was a darker spot. A rusty brown line. Not a circle, like a droplet would be, but as if it had been scuffed.

Chris touched the wood, sliding a single finger along the line. He didn't know enough about construction to be able to feel a difference in the darker area, but he knew enough to put together a theory. Liquid seeped into wood. That was why it was destructive to leave wet clothing on a fine grain.

What if someone had spilled a drop of blood here, and, not noticing, had stepped in it? They would have slipped, and the droplet would have become a scuff. They certainly would have noticed it then, but by that time, it would already have been crushed into the grain. Not hard enough to stain, not yet, but hard enough it would take more than a moment to clean, and someone fleeing from a murder, with a bloody weapon in their hand and spray on their clothes, well, they wouldn't exactly have had time to fetch a mop.

Excitement bubbled up in him as he stared at his discovery. The killer had been here right after they'd done in the Duke. In this hall, and by the direction of the scuff, they'd gone into the very room whose door he now leaned against. Someone had tried to clean the stain, servant or butcher, but by that time, the wood had been ruined and the only way to fix it would have been to replace the entire plank. He might never have noticed if he hadn't been so close, and staring right at it. *This* was something Olivia would find interesting.

He leaned back on the door as he pulled himself to his feet. He needed to find her. The parlour needed to be searched, the staff and the family needed to be questioned, and—

He fell backwards. He let out a strangled sound, wheeling his arms and trying in vain to regain his balance as he fell. His wrist struck something soft, and someone seized it in a rough grip, tight enough to hurt. If that weren't enough, he found himself hauled up by his arm to a standing position, and then he was staring into pale blue eyes.

Ethan Grey may have been more slender than Chris, but he was much, much taller. The iron grip on his wrist retreated, but Chris found himself unable to pull his eyes away from Ethan's. They were standing so close. "Uh." But before he could stammer out an apology, a gentle hand fell on his shoulder, giving him reason to tear his gaze away from Grey's handsome face and the tiny speck of blue paint under his left eye.

Lady Analaea stood with her small hand on his shoulder. Her face was still splotched and her eyes still wounded, but there was a strange softness in her expression. "Mister Buckley..." she murmured, and said nothing more, merely stared at him with that curiously gentle face.

"...my lady," Chris said eventually, and decided it was time to find the apology that had escaped him before. "Forgive me. I shouldn't have said those—"

"Thank you for saying them," Ana interrupted, and she gave him a tremulous smile. It lit her face up like a beacon. "They were only so difficult to hear because I had convinced myself I never would. I know you didn't know my father. I know nothing you said came from a place of authority. But that doesn't matter. Thank you."

"It *is* interesting," Olivia repeated, stepping in another circle around the dark brown mark. "I've seen blood in wood enough times to know this is the real thing."

Behind them, in the parlour where Ana and Ethan had sat, there were now three efficient and smartly uniformed police officers. After Olivia had been summoned and the situation explained, the Deathsniffer's first act had been to get on the val Daren mirror and have Officer Maris Dawson send over some manpower to search the room. The coppers did so now with the determination and skill of industrious ant-men. Furniture was overturned, shelves were disassembled, the grand worldcaught painting was taken off the wall.

"The killer went into the room, then?" Chris asked. He spoke quietly, trying to avoid being overheard by the staff who'd gathered to stare at the activity with wide eyes and affronted expressions. But despite his attempt at subtlety, he couldn't keep the excitement about of his voice.

Olivia nodded. She was trying to hide it, but she was excited, as well. Excited and energized.

"And why would they do that?"

"I don't know." Her response was prompt, as though she'd been waiting for the question. "But it's a question, and for a truthsniffer, a question always has an answer."

"Always?"

"Absolutely, Mister Buckley." She feigned hurt with the coy innocence of a debutante at her coming out ball. "Don't you trust me?"

"Absolutely," he echoed. It occurred to him that he was returning Olivia's grin with one of his own. That same innervated exhilaration he saw sparkling in her eyes like drink or drug was burning in him.

"Miss Faraday," one of the police officers called, and the moment was gone. She turned about, her loose peasant's skirt twirling. "Miss Faraday," the man repeated. The tasteful, dark decor had all been overturned and moved about. "I'm sorry," he said, "we took this place apart, but the only thing we found is this."

One of the other officers stepped forward and extended a gloved hand. Cradled in his palm was an ancient brass key.

Olivia gasped and darted forward, seizing it like a striking snake. "*Yes*," she whispered. "Oh yes, there you are, beautiful. I'd wondered where you got to." She clutched it against her chest. "Officer!" she barked, and he snapped to attention on instinct. "I guarantee you, the killer came to this room after she did the Duke, and that means she left a lot more than just this."

The officer swallowed and glanced over Olivia's shoulder to meet Chris's eyes. "Ah, Miss Faraday—"

"There was some reason for her to come right to this room," she said, her conviction solid as a rock. "Maybe that reason isn't immediately obvious, but we are *going* to find out what it is." She twirled about to give Chris one of her smiles. "Mister Buckley, it's going to be a late night."

CHAPTER TEN

There's something else in that room."

Olivia's back was to the mirror, her gaze trained on Chris at his desk, but it had been a long time since she'd reacted to or acknowledged his presence. When he turned the page and looked up to see if she'd noticed, he wasn't surprised that she hadn't. She was completely lost in her own head.

"The key isn't enough for you?" Officer Dawson's voice asked for what seemed like the hundredth time.

"The key is nothing! All it tells us is that a killer went into a room and left a key. There's something else to this; it's under my skin!"

"Faraday, I trust your gut. But you and my boys took that whole room apart—multiple times—and found nothing."

"I know," Olivia growled. "But there is something. There has to be. Nothing else makes *sense*. Whoever killed Viktor val Daren went to that room before doing anything else, still dripping blood and in such a hurry she didn't take time to fix a hell of a mistake."

They were both quiet for a time. Chris remembered to actually read his paper, but immediately recalled why he'd stopped in the first place. It was an article about the incident at White Clover, and while she wasn't mentioned by name, Rosemary was all over it. By tomorrow, someone would have sniffed out their trail. By Deorday, the flood would be rising over their heads. He wanted to go home to her so badly.

"You're missing a piece, Faraday," Maris said finally. "There isn't anything concrete to any of the 'evidence' you've brought forward so far. There must be something, one major, glaring thing that is completely escaping you."

Olivia made a disgusted sound. "I *know*, Maris."

"Who killed Duke val Daren?"

"Duchess val Daren," Olivia replied immediately.

"Why?"

"Because..." Olivia threw her hands into the air and turned away from the mirror again, slumping back against the table before it. The chimes jingled. "Because she's hiding something. The entire time we talked today, she was going to lengths to not tell me something. I could *feel* it way down deep in my bones. It was..." She shook her head. "You know how it is, Maris. When you can smell it."

"They don't let us make arrests on intuition, Faraday." It was obviously meant as a rebuke, but Officer Dawson's voice was full of sympathy. "Not even us truthsniffers."

"I don't understand why not," Olivia retorted.

"Because you don't know Evelyn val Daren killed her husband. All you know is she's hiding something from you. And if you can't prove she's guilty, that means nothing. Maybe she was just eating a double layer chocolate cheesecake when her husband was killed. People hide things. It's what we do. And Faraday—you've been doing this for long enough that I don't have to explain this. Again."

"It isn't as if—"

"Trail's getting cold, Faraday," Officer Dawson said, and all the tired empathy in her voice was gone. "It's been four full days since the Duke was killed, and you have nothing but a bunch of little pieces that don't fit. Make them fit."

"Oh, yes, ma'am," Olivia said sourly, not exactly in agreement.

"I'll meet you at your office tomorrow morning for our little appointment with Miss Caldwell. Let's make it quick; I have other things to do. And please tell Constance to have a spot of tea ready for me. I refuse to drink that vile, black stuff you keep trying to force on me. Good night."

Chris expected her attention to turn to him when the mirror darkened, but, instead, she deflated. All the life went out of Olivia Faraday, and the complete lack of any soul in her unsettled him more than he could say.

"...M-miss Faraday?"

Her eyes shot to where he sat in his desk. He shrank back. She studied him with the intensity of a hunting snake, and he was as trapped and helpless as a small creature caught in her gaze. "You're still here," she said, with very little expression.

"You said to wait and see if you'd need m—"

"I know what I said." She straightened and shook herself, squared her shoulders, and then looked him in the eye. "Who killed the Duke?" she asked.

He blinked. "Uh."

"You have to tell Maris who to arrest. Right now. Who do you point her towards?"

"I don't know!" Chris responded defensively, but Olivia continued to wait. He met her eyes in stubborn defiance...and then he gave up. She'd have her way in the end.

He took a moment to actually consider it. In his mind, he compiled a list of everyone he believed might have been responsible. The names all swam about and he couldn't make sense of any of it. "I..." He chuckled uncomfortably, "...don't know," he said again, sincerely this time.

"Try."

"I am trying. I just—no one had a reason to kill him now. Not the Duchess, not Analaea, not Miss Caldwell. It doesn't suit any of them. The only thing I can think of is—" He cut himself off suddenly, realizing Olivia still didn't know of his best suspicion.

She didn't miss the implication of his sudden silence. "*Is?*" she pressed. Her fist came down on the edge of his desk and she gave him a meaningful look. "What do you know, Christopher Buckley?"

He shrugged. "What if they had debts?"

Olivia's brow furrowed. "What would give you that idea? The Duchess hasn't said anything about—"

"But she wouldn't, would she? I'd suspect you could go so far as to look at her books, and everything would seem in order. She's obsessed with the family reputation—we established that an hour in." He shook his head. The intensity of Olivia watching was making him very uncomfortable. "It's just something I heard," he finished lamely. "Old Debts."

"You're not making any sense."

"It's a rumour, that's all. I don't know if it's true." He sighed. "The Old Blood are all slaves to their creditors. The sumfinders hold their leashes, letting them off just long enough to reel them back in. Lending and then claiming, generosity and then repossession. They make millions in interest that way. Or..." Chris cleared his throat. "Or so I've heard."

Olivia's eyes gleamed in the dim light. "And just where would you have heard this?"

With the way she was looking at him, it seemed like the most aggressive sort of stupidity to admit he'd overheard a conversation between two anonymous sumfinders at a zoo. He fell back on a half-truth—or quarter-truth. "My father's financial adviser took care of my sister and me after the Floating Castle. He mentioned it when I was explaining the case to him. Er—I didn't tell him anything confidential. No names, or—"

"Why haven't you mentioned this before?"

He shrugged. "He's getting me a list of names. He might be able to actually find the name of the val Darens' creditor for us. I thought if I had something of actual substance..."

"Mn," Olivia hummed noncommittally. Her attention seemed to slip off of him and he could have sighed in relief as she turned and ghosted away; he didn't, sure it would only draw her attention again. "He's getting those names for you now?"

"I think so."

She dropped into one of the well-upholstered chairs, leaning back and closing her eyes. Her long fingers formed claws as she gripped the ends of the arms, the tension there a stark contrast to the way the rest of her relaxed at once.

"A creditor…" she mused. "He misses a payment for the last time, after numerous warnings. His daughter and wife are out of the house for their little gallery. The staff are sparse, discreet, and easy to pay off. The creditor has someone come in under the cover of darkness and show all his other clients what happens when Old Debts go unpaid." She nodded once, to herself. "It doesn't *not* fit. Explains the mutilation. The shock—he thought he was safe. Maybe even the disgust, depending on what the hitman said. And something else, too, something about the way he was laid out, something familiar. It's been bothering me since I first saw him. Maybe…" And then she frowned, her face scrunching up and becoming fearsome in the flickering candlelight. "But not the todger peeping out of his pants. Unless he *was* wanking. The staff didn't feel like they were lying, either. They weren't paid off. I don't think so. And the parlour. The parlour…"

She lapsed into silence, and if not for the death grip her hands held on the arms of the chair, Chris might have thought she'd simply fallen asleep. He folded his newspaper, dropped it into the rubbish bin, and waited for her to speak again.

She did. "And there's still the Duchess. What is she hiding?"

Abruptly, Chris remembered the letter he'd found. "Actually…" he said.

Olivia opened her eyes and sat up.

Chris flipped open his notebook and thumbed through, searching for the copy he'd made. He passed pages and pages of disjointed descriptions and transcriptions until he saw the words, weaved in almost the exact same handwriting as the original. "Here." He slipped out from behind his desk, crossed the room, and handed the notebook to his employer.

She scanned it. "*Evie*," Olivia mused. "Evelyn?"

"That would seem logical."

She nodded, half to herself. "…and who is *HC*?"

"I don't know," Chris replied. He seemed to be saying that an awful lot lately. "And I'm not sure what it's talking about, or why I—why I thought it would be worth your time, but…I don't know. It's something."

"It is that." Olivia looked up at him and the tiniest little spark of her dark fire was back in her eyes. "I'm surprised, Mister Buckley," she continued archly. "You didn't manage to cock up at all today." Before he could so much as flush, she was waving him off. "Go home, then. Tomorrow, hopefully we'll find this one missing piece Maris has so graciously pointed out we're missing." She turned her face away from him, closing her eyes. But a contented little cat's smile was on her lips as she did so, and she hummed quietly to herself as he prepared to leave for the night—finally.

He stopped with one hand on the latch, turning back to where Olivia still rested in the chair. Her fingers drummed out a beat she could only hear along the arms, and while he couldn't pick up any words, he could see her lips moving. Suddenly and inexplicably, he felt not entirely right about leaving her. Would she simply stay all night? Did she usually? It occurred to him he knew very little about Olivia Faraday the woman, who she was aside from her eccentricities and her profession. Where did she live? Who was waiting for her there? Was she married? Did she have children?

"…will you be all right when I go?"

Olivia opened her eyes and swivelled her head to him, and looked surprised before bursting into giggles. "Aren't you sweet!" she exclaimed. "*Yes*, Mister Buckley. I'll be just fine. I appreciate the sentiment, really, but I *only* said you didn't cock up!"

His cheeks burned. "I—"

"Though I did call you pretty, today. Is that what did it?" She *ts*ked. "Am I giving you ideas, Mister Buckley? Should I be—"

"Good *night*, Miss Faraday," Chris interrupted gruffly, and stepped out into the darkness.

He shivered and pulled up the collar of his overcoat to shield his face from the wind. It was too late for a taxi; he'd have to make his way home on foot. The rain had stopped hours ago and stars were sparkling overhead, but he went up to his ankle in more than one puddle. The flicking alp-light from the streetlamps sent the shadows dancing and changing. His steps echoed. The darkness and the solitude and the dark thoughts of murder swirling through his head played havoc with his nerves, and at one point, he swore he heard someone else's steps dogging his own.

He knew it was his imagination, but the mere idea turned him irrational. Every reflection in every puddle made him look about fearfully for the source of movement, and every night bird chirping made him jump near out of his skin. He sped up his pace until he was jogging, and he didn't stop until he passed the soundshield of the Buckley estate.

CHAPTER ELEVEN

The Buckley estate was silent and dark. Chris closed the door as quietly as he could. He laid his umbrella against the wall and hung his bowler on the hat rack, running a hand through his disastrous hair. The dining room table was cleared of all dishes, but the coatroom held a very bulky and unflattering woman's raincoat that must have come in attached to Rosemary's governess. He looked into the parlour where he'd seen her take tea with Fernand that morning, but it was dark and unoccupied. He quietly climbed the stairs and peered into his sister's bedroom, and he could make out her form beneath the covers, see the blankets rising and falling as she breathed in peaceful silence. He saw no sign of anyone else. Frowning, he descended once more.

"Miss Albany?" he called quietly, but there was no response.

When he looked into the parlour again, something caught his eye. A figure was huddled up on the chesterfield, barely identifiable by the alp-light coming in from the street.

Furrowing his brow, Chris pulled off his coat, hanging it with his bowler hat on the rack. Cautiously, he stepped into the parlour. He tapped the small lamp on the pianoforte—which no one had played since his mother had died—and the salamander within flared to light, its dark eyes giving him a peevish glance and its long tongue darting out. Chris gave it only a moment's attention before turning and pacing over to the chesterfield.

For a moment, he thought there was a stranger in his house.

The woman who lay there had long, thick waves of softly curling brown hair that framed her peaceful face. No one would ever call her beautiful, but there was an austere sort of prettiness to her features that would have made any man look twice. And there was a softness, too. Around her eyes, the line of her jaw, in the way her chestnut hair cascaded over her cheek and cast her face into shadow. She was lovely.

He wouldn't have recognized her at all if not for the shoes.

He gaped. *Rachel Albany?* It couldn't be—but it was, for who else would be here, and who else could possibly have thought that colour was a good idea? He could see it, how her hair would look pinned back in a severe bun, how the soft, pretty lines of her face would turn hard and unwelcoming when she set her jaw, thrust her chin forward and up. This *was* Rachel Albany...or, at least, the woman Rachel Albany was underneath the one he saw every day.

As he stared down at her, flabbergasted, her eyelids fluttered open and her brow furrowed in confusion. "Where..." she murmured, throwing up one hand against the dim salamander-light.

Mortified to have been caught leering at a sleeping lady, Chris shot back up so that he was straight as a board. He hoped he was only a silhouette to her in the single light behind him so she couldn't see the heat flooding his cheeks. "Ah, Miss Albany," he whispered, trying not to startle her. "It's Mister Buckley. I'm so sorry. I've only just gotten home now. Can you forgive me for making you stay so late?"

"Mister..." She furrowed her brow and peered up at him, stretching as she did so. She arched her back and he bit his lip. "Mister..." And then her eyes widened and she came awake all at once. She scrambled to a sitting position in the chesterfield, fingers reaching out to straighten the folds of her skirts around her. "Yes," she said, voice still thick with sleep but schooled into propriety of her usual stilted and sensible variety. "Yes, Mister Buckley."

She was trying so hard to claim some dignity for herself that Chris didn't take it from her by pointing out she hadn't in fact responded to a word he'd said. He settled down into the seat across from her. "You can leave if you wish. Thank you so much for staying as long as you have."

Miss Albany twisted about in the chesterfield to look at the clock over the mantelpiece, and then turned back to him with wide eyes. "Yes, I should say *so!*" she said. "It was hours ago when I sat down to rest! How did I manage to…"

"I'm sure you had a very long day," Chris reassured.

But Miss Albany was already climbing to her feet. "No, that is no excuse. I must check on my charge." But she swayed as she stood and fell back into the chair.

Chris didn't move to help her. It wouldn't be proper, not when they were unchaperoned, and when his thoughts towards her had already been so impure. "I was just there," he said, instead. "She's fine. Asleep."

"Yes, she spent most of the day abed. It is difficult to tell, but right now, I would hazard she'll be fine. The few hours she was awake, she was very much her usual self."

"That *is* a relief," he admitted. "I've been thinking about her constantly all day, and if you knew what I've been doing all day…" And she hadn't mentioned reporters. That was good. Of course, one day was only one day. The hounds would not lose so sweet a scent easily. And Lowry would be sniffing about before long. They would be much, much harder to turn away than mere newspapermen. But it was one last day of freedom.

Unable to help himself, Chris let his eyes run along Miss Albany again. The way she changed when she wasn't maintaining her image of respectable solidarity was remarkable. Amazing, really. Now, when she let her guard down, the weight of her image lifted from her. Her countenance softened. Her lips became more full, her eyes less sharp. Her very features seemed to become less angular and more gently made. Her hair fell in hazy coils around her face, trailing down, making her neck seem longer and paler, resting atop the swell of her full, inviting breasts…

At the very moment Chris felt his attention focus there and heat flood his thoughts, Miss Albany quite suddenly flushed and looked away.

He blinked. And then he realized he'd never seen her categorization card. "Oh, Gods," he gasped. "You're a heartreader."

Every unflattering, judgemental, and, most recently, *inappropriate* thought he'd had about her suddenly rushed to the forefront of his mind, and he felt as if he were holding a murder weapon. She couldn't read his thoughts, no, but she could read the feelings behind them as plain as words in a book. And when the emotions were especially strong, or directed at her, they would pour in whether she wanted them to or not.

He raised a hand to press it against his eyes, face burning. He stumbled back a pace and fell into the chair behind him. He wished a hole would open up and swallow him. "Oh, *Gods*," he repeated. "I'm so sorry. I didn't—"

"It's fine," she responded quickly. For the first time, her voice didn't sound calculated or measured. Rather, she sounded as embarrassed as he felt, and when he lowered his hand to look at her, she was not looking back at him. He could see the glow in her face despite the dim light. "There's no need for apologies," she said.

"I'm not—I didn't—" He was and he did. He changed directions. "I know it's hard," he said helplessly. "My…my mother was a heartreader. She said those who want to know what others think of them wouldn't, if they knew what it was like." And then, despite knowing there was no point, he pressed on. "I just—I judge people by their clothing. It's not you. I do it with everyone," he insisted. "*Everyone*. It's awful. I don't know why I do it. I shouldn't. Rosemary teases me for it. Olivia practically calls me an effete. I should listen to both of them. It's the most insubstantial thing to—"

"Please, Mister Buckley," Miss Albany turned her face to look at him. Her expression was pleading. "Really, this isn't necessary."

"Of course," he replied immediately, cursing himself.

"I'd prefer Rosemary doesn't know," Miss Albany said, obviously struggling to recover some of her usual aplomb. "I have implied my proficiency is something passive and unremarkable— which it is. I have not lied to her. It's simply that I find people will try and guard their feelings when they know I can sense them." She gave him a ghost of a smile. "Which I'm sure you can understand, as you're doing it right now."

"I'm sorry," he repeated automatically.

"It's through my proficiency that I am able to read my charges' moods and anticipate their thoughts and actions with such accuracy. Should Rosemary hold herself back from me, I think the connection we've been able to establish would suffer."

"She won't hear a word of it from me," Chris assured her. He tried to mute his embarrassment, sure it was the source of the colour that still rode high in Miss Albany's face despite her obvious attempts to school herself and present her sensible, buttoned-down image. "Could you possibly forgive my complete lapse in courtesy?"

Miss Albany looked at him, then, really looked at him, from head to toe. He shrank back into his chair under her gaze, trying not to feel invaded by the depth of her scrutiny. It would be unfair of him to take offence. After all, hadn't he just done the same to her, and with far more lascivious intent?

"Courtesy matters a great deal to you, doesn't it, Mister Buckley?" Miss Albany asked eventually. She finally disentangled her eyes from him, looking down at the hands she had neatly folded in her lap.

"Yes," he answered.

"It's curious. Rosemary certainly doesn't care for any of it."

"That's…" Chris looked away from her. He was aware of how Miss Albany had to be sensing the old scars that pulled as he phrased the answer. "Our father didn't care much for any of it, either. And Rosemary"—his lips twisted—"does so strive to be his equal."

"Your mother?"

"Very much like me," he murmured. He remembered Julia Buckley sitting in this very parlour, a prettily painted cup of tea cradled in her hands as she entertained one of his father's business associates. Her sweet smile never faltered, the perfectly measured cadences of her voice always made her guests feel welcomed and entertained, and her laughter rang through these rooms like church bells on Godsday morning. Nothing like his father, who would, by sheer force of personality, simply dominate every corner in a room without a thought for anyone but himself.

He supposed he saw things in those extremes. If he wasn't Julia, then he was Michael.

"I just don't feel right having offended you," Chris said in the uncomfortable silence. When she took a very long time to reply, he finally forced himself to look up and found her staring off into the shadows of the room, her expression abstracted and her fingers now plucking absently at the folds of her skirts. She didn't notice his attention focus on her, not even when he knew his curiosity and anxiousness rose. "Miss Albany?" he asked.

"You do press," she murmured, and then she sighed. "If you forgive my saying something very discourteous, Mister Buckley, because it is very late and I am very tired...I find it difficult to give you the absolution you seek when you don't *care* you thought poorly of me, only that I was aware of it."

The wind flew out of him.

For a moment, he was positively incensed. Gods, but he felt badly enough about this as it was, did she need to make it worse? Did it matter why he'd become sorry? She should be grateful he was taking the time to offer a sincere apology to his staff at all, and—

But she was reading all of that, too.

The anger deflated and left guilt. He'd thought awful things about her. Her dress, her manner, the way that she seemed to assume authority over everything in her path. Hadn't he just been *shocked* this morning to realize Fernand enjoyed her company? She'd sensed that. She was right. He hadn't felt badly about any of those thoughts before he'd known.

"I hardly see what it is you want from me, then." It sounded surly and bitter. Immediately, he wanted to apologize. Then he recalled that was pointless. Which made him only more annoyed.

Miss Albany bristled. "Perhaps simply that I have no need for empty courtesies. You congratulate yourself for saying all the correct phrases, but it's meaningless. A facade of kindness, no more."

"A facade of kindness is far better than honest cruelty!" Chris snapped.

"Is it?" she shot back. "Isn't a little harsh, unpleasant honesty better than impersonal and entirely insincere smiles?"

"Would *you* prefer that? If you're so put out because I even thought something bad, how much worse if I'd actually said it?"

"I'm 'so put out' because you *didn't* actually say it!" Miss Albany shouted. Chris realized he'd stood up, then she had in response, and they now stood so closely that her angry breaths fogged his glasses, glaring each other down. Two spots of colour had bloomed high on Miss Albany's cheeks.

Chris took a deep breath. He let it out. He was exhausted. The week had barely started and it was already one of the longest of his life. His fingers uncurled from the fists he'd shaped them into, and his shoulders lowered, the muscles between them loosening. He smoothed his features and took a step back from the governess. "I said I was sorry," he said. Quietly, but not as calmly nor as neutrally as he might have liked. "I said it was wrong of me to think those things. If you would prefer I treated you roughly and ungraciously, that is your decision, but our situation prevents me from fulfilling your wishes. Regardless what you might think of courtesy, I want my sister to value it. I refuse to set an example for her that would encourage her emulation of my father's behaviour."

The twin rose petals in Miss Albany's cheeks slowly disappeared, and she echoed his step back with one of her own, smoothing the lines of her drab grey dress. "Yes, of course," she said, a touch of contrition in her once again well-measured voice. "You must understand, Mister Buckley, I have nothing against the rules of society on principle. Of course not. They serve an important purpose, and I would never advise teaching poor manners to any of my charges. Rosemary could do with a few more."

"And I could do with a few less." The mocking words left his lips before he could so much as note their passage, and he clamped his mouth shut as if to catch them and reel them back. She would feel his shame, he remembered. He'd forgotten what it was like, being so close to a heartreader. It was impossible to cloak intent or reaction.

Miss Albany had the grace to look chagrined, but she gave a short, tight nod. "Perhaps so." Immediately, she turned and started towards the foyer door. "I really do need to be going," she said, speaking just a little too quickly. "It's the middle of the night, and—"

Chris caught her wrist. He didn't tug, nor would he have held her if she fought, but she didn't, merely stood there limp and defeated. "This isn't a conversation I imagined having, especially not today," he told her honestly. He tried to magnify his feelings of sincerity, to push them towards her. His mother had always said that helped her feel him when he was holding back from her.

"...no. I would agree," Miss Albany sighed.

"But it's said, now."

"It shouldn't be, Mister Buckley. I had recently awakened and was speaking without thinking. It would be most appropriate and better for our professional situation if we both forget any of it was said at all."

That isn't very honest, he wanted to say, but reluctantly, he released her wrist. She pulled it up against her, rubbing where he'd held her. She averted her eyes once more, but not before sending him a thankful look under her eyelashes. "Rosemary was extremely happy to know you spent the night at her side. She was disappointed to have missed you." She turned away from him. "The doctor assigned to her was by today. His name is Jameson, and he is very pleasant. Doctor Jameson looked into her blood, bones, and brain, and he assured Mister Spencer and I her recovery is progressing quite well, considering what she did." Chris followed after her. He made a point of not letting his eyes drop to her posterior.

"Will you be all right getting home?" he asked.

"There's no need. I like to walk."

He turned to shoot a dubious glance towards the dark windows, out into the city. "Are you sure?" he asked, watching the flickering alp-light of the streetlamps filter through the frosted windows. "It's dark, and wet, and you'd be alone on the road, and—"

"Mister Buckley," she said firmly, speaking his name like a silencing command. When he turned his gaze back to her, her lips were set in a thin line and her shoulders were squared. The no-nonsense nanny had returned. "Whatever ill-considered moment of weakness you might have seen in me, I am quite capable. I do appreciate your concern, but let me assure you: I can take care of myself, thank you very much."

The thought of simply letting a woman go out into the city this late at night went against all of his gentleman's instincts, but he bit his tongue. He forced a tight nod and a courteous smile up at her, but she glanced past him and frowned, a tiny crease appearing between her brows. She'd felt his dislike of the situation. Did she appreciate his restraint, or was she bemused yet again at his lack of honesty? "I suppose I'll see you in the morrow, then, Miss Al—"

A sharp *crack* from outside cut him off, and then a sound like glass shattering in a thousand shards. He turned to face the door, squinting to see without his spectacles.

One of the warm, orange lights framing the doorway flickered and then died.

"Oh, no," Chris had time to breathe before the sound of crackling flames roared up, and bright orange light flooded into the foyer.

"Oh, Gods!" Miss Albany whispered breathlessly, and Chris was only barely aware of her suddenly pushing up against his side. Instinctively, he wrapped an arm about her shoulders and pulled her against him as they both stood, motionless, not even daring to breathe. They felt the heavy waves of hot light pulse back into the room. Chris could barely make out the form of the freed salamander slithering around its own serpentine body in midair, the friction of its scales putting off heat that radiated outward. No 'binder's song restrained the creature; nothing held it back. Nothing gave it orders. Chris trembled, pulling Miss Albany closer against him—more as a comfort to himself than in any attempt to protect her. If it should choose to wreak havoc in vengeance before going back to the plane then this house, this entire block, he and Miss Albany and *Rosemary*...

The light flared up. A wave of heat like the summer sun fanned back and ruffled his hair. And then those sinuous coils of orange-red light streaked off into the night, vanishing in a sound like the crackle of flames.

Everything instantly went dark and cold. Chris could only stand there, clinging to Miss Albany, afraid it would come back, afraid it wasn't over, but finally, his muscles began to relax. He sagged against the bannister in relief. His face felt too tight. "Oh, Gods," he murmured. "For a moment there, I thought for sure..."

Miss Albany said nothing in response, but the fabric of her gown rustled. There was a muffled *thump* as she dropped down onto the first stair landing, and then the sound of a strangled sob.

Eventually, without saying a word to his sister's governess, Chris gathered himself. He threw open the front door, welcoming the blast of cool night air after the horrible heat of the salamander. He examined the damage while Miss Albany stood in the doorway, peering out into the darkness. The brass support of the light looked as if had been pulled half out of the wall and the enchanted glass circle that had bound the salamander had fallen below, bursting like a thrown snowball.

"I don't know what happened," he murmured. "These are good, solid craftsmanship, and we replace the salamanders annually. I can't imagine why it would just…"

Miss Albany was shaking her head. "No," she said, fear in her voice. "It didn't just break, Mister Buckley. Someone broke it."

A chill went down his spine. He said nothing, allowing her to continue.

She reached up and touched the bronze mount with a shaking hand. "You didn't see. You were facing me. But the moment before it happened, Mister Buckley, I swear to you, I swear I saw a silhouette standing in the window here. Like someone was coming close to the door, listening, watching."

Chris shuddered, remembering the impression he'd had on the way home, that feeling someone was cloaking their steps in his own. He forced himself to shake it off, and found it harder to dismiss than he'd like. "I'm sure it was your imagination, Miss Albany," he said with a confidence he didn't feel. "This is a fine part of the city. We don't have crime, here."

She took a deep, shaking breath, and squared her shoulders. "Of course," she said. "This is a respectable neighbourhood. The mount was just faulty." She hesitated. "But if you don't mind, I—I think I might like to call a taxi service, after all."

He remembered giggling in the cubbyhole beneath the staircase, squirming in the darkness, trying to force himself to remain silent. He remembered the door opening, Julia Buckley reaching out to pull him up into her arms.

He'd buried his face into the crook of her neck. *Oh, but how did you know?*

And she'd stroked her hair and laughed quietly. *I felt you, sweetling. I can always feel you. You can't hide from Mother. She can read your little heart.*

He made sure to check in on Rosemary before retiring, but not even the sight of her sleeping peacefully, safe from all harm, was enough to do away with the feeling of dread he felt growing in the pit of his stomach.

CHAPTER TWELVE

T*he girl who saved White Clover Farms and several bystanders from a disastrous end has been identified as Miss Rosemary Buckley,* the paper read. *Miss Buckley halted the rampage of two cloudlings who had been bound with insufficient skill and broke free of their shackles. If her name sounds familiar, you have a good memory. The Buckley family was once a respected and important part of spiritbinding politics at Lowry, but their name has fallen far from the heights it once soared to. The last vestige of respectability for the family seemed to have been extinguished with the death of outspoken traditionalist, spiritbinder, and socialite Michael Buckley during the Floating Castle Incident. Currently controlled by his young son, Christopher, the Buckley fortune has all but dried up, and no one has rightly given them any thought since their chances at revival died with the elder Mister Buckley.*

Of course, that may change soon. Only days before the six-year anniversary of the Floating Castle Incident, Rosemary Buckley's impressive show at White Clover has the spiritbinding world abuzz. The rogue cloudlings were wild with anger and looking for revenge after their bonds shattered that day, and Miss Buckley is thirteen years old, and not even yet categorized, much less trained. Such a feat would have been impressive from an experienced middle-aged man. For a young girl with a wizard's touch, it seems nearly miraculous. The Buckley family troubles may be nearly over after all, as it likely won't be long until Lowry is beating down their doors, coming after little Miss Rosemary Buckley and her incredible wizardry.

Neither she nor the younger Mister Buckley could be reached for commentary, but traditionalist juggernaut Avery Combs said the following: "We will most certainly be keeping an eye on the girl. We were aware that she existed, as we endeavour to keep careful record of all wizards, but this incident has, of course, shocked and excited us. I suspect you will be printing many stories about Miss Buckley very soon as she works with us to restore the lost balance of our great nation."

We certainly hope so. In an age where even the best spiritbinders are finding their elementals escaping almost daily, someone with this level of skill could be the saviour the traditionalist movement has long been waiting for. Could there be hope for the future of spirit-based technologies after all?

Chris set the paper down. He pulled off his spectacles, threw them down on the desk, and pinched the bridge of his nose. It was far, far too early in the morning to have a headache as strong as this.

He took a deep breath.

So.

After all his years hiding—downplaying his father's boasts, avoiding any contact with Lowry, falsifying accounts of Rosemary's wizardry—it had finally begun.

And only the Three and Three knew how it was going to end. Chris dropped down onto the desk, burying his face in his arms, and choked back the ragged noise of pure panicked uncertainty that rose in his throat.

Gods. How had they ever managed to find out so much? Miss Albany hadn't spoken a word about reporters, and he'd been so relieved. Stupid. Of course they'd find him.

"There's nothing more surreal than reading about yourself in the paper," he muttered unhappily. He leaned against one arm, sliding the paper out from under him and looking at the blurry headline one more time—*WHITE CLOVER SAVIOUR IDENTIFIED*, it read—before he forced himself to straighten. He folded the paper up and dropped it into the rubbish bin beside his desk, wiping his hands of it as though it had been covered in a thin film of grease. If

Olivia had a problem with it disappearing, she could just get a new one. A different one.

If she ever even arrived. He'd made sure to be at his desk a quarter-hour early, but he was sure at least a full half had passed since then. Another barb of irritation stabbed him in the stomach. She'd cattily pointed out when he was just barely on time, yesterday, but he highly doubted it would be appropriate for him to return the favour. Christopher Buckley kept Olivia Faraday's hours, but Olivia Faraday...she, of course, kept her own.

He distracted himself by weaving atrocious limericks onto the back of a useless receipt until he finally heard the sound of the front door opening. It took all of his self-control to keep from saying something clever. "There was post for you," he said instead, using his most polite voice. "I put it just inside the door of your office. One of the notices came from the coppers. You might want to see to that first."

"Oh, she won't," a voice that most certainly did not belong to Olivia Faraday said dryly from the door. "Who are you?"

Chris's head shot up in surprise. A stout, solid-looking woman gave him a small but not unfriendly smile before closing the door and taking off her wrap. She had shoulder-length, orange-red hair, curly like a nest of springs. A splatter of freckles sprinkled across her nose. A Northerner? Most likely. The accent matched the look. Her face had a handsome strength when seen in profile. She hung her wrap on the coat rack. Underneath, she wore the smart blouse, split skirts, and royal insignia of a female police officer.

"You're Maris Dawson," he said aloud, then cursed his lapse and hurried to answer her question. "It's a pleasure to meet you. I'm Christopher Buckley, Miss Faraday's assistant."

When Officer Dawson turned to look at him, it was with renewed interest. She watched him, her sharp green eyes efficiently taking stock of all his strengths and weaknesses. He tried not to cringe under the look. When she glanced away, it was accompanied by a dismissive cluck. "Of course you are," she said, and the acid on her tongue surprised him. There was an awkward pause, and then she walked across the room and settled down into one of the chairs. She sat back, and gave Chris another look. The freckles on her pale skin were like chocolate drops in vanilla. "Where's Faraday?"

"I don't know," Chris admitted. Under those sharp eyes, he felt somehow responsible. "She hasn't been in, yet."

Officer Dawson rolled her eyes. "I swear, that woman just does these things to upset me. She must think she's the only investigative truthsniffer I monitor. Mother Deorwynn forbid I do anything other than hold Olivia Faraday's leash." She eyed him yet again. "I don't suppose you make a decent pot? Constance never could. I'd consider you an upgrade if you could manage that much."

Despite her rough nature, he found himself warming to her. "I've never objected to what I've come up with, myself."

"Well, do your worst," she said. "I suppose I can be grateful I got here before Faraday in this, at least. I don't have to hear her harpying on at me to drink that bitter black poison."

Not long after, they were both seated and sharing the pot Chris had laboured over. Officer Dawson pronounced the tea underwhelming but adequate, which was apparently leagues beyond what the mysterious Constance had ever managed. Chris hid a grin in his cuff when he saw the no-nonsense police officer put not two, not three, but four lumps of sugar into her cup. They drank in companionable silence, both shooting knowing glances to the door and shaking their heads occasionally, until they were interrupted by it finally opening and Olivia Faraday at long last appearing in a flurry of motion.

Today she was dressed like a waggoner woman, with a loose blouse, large golden earrings, and a large patchwork skirt in a riot of colour. Her usually ruler-straight hair was styled into large, looping ringlets that put Rosemary's natural curls to shame. She set down a pile of books, turned to them both, and clasped her hands together in what seemed like all one motion. "Maris!" she exclaimed with great affection. "How are you? How is Emilia?" And without waiting for an answer, she turned to Chris, her jewelry all tinkling. "And Christopher! My handler and my slave, getting on so well! Really, I'm relieved. Maris, I'd worried you'd think he was a fop."

"I like fops well enough," Officer Dawson said evenly, setting down her cup on the table between them. "I certainly like them better than Deathsniffers who make me wait all morning when I have twenty other places to be."

Olivia made a needlessly theatrical gesture with one hand. "Something came up," she proclaimed, looking down her nose at them. Queen Olivia. "I knew you wouldn't mind waiting, since I had to wait an entire *day* for you to find the time for me."

Officer Dawson didn't sidestep the slight. She simply let it bounce off her iron hide and fall, forgotten, to the floor. "What happened to Constance, Faraday?" she asked bluntly. "Why the new assistant?"

A bit of the life seemed to snuff out of Olivia. Her fluttering hands dropped to her sides and her eyes lost their playful, energetic gleam. "She quit," she said. She offered no further explanation and clearly intended the conversation to end there.

It didn't. "Constance? Quit? As if she'd have the courage. What did you do to her?"

Olivia's eyes flashed. Her lips went into a line and she planted her hands on both of her hips. "My assistants aren't any of your business," she said flatly, all of her theatrical good nature gone in a flash. "Constance is gone. I replaced her. Does the Queen's Police have a problem with that, Maris?"

Officer Dawson met Olivia's eyes and held them. It went so long that Chris wondered if Olivia would be the one to back down, if she would relent and tell the story of what had happened to his predecessor—a story he found himself very interested in—just because Maris Dawson's sharp green eyes told her to. If there was anyone who could have cowed Olivia Faraday, it was this woman.

Or maybe not. Because it was Officer Dawson who finally blinked and shrugged. The motion was careless, but Chris noticed she dropped her eye contact with Olivia as she did so. "Well, keep this one, if you would," Officer Dawson said. "He makes a good cup, and he's a proper gentleman."

Olivia smiled to herself, the wicked gleam coming back to her ice-blue eyes. She hadn't missed who had won the exchange. "I'm thinking about it," she declared. "He does the job all right, and oh, he's so nice to look at, isn't he? Much better than plain old Constance." She grinned wickedly. "I was—" she began, but Officer Dawson cut her off.

"No more talk," she said, hauling herself to her feet. "I meant it when I said I'm busy today. I'd prefer to get moving as soon as possible."

"Oh, *Maris*! I wanted to share a cup with the two of you!" Olivia protested with a pout. "I feel so left out."

Officer Dawson brushed past Olivia without a glance back, and Olivia's pout intensified. "If you'd been here on time, I would have considered it." The stout officer retrieved her wrap and swaddled herself, then turned back to Chris and Olivia with her lips folded in a line. "I'm serious. Get ready. We're leaving."

The three of them were soon settled into a taxicab, bouncing along Darrington's cobbled streets. Chris stared listlessly out the window while Olivia slumped in the far seat, the least merry waggoner woman Chris had ever seen. Maris Dawson's presence was authoritative and commanding, deterring any thought of idle conversation with an aura spread over the interior of the car. When the silence was broken, it was Officer Dawson who did the breaking.

"Suspects?" she asked. Or rather, ordered, for it was more command than suggestion.

Olivia perked up, sitting forward in her seat. "Duchess Evelyn val Daren," she announced immediately, eagerly. "The Duke's wife. Cold, arrogant, not in any real mourning, had reason enough to hate him, tampered with my crime scene, Miss Caldwell suspects her, *and* she's hiding something."

Officer Dawson raised an eyebrow. "Other suspects?" she asked mildly.

Olivia rolled her eyes. "Analaea val Daren, I suppose. The Duke's daughter. Classic case of 'Daddy didn't love me,' seems a bit volatile, her grief could easily be guilt, and I personally find it interesting she was squatting in that mysterious room when she knew there was a Deathsniffer in her house. Guarding it from me?"

She began counting the names she'd already listed on her fingers. There was an excited flush rising in her cheeks. "Vanessa Caldwell. The Duke's current protégée. She's a wild card in an unlikely suit. Like she said herself, at first glance, it doesn't seem to make sense, does it? He was patronizing her art. He was her way out of a life she hates. So why kill him? But there's so much we don't know about her, and the whole situation rings suspicious to me. We'll know more in an hour, hopefully!" Her eyes glittered.

Finally, she held up one more finger, and gave Chris a meaningful look. "Lastly, an anonymous enforcer."

The officer raised her other eyebrow at long last. "Oh?"

"It's all just a loose theory!" Olivia said. "And one suggested by my assistant, so it might not have much merit. But apparently, there's some money problems in the Old Blood. Bad ones. The creditors are playing games with them, and since they deserve it, they're following all the rules." She smiled sweetly. "Now, if someone were to *break* the rules…maybe they'd need to be made an example of? So everyone else knows they have to be good?"

"I like that best," Officer Dawson said thoughtfully. "Explains how he was laid out, and it seems tidier and more logical than one of the people he loved killing him."

"Now, Maris," Olivia chided playfully. "If nobody ever killed someone they loved, the second hell would be a lonely place, wouldn't it? Sins of Passion don't come about because the sinner *hates* the one he sticks the knife in." She looked thoughtful. "And then butchers and strings up to the ceiling. I admit, that part is picking the back of my brain in a way that's driving me just mad."

"That's what makes me think this isn't a Sin of Passion," the officer pressed. She looked considerably more alert than she had moments before. She made Chris think of a hound who'd caught a scent. He was reminded that, like all police officers, she was a truthsniffer herself. "Didn't you say he was butchered and strung up *after* he died? That's cold. That's calculated. That's not passion, and it's not rage. That's a Sin of Greed."

"And he had his todger hanging out of his pants," Olivia pointed out. "If *that's* not passion, I don't know what is."

"Was he a heavyset man?"

"Average, I suppose. Why?"

Officer Dawson's lips split into a smile. Her front teeth overlapped ever so slightly. "You list three feminine, frail beauties as your main suspects, but the Duke was strung from the rafters of his study. How did they get him up there? With their fragile, skinny arms?"

Olivia opened her mouth and then closed it. She pushed her nose up into the air. "I don't feel it's relevant."

"You don't get to—"

"I don't *feel* it's relevant, Maris."

Officer Dawson went to reply, and then shrugged and leaned back against the seat. Her increased interest, however, did not go away. It was clear in the tension of her muscles, the set of her shoulders. "I'd like you to look more into it. The creditor theory."

Olivia sighed. "*Yes*, ma'am," she said placatingly. "I'm so grateful I have a generous supervisor to tell me how to do my job!"

Officer Dawson refused to be baited. She grunted and looked away. "You certainly need her to tell you how to do your paperwork."

Olivia fixed Chris with a long-suffering look, tipping her head meaningfully towards her supervisor and rolling her eyes. Chris cleared his throat, coughed, and turned to the window. He intended to stay neutral in this war.

He saw they were already nearing the little hospital where Vanessa Caldwell worked. He squared his shoulders, steeling himself for the sterilized, white walls. Before long, they all jolted as the cab slowed to a halt. The doorman opened the door, and they all filed out.

Chris trailed dutifully behind Officer Dawson and Olivia, holding his notebook open in front of him in case anything needed to be recorded. The same girl at the same desk looked into the same, half-empty book and, once again, directed them to where they might find Vanessa Caldwell. This time, she didn't ask for their categorization cards. Chris wondered if that was because she remembered them, or whether Officer Dawson's sharp police uniform superseded procedure.

They found Miss Caldwell changing the starched white linens on the beds in an empty room. She was so intent on her work—and humming quietly to herself—she didn't notice their entrance until Olivia raised her voice, smug as anything. "I brought the police to make you talk, just like you asked," she sang cheerily. "Are you going to waste less of my time, today?"

"Too much to hope you might have just arrested the Duchess by now," Miss Caldwell said, continuing her work. Her raven-black hair was pulled back in a smart but stylish knot, leaving little strands to fall around her face, and her uniform was as immaculately white as ever.

"I did warn you we'd—" Olivia began, but Officer Dawson cut her off without grace or so much as an apologetic glance.

"There's no evidence to convict Duchess val Daren in this murder," she said. The authority in her voice snapped through the air like a whip, and Chris watched every muscle in Miss Caldwell's body suddenly go rigid. Her hands stilled. "In fact, there's precious little evidence at *all*, something you have not helped in your refusal to assist an authorized investigative truthsniffer. Well, no more. Olivia Faraday has questions for you, Miss Caldwell, and I expect to see you answer them honestly and respectfully. Is that clear?"

Miss Caldwell's flat, disdainful eyes had gone round with surprise, and her lips had parted into a small *o*. She stared at them, and then she shook herself and nodded feebly. "Y-yes, Officer."

"Good," Maris Dawson stated evenly. "Is there a cafeteria where we can sit down and talk?"

Miss Caldwell looked around the empty white room and its empty white beds. "I'm supposed to have all of these changed," she said meekly. Chris could barely glimpse the face of the haughty young poet.

"I'll see to your supervisor," Officer Dawson said, and indicated the door with a quick jerk of her head. "Lead the way, please. I don't have all day to waste. It was inconvenient enough being forced to come at all."

Dutifully, the lifeknitter set the folded sheet down on the bed and walked past them, head lowered, out the door. Officer Dawson followed her at a brisk pace, Olivia at her side. "I knew there was a reason I liked having you along, sometimes," Olivia said in a gleeful little voice to the policewoman, and Chris hurried along after them.

Miss Caldwell led them through white, bleached corridors, and Chris spent the whole time looking down at his feet and breathing very deeply. Eventually, they went through a door marked with the familiar three linked circles into a small dining room. It was warm and lit by orange salamander's fire rather than sterile alp-light, and fragrant with the scent of baking bread. The smell was heavenly, and Chris was immediately hungry for the breakfast he'd foregone.

They took their seats around a little wooden table. "Will you be eating?" Miss Caldwell asked.

"I should hope so!" Olivia said, echoing Chris's thoughts. "I'd have to assume you *were* a killer, if you were cruel enough to not let us have any of that bread!"

"Yes, well," Miss Caldwell said, after craning her neck to look into the kitchen and raising four fingers at whoever she saw there. "I hope you all like tea, eggies and toast. That's all they ever serve. My patients love to complain. The only variation is whether we have jam or marmalade."

"We aren't here to discuss breakfast, Miss Caldwell." Officer Dawson folded her hands on the table.

Miss Caldwell dropped her eyes. "No, of course not," she agreed.

Officer Dawson nodded once to Olivia. That was all she needed.

Olivia leaned across the table, bridging the gap between herself and Miss Caldwell. There was an excited, predatory smile curled around her lips, one Chris found quite unsettling. "Where did you meet the Duke, Vanessa?" she asked.

It wasn't the question Chris had been expecting. It wasn't what Miss Caldwell was expecting, either. She started a little, and then that imperious look reappeared around her eyes and in the tightness of her mouth. "I didn't kill him," she said. "We've been through this, haven't we? I would have been an idiot to have killed him. Ask me about the Duchess. Ask me about the night he died. Ask me—"

"Answer the questions you're asked, please," Maris commanded shortly, and Miss Caldwell's mouth shut instantly.

She sat in her chair, clearly caught between her instinctive desire to do as the police officer said, and her distaste for Olivia and her questions. Chris recorded that silence, the way Miss Caldwell carefully picked an imaginary piece of lint off the sleeve of her uniform, the way she set her shoulders and straightened before she finally began speaking once again. "I…" She hesitated. "I sought him out. He's quite well known, if you care to know," she continued. Her reluctance dripped from every word, and she wouldn't make eye contact with Olivia. "The Duke has made a bit of a name for himself, over the years. Any young artist who's having a difficult time getting noticed, getting *acknowledged*, she starts to ask what she can do, how she can change the situation. And when she asks that question in the right places, a name just keeps coming up. Duke Viktor val Daren. He'll make you into what you only dream you could be, if you can hold his interest for long enough." She shrugged a single slender shoulder, looking almost bashful. "It was no chance meeting. I put myself in his path. Over and over again, until he grew quite tired of seeing me there and had to acknowledge me. I suppose you could say I courted him."

"And how long ago was that?"

"Not long," Miss Caldwell sighed. "Not long enough." Darkness clouded her face. Her plucking at her sleeve grew aggressive, as if it had done something to personally offend. "Half a year. A little more, perhaps. Just long enough for him to"—her lips twisted into something that was not even almost a smile—"to *appreciate* my work, to really know what *direction* to take me in. We were about to start scouting for publications. Finally. And then his wonderful wife had to go and kill him and ruin it all."

"And what did you think of him?"

"He was a sentimental old sop, overwrought, miserable, and unpleasant. His attachment to me was insufferable. He wanted to be a part of every single aspect of my life, putting himself into my personal affairs, and he was always bringing me to his home. I hated him," Miss Caldwell said, entirely without shame. Her dark eyes glittered. Olivia raised an amused eyebrow at Officer Dawson, and Miss Caldwell raised her chin in defiance. "Yes, I admit it. Viktor was a means to an end. I considered it worthwhile. My art is everything to me."

"If you're so good, why did you need a patron?" Olivia asked, her voice mocking. She rested her chin on her palm and drummed her fingers against her cheek.

Miss Caldwell looked up at her, eyes flashing with venom. She shot a quick glance at Officer Dawson, however, and Chris watched her carefully choosing her words before she spoke, despite how badly she clearly wanted to spit out whatever she was feeling. "The...*situation*," she said, "in Darrington. I said this to you yesterday, Miss Faraday. Perhaps you just didn't hear me?" When Olivia said nothing into the silence, Miss Caldwell shook her head and continued. "In case you haven't noticed, it's been a difficult decade. Categorization is failing. No one can decide what to do. Traditionalists and reformists arguing. Have none of you opened a newspaper, lately?" She gestured around the little dining hall, which Chris noticed for the first time, was quite empty. "They've been saying all year this hospital is going to be closed. Not enough doctors. Not enough nurses. Far too many patients, but the new lifeknitters awakening in categorization are all like me—can't even see the bloodstream, good for nothing. Which publication has time for *poetry* when the world is falling apart? An artist has to go the extra mile."

"And bribe people to publish you?" Olivia's eyes sparkled with mirth. "Ah, yes, the artist's dream of an appreciative audience for their work!"

"All it takes is one decent review," Miss Caldwell snapped. "Just *one* word in the right ear. That's what I needed from Viktor. You could be the best painter in Tarland, and it wouldn't matter if nobody ever had a chance to see your bloody painting." The poet's jaw ground. Chris watched her anger grow as she considered her situation. "Gods," she said into her own tortured silence. "She just had to do away with him right before he finally made things happen for me." She shook her head and her pridefully set shoulders slumped, just a little. "I'll be changing linens and stocking closets for the rest of my life, now."

It hit him from nowhere after seeing that defeated drop in her posture. This was a woman who had come close to achieving a lifelong dream, only to have it snatched away. Chris quite suddenly, quite surprisingly, felt badly for her.

Olivia did not.

She lifted her bag into her lap and began pawing through it. "Do you know what the good thing is about you giving me the run-around, Vanessa?" she asked as she rooted about. Miss Caldwell didn't reply, watching the Deathsniffer with wary black eyes. "The *good* thing," Olivia continued, not seeming to notice her question was ignored, "is that I got to spend some time doing research! This morning, for example, while good Officer Dawson and my handsome assistant drank tea and wondered where eccentric old Olivia Faraday had gotten to, *I* was doing my job. Aha!" she announced proudly, and then slapped something down on the table.

It was a copy of *The Daily Herald*, Darrington's most distinguished publication. The headline proclaimed *DOCTOR LIVINGSTONE DECLARES WHITE CLOVER TO BE INDICATIVE OF GREATER CONCERNS*, and it was dated, as indicated by Olivia's finger, for yesterday.

Vanessa Caldwell blanched.

Olivia Faraday smiled.

"Do you know why I have this paper, Miss Caldwell?" she asked, her voice quiet and very sweet. "Why I went to a newsstand and looked for a day-old paper?" When she received no immediate response, she merely shrugged. She took the paper into her hands and opened it, leisurely going through the pages until she found what she was looking for, and then cleared her throat dramatically. "*Sea of White*," she declared, in a voice expressive enough for a theatre. "By Vanessa Caldwell." She gave each of them at the table a pointed look before continuing. "I am standing above the sea of white. The cliff face is sheer beneath me. The sea is eternal. It stretches. It lingers. Oh, how it—"

"Is there a point?" Miss Caldwell bit off. Her hands were folded on the table, and they were shaking.

Olivia smiled slowly, languidly, and dropped the paper. It fluttered in the air before descending with angelic grace to the table. "So, we've already established you really need someone with money to get you noticed in this day and age. The country is in turmoil, after all." She reached out and tapped her finger against the headline. Miss Caldwell refused to look at her directly. "And this, well, this is the *Herald*. You don't get a spot in the *Herald* unless you really earned it! Someone must have dropped quite a few royals to get your ditty in this paper, Vanessa, dear. Now, just who...?" She let the thought dangle in the air, unfinished but clear to all of them. Officer Dawson raised an eyebrow. Chris weaved furiously in his notebook.

"It was one publication," Miss Caldwell protested. She was quite pale now and the bitter venom was all but gone from her eyes and voice. "I hadn't mentioned it because it was barely worth mentioning."

"Hardly the words of a woman getting her lifelong dream. A poem in the *Herald*? I'd be beside myself, and I don't even care about poetry!"

"It was *one* publication!" Miss Caldwell pressed, more insistently. "I still needed him! I still—"

"All it takes is one review!" Olivia said mockingly. "That's what you said, isn't it? We've already established you despised the Duke, and he involved himself in your life. I know all about Viktor val Daren, Vanessa. I know he stays with one artist, entranced by her, loyal to her, until he's tired of her. That can take years." She tapped the newspaper again, grinning ferally. Her teeth glittered in the light from the salamanders along the wall. "Maybe you didn't want to wait years. You had your publication in the *Herald* all lined up to go! You were tired of him, tired of the game, tired of being his little pet, and you had what you wanted. The stir over the Duke's brutal murder...that would make enough talk to get someone looking at your work, wouldn't it?"

"That is not—" Vanessa Caldwell no longer looked imperious. She no longer looked cold. Now, she looked terrified. "That's not how it is," she said, her voice wavering. "Please, you have to listen to me! I knew if I said something about it—it was the Duchess! She hated him, she hates *me*! She's jealous, she's petty, and she's a madwoman! I read about how he was killed, what she did to him. She's capable! She's stronger than she looks, and you haven't seen how angry she can get! She hates it, she hates all of it, everything he does—*did*. She couldn't stand the thought that her husband was sleeping with another woman, and she—"

"Wait," Olivia interrupted. "Wait, wait," she repeated, holding up one hand. "You were *sleeping* with the Duke?"

Olivia's confusion seemed to empower Miss Caldwell. She sat up straighter, and a little bit of the colour returned to her cheeks. "You didn't know?" she asked, and a bit of triumph stole into her dark, dark eyes. "Oh, Miss Faraday," she said sweetly. "Did you never wonder why the Duke never patronized young, talented, attractive *men*?"

CHAPTER THIRTEEN

N o," said Duchess Evelyn val Daren.

Deathly silence filled the room. Chris, Olivia, and Officer Dawson all stood staring down at the noblewoman as she took a deep, shaking breath. One of her hands had gone up to her throat when Olivia had told her. It still hadn't moved.

"No," the Duchess repeated. She took another very long, deep breath, and it, too, shuddered. "That's simply not possible. The girl is lying. I know Viktor. I—*knew* Viktor. He never would have had relations with his girls. They were too unspoiled, that—that was part of what appealed to him, the *art*—" She shook her head firmly, but her breath still trembled. "He wouldn't have."

"Duchess." It was Officer Dawson who spoke, not Olivia. She had her hands folded behind her back, and stood at attention, like she was a soldier rather than a police officer. Her eyes didn't quite meet the Duchess's. It seemed a gesture of respect. "I believe the girl was telling the truth."

"Mn, I'm sure of it," Olivia agreed. "Truthsniffing can't exactly pick out a lie, but that level of certainty is hard to fake."

"That's not *possible*," the Duchess snapped. It might have been a terrible sound, if not for how her voice cracked messily on the last syllable, turning the commanding statement into something pathetic and sad. The Duchess's shoulders shook, just once, and she swallowed the sob that tried to follow, thunder after lightning.

"He would never. He—I—"

She cut herself off there, and said nothing else.

Chris believed her.

He might not have been a truthsniffer like Olivia or Officer Dawson, but he was the son of a heartreader and it had taught him empathy. This wasn't the face of a liar. This was a woman who'd been betrayed. Until the end, she'd trusted her husband, and he hadn't been worthy of it.

The room was quiet. Then Olivia spoke.

"Oh, please," she said, a little too loudly. "You had to have known. How could you not have *known?*" She began to pace, the bracelets on her wrists and ankles all jingling merrily, a stark contrast to how she stalked about. "Vanessa made it clear *she* knew. She knew before she even met him! Everyone knew. Everyone *warned* her. If you want this patron's money, you don't just have to impress him. You have to fuck him!"

Chris jolted at the word, his weaving immediately skidding to an abrupt halt on the page. He snapped his gaze to his employer, eyes wide in shock.

"*Faraday,*" Officer Dawson said sharply. Her face echoed the sick feeling in his stomach. "That's enough."

Olivia ignored her. She marched forward, one finger held out like a weapon, and she stopped only a hair's length from the Duchess's grief-stricken face. "Listen to me," she hissed. "I don't know what it is you think you can *hide,* but I know what you're doing. I can *smell* it."

"*Faraday.*"

"You can tell me you're a sweet innocent lamb all you want, Duchess, but I know you're hiding something. When I find out what it is, you're going to wish you never—"

"Olivia!" Chris cried, unable to quiet himself any longer. The look on the Duchess's face wrung his heart. "*Please!*"

Olivia's shoulders tensed, but where Officer Dawson's protests had bounced off of her, for some reason, Chris's had an effect. She shook her finger at the Duchess once, for good measure, and then turned away with a disgusted growl in the back of her throat. "Fine," she growled. "It makes my poor soft-hearted assistant sniffle to see you get what you deserve. Have your moment of feigned horror." She waved a hand dismissively. "I need to talk to my people. *Alone.*"

The Duchess said nothing. She climbed to her feet, and Chris watched her pull all of her grace and poise around herself like a robe as she stood, her proud, tear-filled eyes staring straight ahead. Without a word, she swept out of the parlour.

Silence reigned in her absence for less than a full heartbeat, and then Officer Dawson was on her feet, storming over to Olivia and grabbing her by the shoulder. "*Too far!*" she challenged as she spun Olivia around to face her. "Too damned far, Faraday! Mother Deorwynn and Father Calhoun, that woman—"

"Is lying," Olivia said firmly. Calmly—eerily so. Olivia's spitting rage from moments before seemed to have evaporated, leaving her implacable and collected. She folded her arms before her, meeting Officer Dawson's challenge with one of her own.

Dawson accepted it. She set her jaw. "If I made arrests based on every truthsniffer's hunch, there would be a lot of innocent people in our prisons. You're being irrational. You have nothing solid, nothing real, just a feeling and a chip on your shoulder, and—"

"And she's *lying,*" Olivia repeated, even more firmly. The force of her words quieted Officer Dawson, and Olivia gave her a tight smile. "You know it, too. You *feel* it, Maris. You feel it like I do. She's all wrapped up around one little nugget of truth, hiding it from us. Don't you *feel* it? Don't you *smell* it?"

Officer Dawson shook her head, just once, stubbornness settling onto her shoulders. "One secret doesn't make someone a killer." Officer Dawson shrugged, but though she pretended not to care, Chris could tell she did. "I sense something." But before

Olivia's triumphant smile could evolve into words, Officer Dawson's voice raised and took on a commanding tone. "And that something could be anything. You don't have *any proof.*"

Olivia's smile vanished and she threw her arms into the air in exasperation. "Oh, come on*!* What could she be hiding that she'd *keep* hiding, even after being accused of murdering her husband? That must be a hell of a secret!"

"You're the Deathsniffer. Isn't it your job to find out?" Officer Dawson shook her head. "You're better than this, Faraday. You are! You have one of the best records in Darrington, and we both know that. Why are you playing the idiot rookie, freshly categorized? You use your hunches to find *evidence.* You don't demand arrests based on nothing else. What's going on?" When Olivia said nothing, the officer shook her head, sending her tight orange curls bouncing in all directions. She took a step closer and shot a quick glance towards Chris. "Does this have something to do with Constance?"

Chris tried to shrink back into himself, but it was no use. That quick glance had reminded Olivia Faraday that he existed, and he immediately found himself the sole recipient of her piercing eyes. Those eyes flashed, and her lips went thin and white in an instant. "Are you taking notes on all of this?" she demanded.

He didn't know what the right answer was, so he gave her the truth, shaking his head meekly.

She snorted. "Am I paying you to stand around and look handsome?" She jabbed a thumb towards the door. "Go make yourself useful."

His eyes flickered where she indicated, and then back. He swallowed. "I—ah, what exactly am I supposed to—?"

"Find. Something," she snapped. "And please make it better than what you turned up the *last* time I sent you off. Useless twit."

If he'd expected defence from Maris Dawson, he was disappointed. She watched him with an even and unreadable gaze as he slunk dutifully out of the parlour and closed the door behind him. Only after he dropped his hand from the latch and a moment passed did he hear their voices pick up from inside the parlour again, too quiet for him to make out.

His shameful contrition instantly melted and reformed into bitter anger. He tucked his notebook beneath his arm and stalked across the foyer, clenching his fists at his sides. Gods, he thought, climbing the stairs, how was this fair? He'd done nothing but dare be in her presence, which was what he was *supposed* to do. And the insult to his work? He'd found the spot of blood. He'd found the curious note. He'd gotten more out of Ana and Mister Grey than Olivia ever would have managed, and even now, Fernand was looking into sumfinders and Old Debts on his behalf.

What had Olivia contributed to the investigation? Truthsniffing seemed very much like stumbling about and hoping for answers to miraculously appear. Her precious damned intuition seemed to amount to little more than an unshakeable belief that the Duchess was guilty. Five days since the Duke had died, and they had nothing but Olivia's unique brand of madness.

He didn't see Analaea val Daren until he tripped over her.

No matter how superior and how angry one felt, it was universally humbling to go flying down a hallway and hit the floor with all the grace of a burlap sack full of cabbages. His notebook skidded across the marble. The *shock* of his hip slamming against the ground felt like pain, but when it passed he realized only his pride was wounded.

"Mister Buckley!" Ana exclaimed as he tried to gather up any remnants of dignity and climb back to his feet. She was at his side in an instant, holding his arm and helping him up. His face burned, and he shook her off as soon as he could without offending her. "Oh, I'm so sorry!" she said. "Mother always tells me someone will hurt themselves tripping over me when I sit there, but…Maiden Maerwald, I'm so sorry…"

"It's fine," he said, his voice gruff with embarrassment. "I should have been watching where I was going." He bent and retrieved the notebook; it seemed no worse for the wear.

"No, *really*," she insisted. "I'm so sorry." He felt her at his side and swallowed his pride enough to look at her. She stared up at him with large, concerned eyes. Today, she was again the pretty waif by the window ledge. No trace of tears marked her cheeks, and she'd taken time and care with her simple gown, cosmetics, and hairstyle. She was also clearly waiting for something from him. He had no choice but to force a comforting smile.

"Well, you are completely forgiven, my lady," he said with a hint of a bow, pulling the notebook close against his chest.

She breathed out in relief and a smile touched her thin lips. Her gaze followed his hands to where he clutched the notebook and she looked up in askance. "Is that where you keep your notes for the Deathsniffer?" Then, before he could answer, she frowned and looked about the empty hallway. "What are you doing here?"

Chris covered the notebook with his hands; if she asked to see it, he didn't want to have to refuse her outright. "Miss Faraday sent me to ask some questions to the staff," he replied, and after a moment's thought, decided he was still angry enough to say something stupid. "She also wanted me to see if I could find anything suspicious."

Something dark fluttered under the surface of Ana's face, but it was there and gone in less than an instant. "Oh," she said, her disinterest stiff and forced. "I suppose you must be very busy with that."

The statement was more leading than the mere words would imply, and Chris immediately recognized an unspoken question—an invitation, even. Analaea val Daren was trying to ask him if he had some time to spend with her. Strange, to say the least. But then, he supposed they *had* formed a brief connection the last time they'd spoken. "Not terribly," he replied. It wasn't as though he had been intending to do as he'd been directed, anyway, and the thought of directly disobeying Olivia's orders was appealing.

Ana's eyes lit up and she broke into a sunny smile. Chris smothered a thoughtful frown. The difference in the girl from the three previous times he'd spoken to her was remarkable. She averted her eyes and a pretty blush touched her cheeks as she asked, "Are you hungry?"

Yes, his stomach clamoured in reply. The scent of fresh bread from the hospital dining room still haunted him. They'd hurried here immediately after Vanessa had revealed the truth of her relationship with the Duke, leaving the promised eggies and marmalade behind. But he kept his voice and face pleasantly neutral as he laughed and replied, "Ah, well, I wouldn't want to insinuate myself."

"No, you wouldn't be!" Ana insisted. "I was just thinking of how I was going to have some scones and jam and tea brought up, and there"—she faltered, and then gathered herself—"and there's something I want to show you. So, please, if you would join me?"

The cryptic promise was too tempting to resist. As was, he had to admit, the mouth-watering thought of scones and jam. "Well, I suppose if you were already having it brought up..."

The young woman clapped her hands and took him by the arm. She led him down the hall and up a flight of grand oaken stairs. She stopped a scurrying maid in the hall and informed her of her wishes, sending the girl off to the kitchen as the two of them continued along their way. Chris watched her from the corner of his eye, taking in the way her steps bounced, the way her eyes were free of all the blotchy veins of shed tears how there was an odd, determined set to her jaw. There had been a change in her since he had spoken to her in the parlour yesterday.

"Where is Mister Grey today?" he asked, trying to make conversation while she steered her through the cavernous hallways of the Old Blood estate.

"Ethan? Oh, he had to get his paintings from the gallery, today. His showing is over," she said with a sad sigh. "I saw him this morning, and he wasn't his usual self at all. He was upset about the gallery closing early and he was so short with me." She shook her head. "He gets like that, sometimes. I give him time to himself, and then he's fine again, but it always worries me. I don't understand why he does it when he knows I'm always here to support him."

"Is that what the two of you fought about on the night his gallery opened?"

Her face darkened. "No. That was…something else. Something…something I should really talk to him about, if I can just only get the courage…" And then she stopped suddenly, tugging at his arm. "Here we are," she said. She released his arm, and then opened the door in front of them, pushing herself in.

He followed her, and immediately recognized which room they were in. "Ah, my lady." Heat flooded his face as he looked around the interior of her bedroom.

"Ana," she insisted, already sitting down in one of two chairs at a quaint little table in the corner. "Please call me Ana. Won't you come sit?"

Chris held his position by the door, weighing his options awkwardly. "This is your bedroom, Ana, and I'm not sure it's appropriate for the two of us to be in here alone without a chaperone."

Her face lit with amusement, and he could see her *almost* laugh. She indicated the empty chair and shook her head. "Oh, I don't have much of a reputation. Carrying on with a poor, struggling artist as I do? I'm not exactly welcome in most proper circles, as my mother is keen to remind me at all turns." And then, to his surprise, she reached under the chair and pulled up a newspaper he hadn't noticed. She laid it down on the table before her. He watched as she smoothed the corners, and he read the headline upside down. *WHITE CLOVER SAVIOR IDENTIFIED.* He recognized the title of the article he'd read that morning. "Is this about you?" she asked, looking up from the sheet to meet his eyes.

He nodded reluctantly, and she returned the gesture with a nod of her own.

"So I doubt anyone will find the time to spread any rumours about you and me, not when there's more than enough already to be said." She gave him a plaintive look. "Please, won't you sit, Mister Buckley?"

He sighed. It was a basic rule of society, not to be left alone with an eligible girl of equal or higher status in a private or personal location. It went against all of his instincts to cross the floor, pull out the chair, and seat himself gingerly at the table.

Ana was reading over the article again, her lips moving silently as her eyes went back and forth across the page. Then she blinked and looked up at him, catching her bottom lip between her teeth. "My…" She lowered her eyes. "My uncle died at the Floating Castle, just like your father did," she said quietly. "My favourite uncle."

I don't want to talk about this. The words jumped into his mouth with so much force it was a trial to keep them trapped there. He struggled to force different words past them into the waiting silence. "I thought no Old Blood had been invited to the Floating Castle opening," he said, his voice even and emotionless even as his stomach churned. "It was a controversy."

But Ana was shaking her head. "No, they weren't," she said. "This was my mother's brother, not my father's."

His interest sparked, and the flame it ignited burned bright enough to scare his ghosts into shadowy corners. He leaned forward in his chair. "The Duchess wasn't born into the Old Blood?"

"No," Ana said, a furrow appearing between her eyes. "I thought you knew. Her maiden name is North. Evelyn North. My grandfather was a big name at Lowry, and my uncle, James, was one of the 'binders who tied a sylph into the Floating Castle net. She met my father when she was sixteen, and she married him before her nineteenth birthday, so she was never categorized." The furrow deepened at the look of confusion she must have seen on his face. "Did she not tell you all of this?"

"No," Chris said, trying not to think of the sylph net at the Floating Castle, trying not to think of cool breeze along his shins and his knuckles white as he gripped the wrought-iron tight enough to feel the tiny bumps biting into his skin. "No, she didn't." He shook his head. "Most likely she didn't think it was relevant to your father's murder. To be honest, I'm not sure how it would be." It might, however, be relevant to the *something* Olivia was so certain the Duchess was hiding.

Ana took a strange, hesitant breath, and she looked like she might say something, but at that moment, a fat old maid bustled in with a tray.

"Just set it here, thank you," Ana said as the woman trundled over. She carried a tray laden to overflowing with fresh scones that smelled like the combined glories of all three heavens, and Chris's mind emptied of anything but his awareness of the pit of his stomach. The sour-smelling old woman took entirely too long setting out the little jars full of different jams and pouring tea into cups for them. When she turned to leave, Chris seized a scone from the tray and took his first bite before she was even halfway to the door.

He closed his eyes in appreciation, barely remembering to keep his mouth politely closed as he chewed the overlarge chunk. "Perfect," he said. He opened his eyes to see Ana watching with a pleased smile on her lips. "Thank you," he said. He made himself set the scone down on the saucer and cut it open like a civilized human being. "This is exactly what I wanted, thank you," he repeated as he spread strawberry jam along the inside of the scone. Steam and a wonderful combination of aromas rose up. "I had to skip breakfast this morning and I've been regretting it ever since."

"You're welcome," Ana said happily.

Chris took another, more dignified bite, and he watched his hostess cut open and butter her own with dainty grace. The girl seesawed so violently between noble elegance and an awkward lack thereof that he never knew what to expect from her, and either always came as a surprise. He took another look around the room, wondering if she'd chosen the furnishings herself. Everything was in pastel colours, lacy and frilly and girlish. It seemed at odds with her simple dress. Either the room or dress reflected the expectations and desires of the Duchess, he was sure, but which?

When his eyes swept over the bed, he felt renewed discomfort twist in his middle, and he winced. "Ana," he said again, more gently than before. "Are you sure this is a good idea? Maybe you don't have a reputation to tarnish for your mother's friends, but what about your own? If they hear about this, they might have their own judgements to weigh."

But the young woman had lowered her eyes in the middle of his question, and when she spoke, her voice was filled with quiet shame. "There's no concern. I don't have friends," she murmured.

He was struck dumb. That couldn't be right. It made no sense. An Old Blooded noble daughter should have been surrounded by peers. She was hardly a poor girl out on a farm, too busy running chores for her family to ever see anyone her own age. She was hardly like *him*, too busy trying to make ends meet and taking care of someone else. But then he thought of that strangeness he had just been remarking on. How *different* she was. And how she clung to her beau like he was her sun and moon and—he realized it with a start—how she seemed to have latched herself onto *him* after barely any time at all.

He tried not to sound pitying as he simply replied, "Well, that's a shame."

She shot him a grateful look from under her lashes, and picked up the other half of her scone. She took a bite and chewed it in silence. "I talked to my mother after you left, yesterday," she said finally. She shot him another look, this one less readable. He watched her pink tongue peek out between her lips to wet them. "I *really* talked to her."

Her eyes were on him and she seemed to be waiting for a response. He made his face the picture of polite interest while he cut and buttered a second scone. "Is that so? What did you say to her, then?"

"I told her I wanted to 'bind." Ana cut into a new scone with a sort of ferocity that made Chris tense. "I told her I *would* 'bind. I said I wouldn't take no for an answer, and I'd spent all my life waiting for her or Father to approve of my choices, and since it was obvious they were never going to, I was just going to start making them for myself."

Chris couldn't help a smile, imagining the conversation as it had taken place. "I don't suppose she liked that very much," he said, trying to keep his amusement at the thought from his voice. It didn't feel right to laugh at the Duchess after what he'd just seen Olivia do to her.

Ana had no such reservations, though, and her eyes twinkled merrily as he looked up at him across the heap of scones. "No," she said, "she didn't."

They sat in repressed mirth as they ate their scones. "Do you think you'll actually do it?" Chris asked eventually.

Ana's nod was emphatic. "I already mirrored Lowry," she said with conviction, stirring cream and sugar into her tea. "I did it this morning after Ethan left in his huff. They're going to be busy with Floating Castle memorial business for the next few days, but I have an appointment to go in and see them next Maerday." She let out a deep breath, and the sound was full of satisfaction and fulfilment. "I..." Chris watched a flush spread across her powdered cheeks. She tried to hide it by picking up her teacup and cradling it in front of her face. "I always thought I'd feel horrible once I finally did this. I'd be going against Mother's wishes. She'd be so angry at me.

But I don't. I feel brave, you know? I feel strong. I think I'm going to talk to Ethan, too. Some of the things my mother has said about him, for so long I didn't want to consider them just because then I'd be doing what she wanted. But I have a right to talk to my own beau, and the truth is I don't care that it's what Mother wants. It doesn't have anything to do with her. See…it doesn't matter to me what she thinks, not anymore."

She set her teacup down, but she didn't take her hands from it. Chris stilled his own motions, watching her. She looked agitated, but as he sat there, wishing he could do something to put her at ease, some of the tension seemed to leave her shoulders and neck. She released her hold on the teacup. "Mister Buckley." She looked up at him, eyes large. "Do you mind if I call you Christopher?"

He did mind, a bit, but he smiled anyway and told her he didn't. If he accepted it from Olivia, he could certainly accept it from this poor girl.

"Christopher," she said, and then retreated back into herself. She dipped her spoon into her tea and idly stirred it. "I feel as if I can trust you," she said slowly, not taking her eyes off the teacup. "I know that might not make any sense, but I do."

She didn't look up at him, but she seemed to be waiting for some kind of response. Chris cleared his throat quietly. "Ah, thank you," he said, not sure what else to say.

Ana nodded. There was another long moment where the only sound was the *clink, clink, clink* each time her spoon touched the edge of her cup. She stirred and stirred, and Chris watched fleeting glimpses of a battle being waged behind her features. When she took a deep breath to speak, her shoulders hunched upwards as if preparing for a blow. "Does the Deathsniffer think my mother killed my father?"

The question caught him so completely off guard that Chris found himself giving her the truth. "I think so. Yes."

186

The girl cringed as if struck. "Yes," she repeated his last word. "Yes, I thought so." She took an unsteady breath. "You don't think it was Vanessa? I was so sure it was Vanessa."

"Miss Faraday hasn't ruled out Miss Caldwell." Chris chose his words delicately. "There's definitely reason to believe it could have been her. But you're right, the Deathsniffer considers your mother her most likely suspect."

Ana nodded. And then she took the spoon out of the teacup, set it carefully aside, and climbed to her feet. Without saying a word, she crossed to her bedside table and opened the drawer in the front. She pulled something out and she stood, clasping whatever she'd retrieved to her chest. Then she turned and retraced her steps back to the table.

She pushed the tray of scones to one side and laid the file she was carrying on top of the newspaper. Her bottom lip was between her teeth. She breathed out a long stream of air. "My mother took this out of her office. She knew you or the Deathsniffer would look in there, so she hid it from you. She didn't know I saw her, but I did." She looked up at Chris with wide eyes and an unreadable expression. "Why would she do that?"

Chris reached out and gingerly took the file into his hand. He flipped open the top and scanned the first page. It was addressed to Duke Viktor val Daren and was full of phrases like *debts accumulated* and *interest owed* and *imperative that this be settled as soon as possible* and *our contract still stands*. He couldn't make out the signature, but the wordweaver who'd composed the letter had carefully spelled out *RAYNER KOLSTON, ESQ.* underneath it.

He flipped the page. The second was very similar to the first. The third was the same, and the fourth, and the fifth. The file seemed to be stuffed with evidence of the val Daren family owing Old Debts, and the identity of the creditor who'd lent the money to them in the first place.

And Evelyn val Daren had hidden it.

His excitement was growing with each page he turned until he reached the middle of the file. This page was not a carefully weaved official notice, but rather a handwritten personal letter with a very familiar salutation.

Evie, it began.

I can't possibly thank you enough for your generous donation at the meeting last night. I had never expected to see such largesse, no matter what our shared history might be. Knowing what you do for the future of Tarland will reward you better than I ever could, and so I will not attempt to do so.

I cannot tell you just how thrilled I am to see you take this cause as your own. These are dark times, Evie, and we have need of every soldier who can take up a weapon and fight. Your weapon may be "merely" your husband's deep pockets, but many different sorts of soldiers are needed for this war to be won. I know both your father and James would be proud of the choices you are making, the stand you have decided to take.

I hope that your first meeting with us will not be your last.

All my love,

HC

Postscript: This may be unnecessary to say, but it would be best, I think, if the Duke is not aware of your involvement. There will be a time when there will be no need for such secrecy, but there are many who do not yet understand how dire this situation is. Your husband is not well known for his realism.

I will thank you in advance for your discretion.

"Do you think it'll be useful?" Ana asked suddenly.

Chris jumped and his heartbeat surged to racing. Quickly, he closed the file and tried to decide where to put it where it wouldn't be noticed. "Yes," he said aloud while he did so. "I think Miss Faraday would very much like to see this."

Ana's voice was quieter when she asked her next question. "Do you think my Mother had a good reason for hiding it?"

Chris looked over to see her looking down at her hands in her lap. He hurt for her, he did. She suspected something horrible, something that no matter how much she hated her mother, she couldn't bear to imagine could be a possibility. But he had to be honest with her. "I haven't the slightest," he said. After all, if the Duke had been killed by his creditors to set an example for other owners of Old Debts, that exonerated the Duchess. Why would she hide the evidence? It had to have something to do with the letters addressed to "Evie," from whoever this "HC" person was. He needed to show this all to Olivia as soon as possible. A touch of smugness licked along the edges of his mind as he considered how she'd react when her little tantrum turned up something so substantial.

Just as he was about to stand up and excuse himself, Ana blurted out, "There—there's one more thing."

Chris tried to hide his eagerness to leave and instead helped himself to another scone. At least the grumbling of his stomach was resolved. "What is it?" he asked.

Ana visibly struggled to raise her eyes to his face, and when she did, she stared up at him from under her eyelashes. She looked defeated, guilty and terrified. "It's..." She took a trembling breath. "On the night my father died, my mother—" And then she deflated, dropping eye contact and sighing all her air out in a great *whoosh*. "My mother *left*," she said in a tiny, pitiful voice. "My mother told me to say she and I walked together after we fought at the gallery, but I lied. She made me lie!" She took a shuddering breath. "We didn't walk. We fought, and Ethan stomped off, and then Mother just left. When I got home...she was already here, and she seemed..." The girl sniffled, and said no more.

The silence in the room rang. Chris clutched the file, trying to put together what he'd just heard. The Duchess's presence at the gallery had been the main thing that had made Olivia's suspicions seem unfounded and paranoid. If she'd left, if no one could vouch for her whereabouts at all, and if she had asked someone to *lie* for her...

"Christopher?" Ana murmured, and when Chris refocused

himself, she was looking up at him again. Unshed tears shone in her dark eyes. "Do *you* think my mother killed my father?"

At the moment, he didn't trust himself to answer.

Darrington passed by, and Chris barely saw it.

Tomorrow, Olivia had said after devouring the file like a starving man at a banquet, *we are going to see this Rayner Kolston fellow, after I've had a good, long look at these files.*

Whatever demon had possessed Olivia Faraday earlier in the day, Maris Dawson had apparently exorcised it. Even before he'd passed her the file and recounted everything Analaea had told him, she'd been brimming with good cheer and playful grins. The police officer had fallen back into her comfortable role as the beleaguered supervisor, and the two of them had bantered back and forth the entire trip to Olivia's office in the winged carriage, arguing endlessly about the contents of the folder and making little progress.

Neither of them had seen fit to involve Chris, and that suited him fine. He'd gathered his shadows around himself and sat in the corner, entertaining ghosts until they'd reached the office. And then he'd left before Olivia could find something for him to do, taking the ghosts with him into his cab; he hadn't trusted himself to walk.

He looked out the window and he saw nothing. He was dizzy and sick to his stomach, and his mind kept going back to the last page in the Duchess's secret file.

Evie, it had begun.

It always pleases me when I have time to write you these longer letters, instead of simply penning quick notes and directions. However, this letter is not a social, pleasant affair, and for that I am sorry.

Two months from now is the anniversary of the night of the Floating Castle. I know it is a difficult time for you, and I will not attempt to understand. James was close to me, as well, but I realize women are made of softer stuff than we men, and I would be amiss if I did not respect that. Nevertheless, I will seek to share wisdom with you so that good can come of this difficult time.

You know that what we do seeks to right the wrongs that were wrought that night. I know it is your instinct to push away painful memories, but I advise that you, instead, bring those memories close to you. Instead of dismissing thoughts of what it must have been like as the Castle fell, entertain them. Use them to strengthen your resolve. Difficult as it may be, you do James's memory a disservice by shying away from the reality of that night.

Force yourself to picture the screaming crowds. Imagine James's terror. Imagine what he must have felt like as he felt the Castle plunge to the ground, how he must have run and tried to escape. Picture him calling out for your father, or even you, to come and save him. Make all of that real to you. And then, know that he was only one of five hundred who were in the Castle that night, good men and women all, their lives permanently cut short. And know, too, that the trauma caused by the fall of the Castle into the city caused the deaths of many, many more.

Those responsible for all of that pain must be brought to justice.

This will not be easy, Evie, but it will be best for all of us.

Yours,

HC

Whether or not the advice had been helpful for Evelyn val Daren, it had not been meant for Christopher Buckley. Like a woman, he was made of soft stuff—softer than the Duchess, for certain. Just remembering it, his fingers gripped to the handle on the door, and he dug the nails of his other hand into the seat cushion to ground himself. His breath came out short and his head spun. He kept trying to push it all aside, to focus on the case, on how he was going home to Rosemary, on being there in time for dinner, on the tide that was rising around them, on the funny, flat expression Officer Dawson wore while dealing with Olivia.

But try as he may, he couldn't get that night from his mind.

Through the fog of distress hanging over his thoughts, he was vaguely aware that the cab had pulled onto his road, that soon he would have to get out and walk and eat and speak to other people like a normal human being. The thought seemed impossible. How could he deal with today when he was always and forever caught reliving that night?

Stop being ridiculous, he told himself, but he wasn't being ridiculous. *Stop living in the past, then,* he tried, but the thought of living anywhere else seemed inconceivable. *Just handle it,* was his last desperate plea to himself, and he made it savagely tear into him, reminding him of where he was, *when* he was, and who was relying on him being able to function.

When he climbed out of the taxi and paid the cabbie, his smile felt not quite feigned, and he managed to unlock the gate and put one foot in front of the other all the way up the walk. The feeling of his hair stirring when he passed through the soundshield and the subsequent peace as the city outside went silent made his world feel real. By the time he opened the front door and stepped into his family's home, he was his usual self, living in stubborn denial of how many jagged pieces swirled dangerously beneath his surface.

There was a stylish bowler hat and a half-cape on the coat rack. Chris blinked at both, trying to piece together what they could mean.

"Mister Buckley?" He heard Miss Albany's prim, controlled voice call to him from the parlour where they'd argued the night before. "Rosemary is resting, for now, and you have a guest."

A guest, of course. He swallowed hard, trying to dismiss the last of his anxiety with it. "Ah, I see," he said, not quite together enough to wonder who his guest was. He set his notebook on the table beneath the magic mirror and strolled into the parlour. Miss Albany set down a biscuit on a tray and met his eyes over the dark hair on the back of the head of the other person in the room. "And who would this guest be?"

The man stood from the chair he occupied and turned about to greet Chris. He was young, darkly handsome, impeccably dressed and stylishly groomed. His face was also very familiar. Chris had seen it a hundred times on the front page of the newspaper, next to articles headlined, *SIR COMBS CALLS LIVINGSTONE THEORY "RIDICULOUS," SENDS SON TO ADDRESS LOWRY*. The man smiled broadly, disarmingly, and extended a welcoming hand. "Christopher Buckley, I presume!" he said in a smooth, pleasant baritone. "My name is Avery Combs. You might have heard of my father? Please, sit down." He grasped Chris's hand, and his grip was like a vice. "I think it's past time you and I talk about dear little Rosemary."

CHAPTER FOURTEEN

C hris's mind raced. Why now? Why did this have to happen *now*?

"I hope you haven't waited overlong, Mister Combs," he said, seating himself and crossing his legs. *Smile*, he reminded himself, and he smiled.

"Oh, not terribly!" Mister Combs replied. His voice was immensely pleasant to listen to, musical and confident. It was well known that Assembly member and traditionalist movement leader Sir Hector Combs sent his son to handle most of his social or public affairs, and it was immediately visible why. Everything about this man projected charisma and solidarity. His smile dismantled Chris even as he clearly recognized what was happening. "I was just talking to your governess, here. I've been trying to convince her there would be no harm in letting me talk to Rosemary, but she's been a bit resistant."

Chris projected his grateful feelings at Miss Albany, and he felt her shift in her chair in response. "I'd prefer if you talked to me first," he replied.

"Well, I suppose that's only reasonable," Mister Combs agreed. He gave a firm nod, as if seeing great wisdom in Chris's words. "You're her guardian, after all." He squinted at Chris suddenly, sincere curiosity and concern displayed on his handsome face. "Has that been difficult for you, Mister Buckley? You were still very much a child yourself, when the Floating Castle happened. I can't imagine just what you've gone through, bringing up a little girl on your own in addition to all the other matters your father left behind. Was there really nowhere else she could go?"

Chris felt himself swaying like a tree facing an axe. "No," he heard himself say, a million miles away. "There were no relatives, and I wouldn't let her go to a home. I'm sure the nuns would have done a wonderful job with her." *Be charming*, something commanded, *act like you normally do,* and he tried to obey. "Probably better than I've done, myself." He forced his practiced rueful laugh, but couldn't tell whether or not it sounded real. "But they're no replacement for family."

"Was there *really* no legal objection? Fourteen, weren't you? Isn't that much too young?"

"My father's financial adviser signed on as secondary guardian, and he vouched for my maturity," Chris said. "He did everything in his power to ensure Rosemary and I weren't separated."

"How fortunate, indeed, yes. You must be so grateful for him." Mister Combs was nodding again. "Still, I can't imagine it's been easy."

"Well…" Chris helplessly searched for something witty and charming to say. *Why* did this have to happen *now?* "No one ever said it would be."

Either that was more winsome than it sounded, or Mister Combs was even better than Chris, because he laughed warmly. A sudden burst of mistrust filled him, and he found himself possessed with the need to know why this well-known man was here. For Rosemary, obviously. For her abilities. But what *exactly* was it that he wanted? "What are you doing here?" *Too sharp,* the part of him that was still coherent realized. *Blunt it.* "I assume you haven't just come for a taste of my famous biscuits." He indicated the tray on the table.

"Did *you* make these?" Mister Combs asked with delight. "They're delicious! Is this what comes of not being able to hire a cook? We should all be so unfortunate."

This time, with his suspicion still running high, Chris recognized the attempt to disarm. "You said something about my sister?" he pressed, and felt a warmth of self-satisfaction at having seen through the clumsy ruse. Just because he wasn't at his best at the moment didn't make him an idiot. He knew all the rules to this game.

"Ah, yes, of course!" Mister Combs said.

"I was just telling Mister Combs," Miss Albany interrupted so smoothly Chris almost didn't notice she hadn't been invited to the conversation. "We're just now only realizing how young and fragile Miss Rosemary actually is. Her heroism at White Clover Farms has left her abed for days, now, and she is still slow to recover. We're all glad it'll be some time before she's doing that sort of work daily."

Chris's eyes bulged against his better judgement. It was impeccably smooth politicking, far better than he'd have thought she was capable of. He sent her another stream of gratitude, and wished he was a heartreader himself so he could have some sense of what she felt back.

Not to mention, some sense of Avery Combs.

Mister Combs nodded attentively. He did a great deal of nodding—Chris knew enough about being an engaged listener to recognize it as a trick. "I'm glad, myself," he said. "But I can't help but be gladder for the three children and two bystanders who she saved from certain death at White Clover—not to mention Mister Buckley, here, and little Rosemary herself." He shook his head in wonder. "It must be *amazing*, knowing someone like her. Wizards are rare enough, but 'binding wizards? Of that sort of power? I can't even bear to think of what would have happened if she hadn't been there, or hadn't been blessed with such a gift. The word may have fallen out of use, but as far as I'm concerned, that's magic. The Gods don't grant that sort of gift without good reason."

They wanted Rosemary.

It was the worst of his fears come true, and he saw it all at once.

Not just for spot work, not just as a figurehead. They wanted her, to take her, to remove her from his custody and put her into their own, where they could do whatever they pleased with her abilities and then discard her when she was empty.

Chris was proud when he didn't immediately stand, wave his arms about, and scream. He wanted to howl at the top of his lungs, demand the man take his expert dissembly and leave them alone. He forced his panic down. It was illegal to make a child work any job not given to her by her family, wizard or no. If Lowry could just take her, they wouldn't be sending their best flatterer to cast a glamour on him.

He considered what to do. He could sit here and talk circles around Avery Combs all evening. But the thought was horrifically exhausting, and even though he knew it was the wiser course, he just couldn't bring himself to do it. Not today. Not now.

He stood up. "Mister Combs," he said, gentle but firm. "I am, of course, flattered and touched that Lowry or the Assembly or whoever else has sent you to check on my sister's well-being. But she is still recovering from her ordeal right now, and isn't seeing anyone." He took a deep breath. *Not too much.* The guiding voice was almost external. *Don't make him feel threatened. He'll fight back. They always do.* "In addition, I want to make something very clear. Rosemary, whatever her remarkable abilities, is a little girl. When she is nineteen, she will be officially categorized, like any other Tarl. Until that day, she will not be doing any 'binding other than what she chooses to do on her own time, for herself. I mean no disrespect, sir, but I do mean to make that clear." He extended his hand for another shake, and he hoped it was plain he meant it to be a farewell. "Thank you very much for coming by."

He expected some sort of fight from the man, but after only a breath's hesitation, Avery Combs climbed to his feet and took Chris's hand in his with a firm grip. "Of course," he said with fierce agreement, so strongly Chris was disoriented. Had he misinterpreted, somehow? "I understand completely. You have to protect your family." He released the hand and stepped back, and there was a moment of silence.

When Combs opened his mouth to say something more, Miss Albany climbed to her feet and extended a hand of her own. "It was very good to meet you, Mister Combs," she said, and her voice was even more a dismissal than Chris's had been. "How exciting to meet someone who's appeared in the papers."

Mister Combs took her hand, and, to Chris's surprise, brought it to his lips rather than shaking it. It surprised Miss Albany, as well. Her eyes widened in shock, and a faint flush suffused her cheeks. Apparently, she wasn't used to being treated as a gentlewoman.

The man looked up at her from over his hand. His eyes flickered over her face, and when he spoke, his voice was just only above a murmur. "What did you say your name was, again, miss?"

Miss Albany took a breath and schooled her features. Her shoulders went straight and her chin went up. "Rachel," she said primly.

And Avery Combs released her hand with a low chuckle and swept a bow. "Of course," he said, and when he straightened, he nodded to Chris as well. "I'm sorry to have disturbed you, Mister Buckley, Miss...Rachel. Do tell little Rosemary a great many people are holding their breaths in the hope that the little heroine recovers." His smile was genuine and sincere as he said, "If we'd had 'binders like her on the Floating Castle, that night would never have happened the way it did. Now, if you'll excuse me."

Chris held himself together until he heard the front door shut quietly, and then he crumpled down into the chair like a balloon losing all of its wind. The strength and clarity that had filled him when he'd clung to his mistrust of Avery Combs all rushed out in a torrent, leaving him shivering. He barely fought off the urge to cry by imagining what his father would have said if he did. Made of softer stuff, he may be, but he was *not* a woman.

THE DEATHSNIFFER'S ASSISTANT

After a moment, he felt a hand on his shoulder and realized with surprise that it was Miss Albany. That lead him to realize she was seeing him like this, and *that* lead him to take a deep, shuddering breath, straighten his shoulders, and look up at her with as much false composure as he could muster.

The softness he'd seen the night before was back as she looked down at him with genuine concern plain on her face. They stared at each other, Chris trying to think of something to say and Miss Albany likely doing the same. It was she who managed first. "I thought you handled yourself very admirably," she said, her rigid voice a clear contrast to her softened features. "That man is extremely good at what he does."

"He wanted to take Rosemary," Chris said. It scraped through his throat like a harsh whisper. "That's why he was here."

Miss Albany nodded, her mouth flattening into an unhappy line. "I'm afraid so." She removed her hand from him and looked over her shoulder, as if she could still see Combs' retreating back. "And that won't be the last we see of him, either. Traditionalist bastards will stop at nothing to get what they want, and Rosemary..." She sighed. "Well, I'm quite frankly shocked it's taken them this long."

Chris closed his eyes, raising his fingers and pressing them against his sockets. "That's because of me. You remember what I told you on that first day, when you'd realized what she was? That's what I've been doing for six years. My father made a lot of noise when he was alive, but I've done everything to downplay how powerful she is." He chuckled without mirth. "I thought I was cocking it up wonderfully. I suppose I should be proud I'd been managing after all." A shiver wracked through his body and he gritted his teeth against it. He rubbed his face with his hands. This was so inappropriate. Rachel Albany was an employee.

But she was an employee who would be able to tell what he was feeling even if he did hide it, and they had already established she wouldn't thank him for that. "I'm sorry," he said, voice muffed by his hands.

"I hardly feel there is a need for apologies," Miss Albany pronounced. "Rosemary is my responsibility now, and I—"

"My mother used to say strong enough emotions could sometimes rush into her like water going down her throat," he interrupted, too—too *everything* to care about the lapse of courtesy. "She said it felt like drowning. I can't imagine emotions any stronger than what I'm feeling right now."

A pause, and then he felt her hand on his shoulder again, and her voice lost some of its characteristic coolness as she said, "Your mother sounds as if she was especially strong. I'm hardly weak, but I've never experienced anything like you describe." She paused, then, softer. "Don't worry, Mister Buckley. You aren't causing me any undue distress."

He nodded. Silly as it was, it was a relief. He was enough of a mess for himself; he would feel horrible sharing what he felt with someone else.

"That said," Miss Albany continued, a touch of hesitation in her voice. "I have no wish to overstep my bounds, Mister Buckley. Already, our relationship has become more personal than I would like. I prefer to maintain professional distance with my clients. But it seems as though the Gods do not have that in mind for you and me, and so I will take the chance and ask...is there anything I could do for you, sir?" As Chris raised his head to look at her, surprised, she didn't meet his gaze and pushed on with determination on her plain face. "I realize you're upset over the thought of that *man*"—and she spat the word with thick venom—"taking your sister away, but I felt your misery all the way from the road. It was not caused by this, only accented. If..."

Chris thought he understood the offer.

"No," he said after a moment's thought. "I don't think there's anything, Miss Albany." If there had been, he probably wouldn't have allowed her to do it. She was right. Already, there was a miserable dearth of professionalism between them, and this wouldn't improve it.

"Yes," she said immediately. "Of course, I understand." But she didn't move, and after a long moment, she set her jaw and spoke again. "It's only—I don't feel *right*, sir, leaving you with Rosemary."

He gaped up at her, and then a flash of incredulous irritation burst forth from him. "I've taken care of Rosemary since—"

She cut in with a rush of words. "I don't feel right leaving you *alone*, Mister Buckley."

Ah. Well. He imagined what he must look like, a miserable, quivering pile of anxiety, a soft man tortured by imagined memories of something that had taken place years ago. *Not all imagined*…a ghost of thought reminded him, and he remembered the rough shingles beneath his hands and knees as he vomited, and then he pushed it away. He pushed it *all* away, and he put it in a room, and he shut the door, and he locked that door, and then he walked away and he left it all in there, as he had for six years.

He climbed to his feet and found his legs mostly steady, and the polite smile he fixed down at Rachel Albany felt as natural as he could have hoped. "I'll be fine, Miss Albany," he said, pleased with how even his voice was. "I've been alone for a very long time."

Rosemary barely stirred when he checked in on her, and only grumbled and shifted when he brushed her bangs back and pressed a kiss to her forehead. Still exhausted, the poor thing. He sighed as he looked down at her. He didn't blame her, but he wanted to speak to her so much. He hadn't since the night of the White Clover Incident, when she'd fallen asleep against his side and had to be carried home. He wanted to ask her how she was feeling, not just hear a report from her governess. He wanted to make sure she could still smile and laugh and tease him for being a baby. He wanted to see that she was still really Rosemary, and still really real.

It was an irrational desire brought on by an overwhelming day. He fought it off and settled for bringing a book into her room and reading by her bedside until the light grew too dim to see by. Instead of tapping one of the lamps and awakening the salamander bound within, he put the book aside and left the room, shutting the door quietly behind him.

He stopped at the wide, western-facing window, watching what he could see of the sunset through the city that had sprung up around the Buckley estate like mushrooms after the rain. Once upon a time, their home had been, if not as grand, as private as the val Daren estate. *Progress,* Michael Buckley had said in his confident voice. But the Buckley family hadn't sold off their land and let the city grow around them for *progress,* just as Fernand hadn't sold most of their ventures to stimulate the economy. Progress felt a lot like decline.

A sudden madness overtook him as he stood there. Perhaps it was thinking of what the Buckley family had once been, or perhaps the imaginary door in his mind hadn't been locked, after all. Whatever the reason, Chris found himself climbing staircases and drifting through halls until he opened the door to his old childhood bedroom. He stood at the threshold, gazing in at the hazy ghosts of his truncated childhood. The room was like a worldcaught painting, a moment frozen in time. Not a single thing had been touched since the day Fernand had gently suggested a young master would be better suited in the master bedroom.

But it wasn't things he'd come for, not his old train set or his book of Tarlish folktales or the miniature pianoforte he'd quit practising when he realized his mother would never teach him another lesson. He walked past all of those things, and he opened the window on the far side of the room. He gazed for a long moment, feeling the breeze ruffle his hair, and then he reached up and gripped the sill in both hands.

That night, he'd needed to put one foot on his toy box and the other on the middle shelf of his bookcase, but six years later, he was tall enough and strong enough to get out of the window by himself. He pulled his body up onto the overhanging roof that the window opened to with minimal effort, and it was strange to imagine how gruelling an ordeal it had seemed when he was a boy.

The roof was littered with the skeletal remains of old leaves and covered in moss and dirt. He sat on the shingles and pulled his legs up against his chest, hugging them to him and resting his chin on his knees. The sky was red and purple and orange, and he could see clearly in all directions. The Buckley fortune and reputation may have dwindled, but their estate was as tall as it ever had been. Some legacies were harder to erode than others.

He didn't know how long he sat there. The orange turned red, the red turned purple, the purple turned black. The black sprouted little tiny pinpricks of light, a hundred thousand alps bound up in the canopy of the sky. When the sun had fully disappeared below the horizon and proud Darrington lit up with all of its nocturnal plumage, Chris climbed to his feet.

With his right hand, he reached up and gripped one of the wrought-iron trimmings decorating the wall that rose beside him. He let his other hand fall to the side, and he gripped the iron hard enough to turn his knuckles white.

And if he breathed deeply enough, gripped tightly enough, he could go back.

Time drained away like the tide retreating to the sea, leaving the last six years scattered on his beach. Blood and murder. Viktor val Daren and Maris Dawson and Olivia Faraday. His year at Lowry refining his skill as a wordweaver. The scientists who had tortured him until the trauma awakened his gift, and no one had ever warned him that was what categorization really meant.

The tide pulled back further and then there was juggling finances he barely understood and his "friends" drifting away as they realized he was a social liability. Dressing like a pauper, eating like a priest, pulling Rosemary into the shadows of life and hiding there, praying no one would see them.

His prayers had all gone unanswered, in the end.

But the thought was gone as the tide pulled back further, and now it was revealing the ugliness of the depths, things not meant for the light of day. The sight of Fernand's face above his bed, the crushing realization that it had all been real, the misery of understanding what was going to be expected of him. And back further, to the long night before, how he had wandered in a slew of crowded hospitals filled with screaming, dying victims, armed only with the knowledge that surely, surely his mother must be here somewhere, surely he'd see her at any moment and it would all be over. All those sterile white halls and appalling wounds and the tide retreated further still.

Scrambling back in through the window, his mouth tasting of vomit and his small body roiling with emotions he couldn't understand.

Watching the Castle hit the ground not so far from where he stood with a shriek of crushing steel. Shattering glass. The way it had crumpled like it had been made of paper and wishes. And, worst of all, the way the sylphs had all joined together to form an exultant tornado, how he could hear their joyous song.

And the moment he'd seen the Castle shudder in the sky. And how he'd thought *I wish it would fall right now so he would just die.*

The tide was out, and for a moment he felt it all at once, all six years of relics on the beach, all the horror and all the pain.

And then it was all gone and he was just Chris, his mother's pride and his father's curse, his sister's most and least favourite person, a boy who'd been too quick to cry, too slow to fight, and never good enough. He was just Chris, angry, dying for a sight of the famous and infamous Castle, crawling out without his nanny's knowledge to stand on the roof and feel the night air ruffling his nightshirt against his skinny, boyish legs.

Even then, he hadn't been happy, but he'd known what it was like to feel *peace*. To not live with a family of ghosts on his back and the constant, never-ending, ridiculous thought in his mind that somehow he'd *caused* the Castle to fall when it just might have righted itself and gone on Floating.

He closed his eyes and breathed deeply. The night smelled like the city, but the only sound was the wind through the trees and the beating of his own heart. He was in the heart of Darrington, but if he couldn't hear it, couldn't see it, maybe it wasn't real.

Waves lapped against him and he floated on the sea, and then he heard a loud, unmistakable *smash*.

His eyes flew open.

The moment vanished, and the last six years crashed into him like a tidal wave. He gasped, flexing his grip on the wrought iron pole. He stood in shock for a moment, trying to place what the sound had been, why it was so distressing to him...and then he remembered.

He thrust the ghosts into the imaginary room, locked the door behind them, and vaulted back through the window. He stumbled when he hit the ground, but caught his footing. He sprinted through his old room, throwing himself against the door, and shouting, "*Rosemary!*"

He heard a clamour a floor down, the sound of someone throwing themselves down a flight of stairs. "*Shit,*" he cursed under his breath and tore off down the hall. "*Rosemary!*" he cried again. Another explosion of sound as the intruder rushed down another flight of stairs, and Chris stood at the mouth of a hallway and the steep servants' staircase. He could either go down the hall and see if his sister was all right, or hurry down this flight of stairs the intruder didn't know existed, cutting him off at the door.

With a tortured, frustrated sound getting stuck in the back of his throat, Chris chose. "Rosemary!" he shouted again, turning away from the staircase and rushing down the hall to Rosemary's room. As he reached it, he heard the sound of the front door slamming, and felt the intruder slip through his fingers. He let him go and pushed open the door to his sister's room.

He'd feared the worst. He'd known she hadn't been taken with the man he'd heard running—no one would be able to move that fast when holding a pudgy thirteen-year-old girl. But he'd prepared himself to see the room in shambles and Rosemary dead or dying. Instead, he was greeted with it being exactly the way he'd left it. Dark, quiet, and peaceful but for Rosemary's beloved music box lying on the ground, open, playing its haunting melody into the stillness.

The light from the hallway fell over his sister's face and pillow, and he saw her stir. She scrunched her features up and squinted at him. "Chris...?" she asked blearily, voice slurred with sleep. "Were you yelling my name...?"

He could have sobbed with relief. He would have, if not for how it would scare her. Breathing in and out steadily, he forced a smile and crossed the room to lean down and kiss her forehead. "I think you were dreaming," he said softly.

She yawned. "Oh..." she said, and blinked. Her eyes took a long time opening again, and she seemed even less alert as she turned on her side and murmured, "Why is my music box playing?" Her eyes slid shut.

"It must have fallen over," Chris replied, bending and closing it, silencing its song. Rosemary didn't reply. When he straightened, holding the box in his hands, her face was once again locked in the embrace of deep, peaceful, healing sleep.

Gently, he set it back on her bedside table. He was grateful it was made of polished mahogany and not some other, more fragile material. Grateful, too, that it had been made by a gearsetter and not a spiritbinder, so there was no risk of a rogue elemental. He carefully put it back exactly where it had been, trying not to think about what had just happened. None of it seemed quite real, anymore, some mad fantasy brought on by his fears and the surreal moment on the rooftop.

He kissed his sister again, turned away, and his heart leaped into his throat. He fell to his knees, barely breathing.

A knife speared a piece of paper to the wall beside the door. In the dim light, he could barely make out the words scrawled there in angry block capitals.

VIKTOR VAL DAREN DESERVED TO DIE.
STOP ASKING QUESTIONS OR I WILL HURT HER.

CHAPTER FIFTEEN

He was pulled from sleep, clawing and dragging, by hands shaking him. "...ckley. Mister Buckley! Christopher!" a woman's voice was saying in a harsh whisper. "Christopher Buckley, I am sorry, but you need to wake up!"

Chris blinked against the light, wanting nothing more than to turn and bury himself in his pillow. He shifted and groaned. Why was he so uncomfortable? Why was his bed so hard? Why did everything smell like flowers...?

He reluctantly opened his eyes and found himself staring up at the sparrowish face of Miss Rachel Albany. Throwing up an arm to ward off the dim grey light, he grunted with surprise when he realized he was in...in Rosemary's room? On the floor? "What?" he asked blearily.

"Mister Buckley," Miss Albany insisted, looking away from him with discomfort plain in her eyes. "Mister Buckley, your employer is on the mirror and she seems extremely distraught. She demands to speak to you immediately. Please, if you would. She refuses to go away."

He was on the floor because he'd slept here. He'd dragged the covers off his own bed and hauled them down to Rosemary's room so he could sleep at her door. Because he'd wanted to protect her. He'd wanted to be sure that if the intruder returned, he'd trip over him on his way in, and then Chris would be up and fighting. The intruder. The music box. The note. Chris swallowed his heart and felt it go all the way down to where his stomach languished in his knees. "Is Rosemary all right?" he asked pathetically.

Miss Albany's eyes snapped with frustrated impatience. "*Yes*, Miss Rosemary is fine. Mister Buckley, Miss Olivia Faraday is on the magic mirror for you, and she needs to speak to you right away."

Olivia? On the mirror? Chris's heart leaped all the way back up into his mouth and he sat up in a rush. "Am I late?" he asked. If he was, there would be no mercy. "What time is it?" But did he even want to go to work?

"You aren't late. It is not long past dawn. I came early today because I was—" she faltered. "I came early today. Please, Mister Buckley, please, get up and see to Miss Faraday." She peered at him. "On the mirror," she clarified.

He didn't blame her for her impatience with him. Still fighting against the last remnants of sleep, he awkwardly climbed to his feet, nearly tangling his legs in the covers he'd heaped onto the floor. He was still fully clothed from the day before save his spectacles, and Miss Albany's features sharpened when he slid those onto his face.

"I'll stay with your sister," Miss Albany offered, and, after shooting a lingering look at Rosemary and fighting with the sour sickness in the pit of his stomach, Chris could do nothing but leave the room and hurry down the stairs to the mirror in the foyer.

When he first slipped in front of it, Olivia didn't seem to notice him. She was staring off to one side, her expression deep in thought. There was a dull greyness to her eyes. Something seemed off in her surroundings. Chris shifted and then cleared his throat loudly.

His employer started, turn, and focus her gaze onto him. Fire sparked back in her eyes, but her expression remained grave. "Thank the Three and Three," she breathed. "I was worried I wouldn't be able to reach you so early."

"I was—"

She didn't even seem to notice him speaking. "I need you. You need to come to the val Daren estate. Now. Immediately."

"The val Daren estate?" That was why her surroundings had seemed odd—she was in Evelyn val Daren's beautifully furnished foyer, not the dim and sparse waiting room of her own office. Chris mentally shook himself. It was too early and he'd slept poorly. "What's going on? Why are you there? Why do you need me? It's barely past dawn."

For just a moment, Olivia broke eye contact with him. When her eyes fluttered back up to his, his heart seized in his chest, and he realized before she opened her mouth that something had gone very, very wrong.

"Is it Rayner Kolston?" he asked, saying the first thing that came to him.

"Kolston?" Olivia blinked, and then muttered an epithet under her breath. "That's right, we were going to see *him* today, weren't we? Well, that will have to wait." She shook her head. "No, Chris, it's something else. Analaea val Daren is dead."

It was as if he'd been punched in the solar plexus. The wind rushed out of him all at once. No. No, that couldn't be right. "No," he said aloud, his voice sounding as if it came from the end of a long tunnel. "That's wrong. I only just spoke to her yesterday. You must have it wrong."

But Olivia was shaking her head. Regretful, and something else. Uncomfortable? "I've seen her body myself. Her blood is all over the walls. She's been dead since yesterday, but no one found her until..." Olivia took a deep breath and then slowly let it out. "Her mother mirrored Maris and then Maris mirrored me. I need you," she repeated.

"This is..."

"This is a complication. Complications can be good, because they're more evidence, and more evidence leads to more solutions. But they can also be bad. They can be very bad. A complication like this adds so much data. It muddies the waters. Everything has to be re-examined, and that's time for the killer to cover their tracks, and—"

"And a young woman is *dead*," Chris snapped. He knew it wasn't in his best interests to say it, but Gods, he'd let himself think for one stupid moment that Olivia's listlessness was a result of grief, of mourning for the awkward, strange, unique young lady whose life had just been cut tragically short. He'd let himself be touched by her humanity. Was he an idiot?

Olivia's eyes flashed, and she met his sharpness with her own. "So? I cry about it and feel very poorly? What good does that do anyone?" She waited for him to respond, and when he didn't, she shook her hair back. It hung loose and straight as wheat, today. "None. What does do some good is finding out who killed her, and who killed her father, and doing something about *that*." Her nostrils flared and she folded her hands carefully on the table before the mirror. "I need you here, Mister Buckley. Now. Come as quickly as you can."

He expected her to release the gnome connecting the mirror and stomp off, but she met his eyes and wrested an unwilling response from him. "*Fine*," he said. "I'll even pay the cabbie extra to hurry, but I want compensation."

She waved him off. "Write it up. I don't care." And *then* she disconnected the mirrors, and her image dissolved into swirling grey mists behind a pane of black glass, which eddied and pulsed for a long moment before solidifying into his own bleary reflection.

Chris could have turned the table over in a combination of fury and grief. *Damn her*, he thought, and then, right on its heels, *Gods save me, Ana.* He thought of the girl, for despite their proximity in age, he couldn't think of her as anything else. He remembered the way her manner and personality would twist and spin between two different people, and he wondered, again, which was her and which was who her mother wanted her to be. The reserved, composed, elegant lady, or the lacy and girlish child. It pained him that he didn't know. It seemed like he should.

There was no way he could simply walk away from this now. Ana was dead, and if there was *anything* he could do to help bring her killer to justice…

"Mister Buckley?"

He looked up, realizing suddenly his fingers were clutching the edges of the table before him and his knuckles had turned white. Miss Albany stood at the head of the staircase, one hand resting on the balustrade, looking down at him with worry plain on her face. "Are you quite all right?" she asked. "I felt your distress hit me hard enough to stagger all the way in Rosemary's room."

"I'm sorry," he murmured, and shook his head. "I—I need to go in. Something's happened."

"Is Miss Faraday quite all right?"

His lips curled into a sneer and he was too exhausted to smooth the expression. "Oh, Miss Faraday is bloody *fine*, as ever."

It hadn't been the right thing to say, and Miss Albany's face pinched with disapproval. "I see," she said, her empathetic concern diving back down beneath the surface of her professional calm. "I suppose you should be on your way then, if it's so serious as that. Do not worry about compensating me for the extra hours today. It was me who chose to come in." She turned to walk away.

Chris rubbed his face with his hand. He couldn't imagine what it was he'd done to upset her, aside from failing in the courtesy she so hated. And he didn't have the time to worry about it. Or the energy, physical or mental. She'd come in early and it was fortunate for him. Her work was looking after Rosemary, and that was precisely what he needed her to do. "Miss Albany."

She stopped, swaying a bit, and then turned to look down at him, her hands gripping the balcony.

"…something happened last night," he said, and as he spoke, the words just tumbled out. "You remember when you said you thought I may have been followed home? I think you were correct. Someone was in here last night, in the house. They"—he closed his eyes, wincing around his fear, the thudding of his heart—"they left a note, you see. They know about the investigation and for some reason, they're coming after me, after Rosemary."

He heard her quiet gasp. Thoughts tumbled around in his head. Analaea val Daren was dead. Had she died before or after the note had been left? Somehow, it suddenly seemed crucially important that he know. He shook his head, trying to clear it, and opened his eyes. Miss Albany stared down at him, all blood drained from her face and her mouth tight. "I need help," he said, and it came out plaintive and weak. "I don't know what to do."

Miss Albany stared down at him for a long moment, and then, slowly, nodded. Just once.

She hitched up her skirts and descended the staircase, and he watched her until she stood beside him and reached out to lay a hand upon his arm. "She needs to be protected," Miss Albany said, her voice chillingly even and composed. It might have unsettled him, if he had anything still settled in him to be affected.

So he just nodded in agreement.

One of Miss Albany's fingers tapped against his shoulder and her gaze unfocused as she visibly dived into her thoughts. They stood in silence until, very slowly, she nodded. "She needs to be protected," she repeated, and then turned her head to meet his eyes. "Yes, I can do that. Leave this in my hands, Mister Buckley. I'll contact the relevant people. I promise you, I will make sure your sister is kept safe."

Something in her voice made him believe so strongly he could taste that she was telling the truth. He sighed and nodded his relief. "Thank you," he breathed, and then, even as it killed him to speak the words, "I have to go."

It took physical effort to leave the house. He didn't so much as go upstairs to change and straighten himself. He hated to be seen in yesterday's clothes *again*, with his hair pressed flat in places and standing up in others. But if he went up, he'd get lost in the maze of it all again. Rachel Albany had proved she'd defend Rosemary yesterday afternoon, and he needed to trust she'd continue to do so.

The grey light of dawn was fading before the yellow light of morning, and the first cabbie he found was cheery and cooperative, agreeing without argument to tear through the streets all the way out to the val Daren estate. Chris held tightly to the hook hanging from the ceiling for the whole trip as his body was thrown from side to side, and he tried to prepare himself for what would be waiting when he arrived.

The estate was quiet and sombre. Chris's steps were unnaturally loud as he walked down the path to the front door. It was still early enough that mist clung to the hills surrounding the house, there was a sharp chill in the air, and dew shimmered from every leaf and blossom in the gardens. He remembered Ana's smile. He remembered her saying, *"I feel as if I can trust you."*

When he went to grip the old lion-faced knocker in his hand, he was startled to have the door burst open. He was nearly bowled over by Officer Maris Dawson and the two policemen who followed after her. The stocky little policewoman stopped in mid-step and looked him up and down. "The Duke's daughter is dead," she said by way of greeting. Matter-of-factually.

Did none of these people really care when someone died? "I heard," Chris said.

Officer Dawson nodded. Discomfort showed in the stiffness of the gesture. "I thought you might have. Olivia's in with her now. Me and my boys"—she gestured back at the men behind her—"are going back to the station to get personnel for an autopsy." She grimaced at the word. "Nasty business, cutting into corpses. I miss the days before we did that." She stepped to one side, and, as her men did the same, beckoned him into the estate. "May as well get in there, Buckley," she said, and cast him a look that wasn't unsympathetic. "Faraday's up in the girl's bedroom, and she's been howling for an assistant all morning. Always been useless on her own, that one."

Chris found Olivia standing in the doorway of Ana's room. She turned to him as if sensing his presence the moment he rounded the corner, and her face broke into a grateful smile. "Oh, good!" she exclaimed, long golden earrings swaying. "Good, good! You're here! Come in, come in, I need you to make some notes."

Without another word, she bustled off into the bedroom. All the gravity she'd displayed on the mirror was long gone. With a coal burning in his stomach and his heart doing somersaults in his chest, Chris started down the long hallway, following after his employer.

He froze at the doorway.

Oh, Gods.

He thought he'd seen blood when he'd first gone into Viktor val Daren's study. He remembered the thick, congealed pool beneath the hanging corpse, the spread of it all down the Duke's front, the way it had smelled like iron and salt, the dark angry red of it. He'd seen less blood in butcher shops. He'd never imagined seeing more.

But now he realized the Duke had died quickly. One slash to the throat, and the blood had spilled out from there. A single clean, killing wound. It had been over in a minute. Life had come out in one steady red stream, and it had all ended up in one place. The Duke's death had been merciful.

Analaea had fought.

His breath went ragged and he raised a hand to his temple. He staggered back a step, heard a strangled noise emerge from his throat. He groped blindly for the door frame.

Olivia must have heard him. She turned about while he found the frame and clung there, resting his cheek against the cool painted wood, unable to draw his eyes away from the scarlet butchery in front of him. He struggled to breathe. He heard Olivia sigh.

"You said you had a strong stomach," she accused. He struggled to bring his eyes to hers. They flashed in irritation. "I remember asking during your interview. You were quite adamant."

He'd gotten quite upset and violently protested her painting him as a swooning maiden, yes, he remembered. He remembered. He forced his eyes closed, taking long, steady breaths, trying to calm his shattered nerves and his racing thoughts and his heaving stomach.

"Mister *Buckley*," Olivia pressed. He could hear her tapping her foot.

"Give me a moment," he said, his voice hoarse.

"You said—"

"I know what I said. I was wrong. Just…just give me a moment."

She huffed.

He could still see it all in his mind's eye. Lines of blood like swirls of strawberry in iced cream going all up the walls, covering the floor, spattered across the ceiling, a red rain falling here and then there. Scuff marks through the blood all over the floor where someone had slipped and fallen and scrambled and fought. Gods, so much blood thrown about, drops and splotches and pools everywhere, the rampage of a scarlet undine.

And Ana.

Ana in the midst of it all, mutilated and cut to pieces. He'd seen little more than that, *wanted* to see little more than that. He feared to look closer, to categorize all of her injuries and hurts, and he knew Olivia would make him do just that.

He trembled against the door frame. He'd dropped his notebook, he realized, in his initial shock. Olivia would not be happy. Had there been blood where it had fallen?

Grandmother Eadwyr, give me strength. It was a more specific prayer than he'd made in many years. Chris took one final steadying breath and opened his eyes.

The room was as sickening and red as it had been before, but his stomach didn't heave and he kept breathing. He released the frame and took a step in, and another. He bent to pick up the notebook, and a cursory inspection revealed it was unharmed. "What do you need?" he asked to Olivia, and his voice only shook a little.

She took another moment studying a line of blood across the ceiling, then turned back to him. She looked him up and down once. "Better," she said, and that was the only comment she made on his moment of weakness.

She directed her attention to the heap on the floor, and clucked her tongue. "Shame," she said, and that was her memorial for the young lady Analaea val Daren had been. She walked in a slow circle around the body. All the blood nearby had been sprawled in and spread about, so it had dried quickly while the thicker droplets remained wet. "She fought," Olivia said, confirming Chris's initial impression. "And she fought hard. She didn't die straight away in shock and disgust like her father did, oh no. The girl gave everything she got."

Chris fought off a surge in his stomach when Olivia reached down and gripped Ana's chin in her hand. She pushed it to one side, making the dead girl's face more visible. "Ugh, so stiff," Olivia said, making a face and wiping her hands on the rag she had tucked into her belt. Chris's heart hurt at the expression Ana had died wearing. Tear tracks went down the blood smeared on the girl's face, and despite the ragged cut in one of her cheeks, it was easy to see that she had died in terror and anguish.

Olivia bent again, this time touching the girl's hands. They were the worst of it. The cuts there were deep and angry, twisted and uneven. Chris could tell the knife had deliberately sawed into them

217

there, and there. Her ring finger and middle on her left hand were hanging off from the palm side, and her index finger on the right was missing from the second knuckle up. "She gripped the knife in both hands," Olivia said, pointing to select cuts. "She tried to push it away from her while the killer tried to push it towards her. They went back and forth." She indicated the ring and middle finger. Then she pointed to the missing index. "Then they changed tack and pulled out while she was reaching to get a better grip. Took the finger off, here. Stabbed again and again, but..." Now Olivia showed him the deep, biting, small cuts peppering the palms of both hands. "But she used her hands to shield her face." One cut went in one side and out the other, a hole right through her hand. "She did not die easy."

Olivia shot him a look. "Are you getting this down?" she asked sharply, and then smiled a feline half smile at him when he indicated his open notebook. "Good boy," she said, pleased. "We're learning."

She turned her attention back to Ana's body. "By now, it's been some time, too long. There's blood going everywhere. So now we're frustrated with her," she said, her voice losing some of its certainty, becoming considering. "We slash low instead of high." She brushed the sliced open fabric of Ana's bodice, in her abdomen. Chris could look there for only a moment before turning his eyes aside. It was too much, too awful, those pale snakes bulging forth from the ruffles of her beautiful, dove-grey gown. "We get her in the stomach, slice. The girl goes into shock at the pain, falls on her bum." Olivia pointed to where the blood on the floor first turned into a smudgy red mess. "But she *still* doesn't stop fighting. The knife keeps falling, and she keeps protecting herself. She turns to one side, tries to dodge, pushes herself back." Chris weaved as quickly as he could, combining the wounds Olivia indicated with the words Olivia said. "Every time the killer pulls back the knife, blood flings to one side, over, up, down." The splatters along the walls and ceilings, of course.

"And the killing blow…" Olivia mused, scanning Ana's body. "The killing blow, the killing blow…"

Chris finally caught up with her tirade, taking a breath of relief and looking up at her. She stood over the body, her face quizzical as she looked up and down and up and down. And then she smiled smally…*almost* sadly. "There was no killing blow," she said. She sounded…impressed? "She tried and tried to get her in the heart or the throat or the temple, but the girl never let her. They struggled here until Analaea bled to death." Olivia looked up and met Chris in the eyes, and her smile widened. There was no doubt this time; she was impressed. "*That* is how I want to die," Olivia stated proudly.

"I want to die old and happy and surrounded by friends," Chris replied automatically, feeling dizzy and ill. "In my bed."

Olivia turned away, skirts swishing behind her and trailing in blood. "That's what everyone says," she said dismissively. "Piss poor way to go, I think. Feeble and weak and unremarkable."

"And happy."

Olivia cracked a small smile. It lasted only an instant. She paced around the wall of the room, studying all the splatters of blood. "I've seen people die scared, people die shocked, people die angry, and people die humiliated." She flickered her eyes over to him and then away once more. "I've never seen anyone die happy. It doesn't matter you're ten or one hundred and ten, you always feel you didn't have enough time."

Christopher thought of his parents, and he kept his mouth shut.

While Olivia walked thoughtfully around the outskirts of the room, studying blood and saying nothing, Chris weaved. His eyes and his thoughts kept coming back to the room, how pastel and girlish it was, how wrong it looked covered in blood. He'd just sat here with her, yesterday, and they'd eaten scones and laughed together. She'd just begun to heal from her father's death, not to mention all the other hurts in her life. What had she done, that had made her deserving of death? Could a creditor be so evil? Or…

Chris looked up sharply. He sought out Olivia and found her on her knees by the door, nose mere inches from the floor. "You said 'she,' " he said.

"Did I?" Olivia didn't look up.

"I wrote it down. 'She tried and tried to get her in the heart,' you said."

"I suppose I must have, then, if you wrote it down."

Chris looked back down at the carved up corpse and shivered. "You still think the Duchess did this," he said quietly. The mere thought made him sick.

Olivia did look up, then, finally. She sat back on her heels and met his eyes from across the room. "Yes," she said with unflinching confidence. "And moreover, I'm more certain today than I was yesterday."

With his heart sinking, Chris used his eyes to trace the wounds in Ana's hands, in her cheek, in her shoulders and arms, and, especially, the one in her belly. It couldn't be, no. Not with this sort of rage.

"Don't tell me you disagree," Olivia continued. "You'd have to be stupid not to find this suspicious. Cwenday afternoon, the girl calls her mother a liar to her Deathsniffer and hands over a folder full of secret information, and then bright and early Deorday morning, she's dead."

"I refuse to believe that. Ana was her daughter."

Olivia shrugged one bared shoulder and seemed to lose interest in him. "A disappointing daughter she couldn't control anymore. And a traitor, too, in her eyes. I've seen a hundred times worse and a thousand times less believable. Come on. We've seen all there is here." She motioned to Chris, and the conversation was dismissed.

Eager to put a list of questions as long as her arm to her prime suspect, Olivia sought out Evelyn val Daren. By then, Maris had arrived with a team of lifeknitters and a heartreader, all wearing the queen's insignias of the Royal Tarlish Police Force. Olivia was happy enough to sign off on Ana's body, leaving it in the hands of the police, before going in search of Duchess val Daren.

It quickly became apparent she was not at the estate.

Servants with apologetic expressions and low voices informed them regretfully than the Duchess had stepped out for the day. No, they didn't know where she had gone. No, they didn't know when she would be returning, either. Was there anything they could do, instead?

"There's nothing I can do about it," Officer Dawson said with flat irritation. They stood in the foyer, and most of the policewoman's attention was taken up with supervising as her men carried Analaea val Daren's litter out to the waiting hearse. "She's free to come and go as she pleases until you order an arrest."

"Can I do that, then?" Olivia asked sourly.

"Don't be difficult, Faraday, you know I wouldn't approve it. You still don't have any evidence."

"She hid evidence from me, she asked people to lie to give her an alibi, she had plenty of reasons to kill him, and her daughter mysteriously shows up dead the day after telling us most of that," Olivia listed. "Can any of *that* be evidence?"

"Don't be smart, either."

Chris couldn't help but watch the lifeknitters with Ana's litter. The hearse would take her to the mortuary, and the lifeknitters would cut even deeper and further into her flesh, searching for anything Olivia had missed. The heartreader would spend the night sleeping at her side, trying to pick up on any strong final emotions that might give the investigation some insight. And then, after a lovely funeral attended by people who never truly knew her, Ana would be taken to a cemetery, somewhere very exclusive and beautiful, and put underground. She'd have a headstone that listed dates too close together and an inscription that said nothing about her. *Beloved daughter,* perhaps.

Ana's body had been covered by a white sheet, and, hidden as it was, it was easy to pretend she had died at peace. Harder, though, to forget the images of her terrified, tear-streaked face and butchered corpse.

Maiden Maerwald, Chris prayed, *Tell her I'm sorry. Tell her I wish we could have figured this before she had to die. Tell her...tell her if I'd had more time, if either of us had had more time, I'd have tried to be a real friend.* He didn't know if the last was true or not. It had been too soon to tell, and neither of them had had much experience with friendship. But he wished it were true. That had to count for something.

Now he'd prayed twice in a single day, he thought ruefully, and the litter was out the front door and being carried down the walk. Fernand would be so proud.

"Wasn't there someone else you were going to see about this case, today?" Officer Dawson was asking. "Reams Kolton? Something..."

Olivia made a nonplussed sound. "Rayner Kolston," she said dismissively. "The val Daren's creditor. I'd really rather talk to the Duchess. Where could she *be?*"

"Didn't you tell me yesterday she had a brother who died at the Floating Castle?" Officer Dawson asked. "The six year anniversary is tomorrow. Isn't it likely she's preparing for one of the memorials?"

"I'd think she should be a little more concerned with the daughter who died today than the brother who died six years ago, Maris."

"Maybe she just didn't want to be called a murderer on the day when the two coincide," Chris spoke up, against his better judgement.

"Maybe," Officer Dawson agreed before Olivia could say a word, and then continued to speak, cutting off any chance to change that. "Go and see the creditor today, Faraday. As I recall, you were quite excited about that this morning. You can talk to the Duchess later today, or tomorrow."

"Once she'd had all day to practice her lies," Olivia muttered, but in the end she had no choice.

Without the Duchess there to authorize the use of the estate's vehicles, and with Olivia in no fit mood to wait an hour while they mirrored in a hackney cab from the city, Officer Dawson offered to let them sit in the back of the police car she and her boys had come out in. The rest of the police officers would be attending the hearse, making the police car free but for Officer Dawson and the driver, who were seated in the front. Chris was grateful for the offer—he was nearly as disinclined to sit at the estate for an hour as Olivia was—but the bars on the windows and the clattering manacles attached to the seats made him painfully uncomfortable once they'd started moving.

Olivia didn't seem to notice the grim surroundings. Chris sat back in his seat and let her voice wash over him, thinking about Ana. He thought about how her life might have been about to change, about how desperately lonely she had been. He wondered about her beau, Ethan Grey, and what he felt on a day like today. And he couldn't help but wonder what expression he, himself, might have had on his own face if his father had come at him with a knife. Would he have had cuts all over his hands from fighting, or would he have been split in one slice, like the Duke? He didn't have an answer.

CHAPTER SIXTEEN

The doors to the police carriage didn't open from the inside, which Chris discovered with some horror when he went to let himself out. Officer Dawson was there in mere moments to release them, but Chris still found the fresh air and the feeling of stretching his legs especially welcome after the experience.

It was mid-morning by then, and Darrington was loud and boisterous and full of people streaming in all directions. Chris looked around him, trying to place where exactly they were. It was the banking district, of that he was certain, but he couldn't pin down more. The building they'd stopped in front of had clearly been a house, once, before it had suddenly found itself in the midst of a busy trade district and had been offered a sizable sum to join the crowd. It was small and quaint, but, very, very old.

Olivia jumped down behind him and turned about to survey the area as Chris had. Her dress today was modern and stylish, off the shoulder, tight in the waist and bust, long slender skirts ending in a small train. For once, she could have blended in with all the other ladies of Darrington, if it weren't for the blood coating the hem of her skirts. "It's hard not to feel like a criminal back there," she said, retrieving her stylish lace gloves from her handbag, pulling them daintily onto her long fingers. "Though I should thank you for not locking us into the manacles, I suppose." She fluttered her eyelashes at Officer Dawson.

The policewoman turned her back. "It was tempting."

"I appreciate your restraint, Maris, as always," Olivia gushed.

Officer Dawson tipped her chin towards the old building that had once been a house. "The offices of Rayner Kolston," she said. "As you requested. You're lucky it was along the way, or I'd have put you out at the station and let you get a hackney here."

"Are you going to wait for us, then?" Olivia laid a hand on the policewoman's forearm, who shook her off irritably.

"Hardly," she grunted and started to walk off. "Let me know how it went when you get back to the office. This is still my favourite theory of them, especially with what you told me this morning. I want to know everything."

"Aye, aye, captain," Olivia saluted Officer Dawson's back mockingly.

"Oh, and one last thing…" Officer Dawson said, turning about and looking Chris right in the eye. He couldn't help but start at the unexpected attention. The police officer gave him a grim smile and a nod. "You didn't do half bad in there this morning, Buckley. Constance puked her guts at her first messy one, and she didn't even know the victim." She turned her attention to Olivia. "Keep this one. I mean it."

From the corner of his eye, Chris saw Olivia give an awkward half shrug with one of her bared shoulders. The driver helped Officer Dawson up beside him, the whip was cracking, and the unicorns were trotting off down the road.

There was an uncomfortable moment where Maris Dawson's compliment hung between the two of them like a fading perfume. The police carriage vanished into traffic and Chris tightened his grip on his notebook, clearing his throat. "So," he said, trying to sound conversational. "Ah, after what we've already seen today, I doubt this is going to be very enlightening."

Olivia chuckled. She reached into the satchel she carried at her side and pulled out a yellow and crinkling newspaper. She waved it in his general direction, just long enough for him to make out half of the headline, *MESSAGE TO OTHER DEBTORS,* before she was off down the walk at a brisk, swishing pace, and he was hurrying to catch up with her.

The reception room of the house-turned-office was dimly lit and grey, and it smelled like ancient mold. A pinched middle-aged woman sat behind the reception desk. She pointedly ignored them until Olivia walked directly up to her and put her categorization card on the surface between them. "I'm here to talk to Mister Kolston, please and thank you," she said sweetly. The sour-faced woman stared up at her with pursed lips and flat eyes for a long time. Then she stood up and wordlessly bustled off down a hallway. The floors creaked and groaned and sagged under her weight.

"What does the paper say?" Chris couldn't help but ask, now incredibly curious.

Olivia shot him an impish smile. "You'll see. Oh, but it's good. It's *so* good."

When the secretary came back out into the room, her belligerence seemed slightly reduced. "Mister Kolston will see you," she mumbled, and started back down the hall. Olivia and Chris hurried after her. She led them down a long hallway lit with very old, dim, flickering alp-lights, their dark nimbuses fuzzy and undefined with age. As relatively harmless as alps were, the uncertainty of their bindings put Chris's heart in his throat. Then he thought about Analaea val Daren singing to the one, and a moment of blinding grief overtook him.

The secretary pushed a door open. "Here they are," she said, and, pushing past Olivia and Chris, turned back down the hall to the safety of her musty reception room without another word.

Chris hung back from the open door and Olivia shouldered past him and through the frame. He saw her put a friendly smile on her lips and tilt her head at the man inside before she vanished into the room, and he followed after her, opening his notebook to the first empty page. The one before it was full of descriptions of Ana's death, and he tried not to look at it.

The room was very big, and it dwarfed Rayner Kolston. He was a small, furtive-looking man with sharp, narrow features. He wore a well-tailored but faded suit and a smart little bowler hat, just slightly too small for his already tiny head. He had a waxed and pointed little goatee that matched the slicked black hair poking out from beneath the back of his hat. His smile was oily and his eyes searching as he steepled his fingers over the papers spread across his desk. "Now," he said, and his east-end Vernellan accent was thick as stew, "what do I owe the fine pleasure of such a lovely lady's compan—"

Olivia dropped the paper down onto the desk. The headline was facing Mister Kolston, but Chris could read it upside down. *DUKE HERBERT VAL FRENTON MURDERED BY CREDITOR, MESSAGE TO OTHER DEBTORS.*

Kolston took one glance at the article and then threw his hands up helplessly. "Right," he said. "Not like I didn't see this one coming." Olivia watched him while he pushed up from his desk, sidestepped Chris, and shut the door behind them. "Look, I know it all smells plenty bad, but it weren't me that killed Vik, okay?"

Delicately, Olivia picked the paper back up. It crinkled and a fleck of yellowed paper spiralled down to the rickety floor at her feet. "Let's see here," she said pleasantly, scanning the article with one finger. She cleared her throat and began to read, her voice musing and thoughtful. "Duke val Frenton's arms were split from palm to armpit, dislocated, and then hung from the ceiling by the wrists." She looked at Chris, a furrow appearing between her eyes. "That sounds familiar, doesn't it, Christopher? Why does that sound so familiar?"

"Herbert's neck weren't cut, and he bled out from the slices down his arms," Kolston protested. "Plenty different from Vik. Plenty different, love."

Olivia continued to read. "Deathsniffer Trenton Gavril has put in for the arrest of categorized sumfinder *Rayner Kolston*, val Frenton's creditor..." She focused her eyes on the rat-man leaning against his office door as if he could keep them in there with his diminutive frame.

"That's a mighty old paper."

"Oh, come on," Olivia begged him. She folded her arms, crunching the paper, and settled her behind back on the edge of Kolston's desk. "Don't be such an amateur. I know a slimy sumfinder like you can do *way* better. Aren't you creditors supposed to be smooth talkers? Try again."

Kolston pushed off the door and paced towards them. The floorboards squealed. "All right, lovely," he said, holding his hands before him, his face begging them to believe his harmlessness. "How's this. If you bothered to read a paper a week later than that one, you'd see Gavril never got approved for that arrest. And a bit later, you'd know I got framed, see? Val Frenton's wife came out and admitted she staged the whole thing, confessed, and got herself crisped up nice and good by a cloudling." He rolled his eyes. "Old Blood, eh? Frying is a status symbol for those bunch. If it had been me, I'd just been hung."

"I'm not convinced it wasn't you." Olivia cocked her head, not giving an inch.

"I'd be pretty bent in the head if it were, don't you think?" Kolston asked. Something changed in his voice, and Chris felt the curious sensation of being wheedled and directed, like he was a sheep and Kolston was a little herding dog. "What kind of idiot would I have to be? Look at it, love, you'll see. So I'm angry that Herbert ain't paid up and I'm pretty sure he's never going to, so I think, sure, I'll turn him into an example, maybe use him to squeeze something out of all the other Old Debts I've got on my plate. I kill Herbert in the most needlessly grotesque way I can come up with, somehow manage to pull a vanishing act on the

Deathsniffer who comes after me, and get away free as a bird. So then, what?"

Olivia raised her eyebrows and waited.

Kolston sighed and dropped his hands. "So, I wait eight years and kill another client with the same profile in the same way? Come on, now, you look like a smart lady. Smart enough to see *I'm* too smart to pull something that *stupid.* If I were to kill Vik, smart thing would be to do it as different as possible, eh? Doing it the same way, now, that's just asking for a Deathsniffer to show up on my doorstep." He peered at her for a moment and then gave her a sideways sort of grin, reaching up to straighten his ascot tie. "Course, if I'd known she'd be so fine a creature, maybe it would have been worth it."

Chris expected Olivia to react poorly to the flirting, but, to his utter shock, she actually chuckled and rolled her eyes playfully. "Oh, don't even try," she said. "I'm a Deathsniffer. You're a murderer. It would really never work."

Kolston's slimy grin widened. "Well, we never know till we give it a spin, eh?" He looked her up and down *very* slowly, and his eyes lingered in places that made Chris blush and focus his attention down on his notebook, where he almost tripped over himself weaving something very unflattering about the both of them. "Never did get your names."

"Olivia Faraday, Deathsniffer. And this is my assistant, Christopher Buckley. Better looking than *yours.*" Olivia poked a finger at him accusingly, and Chris was grateful she silenced whatever remark Kolston was about to make. "You won't distract me, Mister Kolston. I'm much too good." She tapped one finger against her upper arm and raised her eyebrows. "Tell me about the val Darens."

"What do you want me to tell?"

"Whatever you have. Start with their debts. I'm very interested."

Kolston sighed. The floor groaned in protest as he went to sit behind the desk once more. "Old Debts," he said, and then looked consideringly at the papers all spread out before him. He shuffled through a stack, moved pages about, thumbed through another. "I could tell you there was nothing special about the val Darens', but I like you, even though you think I'm a killer, so I'll be honest."

"That's ever so sweet of you."

Kolston cracked a smile. "I hear that sometimes." He finally stopped mussing with his papers and leaned back in his chair. "Old Blood nobles are idiots," he said. "Blasted chuckleheads, they are. Boil on the arse of society. We tell them they're special from the day they're born and they're too puffed up with that to see they're not. They shit and piss and bleed like all the rest of us do, and the only thing not getting categorized does for them is ensure they're piss poor." He rubbed two imaginary coins together between his thumb and forefinger and grinned. "All their money is vapour and mist, and it's a creditor's dream and nightmare both at the same time."

"I do understand the principle of Old Debts."

"Aye, you look like the sort of fine lady who puts things together quickly. Sure, course you do. Ain't hard to figure out, eh? Well." He straightened his hat. "You get the basic gist, then. Them idiots are always spending money they don't have like it's going out of style. There's never been an Old Blood noble seen a price tag they didn't like. Old Debts run in Old Blood, is how the saying goes, and any Tarl who knows the first thing about sumfinding can tell it to you. Now, though, here's the thing about the val Darens." He leaned forward, and Chris couldn't help but do the same, leaning towards him, drawn in by the oily little man's vulgar storytelling. "Every Old Blood family is leaking money. But the val Darens, now…the val Darens are *haemorrhaging* it."

Olivia furrowed her brow, disappointed. "Yes," she said. "Because of the Duke's hobby."

But Kolston was shaking his head. "No, Liv, I don't think you're getting what I'm saying. Vik could have had ten girls a year and bought every single one of them their own personal Floating Castle and still not been gushing out royals like he was. I juggle two dozen Old Debts and I could put all their expenses together and still not equal how much the val Darens spend in a year."

"Hm." When Chris looked over, Olivia was chewing her lip. "That's interesting," she admitted, and then fixed Kolston with a shrewd look. "It would be a good reason to kill him."

Kolston gave an exaggerated sigh. "Now here I thought we were getting past that."

"No, really," Olivia said. She reached out and tapped the crumbled paper on his desk, the headline still easily readable. "Explain this, why don't you? No neck wound or not, that's much too similar to be a coincidence."

Kolston shrugged. "You're the Deathsniffer, not me," he said. "Ask me to add ten digit numbers in my head and I'll get back to you in half a wink but tell me to explain a murderer and I'm stumped." He scratched his goatee. "I was there myself when they blackened old Lizzie val Frenton, so it sure weren't her." He peered searchingly at Olivia. "Don't you have a notion?"

"I have a theory."

"Already told you, lovely, it weren't me."

"I didn't say that was the theory."

Kolston leaned back in his chair, far enough that the front legs came off the ground and the floorboards moaned. "I got a theory of my own," he said. "Theory is when Lowry goes to categorize somebody and nothing happens, they send the stupid ones to the church...and call the smart ones truthsniffers. Seems like you're wrong at least as often as us mere mortals."

Olivia giggled. "Don't voice that theory too loudly, now. Lowry doesn't like that sort of talk. Categorization is a flawless system, didn't you know?"

"Funny time of year to be saying that," Kolston said with a laugh of his own. "Try telling it to the blokes and misses who thought they was going to a fine party at a castle in the sky."

Chris's weaving slammed to a halt. His body tensed. Kolston might not know any better, but *Olivia* did. Let them banter over the val Daren case when Ana was dead. Fine. He didn't have to like it, but he could keep his mouth shut and realize he was sensitive; he *knew* the girl. But the Floating Castle...no. That was too cruel of them.

He went so far as to move one of his feet, starting for the exit, but he forced himself calm. Olivia would not be pleased if he left. He still needed this job, for Rosemary. *You'd be just as well leaving this job for Rosemary,* something murmured. *Remember the note.*

No. He trusted Miss Albany.

"Miss Faraday," he said quietly. "The letters addressed to the Duchess..."

Olivia shot him a dark look. "*Yes,* Christopher," she said sharply. "I realized."

Kolston raised his eyebrows. "What's this, now?"

Olivia's disapproving glare lingered on Chris for a long moment, but then she sighed and reached back into the satchel she carried. "You don't need to see this," she said. "But since my assistant has seen fit to involve you, I can't see the harm." She pulled out the file Ana had given Chris and handed it to the creditor, who took it and opened the first page. A furrow appeared in his brow as he read it, and then he made a face and closed it.

"Letters from my office," he said. "I don't get it."

Olivia reached across the desk and flipped the pages until she reached the first personal letter addressed to *Evie.* "This is more what I had in mind," she said, and this time, Kolston's expression deepened in interest as he read it.

"'Your weapon may merely be your husband's deep pockets,'" he read aloud, then whistled lowly. "Well, this explains a mystery that's driven me off my nut in the last decade. Much obliged, Liv." He licked his thumb and rubbed the signature at the base of the letter until it smudged. "HC," he mused. "Who the bloody hell is HC?"

Olivia reached out and snatched the folder back, giving him an admonishing look. "We're not sure," she replied. "And we certainly wouldn't tell it to a suspect who licks evidence."

Kolston feigned hurt. "Still a suspect?" he mourned.

"I know better than to let my guard down around a man who oils his facial hair," Olivia said with a knowing smile. She ran her fingers along the edge of his desk. "Do you have anything else useful for me?"

The creditor shrugged. "Might have. There's another old saying amongst us sumfinders, you know. 'If you want to know who a man wants to be, talk to his wife. If you want to know who a man really is, talk to his creditor.' " His eyes watched Olivia's marching fingers hungrily. "I knew Vik better than most, I'd say."

"And did that knowledge earn you any insight?"

"Might have," Kolston said again.

Olivia's fingers stilled, and slowly, she flattened her hand against the desk. Her head tilted and her brows knitted together, but a small smile was pulling at the corners of her mouth. "Are you getting at what I think you are?" she asked.

Kolton broke into a wide grin. "Might be," he said with obvious savour.

"You realize I can come back here with my police supervisor and *make* you talk," Olivia informed him tartly, her tiny smile never wavering. "I already had to do that with the Duke's mistress. Officer Maris Dawson is a tiny ginger anvil, and she'll make you feel *very* sheepish. Or worse, if I tell her about what you're asking."

"I ain't asked for anything." Kolston's teeth and eyes glittered in identical delight.

"Wicked man," Olivia said, and, with an exaggerated sigh, she reached into her satchel and pulled out a dainty, lacy billfold. Chris watched in utter shock as she opened it, pulled out a five royal note, and extended it out to the ratty little man in the oiled goatee and the tiny bowler hat.

"What are you doing?" he asked, unable to help himself, and they turned to look at him as if they'd forgotten he was there.

"Bribing the bloody swindler, obviously," Olivia said, and Kolston reached out and snatched the note from her fingers. Chris could only stand with his mouth hanging open while the creditor examined the bill from all angles, and then swept his bowler hat off in a sitting bow before tucking it into his vest. "I hope that's good enough and you didn't just make my money disappear," Olivia said, voice warm with mirth. "Or I might go and get my supervisor after all."

"No worries, love," Kolston replied, settling back again. He set his hat on one finger, hiding his hand like a lampshade, and twirled it about, studying it as if it were the most interesting thing in the world. "Vik was a real scoundrel under all his maudlin posturing," he said. "Weren't nobody he could talk to about all them little butterflies he took a shining to, so he'd tell it to the one man who couldn't ever judge him for it. Every one of them, he told me about, in enough detail to make your little assistant there blush all the way down to his baby toes. There were dozens of them, a new one every year, sometimes twice a year."

"Do you always talk about obvious things before you get to the interesting part of your stories?" Olivia asked, eyes wide with innocence.

Kolston laughed. "Ruins the story if you just jump right in," he said. "But for you, I guess, I can skip to the good part." He smiled up at her. "Vik's burned his way through a whole lot of girls, let me tell you ...but there ain't never been a one he was half so in love with as little Vanessa Caldwell."

"Is that so?" Olivia asked, the innocent curiosity in her expression fading to practiced disinterest. She picked at the lace of her gloves. "She didn't seem so enamoured with him."

"He didn't know it. He was always going on about her. He could talk a big game all he liked about purity and guilelessness and

234

all that rubbish, but you've met his wife. Vik may be drawn to freshly fallen snow, but it's the play of ice and fire that really captivated him. Vanessa had enough of that to put even Evelyn to shame. Hot and cold, perfect balance. Doubt she ever knew just how perfect she was, but the girl swept him right off his feet."

"This is gossip," Olivia droned, looking up from her gloves. "This isn't useful. I'd like my five royals back, please."

Kolston held up his hands, his hat used like a shield. "All right, all right, hold your horses there, lovey. I guess I'll wreck all the tension and go right to the end, but you're missing out. Everyone says I spin a good tale." When Olivia's expression didn't change, he sighed. "Vik told me he was going to go out and get himself a divorce."

Olivia's features changed instantly. Her feigned indifference melted immediately, draining away and leaving eager fascination in its place. She put both her hands on the surface of Kolston's desk and leaned forward, eyes sparkling. "To marry Vanessa Caldwell," she said breathlessly.

"So he claimed."

"But she's just a lifeknitter with some aspirations to poetry. Sure, Evelyn North had no Old Bloodline to speak of, but her family was rich and well-regarded before the Floating Castle. The Duke couldn't have been so stupid as to marry someone like that..."

Kolton raised an eyebrow. "Would he?" he asked. "I told you the Old Blood were stupid, didn't I? It ain't just about money."

Olivia straightened. She shot Chris a triumphant smile, her eyes darting from the notebook to his face as if to say *are you getting this?* He nodded once in reply, and went back to weaving, unsure of what he thought of this development himself. "Well, Mister Kolston," Olivia pronounced. "That's very helpful information. Certainly worth five royals. Thank you."

Kolston finally set his hat back on his head. He straightened it, looking up at Olivia with something that was nearly a leer. "Didn't think you'd pay."

Olivia returned his leer with a flash of playful half smile before turning about in a flounce of straight yellow hair and cleanly cut skirts. "It was presumptuous of you to even ask," she said, starting for the door. Chris flipped the notebook shut and started after her, but bumped into her when she stopped to shoot one last look over her shoulder at the oily little man. "I like presumptuous," she said. Her eyes said much more.

They were out in the busy banking district minutes later. Chris straightened his topcoat and ran a hand through his hair, feeling as though there were a thin coating of grease all over his body. "That man makes me feel as though I need a bath," he muttered.

"Mm. Tell me about it," Olivia purred, staring back at the old, old house, and the look on her face made it all the worse.

CHAPTER SEVENTEEN

They spent the rest of the day looking for people who seemed to be purposely avoiding them.

Vanessa Caldwell had left work early and wasn't at her old tenement house. The Duchess never returned to the estate, and the staff stopped answering the mirror in the afternoon. A quick trip to the station told them Ana's autopsy was taking longer than expected, but so far, nothing revealing had been discovered. By suppertime, Chris was exhausted and would have done anything for a day just sitting behind the desk in Olivia's windowless waiting room, bored. As his exhaustion grew, his control over his emotions waned, and he found himself choking back tears in their last cab ride of the day. If Olivia noticed, she pretended not to. For that reason, he felt she didn't.

The fine weather of the morning had clouded over at noon, and by the time they reached the office of O. Faraday, Deathsniffer, with its strange dark mist, the sky was dark and the air smelled heavily of the metallic twinge that came before a rain. Chris tried to brush unfallen tears from his eyes without Olivia seeing while she climbed out of the cab after him and paid the cabbie, who was only too eager to be on his way.

As their taxi merged into the flow of traffic and disappeared into the ebb and flow of Darrington city, Olivia stood there by the roadside. She didn't notice the smell of rain to come, nor how Chris simply stood there, waiting for her. Her shoulders were stooped and her eyes seemed to be looking at something very far away.

Chris chased the darkness from his thoughts and reached out to lay a hand on his employer's forearm. She started, twisting her head about to stare at him with slightly widened eyes, as if surprised to see him there—or, in fact, to see *herself* there. "Oh," she said, blinking. And then her eyebrows pulled together and she shook his hand off irritably. She turned away from him and started down the walk to the office, clearly expecting him to follow after her.

"I don't think it was Kolston," she said with conviction, whatever spell had overtaken her vanishing and business flooding into the empty space left behind. "He's right. It would be stupid to recreate a murder he got away with if it could be linked to him so easily. He was lucky enough to avoid hanging the first time."

"Then—"

"It had to have been someone who was trying to use the val Frenton murder as a cover-up, but they didn't plan it that way. It occurred to them only after the fact." Olivia stopped to turn the knob and push the door open with her hip. She had the gleam of the hunt in her eye when she turned to meet him and held one finger up. "Do you know how I know that?"

Wearily, Chris shook his head. "I haven't the foggiest."

Olivia smiled and bustled away into her office. "The Duke died from his neck wound. Bled out in almost an instant. You wouldn't believe how much blood comes out of someone's neck, Mister Buckley. It's absolutely obscene." She deposited her satchel by the hat rack and ran the fingers of one hand through her long, straight hair. "And I don't think the killer knew, either. I think she didn't intend to kill the Duke at all. She went into the study that night to talk to him, not to kill him. Then something happened, something went wrong. He reacted poorly, or said something to enrage her. She pulled the knife and did him across the throat."

She whirled about again and gave him a shrewd look. "You're not getting any of this are you?" she asked with a disappointed shake of her head.

He brought his chin up in defiance. "I'm memorizing."

"Suit yourself, but if there's details missing from my notes, I'm going to be *very* angry," she said, and dropped into one of her beautifully upholstered chairs. She continued to look at him, as if waiting for something. Just what, exactly, he couldn't say. Finally, she shrugged and stretched. "She panics. She didn't intend to kill him, but now he's dead, and what's there to be done? So while she's standing there, panicking, something occurs to her. She remembers Old Debts, and remembers his creditor almost got himself into trouble for sending a message almost a decade ago. She thinks she can take some heat off herself and shine it onto him if she can recreate that little event." She turned her attention back to Chris, that same expectant look on her face.

"...that does sound plausible," Chris admitted after a long time where the ticking clock had been the only sound. "More plausible than Kolston." As much as he disliked the man.

"That's all?"

"Is there something else?"

Olivia kept his gaze until she grew bored. She clucked her tongue and set about pulling off her lace gloves, finger by finger. "No one ever notices the really obvious bits," she complained. "I just spelled it all out for you, and you still don't put it together. Well, here, think about this, won't you?" She dropped one glove onto the table between the chairs and started on the other one. "The val Frenton murder happened ages ago. Anything before the Floating Castle is ancient history. What's more, no one immediately remembered it even when a murder so strangely like it happened. That means it's gone from the public consciousness—nobody cares anymore." Her eyes sparkled when she brought them back to his, and he could see her teeth gleam through her dark smile. "So how did the murderer think of it? Think of it in a blink and use it as a defence, hitting the ground running?"

She dropped her second glove onto the table, and his breath caught.

He had to admit, it was impressive. He'd never have put it together himself, but the line that lead from one point to the next to the next was unbroken and undeniable. "It was someone who knew everything about the Duke," he said quietly.

"*Everything*," Olivia stressed. "Someone who didn't just know his creditor's name, but knew his creditor's history. From memory, recalled at the drop of a hat. Now," she said, giving him a sideways smile and stressing the consideration in her voice, "who might know a man so well as that? His wife, maybe?"

"Or his mistress," Chris supplied.

"Or his mistress, I suppose," she allowed. "I admit, Vanessa Caldwell is getting a grand list of charges against her, herself. She hated the man. If *she* knew he was going to marry her…" But then she waved the thought away with one hand. "I like the Duchess better, though. It all fits together so well. Everything is circumstantial, but enough of that, and it doesn't matter. Maris will make the arrest if I order it, soon. She's done it for less." Her face darkened.

"…will you?" he couldn't help but ask. "Order it?"

"Hmm, maybe," Olivia mused. "But I don't know if the arrest would hold with what I have. No, not yet. I need to know if she knew. About the divorce, about Vanessa. I need to know what she and Ana fought about, just before she went home and he died. But that's a lost cause. I can't trust anything the Duchess says, and the girl, well." She sighed. "I should have asked before it was too late."

At least she didn't say "you" should have asked. Chris didn't know how he might have responded, if she had. Already, he felt darkness clouding him again at the thought of Analaea. The image of her pastel room drenched in blood flashed through his mind.

But even through that, he was thinking about what Olivia had said, and he fixed her with a look as he pinpointed the source of the restless thought. "Ana wasn't the only one there, though," he said, hearing a touch of excitement in his own voice. "*Ethan* was, too. Er, Ethan Grey, Ana's beau."

Olivia's eyes lit up. She vaulted from her chair and near-ran across the room to the mirror, spinning once and pinching his cheek like a doting grandmother along the way. She seized the mallet for the little set of chimes resting on the table before the mirror, and then she impatiently struck the lowest note over and over until clouds suffused the mirror and the reflection faded. "Oh, hurry up, you lazy thing," Olivia muttered impatiently to the gnome whose brown glow suffused the edges of the mirror.

The mists within the mirror spun and danced for considerably longer than usual, but eventually, they burned off, revealing a frazzled-looking young woman with glasses resting at the end of her nose and a mess of freckles covering her homely face. "Hello," she said, her voice rushed. "This is the Darrington City mirror operator, do you need assistance?"

"Well, obviously," Olivia laughed, and the girl's face screwed up like she might cry. "I need the mirror frequency for an *Ethan Grey*, worldcatcher categorization, Darrington City!"

"One moment, please," the girl said plaintively, and the mirror went back to cloudy fog while she rifled through whatever plethora of records she had set before her. Most mirror operators were, to Chris's knowledge, very low-power truthsniffers, to help them reach the information they sought more quickly. However, that couldn't make the task of sorting through so much data under such time restraints very easy.

The clouding in the mirror seemed to stretch far longer than it ever had for Chris. Olivia huffed and drummed her fingers along the table, then tapped one foot, then hummed off-tone under her breath, until just watching her made Chris irritable by association.

And still the mirror stayed locked in its swirling, smoky depths, silent and blank, until finally, when Chris thought Olivia might be about to explode, the young woman reappeared, now looking even more frazzled. "I'm sorry, could you repeat your request?"

Olivia slammed one hand down on the table. The chimes rang. "You *have* to be kidding me."

The girl sniffled. "Miss, I just need you to repeat your request, please."

Olivia rolled her eyes. "Ethan Grey," she said, enunciating every syllable and sound as if the girl were stupid, and then spelling it, for good measure. "Worldcatcher categorization. Darrington City."

Chris thought the girl really might burst into tears. She lowered her head and said, very quietly, "There's no one matching that name and categorization in our records for Darrington City, miss."

"That's—" Olivia started sharply, causing the girl to duck between her shoulders and physically cringe away from the opposite mirror...but then Olivia's voice dropped and her face softened. "Interesting," she concluded. "That's very interesting." She frowned and Chris saw her chewing the inside of her cheek while she thought. "Do you have anything in that name and categorization for another city?"

"I can't give you that information unless you're mirroring from that city," the girl said, and instantly, Olivia was back to her outrage, throwing up her hands in frustration.

"Oh, of course not. Useless as a unicorn's fart," she spat, and, before the poor young woman could say anything else, she was dragging the mallet along the chimes and sending off a cascade of sound. The nimbus surrounding the mirror faded, and the girl's face winked out, fading to first misty darkness, and then to Olivia's deeply frowning face.

"He must still be registered in the town where he was categorized," Chris said eventually, more to fill the silence than anything else. "But the Duchess may know where he lives, or someone else at the val Daren estate, or—"

"Just what do we know about Ethan Grey?" Olivia interrupted as if she hadn't heard him speak at all. Her face was locked deep in thought, and she gripped the table before her as if it were all keeping her in the world.

Chris quickly changed directions, searching through his thoughts for all the information he'd filed away about the handsome young man Ana had loved so dearly. "He's a painter," he said, and Olivia nodded encouragingly. "He had his work displayed at a gallery in the city that opened the night the Duke died, and closed yesterday. It was the first time. He seemed very devoted to Ana. The Duchess doesn't like him—"

"Why?"

Chris stammered. "I-I don't know. I mean, I don't think we know."

"And which gallery were his paintings displayed at?"

"I don't think we know that, either."

"How did he and Analaea meet?"

"Or...or that." Chris shook his head and raised his hands helplessly, hoping to fend off more questions. "We don't know much of anything about him, Olivia. We didn't ask." He studied her thoughtful expression, trying to discern just what she was thinking. "Do you think he might have...?" And he shook his head. "No, it makes no sense. He had no reason to harm the Duke. And he wouldn't have hurt Ana. Tell me that's not what you're trying to say."

Olivia seemed to come back to herself. She released her hold on the table and turned away from the mirror, leaning back and folding her arms. "I'm not saying anything," she said, reaching up to tuck her hair behind her ears. "I just suddenly realized that despite being threaded all through this thing, we know next to nothing about him." She gave him a tight smile. "I don't like unknowns. They *always* end up being important."

Before he could say anything, she pushed herself off and started across the room. Her eyes listlessly went here and there: from the chairs to the clock to the desk and back to him. She focused them, then, and stopped in her tracks. "Tomorrow is—" she began.

He cut her off, his heartbeat speeding in his chest. "I know what tomorrow is," he said, sharper than he intended.

She narrowed her eyes and took her time looking him up and down before shrugging. "I suppose you'll want it off," she said with a disdainful wave of her hand. "Take the time to go to a memorial. Well, I'm not cruel. If you—"

"Miss Faraday," Chris said, very quiet. He found he couldn't quite look at her, and focused on his hands folded before him, instead. "If you don't disagree, I'd really prefer to work tomorrow." He lifted his head to offer her a tremulous smile, and saw her considering him as if he'd just told her something very revealing. Maybe he had. "After all, we have so much to do, and it's been nearly a week since the Duke passed."

She raised her eyebrows in a silent question, one he chose not to answer. They watched one another, holding their ground, until finally, Olivia stirred. She shrugged one shoulder and started forward, brushing past him on her way deeper into the office. "Fine," she said. "I prefer it, myself. Spending a day crying over the dead won't bring them back." She opened the door to the flickering light of the hallway, turning back to meet his eyes over the curve of her shoulder. "You're dismissed. Try to organize all of today's notes into something readable for tomorrow, won't you? I want to read over everything and get my bearings." She turned away. "Good evening, Mister Buckley," she murmured, and then the door closed behind her.

Chris walked with his notebook held before his nose. It was perhaps not the most dignified way to travel, and he was sure he drew baffled looks from passersby, but for once, he didn't care. It seemed a waste to spend the entire walk simply staring at nothing, mind wandering, heart clouding, when he could be working.

True to his hastily given word, he remembered most of the summary of events she'd given in the reception room of her office. Perhaps it wasn't accurate to the letter, and the possibility existed he'd forgotten a word here or a phrase there, but he thought he'd gotten most of the beats down. He was putting the finishing touches on the end of their exchange about Ethan Grey, weaving, *we know next to nothing about him find out more* when he had to use one of his hands to fumble with the gate to the Buckley manor. He went over what he'd weaved while he made his way down the front walk, feeling the city go silent and the sylphs ruffle his hair and coat as he passed the soundshield, and taking note of the sound of a horse or unicorn whinnying in the carriage house before he reached the door and tucked the notebook under his arm. Fernand would be here, then. The thought put a smile on his face. They could all have dinner together. Perhaps Miss Albany would be willing to stay for it. She'd proven herself an ally, and he needed those…

He noticed a moment after hanging up his coat that one of the voices that had stopped talking in the parlour at his entrance did not belong to Fernand Spencer at all.

He turned towards the parlour, feeling as if he was moving through gel, half expecting to see Avery Combs sitting there once again with his snake's smile and fancy words and unwelcome intentions. But there was a different stranger sitting across from Rosemary's governess, today, an older, warmer, less urbane man, whose lined, smiling face Christopher recognized in an instant.

The man stood and inclined his head with respect. "Christopher Buckley," he said. "I'm—"

"I know who you are," Chris interrupted. He still held the doorknob with one hand, and he found himself gripping it like a lifeline so as to not fling himself at the man in a rage. His arm trembled. Yesterday, well, he had not been himself. Today would be different. Today, he would stop this before the snake oil salesman got two words out of his mouth. He was *not* going to let *anyone* use Rosemary. "Doctor Francis Livingstone," Chris said, and the famous scientist had the grace to look abashed as he smiled.

"It does get hard to be anonymous when your face so often appears in the papers," he said mildly, and Chris allowed himself to release the doorknob and start into the parlour. What he was feeling must have showed on his face, because Doctor Livingstone's voice trailed off the moment he opened his mouth to speak again, and his smile wilted.

"I don't know what exactly it is you want," Chris began, his voice a low growl of a threat, vibrating through his throat. "But I know it has to do with Rosemary, and all the clever little ways she can be used to benefit *someone's* agenda." He balled his hand into a fist. "Rosemary is *not* a pawn," he declared, letting his voice carry. "She is a *girl*, a sweet little girl who isn't old enough to have to deal with *any* of this. She *deserves* a chance at a normal life."

He could have kept going, but— "I completely agree with you," Doctor Livingstone was saying, making calming gestures with his hands. "I couldn't possibly agree *more*, Mister Buckley. That's why I've come."

Chris blinked and choked down a laugh. It was too impossible, too unbelievable. Did this man, this ubiquitous speaker and figurehead, known to all and sundry to be the undisputed leader of the reformist movement, think he would be *believed?* "Are you *insane?*" he asked. Dimly, he was aware he should speak more quietly, so Rosemary didn't hear the upraised voices from below, but all he could see was white-hot anger. "Do you think I'll *believe* that? I know who you are. I know *what* you are. You show up here, uninvited, with your agenda in hand—if you think I'll believe my sister is *anything* to you but a piece to be played against the traditionalists, you must think I'm an *idiot*. And if you honestly, actually think you're *any* different from Avery bloody Combs—"

"Mister Buckley!" Miss Albany's voice registered through his rage, and he felt her hands on his arm. "Mister Buckley, *please*, listen to me!" She tugged at him.

Some sanity came back to him. He remembered where he was, took note of his surroundings. Doctor Livingstone was looking back at him gravely, and Miss Albany was at his side, clinging to his upraised arm. He'd been shaking his fist in the doctor's face, he dimly remembered. Miss Albany's fingers dug into his topcoat like claws.

He swallowed, trying to contain his emotions and hold onto the clarity he felt now. His eyes slipped from the doctor's, turning to meet his governess's. She stared up at him, brown eyes wide, expression pleading. She quailed a bit under his gaze, slightly relaxing her grip on his arm and settling back onto her heels. "Please, Mister Buckley," she murmured. "He didn't just show up. I..." Her eyelids fluttered, and she looked away. Colour touched her cheeks. "I asked him to come."

CHAPTER EIGHTEEN

What?" Chris tore his arm from Miss Albany's grasp. "You—" Rage contorted his face. "You had no *right!*" He all but roared into her face. "You're nothing but her nanny! I am her brother. *I* decide who—"

"You asked me to help protect her!"

"I assumed you would go to the police!"

"The police?" Miss Albany crossed her arms, eyes narrowing. "Well, you work with them, sir. Why didn't *you* go to the police?"

The question stymied him. He blinked. True enough, he'd spoken to police of all stripes today. Officer Dawson and her unit had featured prominently in his actions. But they were so flawed, so human; they were a normal part of his daily life. They couldn't protect Rosemary. "I..." he stammered.

Miss Albany shook her head, frustration on her face. "Exactly. Perhaps you sensed the truth. All you have to do to give up your authority of Rosemary is to put her into someone else's custody. *Anyone* else's custody. And the police are not a flawless body of protectors! They are people with agendas and wishes, and they are almost all traditionalists. They'd have used this to bring her in 'for her protection' and before sunset, she'd be in Sir Combs's grasp!"

His heart rejected the logic of her words even as his head understood it. "So you brought *him* here?" He jabbed a finger in the direction of the silent doctor. "You brought *Francis Livingstone* into my home? How can you possibly think I'd—"

"Please, Mister Buckley, just listen to what he has to say!" Miss Albany pleaded, her voice loud enough to drown his out. Her eyes were wild and her cheeks flush. "He can help. I swear he can help! It's not like the Combses. It's nothing like that. Please. You asked me to protect Rosemary. Can you trust me just a little further?" As she spoke, her voice grew quieter and quieter, until she was all but whispering as she repeated her entreaty. *"Please."*

He stared at her. He met her eyes with all the intensity he could muster, searching as deep as he could go for something that would tell him whether to believe her or not. He wished he could read her like she could read him. If he could just tell what she was feeling, know if she was *honest*, if he could *believe* her...

But he couldn't find what he looked for. He blinked hard and pulled his gaze away, and set his jaw. "Go to Rosemary," he said tightly. "Whatever you're about, I don't want you here."

Miss Albany's lips thinned and her grip tightened on his arm, but then, stiffly, she bowed her head and hurried away, grey skirts rustling. Chris watched her go out of the corner of his eye, and then, when he could see her no longer, turned his attention to the unwanted guest.

The doctor wore an apologetic smile. It seemed sincere. His hands were folded before him. They studied one another in silence, and Chris searched the man as he had Miss Albany. He found just as much.

The doctor blinked rapidly and turned his face away. "Rachel told the truth," he said.

"Rachel." The use of her given name was not lost on him. "How do you know her?"

"Her elder brother is a friend of mine," the doctor said, and his lips twisted slightly at those words, like he'd tasted something foul. "No. Garrett Albany is an indispensable ally, but I should never call him a friend. Rachel, however...well, I hold her in much higher esteem. I rarely hear from her, and our paths rarely intersect, but she never has something to say that I regret hearing."

What do you want? Chris wanted to ask. *What help could you possibly offer Rosemary?* But now that his blood was flowing normally and the red haze over his vision had cleared somewhat, his instincts were returning in full force. He forced a smile. It felt tight and false, but it was a smile. "I had a very trying day at work," he said, in way of explanation for his previous outburst. "And my sister..."

"Your sister is at a very delicate time in her life," the doctor finished the thought easily. His smile was warm and seemed genuine, but Chris wouldn't be fooled by it. A man like this could hardly do what he did without learning to fake a smile. "She's caught the attention of many important people, all of whom have plans and schemes she would fit nicely into."

"And you mean to tell me you aren't one of those people." Chris tried to let only the faintest edge of a threat touch his voice, but he could tell from the way the doctor's smile flickered that he'd been more direct than he'd intended. He checked his smile, found it still hanging on his lips, and pushed onwards. "Doctor, I am perfectly aware Lowry has been sniffing around our door for most of Rosemary's life. My father didn't do a thing to keep her abilities quiet. He did everything but take out advertisements in the papers." He met the doctor's eye, issuing forth a challenge. "I'm also perfectly aware *you* work at Lowry."

"The Richard Lowry Academy of Proficiency Categorization is a very large institution, Mister Buckley." There was no answering challenge in Doctor Livingstone's voice, only gentle correction. "It is what it is, a monument built to house a flawed, old system, but it isn't only that. It's a place of learning, of study, and of forward-thinking people who recognize the work Doctor Lowry did all those years ago may have served us well, but the risks of hanging our society upon it have come to outweigh the benefits."

Chris held up a hand. "Please," he said. "Please, I've read all the interviews and speeches. I've even heard some aloud. You aren't going to convince me of anything."

"No," the doctor said, having the grace to look abashed. "Of course not, and forgive me. Giving the same talks over and over can become a bit of a habit." He shot a look behind him and then turned his attention back to Chris with a question on his face. "Can we sit, Mister Buckley? Circling about one another like wild animals is very tiring. I'd rather speak to one another like civilized men."

The open honesty in his face caught Chris off guard. He reminded himself this was all second nature to Doctor Francis Livingstone, who'd spent years perfecting all the ways to make people trust him. Avery Combs had been very convincing, too. But even as he carefully told himself that, he found himself inexorably drawn to the older man, his gentle demeanour and the frank openness of his face and speech. He raised a hand to cover his tired, strained eyes, and gave the inevitable answer. "Yes. Yes, that's fine, Doctor. Please do."

When he lowered his hand, the doctor had eased himself into a chair, and Chris knew he couldn't do this alone.

"Just a moment, please," he said, backing away ungracefully. "I need to use the mirror."

The doctor's face clouded. He stopped relaxing back into the chair he'd taken and leaned forward, a furrow creasing his brow. "If I'm not welcome, tell me now, and I'll leave," he said urgently. "I was invited here by your nanny. I didn't know she didn't have permission to offer."

After a brief moment of confusion, Chris couldn't help his chuckle. He folded his lips, swallowing the rest of his mirth. "Please, relax, Doctor," he said, turning away to hide his amusement. "I'm not contacting the police."

He mirrored Fernand.

Before the old man could greet him, Chris grabbed the edge of the table and leaned forward, so close his nose brushed the glass. Keeping his voice very low, he shot a look over his shoulder to tell Fernand he wasn't alone. "I need you here," he murmured.

Fernand's brows pulled down into a confused expression. "Chris?" he asked, his own voice a bare whisper. "What is going on? Who's there with you?"

Chris debated his answer. Fernand was a stolid old traditionalist, frowning mightily whenever he heard tales of that new radical way of thinking. Chris had seen him turn up his nose at many a headline that mentioned the man now sitting in his parlour, muttering about how there was no wrong in using the gifts the Three and Three provided. There were different ways to approach this...

He settled on honesty. "Doctor Francis Livingstone," he said, and while Fernand's eyes widened and his brows pulled down even further, Chris hurried on in hushed tones before he could say anything else. "I know you don't agree with his politics or his movement. I know you're a defender of the old ways until the end, just like all the Buckley men you've served." *Except me.* Chris took a deep breath. "I also know," he said, "that you're not my father. You'll give anyone a fair shake, Fernand, especially when they have something to say that can help someone you care about. That's the sort of man you are." Chris saw a tiny softening around the mouth and eyes of the old man, and that would have to be good enough. "The doctor says he can help Rosemary."

Fernand hesitated only a moment. His voice was gruff when he spoke, but Chris already saw him pulling away from the mirror, grabbing his cane and hobbling towards his coat and hat. "I'll be there within ten minutes," he said. "Don't let the man say a bloody word until I'm there."

When Chris returned to the parlour, he felt his shoulders squarer, his back straighter, and his heart lighter. He felt like his normal self once again. He smiled at the doctor and settled into the chair across from him. "I apologize for my outburst when I first came in," he said. He felt his words flow from him, smooth and controlled, like he was accustomed to.

"You had a trying day, you said."

"Worse than you could probably imagine." The image of Ana's tattered body flashed before his eyes again, and he forced it down. "But it still doesn't excuse just how rudely I behaved. Whoever may have invited you, and whatever circumstances you might have come under, you're a guest here." He held up a hand to forestall the words he could all but see the doctor gathering on his tongue. "I'll hear what you have to say, but not yet," he said. "My…" *My financial adviser* certainly didn't give the right impression. "A friend of our family is going to come and sit with us while you talk. I've been told I'm an overly pliable sort of fellow. I don't want to be talked into anything."

"I think that's very fair," the doctor agreed, and then, without missing a beat, "why don't you tell me about yourself, Mister Buckley?"

Chris considered. Making small talk certainly sounded more compelling than sitting and waiting for Fernand for ten minutes. "Well," he said, giving in to his desire to lose himself in simple conversation, "I'm wordweaver categorization. Very strong." He always felt the need to add that, as if it made his proficiency any less menial. "I work as the personal assistant and secretary of an investigative truthsniffer."

"Oh? How long have you been doing that?"

"Less than a month."

"And do you like it?"

Chris managed a smile. "As I've said…it's trying work."

"Of course, naturally." There was a sincerity to the doctor that Chris was finding it very hard to remain suspicious of, a sort of latent integrity that shone through everything he did. It could have been feigned, but he found himself losing to it, being pulled in by it. The doctor smiled. "Any friends?"

Chris shook his head.

"Hobbies?"

Again. "Only Rosemary," Chris said, injecting all the meaning possible into the statement.

The doctor didn't miss it. "There's nothing more important than family," he said with surprising ferocity. "I've done everything I can to keep my wife and children away from the risks of my name, and if I thought for a moment they were at risk, I'd give it all up. Hand it down to some younger bloke who doesn't have as much to lose."

Too personal, too close to the mark. Chris tried his best to push the conversation back to the meaningless and friendly, feeling as though he was trying to divert the course of a river. He forced himself to not look at the clock. "And what about you?" he asked. "Tell me something I don't know from the papers."

Doctor Livingstone smiled. "I have a granddaughter," he said, a conspiratorial twinkle in his eye. "She was born last month, and she's the prettiest screaming bald creature that ever lived."

Chris had to laugh. He had been old enough when Rosemary was born to remember her in that stage. He'd heard some elder siblings were jealous of new babies, but never him. Julia had told him stories until the day she died about how fiercely he'd loved his new sister. Her favourite had been the time he'd had a dream about harpies flying in through her window and carrying her off. He'd pulled all the blankets off his bed, dragged them into the nursery, and slept leaning up against her cradle to the sound of a fiaran's icicle chimes tinkling over their heads, determined to protect his baby sister from anyone who might harm her.

The smile that had crept onto his face vanished as he couldn't help but draw parallels between that evening long ago and last night's events. He looked over Francis Livingstone again, and was unable to help himself from noticing, once again, the aura of trustworthiness the man exuded. Rosemary *was* in very real danger, and not only from the traditionalists. If this man could do something to help…

A commotion at the front door caused both of them to turn their heads. Moments later, Fernand was limping in, huffing and puffing and leaning heavily on his cane. His gaze went stormy when it connected with the doctor. He stopped in the entryway to the parlour, hunching over his cane and putting all his weight upon it. His face was red.

Chris got to his feet and hurried over to his old friend. "Fernand?" he asked gently, laying a hand on the old man's arm, but he was irritably waved off.

"I'm fine, Chris," Fernand insisted, straightening—mostly—and hobbling over to the nearest chair. "I just decided to get on horseback and make my way here as fast as I could." He shot a glare at the doctor. "I didn't want anyone filling your head while you were waiting."

"We've only been making nice," the doctor assured him.

Chris hovered near Fernand's chair. Despite the insistence of health, he couldn't help but notice how the old sumfinder's fingers trembled where they gripped the cane, how the colour in his cheeks was set off by the grave-white of his hands. He'd never seen the old man looking quite so fragile, and it seemed wrong to just go and sit. "Fernand," he said delicately. "Do you need a glass of water, or…"

"Oh, sit down, young master." Fernand waved him off again, more insistently this time. As Chris awkwardly moved to his seat, trying not to stare at the old man's feeble appearance, Fernand turned his attention to the doctor and his chin jutted forward. "I'm Fernand Spencer. I knew Master Christopher's grandfather. I hear you can help little Miss Rosemary."

Chris took his seat. He watched Doctor Livingstone nod slowly and lean forward, steepling his hands before him. "By now," he said, "you've realized Combs and his supporters aren't going to leave your sister alone. You did a fine job keeping her out of the spotlight for as long as you did, Mister Buckley, but that time has passed, and you won't get it back. They knew the girl was a wizard, but they also knew your father to be a man who made tall claims. They gravely underestimated her potential all these years, and are currently berating themselves for all the possibilities they let go by. Well, no more. White Clover changed that for good."

The doctor looked at each of them in turn, seemingly searching for some question, some protest from either of them. But Chris had nothing, and Fernand didn't appear to, either, for he kept his silence. The doctor continued. "No matter your affiliation or your politics," he said, "you have to know Combs and his lot will do anything for their cause."

"The same thing has been said about the reformists," Fernand put in then, unable to help himself.

"There are certainly factions of the movement who could be accused of that," the doctor agreed without missing a beat. "And nothing to be done about it, I know. But please, Mister Spencer, don't group me with them. Whatever can be said about this group I've somehow ended up heading, not every arm of it speaks for me. I don't believe in unwilling sacrifices." He folded his hands before him and his voice was impossibly clear as he said, "Rosemary can't stay in Darrington. She needs to leave, and soon."

Chris's heart sank. "That's…" He shook his head. "No. I'm sorry, but no. Our family home is in Darrington. *I* am in Darrington. Where would you have us go, Vernella? From what I've heard, it's nearly worse."

"Not Vernella, no." The doctor shook his head. "Cooperton. Now, don't blanch, young man. I realize it's not exactly an urban centre, but it's small, it's honest, a lovely little university town, and it's far from the reach of Combs and his ilk. Your family home will do just fine here by itself, and Rosemary could find a good life there. A peaceful life, out of reach of those who would use her."

"No," Chris repeated. "I can't be separated from her. I've raised her. I'm all she has."

"You're a wordweaver, you said?" The doctor looked him up and down and nodded consideringly. "My cousin is a truthsniffer working in a laboratory in Cooperton. She needs a technician and an aide. You could do just fine." He misinterpreted the expression that must have showed on Chris's face. "You'd be well paid, of course."

Chris raised a hand to his temple. "This isn't exactly what I was expecting," he murmured, dazed. Leave Darrington? No, of course not. The Buckley family had been in Darrington since Reginald Buckley had served as a lab technician to Richard Lowry, all those centuries ago. Everything they had was here, all their assets, all their investments, all their ties…

But he remembered Fernand with the file and the low voice, saying all the money had dried up and he was liquidizing whatever was left. He remembered all the times he'd shyly admitted to having had no friends, remembered how all the old Buckley family steadfasts had dried up and blow away as the money had evaporated in the six years since the Floating Castle.

When he really looked at his life, there were only two things tying them to Darrington: the home, which could be shut up and left until Rosemary was old enough to fend for herself, and his position with Olivia Faraday as a Deathsniffer's assistant. A job that had directly resulted in an intruder in Rosemary's room, her music box tipped on its side, and the note and knife.

When he really took his life apart in his mind, in fact, the offer didn't seem as unacceptable as it felt it should.

The doctor looked at the both of them. "Well," he said. "What do you think?"

Chris watched Fernand steer his horse out to the road. The old man's hair shone gold and orange in the light of the sunset, and for a moment, strong on the animal's back, with his hair turned auburn and his shoulders back, he looked like the strong young man he hadn't been in an age, a man Chris had never actually met.

And then he wheeled the handsome horse, turned about, and vanished into the crowd.

Chris ran a hand through his hair, squinting through the ache that threatened to split his head apart at the temples. He and Fernand had spent the last hour discussing the offer, long after Doctor Livingstone had left, and Chris felt no more clarity than he had when the man had first offered the extreme solution to all their problems.

He hadn't expected Fernand's open willingness to consider the option. "I'm a traditionalist man to the bone," he'd said gruffly at the end. "I support Sir Hector Combs tirelessly because he'll do anything he has to, to get things done, to maintain the way of life that's made Tarland the greatest nation in the world." His face had softened and his voice had gone quiet, then, and Chris had seen pain flickering deep in his eyes. "And I don't want him anywhere near Miss Rosemary, young master, for all those very same reasons. I can't tell you what to do. I don't know, myself. But don't you just dismiss this out of hand. Give this thought."

As if he could do anything else. Chris rubbed at his temples with his index and middle fingers, trying to soothe away the ache to no avail. Cooperton. A small university town over three hours up along the eastern seaboard. Nothing much there other than scholars and researchers. No parties, no shops, no theatres. Nothing a young lady with as much personality and beauty and charisma as Rosemary would need growing up.

But it wasn't as though he'd be able to afford those things for her, anyway. The idea of Rosemary having a debutante's ball, with a personally designed gown and a hat that wasn't years out of style was a pipe dream at best, a sad fantasy at worst. They could be safe in Cooperton. Far from Hector and Avery Combs and their ambitions, from Olivia Faraday and the darkness that followed her about like the mist hanging around her office—even far from Francis Livingstone, though it was frustratingly difficult not to trust the man.

"Mister Buckley?"

Startled, Chris looked up.

He shouldn't have been so shocked to see Miss Albany standing at the foot of the staircase, but somehow, he'd completely forgotten about her. How she'd started all of this, the doctor's cryptic remarks about some unpleasant brother, and how Chris had sent her to Rosemary to await her fate like a misbehaving child. His face burned at the memory of the last, but he tried to keep his expression neutral as he studied her.

Despite how their last encounter had ended, she met his gaze with her chin held high, a challenge in her eyes. The only sign that she was uncomfortable was the hand knotted into her plain grey skirts. "Mister Buckley," she repeated, her voice low and filled to brimming with discomfort. "I would like to know whether or not I'll be coming in tomorrow."

She was asking if she was fired, Chris realized with a start.

And then, to his shame, he considered actually doing it. He almost opened his mouth to tell her, "No, don't bother." He'd find a nice, simple, uncomplicated nanny who'd do only what was required of her, who'd teach Rosemary history and geography and arithmetic without filling her head with ideas, who didn't have any political affiliation, who dressed in stylish skirts and wore lace gloves and large hats with fake flowers and real feathers.

But he didn't want that nanny. He didn't want just a nanny at all.

She hadn't even hesitated that morning when he'd asked her to take care of the situation. For all his righteous outrage, he'd just left Rosemary here, and he'd trusted Miss Albany enough to take care of her, and no matter how she'd done it, she'd come through. If he'd had the time, he would have called the police, never even thinking through the logic of what she told him. She'd risked a good, steady job in an economy that had people on the streets to take care of his sister.

If he dismissed her, he was an idiot.

"I think," he pronounced, mulling over each word, "that I actually might owe you an apology. And a thank you."

"If I cared about either of those, I wouldn't have taken such a risk." Miss Albany's words were carefully selected and tightly delivered, but her hand slowly uncurled from her skirts, belying her relief. "I care about your sister, I care about Avery Combs not getting what he wants, and I care about this job." She took a deep breath. "So. Am I coming in tomorrow morning?"

A rueful smile tugged at Chris's lips. "If you can stand to," he murmured.

"Then I'll be on time, as usual." She used both hands and smoothed her skirts. "Miss Rosemary was up and about today," she reported. "That lifeknitter who's been seeing to her, Doctor Jameson, was here just after noon, and after a brief examination, he concluded her recovery is coming along very nicely. She should be fully restored from her burn out by Godsday. She's a little groggy right now, because I gave her a tincture, but she's awake." Still as self-possessed as the Queen, she glided past him.

"Miss Albany," he said, stopping her as she went to take her shapeless coat off the rack. "Whether you care about it or not, thank you. And I'm sorry." Ears burning, he hurried up the stairs, too embarrassed to stay and hear what she might have to say in reply.

Rosemary's big blue eyes flickered open as he brushed black ringlets off her forehead. She owlishly peered up at him in confusion for a long moment. Her gaze sharpened and her lips spread into a wide, happy smile. "Chris!" she exclaimed. There was a thickness to her words, and her eyes could stay focused for only a moment before her lids fluttered shut again, but there was also real excitement in her voice, and he smiled to think she brightened so just seeing his face.

"I hardly recognize you, stranger," Chris said lightly. Her hair felt as soft as gryphon down.

She didn't open her eyes, but her smile turned into a pout. "You're always at work," she drawled. "I was up for hours today and you weren't here."

"Well," Chris said, feeling a pang of guilt. "Olivia Faraday is a very demanding woman. She keeps me on my toes all day long."

The pout flipped back into a smile, and Rosemary blinked up at him again for several long moments, trying to orient herself. "Did you find out who did it?" she asked with a yawn.

Even now, she was thinking about his grand mystery. He smiled. "No," he said quietly. "Not yet."

"So slow!"

He chuckled, and then lapsed into silence as he thought about the most recent things whirling through his mind. "Hey...tell me, Rosemary," he said hesitantly. "Do you want to be in Darrington? Do you love it here? Would...could you be happy somewhere else?"

When Rosemary didn't immediately respond again, Chris assumed, with a sad little twinge, that she'd fallen asleep. But then she squirmed about beneath her blankets and her eyes opened and then closed once again. "I'm happy wherever you are, silly goose."

He smiled.

She nuzzled down into her pillow and her bedding muffled her tiny voice. "Were you...were you in my room last night, Chris?"

His heart stopped. His hand stilled in her hair. *I was,* he reminded himself. *I was.* "Yes," he answered quietly, forcing himself to resume his stroking, to act as though nothing was wrong. "Your music box had fallen, and I told you to go back to sleep. Do you remember?"

She managed a tiny nodded, drifting off into the safe embrace of sleep. "Then that *was* you standing over me all quiet in the dark." And his breath all went out of his lungs. "It looked like you. I'm glad...I was scared..."

Chris drifted from the room in a daze, his head pounding. He went about his evening tasks in a stupor, those words echoing in his skull until they reached a fever pitch and he made a decision.

He put the note and the knife with his finished reports for Olivia.

CHAPTER NINETEEN

Olivia's eyes widened and her breath quickened as her gaze darted back and forth across the note. She gripped the paper so hard it crumpled in her hand, and her lips parted slightly in shock or delight or both. "This is incredible," she breathed.

Chris fought to keep his cool. "*This*," he reminded her, "was beside my sister's bed. The person who wrote this was in my home, in her room, looming over her in the dark. I brought you this because I want you to tell me how we can take care of her." *Until we leave Darrington.*

Olivia didn't seem to hear him. She brushed past him, eyes fixated on the page as if it held the ingredients to the Elixir of Life. "Why you?" she mused, her movements too quick to be called pacing. "Why not me? I'm the Deathsniffer. You're just my assistant. Why would they go into *your* house, threaten *your* sister? It doesn't make any sense!" She halted and dropped her arm to her side so quickly it looked spring-loaded. She fixed him with a look, eyebrows pulling down. "Cwenday, you said?"

"Yes."

"The day you talked to Analaea?"

A twinge in his middle. "Yes..."

She snapped the note back to her face, looking at it once more. "'Deserved to die,'" she read. "Why? And why tell you that? Why would that make a difference? Why tell *you* anything?" She swirled away. She wore a gown that would have been outdated two hundred years ago, and she looked like she was going to a costume party. Her hair was held back with a net of pearls, discoloured with age, and her massive skirts rustled and moved like a living thing about her legs. "Did you see anything?" she asked him again.

"No," he repeated.

"Did your *sister* see anything?"

"*No.*" His voice rose, but she was oblivious to his tone, turning the note over and over in her hands. "She saw someone standing over her in the dark. She's exhausted, remember, and she's sedated."

"Has there been anything else odd?" she asked. She turned in circles like an agitated cat. He could practically see her tail lashing and whiskers twitching. "Has anything happened out of the ordinary?"

So much of both that he didn't even know how to begin filtering it. Doctor Francis Livingston and his strange but increasingly tempting offer were hardly relevant. Nor was Avery Combs, with his slimy smile and poison charm. The rapport growing between him and his governess was nothing Olivia wanted to hear about. Fernand telling him they'd run out of money, White Clover Farms and rogue cloudlings, reporters showing up late in the evening to try and talk to the little wizardling, salamanders in the night…

He halted at the last, remembering. Miss Albany against his side, the two of them standing in the dim light, barely breathing, while the hot orange glow pulsed right outside the door. He'd thought of it the morning after the home invasion, but things had been so mad ever since Ana had died.

"Someone followed me home," he said. "The day before that. Maerday. They broke a light and ran off."

She snapped her eyes to his again. "And what else did you do Maerday. *No*—" She held up a hand when he opened his mouth to respond. "No, I remember. I sent you snooping. You found the room, with the drop of blood." Her gaze sharpened. "You talked to Analaea that day, too, didn't you?" And before he could respond, she set off again. "I don't understand," she murmured. "I don't understand. Why you? Why the assistant? Why threaten *you?*"

My sister, he wanted to crow. *They threatened my sister! I didn't bring this to you for evidence. I brought it so you could help me!* With all his restraint, he produced the latching wooden case lined with fine velvet he'd purloined from the kitchens. "It was pinned to the door frame. With this," he said.

Olivia barely looked up at his voice. She looked at the case with disinterest. "What's in it?" she asked, and, when he didn't immediately reply, stormed up and seized it. One-handed, she threw the latch and flung it open, and then looked down into the box at the single large, sharp knife tucked in where normally an entire cooking set would be. No one had used the box for a decade. It had seemed as good a way as any to transport a potential weapon.

He didn't know what sort of reaction he'd expected. But at the sight of the knife, Olivia's breath all left her lungs like a rush of sylphwind. Her eyes bulged and her mouth fell open, and she stared down into the box like it held the crown jewels themselves. "A knife," she breathed, with such reverence she could have been speaking the name of a god.

She dropped the note as if it were nothing and it fluttered away. Her second hand came up to cradle the old knife case like a holy relic. Once again indifferent to his presence, she started off toward the mirror, eyes never leaving the precious artifact she held before her. She set it down on the table gently and she struck out a frequency on the chimes. Clouds filled the mirror as the gnome reached out, searching for its cousin to link with, and Olivia's gaze never left the knife.

If we had that knife…

Against his better sense, he felt a tiny ball of rolled up excitement quivering in the pit of his stomach. He saw what she did.

When the mist in the mirror cleared, Chris could barely make out the freckled face of Officer Maris Dawson. "Faraday," she said, sounding confused. "What can I help you with? Is it the daughter's autopsy report? We have it, but there isn't anything especially—"

"I need to see William," Olivia interrupted in a rush, raising her eyes eagerly to the policewoman's. "Today. Right now. As soon as humanly possible, I need to see him."

A silence. Then, "William? Today?"

Olivia took the knife in both hands, blade and hilt both balanced on her index fingers. She raised it to the mirror, and what Chris could see of Officer Dawson's face transformed immediately. "Where did you get that?"

"Somewhere suspicious enough to try," Olivia replied. Her voice had a ragged edge of excitement.

The policewoman's reply was slow and uncertain. "Faraday," she said. "There are channels. There's a process. Paperwork, set-up, appointments. Mister Cartwright isn't even working today. We'd need to call him in. We'd need to push a lot of important clerical things to one side, and—"

"Maris, please!" Olivia's voice was sharp, and Chris started at the genuine desperation he heard in it. "Please! You've pushed it before, when it was necessary. I'm *floundering*, here. I know who did it. I do. I just need proof, but it's been almost a week and everything is getting cold and who knows when another body might show up?" There was a pause, and whatever Olivia saw on the policewoman's face must have encouraged her. "We could end this case right now, today. If I see the Duchess in this, that's it. We all go home!"

"And if you don't see the Duchess?"

"We arrest whoever we see, instead." One final pause, and Olivia extended the knife forward further as though offering it. "Maris, come on. You saw the girl yesterday. Don't you want to put this one away?"

A growl, then, "I want every piece of paperwork you owe me

THE DEATHSNIFFER'S ASSISTANT

in on time without delay for the next month, or we're going to have a problem."

Olivia would have clapped her hands if she weren't holding a possible murder weapon. "Yes! Of course!"

"Done by you," Officer Dawson elaborated. "Not Buckley, *you*."

"Naturally!"

Officer Dawson sighed. "Be here in an hour," she grunted. "And *you* can deal with Cartwright."

The moment the policewoman's face was no longer visible in the mirror, Chris could no longer keep his silence. The tiny centre of excitement he'd felt before was growing, and despite all that had happened, despite how little she seemed to care that Rosemary had been threatened, he felt an eagerness, a thrill at the thought that they may actually be making progress. "You think that's *the* knife," he said.

She set it back into case, arranging it and then closing the cover and flipping the latch with a quiet *snap*. When she turned back to him, she was grinning. The feelings he was experiencing himself were plain on her face, though the animalistic gleam in her pointed canine teeth was unsettling enough that he didn't like to think of himself exhibiting anything similar. "I'm surprised you didn't think of it," she said.

It seemed as good a time as any to remind her why, exactly, he'd brought it to her. "My sister..." he said, letting his voice trail off and hoping she'd take the rest of his meaning from there. He watched her as she stopped at the door and slipped the knife case into her handbag. She didn't seem to be drawing any conclusions. She reached for her still-dripping wrap and rain-speckled umbrella. "My *sister*," he said again, and then, furrowing his brow. "What are you doing?"

As she turned to him, she popped the umbrella and a shower of droplets peppered the room and his suit. She met his indignant stare with an innervated grin. "We're walking to the station," she chirped, and then looked him up and down imperiously. "Get your boots on, Mister Buckley!"

Olivia's whim to walk could not be discouraged. Chris huddled beneath his umbrella, feet soaked even in his rubber boots, as they made their way down slick, soused sidewalks and splashed through puddles that were growing larger by the moment. All the fury the clouds had held back the day before was unleashed, and the world couldn't have been greyer or wetter if it was the tears of Mother Deorwynn herself falling on Darrington.

Despite the truly horrific weather, Olivia seemed possibly more energetic than Chris had ever seen her. While he tried to make himself as small as possible, miserable in his drenched coat and trousers soaked up to the calves, Olivia danced along the street like it was a warm, sunny summer day. She splashed in puddles, cheerfully greeted every other person stupid enough to be outside, and didn't seem to even notice the rain. For once, however, she didn't chatter on about all the little trivia she usually heaped upon him when she was in these moods. She was silent, and, whenever he looked over at her, her face was animated with manic glee, her eyes far away.

She was an animal on the hunt.

He didn't long for conversation. There were things he wanted to ask, but he had no desire to speak them. All he wanted was to be dry, and warm, and since Olivia Faraday was the person who'd contrived to make him wet and cold, he entertained himself for most of the walk by quietly hating her.

It was easier than looking at Darrington around them.

Every church they passed streamed hymns and prayers into the road, soundshields deactivated. The faces of those they passed were sombre, and many were red and blotchy with tears. Most shops were closed, and a great number of buildings were dark and strange and empty looking from the road. The rain had chased most of the usual loud doomsayers, lamenters, and sneering traditionalist malcontents off the streets and into teashops and cigar parlours, but that didn't make it any less obviously the day it was.

The station itself was one of the mildest offenders they saw. Brightly lit against the gloom that rain like this always brought with it, streaming with police officers going about their business as usual, the only sign of the date whatsoever was a small display near the door bearing the Mark of Three and surrounded with drooping flowers experiencing various degrees of water log. Olivia stopped to stare at it as curious police officers passed them by, crooking one eyebrow. "Yes," she murmured, as if to herself, "I'm sure that's very comforting to everyone you're making work today, Your Majesty." She slipped past a handsome young officer entering the building, thanking him and batting her eyelashes. Chris had to catch the door for himself to follow after her.

He'd never been in a police station before. He looked around, a bit awed at how such a well-organized work area could be so dishevelled and confused by the presence of its workers. One long counter extended in the front, and then there were desks and workstations all spread out around the room behind it, filled with shouting, gesturing, gossiping, laughing, quiet, considering, hard at work police officers. The man at the front bent over a scattering of papers. He was a homely, middle-aged fellow with a mole on his cheek that could draw the eyes of a blind man. He looked up at their entrance, saw Olivia, and shook his head, turning back to his work without saying a single word.

Olivia stopped for only long enough to pull down her umbrella. She left ghastly puddles as she brushed past the counter into the loud, chaotic mess of police officers. Chris had no choice but to follow after her, lest he somehow manage to lose her and her ridiculous costume amidst the cacophony of sound and herds of moving officers that assaulted his senses.

Officer Dawson didn't look up until Olivia laid a hand on her desk. She raised her head, blinked, took a second look, and one eyebrow crept upwards while her mouth pulled into a purposeful frown that seemed to be hiding some other expression. "Did you *walk*?" she asked.

"We did walk," Olivia agreed pleasantly. She looked about rather than meet the officer's eyes. "Where is he? It's been at least an hour, hasn't it?"

Officer Dawson's eyes slid past Olivia, meeting Chris and giving him a commiserating shake of her head. "You're soaked," she said, looking at him and not her. "You're *both* soaked," she repeated after Olivia didn't immediately say something, clarifying her point.

"Well, Maris, we're not made of sugar and baking soda. I'm sure we'll survive." Olivia reached into her handbag and pulled out just the corner of the knife case, letting Officer Dawson get a look at it.

The policewoman ignored Olivia for a good minute, looking down at her desk and writing away. He felt Olivia tensing and shifting beside him, but by her silence, he sensed this was another game between the two of them. Officer Dawson was defining who was in charge of this situation. Olivia could either accept it and get what she wanted, or throw a tantrum and be told to come back later.

When the policewoman finally capped her pen and stood up, pushing her chair back, Olivia heaved an exaggerated sigh of relief, but wisely said nothing. Officer Dawson made a jerking motion with her head and then set out at a brisk walk in the direction she'd indicated.

She led them to a back room, indicating they should enter before her and then closing it after them. The chaotic noise of the big room behind them faded to a murmur immediately. Sterile, white alp-light filled the room, and Chris looked up nervously when the illumination flickered. The black nimbuses surrounding the glass balls overhead *seemed* solid enough, but...

There were two other occupants in the room. One was a second female police officer in the same split skirt uniform Officer Dawson wore. That was where the similarities ended. Where Officer Dawson was short, stout, handsome, and tough looking, this woman was tall, slender, beautiful, and long-limbed. Officer Dawson's bright red curls and freckles were contrasted by flowing white-blonde locks and skin as clear as cream. Everything about her exuded an aura of fragile, demure femininity, and she stood with her hands folded before her and her eyes cast downwards.

The second person was a young man. A *very* young man. He looked no older than sixteen, which was impossible, because he was outfitted in the uniform of a police officer which meant he was categorized and of age for employment. But Chris couldn't even make out roughness in his cheeks to indicate he shaved. His hair was dark and long around his shoulders, and his build was slight and waifish. "Pretty" was the word he would be called. *Not* handsome, like Chris was so often named. This was something else entirely. The long lashes framing his flat stare were almost girlish, like the fullness of his pouting lips, or the slenderness of the hands he drummed impatiently along the surface of the table he sat at.

"Hannah," Olivia said by way of greeting to the tall, lovely woman. She laid the still-soaked umbrella down on the table.

"Miss Faraday," the woman replied in a quiet voice that reminded Chris of a soft autumn breeze. She inclined her head respectfully.

"William." Olivia turned her attention to the young man and unwrapped her coat.

The fellow ceased his tapping on the table. His eyes sharpened and his pout became a lips-folded glare. "I was supposed to have today off, Olivia," he said, his voice a pleasant alto with an unpleasantly bitter flavour.

"Yes, and now you're getting paid," Olivia sang, throwing her wet wrap down onto the table and sending up a cloud of moisture. "Aren't you grateful you have me?"

While Olivia went elbow—and nose—deep into her satchel, the pretty young man turned his attention to Chris. He looked him up and down, assessing him. "Who's this?"

"This is Christopher Buckley," Officer Dawson replied before either Chris or Olivia could. "Previously known as Constance, yes. Let's not ask uncomfortable questions about it. This one is good." Without missing a beat, Dawson half-turned and directed her next words at Chris. "Buckley, this is Hannah Burke, one of our officers." She indicated the woman. "Officer Burke is special in that she oversees our more clandestine matters of business, which includes this charming fellow"—she indicated the young man—"William Cartwright. He's our timeseer, but if anyone asks, he's just one more weak truthsniffing police officer who fills for the more important ones."

"Buckley," Officer Cartwright tasted the name. He took a longer look at Chris, one that started at his toes and ended looking deeply into his eyes. Sharp intellect glimmered, and Chris saw a spark of recognition. For a moment, he was confused. But when the young man's gaze flickered from Chris, to Maris, to Olivia, and then back to Chris, he understood. The papers. The stories that had been running. White Clover.

His realization must have showed, because something changed in Officer Cartwright's expression. He fluttered his long eyelashes and shrugged one slender shoulder. "Less cringing than Constance, not that it's hard. He'll do, I suppose." The boy turned away, appearing to dismiss the unimportant secretary even as Chris still tingled from the unspoken exchange that had passed between them. He wished he could define what had just happened. Not knowing made him nervous.

Officer Cartwright focused his attention on Olivia. "I hear you have something for me," he said, and even as he did, Olivia produced the knife case and pushed it across the table. It slid like a stone on ice and stopped right before the timeseer. He took his time opening it and studying the weapon cradled lovingly inside before taking it into his hand. He wielded it like the weapon it was, holding it by the hilt, and turned his wrist about to examine it at all sides. A chill crawled up Chris's spine. This was not just an examination. Something about the way the other man held the weapon made it obvious he was used to such weight in his hands.

"It belonged to a killer," Olivia supplied when the silence dragged. "It doesn't appear to be an antique, so it probably doesn't have a long history." Officer Cartwright didn't respond. He kept turning the weapon about, as if trying to be sure he saw every last speck of its surface. "Do you think—"

"I'm *trying* to," the timeseer snapped. "Stop talking."

And she did. Just like that, Olivia closed her mouth and said nothing else.

"I can do it," Officer Cartwright said, finally. Olivia let out the breath she'd been holding. She clapped her hands before her, exactly once, and then stood still and silent, awaiting more instructions.

Officer Cartwright set the knife back down. He looked up at Olivia, and then turned his gaze to Chris. "You sit to my left," he said. For a moment, Chris thought he was talking to Olivia, but he realized the young man was still looking at him...and that everyone else in the room was, too.

"Will," Officer Burke murmured into the silence. "It's very important I receive as clear a picture as possible. You know I am required to write a report on every timeseeing you do for Her Majesty's peace."

"You can sit by him," Officer Cartwright said. "Your image will be clean enough for your report, Hannah, I promise."

"Then surely that position will be more than suitable for Miss Faraday's new assistant, Will," Officer Burke offered. "My reports are required to be as exhaustive as possible, and—"

"He sits by me," Officer Cartwright insisted. The set of his jaw and the way he folded his arms reminded Chris of something...of Rosemary, he realized. It was the look of someone who was used to getting their way.

He had his way this time, as well.

They arranged themselves around the table. William Cartwright sat at the head, with Olivia on his right and Chris on his left. Officer Hannah Burke sat beside Chris, looking none too bothered by her having been overruled, while Officer Maris Dawson sat beside Olivia, looking the opposite. Chris suspected she disliked the apparent breach in procedure more than anything else. He hoped he wasn't going to cause anyone work or trouble.

Officer Cartwright extended his hands, and, tentatively, when he saw what Olivia did, Chris reached out and took the one offered to him. It was warm and soft and strangely familiar, somehow. Chris shook himself and, continuing to take his cue from Olivia, he offered his other hand to Officer Burke. Her fingers felt like the bones of a bird.

"Christopher," Olivia purred, one eyebrow quirked, "don't be alarmed. This can be *very* surreal the first time you experience it."

Before he could open his mouth and ask just what, exactly, that meant—

—everything plunged into darkness.

CHAPTER TWENTY

Shadowy shapes moved just beyond his vision. Blurred patches of near-white against the black. Dimly—very, very dimly—he was aware of his body, aware of the room, of Hannah Burke's small, delicate hand clasped in his. Dimly, he was aware that he was Christopher Buckley. But those things were far away, strange, unimportant.

His vision focused slightly and then went blurred again. There was a banister against his hand. He was climbing steps. His vision focused again and he saw the very last moments of twilight through a window, familiar carpeting beneath his feet, a painting on the wall he knew well. The world surged, then stopped, then raced, then slowed, then crawled. He was looking down at Rosemary in bed. She turned on her side. Her lashes fluttered and they made eye contact. "Chris?" She yawned, and he tightened his grip around the knife in his hand, flexing each finger…

"No," he heard Olivia Faraday's voice, a lifetime away, and Rosemary dissolved into haze and mist, leaving nothing but darkness and the feeling of gripping the hilt of the knife. "That's not it. Go back further, William. Not far. Just a bit."

An odd, dizzying sensation of walking backwards. Back down steps and across a floor and through streets, walking and walking, an hour of walking, all in an instant. The only images he glimpsed were seen through a thick haze. Trying to focus on anything was impossible. The vision moved of its own accord, someone else sifting through and pilfering a story, skimming a book, looking for the important parts. They recognized and dismissed things before he even knew he what was looking at, and they were moving again before he knew they'd been there, sliding through barely visible, half-obscured images he didn't understand.

Ana's face flashed before him, her mouth a rictus of terrible pain.

She clutched at her stomach, trying to keep her insides in. She scrambled away from him, eyes wide and tears streaming down her face. The knife was slick and sticky in his hand, and he stabbed again, and again, meeting her forearm, her hands, never anything important. The image jumped and popped and fizzed like a photograph held over a flame. The edges hopped and doubled. Ana sobbed. "I don't understand," she howled. "I don't understand!"

"Gods, yes, *yes*." Olivia's voice was at the very end of a long tunnel, so far away nothing she was saying could possibly matter. "This is it. This is the knife she used! Go deeper. There's something here. We need to find it, William! Just a little more."

The image snapped into focus, and there was blood everywhere, blood all over his face, and he twisted the knife and there was blood on his hands, blood on his knees, blood all over the walls, and blood splattering Ana's face like rain from Olivia's umbrella. For that instant, everything was sharp and real and immediate and Chris could have put his head in his hands and wailed for how horrible, how visceral, how brutal it was.

He was faintly aware of someone gasping, and it all slid away into blurred red shapes, nothing visible but blood, blood, blood through a haze of tears. "I can't," Officer Cartwright's voice had lost its superior, smug polish. He sounded small and weak and terrified. "Oh, Gods, it's too much. It's too much. I can't connect. There's too much blood. I *can't*."

Olivia was protesting. What she was saying didn't matter.

The red faded and he was moving back again, back and then forward, always with the knife in hand. There were periods of complete blackness, then periods of movement and shapes and colours, and then blackness, a feeling of utter disconnection, of loss of identity. Time blurred past like they were running a race through it, backward and forward, and nothing was definite enough to put words to, nothing at all.

He was holding the knife. His other hand pressed against a rough grain of wood. Birds chirped out a window framed with gently wafting curtains, and his hands were covered in red pulp. He brought the knife down again, and again, and again. Moisture bloomed in his hands and there was red everywhere.

"Tomatoes," Officer Dawson's voice said, full of contempt. The smell of something sweet baking reached his nose and he breathed deeply. He wiped one hand on his apron, keeping the other firmly holding the knife, and then pushed strands of long hair back from his face. "Too far."

The curtains and the birdsong and the hands covered in seeds melted away. More movement, more meaningless images, back and forward, now and then, come and go.

He suddenly gripped the knife at his side. He opened his eyes just a crack and found himself staring into the face of Duke Viktor val Daren. Strong arms surrounded him, cradled him, and his lips and tongue were entwined with those of the Duke, the roughness of his stubbled chin coarse against his face. He released the hilt of the knife to reach for the front of the Duke's pants and the colour all ran together and vanished all at once.

"Oh," Chris heard himself say faintly.

He'd never been kissed in his life.

The image *connected* again like being slammed into by a carriage, trampled by hooves and wheels both. He *slashed* out with the knife, and the Duke's throat opened, whatever vocalization he'd been about to make turning into a horrific gurgle as blood bubbled up and squirted out like an undine's eternal fountain. Blood splattered his face. It got in his eyes, in his mouth. It tasted like iron and salt, and the Duke's eyes were horrified and terrified both as the light faded from them, before—

"I'm *sorry*," Officer Cartwright moaned, and it washed away.

"No, *no*, stay with it!" Olivia roared. "Go *back!* Reconnect, do it again!"

"I'm sorry," Officer Cartwright was panting like an exhausted dog. "Oh Gods, it's too much."

Back. A flash of the val Darens' beautiful foyer.

Forward. The little room Ana and Ethan had laid together on the chesterfield in, covered in bloody rags and red smears.

Back. Fitting an antique key into an antique lock.

Forward. Carving long lines into a dead man's arms.

The picture jumped and skipped and hopped and settled for only flashes at a time, and Chris could hear someone sobbing a universe away, sobbing and muttering, "Too much, too much." Back, pushing aside the curtain in a taxi cab. Forward, tying him to the rafters. Back, skirts swirling in the dark along the walk. Forward, skirts heaped in a pile covered in blood. Back. Forward. Back. Forward.

Back.

He caught his reflection in the magic mirror gracing the wall of the val Darens' foyer.

"*There!*" Olivia cried.

"Gods," Maris Dawson breathed.

"*Hold*, William," Officer Burke's soft voice was sharp.

The image held.

His wavy, ebony hair was caught up with pins of diamond. His slight but shapely body filled the lines of his dark green velvets perfectly. One of his lace-gloved hands gripped the knife hidden in the belt beneath his skirts, sheathed but ready, and the other held tightly to an antique iron key.

Chris stared into the dark-as-black eyes of Vanessa Caldwell.

He blinked at the image. The lines of Miss Caldwell's beautiful face shimmered and blurred, and he heard Officer Cartwright make a tortured sound somewhere very far away. But there was no denying it was her. That meant something, he knew. That meant…that meant…

He slammed back into himself with a physical jolt. His hands gripped Officer Burke and Officer Cartwright's, and he felt the polished wood of the table cool against his forehead. He breathed unsteadily. He had some mild awareness of chairs scraping, Officer Burke gently prying his fingers from hers, quiet conversation. He breathed, breathed. He couldn't seem to grab hold of and identify a single thought in his head. When he reached for them, they fluttered away playfully, like shy maidens or pesky flies.

"Mister Buckley," he heard Olivia say at his ear, and the thought of responding to her seemed absurd. "*Christopher.*"

He should just tell her to call him by his first name after all. She did it anyway. Still, it would feel like losing a battle. He was inordinately pleased with himself for having actually framed the thought, but he only noticed Olivia had left his side minutes later, when he finally tried to respond.

Bits of stimulus floated through him and registered faintly. The door to the room opening and closing, chaos leaking in from outside, Officer Dawson and Olivia speaking heatedly in the corner, Officer Burke's quiet tones being there and then being gone. He became aware of the fact that he was still holding someone's hand. Curious. He no longer gripped the hand in a white-knuckled stranglehold, but rather, their threaded fingers rested gently on the surface of the table between them. Chris concentrated on that, flexing each of his fingers one after the other, and felt a jolt at self-realization go through him when the hand he held squeezed his in response.

He turned his head to one side, pressing his cheek against the table. At some point, somehow, his spectacles had come off. They lay on the table beside him, and his vision was so blurred he could barely make out Officer Cartwright's face, but he could see enough to tell the boy looked as bad as he felt.

"I'm sorry."

The words seemed to come from the world away, but Chris heard them and processed them. His brows knotted together.

"I probably should have warned you."

Chris's tongue finally remembered how to move and form words, though they sounded slurred and distant. "You wanted me to sit by you…"

"Yes. The closer you are to the seer, the more strongly you experience the flashes."

Chris frowned, trying to warp his mind around that. Yes. Yes, that was the conclusion he'd come to, before this started. He nodded, the flesh of his cheek squashed up against the table. He kept nodding. Some of the cobwebs seemed to be clearing from his mind, bit by precious bit. "Why?" The obvious question took some time reaching him.

He saw the young man hesitate. "Your mother died at the Floating Castle."

"My mother…" His mother. They only ever mentioned Michael. He was the important one, and she'd just been his wife. Everyone assumed it was his father he mourned, but he could have handled losing Michael. It would have been awful, but if Julia had survived…

He flinched away from the thoughts despite his state. That path always lead to shadowy dead end alleys, and *nobody* who'd been inside had survived the Floating Castle. He shook it off, and tried to push himself up from the table. He groped with his empty hand for his glasses. Only after he'd slipped them onto his nose and blinked in shock at how real everything looked did he realize he hadn't even considered breaking the link between himself and the timeseer.

The other man was watching him intently, *something* in his eyes.

Chris cleared his throat quietly. "Officer…" He shook himself and tried again. "Officer Cartwright…" he began.

"Please, William."

No, that would be rude. I barely know you. I'd hate to be rude. "William, then. I…"

It was then that Olivia seemed to notice he'd come up out of his trance. She'd been speaking heatedly with Officer Dawson in the corner, and now whirled about to look at him. "*Finally*," she said, abandoning Officer Dawson to start towards him. "I could hang you up by your toes, Will, for putting my assistant out of commission for so long." She stopped before him, drumming her fingers on the surface of the table and looking down at him. She barely seemed affected by what they'd just seen at all. Perhaps she was used to it. Or perhaps it had never bothered her. "We need to go," she said.

"Where?"

Olivia rolled her eyes and increased the rhythm of her fingers. "Does it *matter*? We're *going*."

Officer Dawson appeared behind her. "Vanessa Caldwell isn't at the hospital, today. She didn't show up this morning, and she was scheduled to. We mirrored her apartment, and there was no response. We'll be taking a team there, now. You're not *really* needed, but Olivia should be there, as investigator for the case."

"Miss Caldwell…" Chris murmured.

"Gods, Will, did you put all of his brains back in *backwards*?" Chris grunted in surprise when Olivia reached down, looped her hands around the crook of his arm, and *pulled*. He half-stumbled to his feet, twisting his arm backwards before he thought to release William's hand. "*Apparently*," Olivia's mouth pulled down in disgust, "Vanessa Caldwell killed the Duke. We need to make an arrest."

"Stop sulking," Officer Dawson snapped.

Olivia rounded on her, glaring fury. "It doesn't *feel* right!"

"We have her at his house, with the key to his locked study, hand on the hilt of the knife that killed him, Faraday. I'm done talking about this. If you're not calling an arrest, I am."

Olivia clenched her jaw hard enough they all heard it grind, and turned all her stormy attention back on Chris. "As I said," she spat. "*Apparently*. So let's go."

Chris turned to look back at William Cartwright before they left the room. The boy met his eyes, his head still resting against the table, his hand exactly where Chris had dropped it. Their gazes locked.

They emerged into utter chaos.

The room had been a whirlwind of activity before. Now, it was a hurricane. Officers ran in all directions, and the room rang with shouts, commands, and short, clipped replies. All the chairs and desks were empty as every police officer in Darrington scurried about the room like mice in a maze. Most of the activity seemed concentrated up where they had come in.

Officer Dawson stopped in her tracks. She scanned about. When a short, skinny boy with hair as orange as hers rushed by, arms full of papers, she grabbed him by his arm and yanked him back so hard he stumbled and his cargo went flying everywhere. "Aw, damn, Officer!" The youth cried, trying to dart after the snowing papers.

She held him tight. "What in the three hells is going on?" she demanded.

He let the snow continue with a sigh. To his credit, he didn't cringe in the face of Officer Dawson's fury. "Bringing him in now, Dawson," he said, indicating the confusion up near the doors with a jerk of his chin.

"What are you talking about?" Officer Dawson demanded, shaking the boy as if he were a misbehaving puppy she held by the scruff of the neck. "Bringing *who* in? Why?"

The boy gaped at her. "Where you been all morning, ma'am?" he asked uncertainly. "Didn't think there was a body here who hadn't heard about what Doctor Livingstone did."

Cold fear paralysed Chris's heart. "*Francis* Livingstone?" he demanded sharply. The last of his fog cleared from his mind, and he thought of Rosemary. Had his read on the man been wrong? Had he made a horrible mistake to have trusted him? To have trusted Miss *Albany*? What if...

But what the boy said next made Chris's absolute worst, wildest fears seem like paper tigers. He nodded vigorously, seeing their perplexed expressions, and tore himself free of Officer Dawson's grip. "Got him on sabotaging the Floating Castle, would you believe it? All these years talking like he has, and he crashed the damn thing hisself."

Chris couldn't have stopped if he tried. His mind went blank and his legs just seemed to carry him themselves. He pushed past the boy, brushed Olivia off as she went to grab him, sidestepped desks and chairs and harried police officers and their assistants. He was curiously focused, and all the ringing sound in the room faded to nothing but a muted buzz underscoring the thumping of his own heart. Everything seemed to move both very slowly and very quickly, and the crowd somehow parted for him like grass bowing before the wind.

He met the doctor's eyes as he was escorted into the building, bound in shackles and flanked by five police officers.

The sound all roared back to life. He could hear a crowd gathered outside, screaming and jeering and wailing. Reporters with flashbulbs pounded at the doors that closed behind them, shouting questions through the glass at the top of their lungs. "Doctor!" they cried. "Doctor!" Officers moved in all directions, some moving away, some pulling forward, some moving up to assist their peers in escorting the doctor. Most of the officers seemed to forget what and who they were, and called questions after the doctor just as openly as the crowd and the reporters had.

"How *could* you?" one woman screamed, and spat in his direction.

"*Bastard*," howled another. "My son and his wife died that night! They weren't even there, they had nothing to *do* with that damn castle! Your *statement* crashed right through their roof!"

"Doctor!" The man's voice was desperate. "Doctor, we *know* you didn't do this! I'll do everything I can! I'll clear you!"

"*Fuck* you, murderer! Piss on you and all you've done!"

He felt rather than saw Olivia's presence beside him. He took a deep, gulping breath, leaning back into her strong bearing without thinking, trying to gain some grounding from it. He couldn't get the sound of screeching metal out of his head, nor the taste of his own vomit out of his mouth. "Olivia..." he said hoarsely, but there was nothing Olivia could do, and she wouldn't provide comfort for him even if he asked. He closed his eyes tightly, sucking in air. *Mother...*

Very close at hand, he heard a woman's voice in an angry mutter that cut through all the rest of the chaos around them. "I wonder whose pockets that monster Hector Combs had to reach into to pull *this* off. Is there nothing he wouldn't do?"

Olivia heard it too.

"Oh Gods," she breathed close at his ear, and she seized his upper arm in a grip tight enough to crush steel. He saw her in the corner of his eye as she fished about and then flipped open the file Ana had given him, on her person as always. He looked down as she ran her finger over the initials that signed the letter on top of the file, smudged where Kolston had licked his thumb and rubbed the page. "Oh Gods," Olivia repeated, fire in her voice. "I know who HC is."

CHAPTER TWENTY-ONE

The city's sombre, quiet tone of mourning was gone.
Chris murmured to the unicorn that had pulled their
police car to the old tenement. The animal danced and
sidled and rolled its beautiful blue eyes, but Chris's low
voice seemed to keep it sane in the face of the chaos boiling around
them. No longer reverent, Darrington churned and roiled. The
streets were so congested with swarming people, all muttering and
babbling to one another, drivers were using whips on the crowds
more than their animals.

Two young women jostled him as they jogged past, gesturing
wildly between one another. A tattered-looking man pushed a
finely dressed lady onto her knees and didn't stop to apologize.
Down at the corner, a newsboy was hawking his papers loudly, his
young countertenor shrill enough to pierce through the chaos.
"Doctor Livingstone charged for the murder of hundreds!" he
cried. "Darrington Arrow's got the full story, read all about it! Ten
coppers! Ten coppers!"

"Come on, now," Olivia muttered. Chris barely picked out her
voice over the excited hum of the city around him, and she stood
less than four paces away. She stared at the door of the building
and one of her feet tapped anxiously. Water splashed up all over
her soaked skirts. "Come on, Maris, I don't have all bloody day."

The unicorn sensed his change in focus. It whickered and threw
its head about nervously, and Chris grabbed the bridle and hushed

the poor thing. Its pearly horn dripped with rain, and it didn't look so special all muddy and reeking of horse. He patted its nose and whispered encouraging words, but it barely seemed to see him.

Chris sighed and pressed his forehead against the animal's cheek. When he closed his eyes against the rain sluicing down his face, he saw the Doctor's eyes. They bored into his, and he tried to name what he'd seen there. Apology? Defiance? Pleading? His memory of the instant kept changing with what he wanted to believe. In one breath, he saw the good Doctor as a victim. Darrington had wanted a believable scapegoat for six years; a set-up would have been easy. But in the next, he saw a man so good at his bloody politics he'd almost convinced Chris to leave his life and take his sister to a reformist laboratory Gods knew where.

The unicorn sidled. Chris half-heartedly tugged on the bridle. "Do you think he did it?" he said, dropping his voice into the whirlpool of sound and motion.

Olivia snorted. "Absolutely not."

She sounded so sure. "Why? How can you know?"

"I can't *know*," she replied. "But it just doesn't feel right. I don't care we saw her in his house, with the knife, with the *key*. Gods, we all but saw her slashing his throat and cutting up the daughter, too, didn't we? But it doesn't *feel* right. What does that *mean*?"

Chris sighed and shook his head. She was talking about the val Daren case. Well, of course she was. Olivia was single-minded and the val Daren case was her job. Why *should* she care about Francis Livingstone and the Floating Castle?

"Do *you* think she did it?"

"I don't know," he said. He didn't even know what he wanted to think. The thought of having someone to blame after all these years, a real villain to hate...

He felt Olivia stiffen and then straighten beside him. "*Finally*," she said, and in moments, they were surrounded by police officers and their rustling raincoats. Chris envied them those. He was soaked to the skin and freezing cold. "Where is she?"

Officer Dawson growled. "She's not here." The stout little woman was nothing but a bristle of dripping orange curls poking out of a hood. "Her landlady says she vanishes for days a lot, but I'll bet it's not so simple, this time. She was scheduled to work, like I said." The officer growled. "You showed your hand too early with that poem in the Herald, Faraday, and she bolted off into her warren."

When Olivia didn't reply to the implicit accusation, Officer Dawson snarled and turned to the lower-ranking coppers who surrounded her. "You two," she barked. "Get on mirrors to our stations in every damn village, town, and city from sea to sea. Clarkson, Cuthberry, the two of you are going to take men and scour *this* city top to bottom. Monkton, you go back and get whatever evidence you can find from her apartment. Pry the key off the landlady with your weapon if you have to."

A chorus of quite *yes, ma'am*s answered her words, and the officers all scurried off in different directions to accomplish the tasks set before them. Officer Dawson turned back to Chris and Olivia. "She did it," Officer Dawson said.

"You keep saying so," Olivia muttered.

Officer Dawson scanned the crowds rushing past them, coursing around in both directions like two rivers colliding. Then she folded her arms and sighed. "You want to go talk to that poor woman."

"*Yes*," Olivia said. She whipped out the folder once again, indicating the smudged *HC* at the base of the page. "I just want to lay it all to rest," she insisted. "If this is what she's been hiding the entire time, I'll even admit it was probably Caldwell. I just need to *know*."

Officer Dawson watched the rain soak through the page. The page was handwritten; the ink ran and made the smudged initials seem right at home.

Olivia didn't seem to notice.

"If the Duchess funded some sort of high-concept framing of Doctor Livingstone…" the policewoman mused.

"Her Majesty's police would like to know, wouldn't they?" Olivia wheedled.

"It wouldn't be your case," Officer Dawson warned.

Olivia shrugged. She finally seemed to notice the rain turning the words on the page to sludge and closed the folder with a wince, vanishing it away into her clothes with a small flourish. "Conspiracies bore me, anyway," she said, and bared her teeth. "Not nearly enough blood."

Did Chris imagine the way he saw Officer Dawson pale? "If there aren't enough bodies on this one for you, Olivia," she murmured, "I don't know what to tell you." And then, louder, as she shouldered Chris aside to grab the unicorn's bridle, "Fine, go talk to her. But this time, you can call a taxi. I have an actual murderer to chase."

Once they were sheltered inside a dry hackney, Chris asked again. "Do you think the Doctor is guilty, Olivia?"

"Oh, of course," she said without a thought, crossing her legs and arranging her skirts as though they weren't sodden and covered in muck up to the knees. "I just haven't decided if it's for the crime he just got arrested for or not."

The handwritten note was nigh unreadable from the rain, but there could be no doubt Evelyn val Daren knew exactly what she was looking at. She blinked down at where Olivia had dropped the file on the table before her. The colour drained from her face, and one hand went up to clutch at the string of pearls surrounding her neck. Her throat worked, but no sound came out.

Olivia smiled with sickening sweetness. She reached down and straightened the papers slightly, brushing a bit of imagined dirt from the top of the page. "Have you heard the news?" she chirped. "Francis Livingstone was arrested this morning for sabotaging the Floating Castle! I'm sure you know absolutely nothing about this!"

The Duchess took a deep breath. It shook. So did the hand she untangled from her pearls to smooth her hair. "We won't be needing your services, Laurie. You're dismissed for now." Her voice, at the least, was very steady. The maid dipped a quick curtsey and slipped out, closing the door behind her.

"I'm very curious," Olivia said into the stretching silence.

The Duchess spidered her fingers atop the note and pushed it back across the table to Olivia. "These notes," she said, her voice clear and authoritative, "are private business, and in no way related to the investigation I solicited you to perform."

"No? Now I'm even *more* curious. If they're unrelated, why *exactly* did you take them and hide them so I wouldn't find them?"

Duchess val Daren's eyes flashed. "Precisely *because* they are unrelated, Miss Faraday!" she said, voice ringing along the walls of the empty parlour. There were finally cracks in her perfect demeanour. One cheek was brighter blushed than the other. Her hands were bare of rings or gloves. He saw crumbs from biscuits or scones in the folds of her right cuff. Finally, she looked like a woman who'd actually lost something. The Duchess folded her hands before her. They looked terribly wrong without their usual adornments, an ageing woman's hands, not those of a beautiful lady of society. "I knew you would latch onto them. They would taint your investigation. You'd look for answers where there are *none.*"

"And the letters from the offices of Rayner Kolston?" Olivia asked mildly, and the Duchess blanched again. Olivia's teeth glittered when she smiled. "Those are in the file, too. I find it interesting you didn't think *those* were unrelated, considering how your husband's body was laid out. I'm assuming you knew about the val Frenton murder?"

"It was ruled unrelated!" the Duchess protested. Her voice was shrill and her fingers were clawed into her skirts. "I—this family has a reputation to maintain, and our debts are not the affair of, of—" Her face twisted and she growled. Reaching out, she *shoved* the file, and papers flew up into the air like a furious flock of birds. "*Where* did you get these?"

"That's none of your concern."

"I *demand* to know where—"

"I want to hear about Hector Combs." Olivia said.

The fight went out of the Duchess. Her shoulders sagged and her eyes closed and a puff of air came out from between her parted lips. Olivia tapped her long fingers on the table between them.

The Duchess opened her eyes. "I would prefer to sit," she said quietly. She walked to the box seat at the window, the seat where Chris and Olivia had first spoken to Analaea. When the Duchess sat in it, pulled her legs up to her chest like a very young girl, Chris saw the resemblance between her and her daughter for the first time.

Olivia said nothing and waited for the older woman to speak. She wasn't disappointed. When the Duchess's voice came, it was from somewhere very far away. "He was one of my father's protégés," she said. "At Lowry. He was my father's favourite, and so they were very close. Hector was frequently at our home for dinners and other social events, accompanying my father. I think they hoped he and I would fall for one another, but Hector was ten years my senior, and I already had my eye on a particular man. An Old Blood noble. Still, we became close friends. The three of us."

"You, Hector, and your brother, James North," Olivia said.

The Duchess nodded. "James and he were especially very dear to one another. They were closer in age, you see. I was a girl and a tag along, but they tolerated me." She reached out to brush the pane of the window as if trying to touch something that wasn't there. "I didn't care a whit about their politics. James and Hector were always talking about the reformists, about Lowry. Later, about the Floating Castle. They spoke of how it was going to be a monument to everything the traditionalists stood for. Categorization *isn't* a stagnating, depreciating system. It's still evolving, still growing, able to accomplish more and more new, impressive feats. The sylph net…it was going to be the grandest thing ever done since the days of the old wizards. It was going to be a statement."

Chris couldn't help himself. "I don't understand!" he cried. "The way you talk about it—you obviously *care*. Why have you always spat at Ana's dreams? There's nothing she wanted so badly as to 'bind, and they're *desperate* for *anyone*."

The Duchess twisted about to look at him. Her eyes glittered like steel. "Ironic, hearing that from you of all people." She smirked at his reaction. "*Yes*, I know who you are. Haven't you been paying attention? I'm part of a vast traditionalist conspiracy. We all know about Michael's little rose. He was obsessed with seeming more than he was. We assumed his little wizardling was just more of that. I'll admit, you did a good job keeping her potential hidden until White Clover." She clucked her tongue. "All the things she can do for this country, and you've kept her hidden away from the people who need her the most."

Chris clenched his fists. He went so far as to take a step towards her, but Olivia's hand on his shoulder stopped him. "She's my sister." He hung the words like a net, hoping to tangle her in them. "I'm all she has. It's my job to protect her."

"Yes, I know. Just as I protected my own daughter," the Duchess flung the net back at him, and he found he was the one trapped. "You don't know anything about the Old Blood. And you certainly don't have the first idea of what it was like to go from being Evelyn North to Evelyn val Daren. It isn't done, you know. Old Blood marry their own. It doesn't matter how rich or high class or well-provisioned you are, common is common. Ana was always strange enough on her own. I would not—I *could not*—allow her to be seen as *common*."

"It was *her* choice to *make*!"

"And your sister? What would *her* choice be? Or have you ever thought to ask?"

She's a child, he went to say, but she'd have a response to that. *She doesn't know what she wants.* No, that too. *I understand the situation. I'm the one to make that decision.* And that, as well. Chris ground his teeth, glaring fury at the Duchess, but every direction he turned in, there was just another wall. The tension left his shoulders and his face went slack as he realized, suddenly, that Evelyn val Daren was not and had never been any worse than he, himself.

The Duchess nodded her satisfaction. "I couldn't explain myself to her," she continued. "Naturally, I couldn't. It was important her father never find out where his money was going, and so I had to keep her ignorant to keep him ignorant. He'd have just used her against me."

He cast about for one last weapon to throw at her. "What about Ethan Grey?" he demanded. "He adored her and just because you hated her father's interest in artists, you—"

She laughed at him, a mirthless, angry laugh. "*Ethan Grey,*" she spat, her voice dripping with the usual scorn and barbed hatred. "My complaints with that *pervert* have absolutely nothing to do with what I may or may not have thought of my husband's little hobby. Of course, there's some *irony* to it, but it was never my concern."

Chris felt Olivia step up beside him. "What did the three of you argue about that night?" she asked quietly. "The night at the gallery. The night your husband died."

The Duchess waved the question off and turned to look out to the countryside. "The same thing we always argued about. I pointed Ana towards something very obvious and Ethan was quick as a clever little fox to convince her I was being petty."

"And what was that?" Olivia pressed.

The Duchess shrugged. "The boy is a sodomite." Despite her air of nonchalance, the words were forced, dripping venom, from her mouth. "He used his courtship of my poor daughter as a way to—to appear *normal* before potential buyers and art collectors and gallery owners, but, *oh*, the moment no one important was watching—" She cut herself off, disgust thick in her voice.

Olivia shook her head. "Really? Hmph. I suppose I should have guessed you'd be a bigot, too. All that hatred over something so unimportant."

The Duchess glanced up, shocked. "*Unimportant?* Did you hear what I just said, Miss Faraday? Ethan Grey is a…a…"

"An adult man whose private business doesn't affect you in any way?" Olivia filled in mildly.

"If that were only the truth! That night, he and this—this other young fellow who was carrying the paintings about, hanging them for display, *Gods*, you should have seen them carrying on. And my Ana just standing there, staring up at him as if he were Cwenraed the Youth. Was it not my duty as her mother, to point out what was happening right before her eyes?"

Chris remembered the feeling of the Duke's rough cheeks against his face, his tongue in his mouth. He felt a telltale burning in his cheeks. It had been *Vanessa's* face, Vanessa's mouth. It wasn't the same.

Olivia sighed. "And that, something that stupid, is what you fought over?"

"In the end Ana always believed him. Over me, her own mother!"

"You left the gallery early. You told Ana not to tell anyone. You told her to lie for you." The Duchess squeezed her eyes tightly shut and said nothing. Olivia's voice came sharper as she pressed the issue. "Where did you go, Duchess? Why did you make Ana cover?"

The Duchess leaned her head against the windowpane. "You know where I went. To our final meeting before everything came together. Hah, and you know, I didn't even think twice about leaving her. He had stormed off in a huff and she wanted to go after him and I was so *angry*. She never *listened* to me. She was always so convinced I was her enemy." A weak, quivering breath. "She died—she died thinking I killed her father. She died thinking I was a murderer. Because of you, she—" And suddenly, her voice caught and her shoulders trembled, then shook. Chris's heart skipped a beat. He opened his mouth to say something, some word of comfort, but none came. The Duchess shook with silent tears.

"Duchess," Olivia said after a very long time, not unkindly.

"They're both gone," the Duchess whispered. She drew a black lace handkerchief from inside her bodice, using it to delicately dab tears from her face. Cosmetics smeared on her grey skin. "Gods, the both of them are truly gone, and I'm all alone in the world, after all."

"Well, not completely alone. You do have your co-conspirators." When the wounded bird that had been the haughty Duchess raised her head, Olivia's voice lost a bit of its mockery and became almost gentle. "Tell me just one thing, Duchess," she said. "Did the Doctor actually sabotage the Castle, or did you and your friends all just use that lovely Old Money to make it look like he did?"

The Duchess blinked away tears and gave them a tired smile with no life, love, or hope behind it. "You know, I honestly don't know," she murmured, and then chuckled. "And I don't care."

Olivia nodded. Just once. She gathered the papers from the table, put them back in the file, and closed it. "Come along, then, Mister Buckley." She stopped at the door. With her hand resting on the latch, she turned just far enough to let the Duchess see the line of her profile. "Vanessa Caldwell killed your husband and daughter," she said. "There's an arrest been ordered. We're out looking for her now. It shouldn't take too long."

Stunned silence. Then, haltingly. "Then…then…" A shuddering breath, and then a sigh of great relief. "Then this is all over?"

"Apparently," Olivia breathed, and they left the broken Duchess sitting alone by the window.

CHAPTER TWENTY-TWO

T he maid who had been quickly and indelicately dismissed from her lady's presence was standing at the mirror when the two of them found their way to the main entrance hall. "Ah, ma'am, they're coming out, now. Do you still wish to—"

Officer Dawson's excited voice stomped all over the maid's respectful, quiet tones. "Faraday? Are you there? Get over here."

Olivia waved the poor girl aside like a pesky fly and then took her place at the mirror. "What is it?" she droned.

If Officer Dawson noticed the disinterest in Olivia's tone, she certainly didn't show it. "We got her. Caldwell. In Vernella."

Olivia crooked an eyebrow. Chris came to stand slightly beside and to one side of her, so he could see both her and Officer Dawson's faces. He was still putting the finishing touches on his notes from their last conversation with Duchess val Daren. "Fleeing Her Majesty's justice by rushing to Her Majesty's side? Very peculiar."

Maris Dawson did not have a flattering blush. Her red skin made her orange hair look ludicrous, and her freckles stood out like chunks of carrot in a tomato soup. "She *claims* to be there visiting her sick mother. She received word Missus Caldwell was finally getting about dying and dropped everything to rush to her bedside."

"Does the story check?"

"We're still not sure," the policewoman muttered. When Chris looked up from his notebook, her bushy orange eyebrows were pulled down like angry caterpillars. "We just picked her up ten minutes ago. The first thing I did after finishing on the mirror was to try and get in touch with you."

"So," Olivia said. She raised her hand and studied her fingernails clinically. "What *do* we know?"

"She's denying everything," Officer Dawson said. "But as we've already established, she doesn't have an alibi, and Gods, Faraday, we have her at the *house*, in the *room*, with the *knife*. What else do you need?"

Olivia shrugged one shoulder. "What does the heartreader say? Is she telling the truth?"

"He can't tell. She's projecting sincerity, but he says it feels forced. He'll need more time with her. He swears she's shocked, but again, he can't say if it's because she's innocent, or if it's because she didn't expect anyone to find out she was guilty, or even just because her mother is dying."

Olivia finished her study of her hand and finally deigned to meet Officer Dawson's eyes. "We're going to need more than the seeing," she said. "We can't use it in court. You know that. All it takes it one pushy reporter, and then press latches onto it, and no more ace in the—"

"I know, I know," Officer Dawson growled. "Trust me, Faraday, I bloody know. We'll find something. She was *there*; she *did* it. We damn well saw her." She shook her head and glared at her charge accusingly. "You certainly know how to kill a woman's enthusiasm. We got her, Faraday. You got your man, as always. Aren't you glad?" Olivia said nothing, only stared mildly into the mirror, until the policewoman sighed and lowered her gaze, pretending to fuss with the papers on the desk between them. "Did you talk to the Duchess?"

Now it was Olivia's turn to deflate. She dropped her eyes and ran her finger along the surface of the table before them. "Yes."

"And what did she say?"

Olivia raised the finger, checked it for dust. When she found none, she made a face and sighed. "She says she's been funding the traditionalists for years. She's a long-time friend of Hector Combs. She was with her cronies planning the exposure of Doctor Livingstone on the night the Duke was killed, not that any of them can speak in her defence without admitting some awkward truths. The fight at the gallery was because her daughter's beau enjoys the company of other men, which apparently is a very big deal to some people, and everything neatly wraps up together."

"Do you believe it all?"

Olivia's shoulders slumped like she was suddenly carrying the weight of the world. She closed her eyes and raised one of those elegant hands to rub at her temple. "It all feels right," she murmured unhappily, and shook her head. "Gods damn me, but it *feels* right."

"All along, you—"

A bit of the spark appeared in Olivia again, and her shoulders tensed. "I *said* I knew she was hiding something," she interrupted accusingly. "And I was right. Was it so big a stretch to assume it was the obvious thing? I'm never wrong in my feeling, Maris, *never.*" When Officer Dawson inclined her head in agreement, Olivia continued. "Vanessa Caldwell doesn't *feel* right."

The policewoman sighed. "No? Then who, Faraday? Who killed the Duke and the girl? Was it the creditor? One of the staff? Someone we haven't even looked at?"

"I don't..." Olivia growled in frustration. "I don't know."

"I'll tell you who it was. It was the mistress. It's always the mistress. We should just arrest them as part of procedure." Officer Dawson looked over her shoulder for a long moment, staring at something far away, and then turned back to the mirror. "We're going to hold her in Vernella overnight, try to get some more information over her, and then have her brought to Darrington. *You* can ask her some questions, see what you can get out of her.

Go to the hospital tomorrow. Talk to her friends. Talk to her landlady. Just get *something*. It was her. We know it. We just have to find proof we can use to put her in jail for it. You understand me?"

"Naturally."

"Good, I'll talk to you—"

Just do it now, Chris told himself, and, before he lost his nerve, pushed himself forward, elbowing Olivia aside to take her place in front of the mirror. "Officer Dawson," he got out, "I'm very sorry to take up your time, but I need to ask you for a favour."

The policewoman's eyebrow shot up into her hair. "Do you, now?"

"Yes." He took a deep breath. "I—I need to speak to Doctor Livingstone."

Officer Dawson stared at him for a long moment, and, just before he went to hesitantly repeat his question, she barked the sort of laugh that could set half the dogs in a neighbourhood howling. "You and everybody else!"

He licked his lips and tried again. "I just need to ask him a question. It won't take—"

"Buckley." Her tone turned flat and the amusement vanished. "Don't waste my time. A reporter from every paper in the country is converging on this police station, and they're the least of it. I've got Lowry bigwigs and investigators and politickers from both sides pouring in through the damn windows. And on top of it all, I've got the Livingstone family. And you know what?" She shook her head. "It's not even my case. It doesn't have anything to *do* with me."

He longed to reach through the mirror, grab her shoulders, force her to understand. "This is important. I spoke to him just yesterday. He was at my house! Please, I—"

"I like you, Buckley." Officer Dawson pointed an accusing finger. "Stop making me not like you." Before he could say another word, she reached out and rang the chimes, and her face in the mirror was enveloped into the mist.

Chris could have howled. His tenuous connection with Officer Dawson was the only way he could think of to get in and see the Doctor. He had to know if it was true, any of it. At the very least, if he could hear the Doctor say for himself whether or not he was actually responsible, he felt he could have some idea of what to do. The danger had grown only greater; the traditionalist movement would strike while the iron was hot.

He shook his head in defeat. Surely, a plan would come to him. He could talk to Miss Albany when he got home this evening. She might know what to do.

He forced himself to straighten. He murmured a quiet apology to Olivia while making a show of opening his notebook and checking his notes from the conversation he'd just witnessed. When he was sure everything was in order, he looked back over at Olivia, who was watching him with a dull gleam in her eyes, seemingly half a world away. "Well," he said, trying to sound professional and collected. "Who else do we have to talk to today?"

Olivia turned away from him, drifting towards the door. She looked like a leaf carried by a current, dancing on a wind, floating in a pool. Directionless and lifeless. "No one," she said quietly. "Nowhere."

Chris frowned. "But Officer Dawson said—"

"I know what she said. I don't have any intention of wasting my time." She shook her head and opened the front door. "Go home, Mister Buckley. I'll see you in the morning. Maybe once I've slept on this…maybe once I've slept on this, I'll have any damned idea of what to do with myself."

She didn't even let him share her taxi.

Chris had gotten used to returning to the estate to either silence or chaos, dark echoing corners or important men with lies on their lips. When he pushed open the door and was greeted by a sweet voice calling his name, he felt as if he'd been given a gift.

"Rosemary!" he cried. He dropped his things in an untidy lump by the door and before he'd even managed to wrestle out of his topcoat and shoes, he was barrelled over by a ball of blue cotton and black curls.

She wrapped her arms around him and he held her tight, tears prickling the back of his eyes. Was it ridiculous that she seemed taller? Had her curls always been so soft, and had she ever allowed him to stroke them without pouting? He pressed his cheek against her dark crown and felt her link her pinkie fingers behind his back. "It feels like I was asleep forever," she said quietly, and he thought he could almost hear a ragged edge of tears in her sweet voice. "And every time I woke up, you weren't here."

"I'm here now, Rosie," he murmured, and she sighed contentedly, and that was all either of them needed.

He could have stayed forever, everything simple and familiar, but Rosemary was always restless. She untangled herself from him and grabbed one of his hands in both of hers. "Come on!" she insisted. He struggled to at least kick off his muddy shoes while she dragged him into the dining room. He was surprised to see, not Miss Albany, but Fernand sitting at the head of the table with a book spread out in front of him. Rosemary's empty seat was also parked before an open book, and her workspace was littered with graphite pencils strewn in all directions. Rosemary's favourite tea set—it has been their mother's favourite, as well—was in the centre of the table between them.

Chris laid his hand on the top of Rosemary's head, feeling her springy ringlets depress beneath the weight. "Fernand," he faltered. "What are you doing here today? Is there something with the investments, or…"

The old man shook his head. "No, young master, I'm just here for little Rosemary."

"Oh no!" Rosemary cried, and Chris followed her gaze down to the puddle his topcoat was making on the floor. "You're soaked!" The outline of one of the buttons of his shirt was pressed into her cheek, he noticed with a smile. "Were you walking out in the rain all day?"

"Yes, actually," he said, gingerly pulling off the wet coat and tossing it back towards the rack. It hit the ground with a wet *thunk* and he cringed. "Where's the nanny?" he asked, following Rosemary into the room. "I wanted to talk to her about something."

Fernand reached for the tea set in the centre of the table. Chris saw the discontent he tried to hide in the curve of his lips, the set of his eyebrows, and the tension in his jaw. "She mirrored me," he grumbled. "She said she had a family emergency and had to leave work immediately. I thought nothing of it, not until what I learned happened today. And until..." He dropped a sugar cube into his tea. "Tell your brother what you told me, Rosemary."

The girl turned her bright blue eyes onto Chris. "Someone mirrored for her. The gnome liked him. He said he wanted to set him free."

A reformist. Chris tried to recall what the doctor had said. "I think her brother is an associate of the doctor," he told Fernand, and, when Fernand's cloudy expression didn't dissipate, continued. "Fernand, please. I'm not going to dismiss someone for their politics."

"After what happened today, it's hardly just politics," Fernand muttered, sipping his tea.

"We still don't know *what* happened today," Chris insisted. "All I know right now is that Miss Albany has done her best for Rosemary."

Rosemary seized his arm, tugging his wrist towards the table. He trailed after her as she pulled him along to the empty chair across from her own, with their mother's tea set between them. "Is it true, Chris?" she demanded. "Did they really arrest that Livingstone bastard for the Floating Castle?"

"Language," Chris warned. She murmured an apology and he pinched the bridge of his nose. She sounded much too excited about all of this, like it was a thrilling event and not...whatever it was.

"*Is* it true?" Fernand asked. "I've had that mirror going off all day, reporter after reporter trying to hear the little wizard's commentary on the big event."

"He wouldn't let me talk to any of them, Chris," Rosemary pouted, leaning against his shoulder.

"Good," Chris said, and held up a hand to forestall her protests. He pointed to the chair across from him, and she skulked back over. He was very aware of first Fernand, and then Rosemary watching him intently as he took his time pouring hot water into his cup. The salamander in the glass at the base of the teapot slowly blinked at him, and he avoided locking gazes with it.

He would have waited until his tea was fully prepared before saying anything, but he felt the tension about to explode. "I don't know what exactly you've heard." He reached for a bag of leaves. Fernand picked one up and handed it to him, and Chris smiled at him thankfully. "But, yes, Francis Livingstone has been—has been arrested on suspicion of sabotaging the Floating Castle."

"Oh, wow," Rosemary breathed.

Chris dropped the bag into his cup and held it under with his spoon. Colour ran into the water, staining it orange and brown. "I was at the station when he was brought in—"

"*Really?*" Rosemary squeaked.

"—but I don't know much more, except that at this point, it's only suspicion." Even if he could tell them about the Duchess or the conspiracy or all the Old Blood money that had been poured into making this a reality, he wouldn't. To Rosemary, it would sound too exciting for something so awful. To Fernand, it would sound like the paranoid ranting of a reformist sympathizer.

Fernand caught his eye as he went to raise the tea to his lips. "I suppose that takes the offer of Cooperton off the table," he said quietly.

Chris flicked his gaze to Rosemary, who stared up at him, big eyes filled with curiosity. "I suppose," he agreed, and, hoping that would be the end of it, took a long draught of the tea to forestall any further questions.

His eyes watered and bulged. He coughed and sputtered, trying not to spit. *"Gods,"* he cried after forcing himself to swallow it. *"Gods,* that's bitter." Rosemary giggled at his distress while he peered into the cup, looking for some explanation for the acrid taste. It *looked* normal enough, though now that he was paying attention, the scent was a little spicier than he was used to…

Fernand blinked. He took another bag of leaves from the tray and sniffed at it thoughtfully. "Mine was fine," he said.

"Mine, too!" Rosemary supplied.

Chris set the cup down on the table and pushed it over to Fernand, trying to scrub the taste from his teeth with his tongue. The old man lifted the cup to his lips, took a thoughtful sip, and then peered down into the cup. He shrugged. "I don't know, young master," he said, and then sighed and reached over to set the cup back down before him. "It tastes just fine to me."

Chris eyed the teacup as though it might bite him. He didn't reach for it.

"Do you think they'll get him for it?" Fernand was asking, and Chris dragged himself back to the unpleasant matter before him. He gave his adviser a pleading look, but the old man either didn't notice or didn't care.

"I honestly don't know." He trailed his finger around the rim of his cup. "The whole thing is just…unbelievable. And…and tragic. Whether he did it or not, it's *very* tragic, actually. I wish everyone could stop treating the whole thing like a carnival. This is the anniversary of the—of the worst and most tragic disaster in Tarlish *history,* and instead of treating it with the gravity it deserves, we're all just sitting around *gossiping* about—"

He cut himself off. Too late, he heard the way his volume had risen. Fernand watched him with mild reproach while Rosemary blinked wide eyes and wrapped her hands around her teacup. Chris looked back and forth between them, searching for the best way to smooth it over, but his social instincts seemed broken or just gone.

He reached for his cup. The steam rose and be breathed deeply its spicy scent. "Honestly," he murmured, staring into his tea. His head suddenly felt very heavy. "I'd rather not talk about it. Any of it. Today has been so long and so full and I—" *I can't.* He swallowed the words and looked up. "What I *would* rather," he said with false cheer, "is to *finally* spend some time with my little sister! Especially since our Uncle Fernand is here!"

Rosemary brightened. "I've *really* missed you," she said, eyes shining.

"I suppose there are things more important than politics and scandals," Fernand allowed.

Life always goes on, Chris reminded himself. *You can lose control of yourself now, but you'll just regret it tomorrow when life keeps going on.* "I'm in the mood some for cribbage," he said, and was rewarded with a happy squeal from Rosemary. "Who wants to go and fetch the board?" He took another drink of his tea without thinking, and then blinked and smacked his mouth. "...and this is perfectly fine, actually," he said as his sister scampered away in search of the board and a deck of cards. "Quite good."

"I thought as much," Fernand said. A furrow of worry creased his brow. "If you don't mind me saying, young master...you seem a bit frazzled, today."

It was all Chris could do not to reach out and slap the old man up the side of the head. As if there was any wonder why. But he forced a smile, like he always did, and took another drink of the tea. The spice and mildness combined to swirl down to his toes and make him curl them in bliss. "I'm just going a little mad, I think," he said, and that was the truth.

He floated on a lake of consciousness, just barely above the waterline, dipping down and then up, falling and rising, unable to grip onto either state. It was dark and he was in his room and he was dreaming. Olivia sat at a table with Doctor Livingstone, saying, "Fifteen two, fifteen four, and a pair is six." The doctor looked up and said, "Ah, here she is," as Rosemary was led into the room by a man without a face, and then someone was breathing heavily, and they were doing it right by his ear.

He twisted to tap the salamander-lantern on his bedside table and he couldn't move.

Panic rose in his throat and he felt a scream bubble in from all the way down in his toes, fanning out in his stomach, filling his lungs, surging up his throat and then cresting on his tongue. A hand clamped down over his mouth and trapped it inside of him.

"You're asleep."

That made him feel better. He sighed and the faceless man led him into the room, where William Cartwright and Evelyn val Daren were still playing cards. "Buckley," Officer Cartwright said, then frowned. "I told you to call me William." The Duchess wept, her shoulders shaking.

The faceless man sat Chris down at the foot of the table, and he could feel hot breath stirring his hair. "Where is the list?" a voice growled.

His bedroom was black and still. Someone was in bed beside him and a hand was clamped over his mouth. Chris went to brush hair from his forehead where it clung with nervous sweat, but he couldn't move his hand. Was he awake? "What…" he whispered into the darkness. "What list?"

A grunt of impatience. "Your father's list. Whose names are on it?"

His eyelids fluttered closed, and he was waltzing with Rachel Albany in a grand ballroom. She wore green and it brought out the golden flecks in her eyes. Her skirts swirled around his legs and her face was soft and beautiful in the lamplight. Her eyes sparkled as she stared up at him. They moved together like they were made for one another and his hand was on the small of her back. He leaned in and murmured against her ear. "Am I awake?"

His partner pulled away from him to look into his eyes. William Cartwright hummed and sighed. "What did your father tell you about the Floating Castle?" he whispered. "Where is the list, Christopher?"

He smelled like heather and sunlight. Chris buried his nose in the young man's hair and felt his lips on his neck. "I don't know about any list."

His bed springs groaned and the floor squeaked. He heard the door of his room close. The wind blew the curtains at his window. He could see them dancing like ghosts in the corner of his eye. He couldn't move…he couldn't move…

Am I awake?

The next thing he knew, birds were singing, sunlight was streaming in, and another year post-Castle to face was laid out before him. He raised a hand to rub his eyes, remembering vivid and confusing dreams, but unable to recall much of anything.

He pulled himself up from bed. Another long day ahead of him.

CHAPTER TWENTY-THREE

Why are you here, Liv?"

Chris glanced up from his notebook just in time to see Olivia's jaw tighten. He slid his eyes to Rayner Kolston, who was holding up a copy of that morning's paper, its headline proclaiming: ASPIRING POETESS ACCUSED OF BRUTALLY MURDERING DUKE VAL DAREN, INVESTIGATIVE TRUTHSNIFFER OLIVIA FARADAY ORDERS ARREST. The little man raised his eyebrows and shook the paper. Olivia folded her arms. Chris held his breath. That question had been hovering at the tip of his tongue since the two of them had climbed out of the hackney.

"I don't know," Olivia grumbled.

"Ah." Kolston set the paper back down on his desk and spread his hands helplessly before him. "Well," he said. "Only so much I can do to help you out, then, ain't there?"

Olivia growled and turned on her heel. She paced. She wrung her hands as she did so, a gesture of restless energy rather than distress, and her trailing skirts rustled and bunched behind her as she moved. Chris could almost see her tail twitching. "I *didn't* order that arrest. My supervisor did."

"Eh, I know how these things work. You must have authorized it. Can't do it otherwise."

"I had no choice!" Olivia stopped to bark, and then immediately set off again. The old floorboards squeaked and moaned. "I had no choice," she repeated. "Maris believes it was her. It *looks* like it was her, Gods, how could it not be her? It had to be here. It wasn't her."

Kolston scanned the article. His mouth moved in time with the words he read, but Chris could tell the man was making a deliberate show of it. He'd already read the article. And why not? The headline must have caused him no small relief. He was barely a suspect, but he was a suspect. He'd sleep better with someone else under arrest.

In fact, it was beginning to seem the only person who wouldn't rest well with Vanessa Caldwell behind bars was Olivia Faraday.

When the creditor looked up from the paper again, Chris's hand itched to slap his face. His simpering expression was so obviously feigned that it was more insulting than a smug grin. "This all seems sorted as gets, to me, love," he drawled. "The girl had her poem in the *Herald*, found out her unwanted suitor was thinking he might become her unwanted husband, and the poor dearie couldn't handle it." He shrugged one shoulder. "Don't really blame her, I suppose. I'd have shivved Vik myself if I thought I'd have to swear vows to him."

Olivia paused long enough to regard him shrewdly through the black lace of her veil. "Is that a confession?" she asked.

"You wish it were."

Olivia sighed. "I do," she said, and she stopped moving. She dropped her hands to her sides. "I really do."

No one moved for a long moment. *Can we leave, now?* Chris wanted to ask. He hated this man and this office. Vanessa Caldwell was shackled into a police car on her way from Vernella as they spoke. When she arrived, Officer Dawson would be irritated if they hadn't questioned her connections. Not that Olivia showed any inclination to. When Christopher had arrived at the office, still shaking off bizarre, half-remembered nightmares, Olivia had been waiting at the curb with a taxicab, restless and innervated. Chris had let himself think she'd had some epiphany during the night and they were on their way to entrap the real culprit. He'd even let himself keep thinking that when they arrived here, right up until the moment Olivia had opened her mouth to speak and nothing had come out.

Now the creditor and the Deathsniffer regarded one another, him all amused bewilderment, her all peckish desperation. When Kolston finally sighed and went to speak, Olivia leaned toward him like a flower stretching for a ray of sunlight. It was almost heartbreaking.

"Tell me, Liv, you ever heard the story of the Faceless Rogue, faceshifting sonabitch and best conman in all Tarland?"

A small, unwilling smile crossed Olivia's angry face. "Was his real name Rayner Kolston?" she asked lightly.

The sumfinder gave a laugh. "Oh, I only just wish," he said. "You know why there are so many laws and taboos on faceshifting, lovely? Because any seeshifter brave enough to go ahead and do it is going to rob the trousers off every single person he walks past. When you can be anyone in the world, well...it's no wonder the Faceless Rogue were the best conman Tarland ever did see, until he made his great mistake."

Olivia's burgeoning smile faded. "And what mistake would that be?" she asked.

"It's a good one," Kolston said leadingly, but when her icy gaze didn't melt, he threw up his hands helplessly and sighed with dramatic exaggeration. "Short version, then, right," he said. "Well. The Faceless Rogue was a right bastard of a criminal. He'd walk into banks looking like the banker and walk out with thousands of royals in his bags. He'd go to appointments meant for members of the Assembly, learn all about their plans, and sell them to the other side. And he'd tumble all the highborn Old Blood ladies by wearing the face of their husbands and slipping right into their beds like it were nothing. He were the best at it, and he were so good, near fifty years of doing it and he never once got caught.

"Well, time comes, the Faceless Rogue wants to retire. He's getting on in years and ain't got the stamina for it anymore. But he don't want to just fade away, eh? He wants one last take that'll make him into a real legend. He starts looking about here and there for a good score, something that'll stand out, and he looks and looks and—"

"This is the short version?" Olivia asked. She tapped her foot.

Kolston threw his hands in the air. "You know how to ruin a good story, Liv, let me tell you. Fine, to the good part. He decides to go after the Prince Royal's favourite cousin. He's a famous face at court, known to be a bit of a show-off. He's always talking about his collection. Art, mostly, and worth a bloody fortune, if you fence it outside of Tarland. And why not, if you're retiring? Civilization is overrated.

"Well, he pulls off the take. Biggest and best heist of the century. He even gives the jackanape's wife a go while he's in there, because why not? He's wearing the fellow's face, and everyone knows she's a sight to see. He's managed to do the impossible, and now all he's got to do is take all the priceless junk he's gathered up and get hisself out.

"Only, the thing is, as he's getting ready to leave Tarlish biscuits for Frelsh cheese, he hears he missed one piece. The crown of the collection, a sculpture that's renowned throughout the whole world. He could have just let it go, because it was all a bit suspicious, but—"

"Oh, Godssakes, this is ridiculous," Olivia snapped, startling Chris out of the trance the creditor's voice had lulled him into. He blinked and then raised a hand to his mouth to cover his surprise at having been pulled into the story so completely. Olivia, apparently, hadn't bought in for even a second, and she *liked* the vile man. She was scoffing aloud in anger, and shaking a finger at the man behind the desk. "I can finish this one for you and I've never even heard it before. The Faceless Rogue, in his infinite stupidity, can't just accept what he's been given, because he needs more! He needs to be *satisfied*. So he goes back to the estate, only to find it was a big dumb trap and he's a big dumb idiot for falling for it, and then he loses *everything* and he deserves it for being so big and so dumb."

"Something like that."

"If he'd *only* just taken his score and gotten out while he could!" Olivia cried in mock despair. "Please. Moralizing doesn't suit you."

"No *moralizing* about it, love," Kolston said. Chris couldn't help but note how there was a dark edge to the man's voice. Whatever sort of happy fool the creditor considered himself to be, he was not one who abided being laughed at. "Like I said, I know how it works. All that matters is your accuracy record, and anyone would believe little Vanessa were the one who put the knife into Vik. Just take what you've been given and move onto your next body, eh?"

"You have no idea what it's like!" Olivia spat. "Nobody does. When something is off, when it doesn't add up, when it doesn't *feel* right, Gods, it's like an itch you can't scratch. When everything is racing towards the wrong conclusion, it's like—it's like doing a jigsaw puzzle with half the pieces from another one, and they don't fit and they *won't* fit, and everyone is cooing over how nice the puzzle is! It's awful. It's bloody *awful!*"

Kolston met her eyes for a long moment. Something passed between them. Then the creditor picked up his paper, and opened it to a page seemingly at random. He sat back in his chair and, in shocking display of rudeness, propped one booted foot up on his desk. Chris could make out flecks of dirt falling onto the papers below, but the ratty little man didn't seem to care. "Well," he said to the paper. "Truthsniffers are wrong, sometimes, too."

Olivia made a growling noise and took one step towards the man. For a moment, Chris thought she'd do more, but she stopped herself in midmotion. "Well," she said, instead, her voice tight. "Thank you for nothing, Mister Kolston."

She turned to flounce out of the office, and Chris followed her, but Kolston's voice followed after them, and Chris saw Olivia's shoulders bunch in barely deflected rage. "To be fair, lovey, that's what you came here for."

By the time they settled into the back of a fresh taxi and it jostled to a start, Olivia was like a pocket watch wound and wound and wound until every gear inside was creaking and straining and begging to be released. The staccato *clok clok clok* of the palfreys' hooves made her flinch with every iteration. Chris tried very hard not to so much as breathe, willing himself beneath her notice. The last thing he wanted was for all that energy to snap and spring back full force at *him*. He wished she'd be *calm*, that she'd see it would all work out, somehow. Against all reason, Chris believed they'd find an answer that satisfied her. Somehow, despite or perhaps because of her wild eccentricities, he had faith in her. He wished she could have the same faith in herself.

To his surprise, her mood actually did seem to change. Her icy blue eyes lost their flintiness and became thoughtful, and the wood-stiffness went out of her shoulders. As the anger left, sadness seemed to rush in, filling the void, and he stopped wishing she would ignore him and not see him there. Instead, he started wishing that, somehow, he could do something for her.

These mercurial moods of hers, the way she hopped between manic cheer, popping rage, and this sort of…emptiness…well, he couldn't imagine living that way. As the grinning, fey trickster, she was infectious or infuriating, and as the blazing firestorm of undirected umbrage, she was frightening. But as the listless, staring, blank-faced wanderer, he could never help but feel anything but sympathy, and wish for some way to pull her back to herself.

"I don't know why I went there," Olivia spoke into his ruminations. She didn't look at him. "I knew he didn't do it." She scoffed. "Look, I can tell who didn't do it. So useful."

"Maybe you were…just looking for some guidance," he said.

"It did *wonders*," she muttered. Then, however, she stole him a look, and the apology in her eyes made it clear her ire was not aimed at him. She turned in her seat, away from him. "I'm always looking for some guidance," she said. "I reach a dead end, and then..."

"I think it would drive me mad," Chris said.

"What?"

"Knowing something is wrong, and not knowing what." He reached up to run a hand through his hair, felt it fall back into its tousled waves. "I think about it, and I can't even imagine. Being able to pretend things are good...even when they're not..." He let it hang there, because there was no way to finish the thought without revealing more about himself than he felt comfortable. *It's all I have. It's the only way I get through each day.*

Olivia delicately shrugged one shoulder. It barely moved. "There are worse things," she said. "I was *born* to be a truthsniffer. My Da always said I came into the world asking questions." She blinked slowly. "I'd rather be aware of what I don't know than just not know it. There's nothing worse than ignorance. Nothing."

Maybe if Chris were a truthsniffer, he'd have been able to tell whether or not he'd just been insulted. He wasn't, though, and he couldn't. "What..." He cleared his throat and tried again. "What about Doctor Livingstone?" he asked.

She blinked, and then her brow furrowed in confusion and she turned to give him a puzzled look. "What does he have to do with anything at all?" she asked.

He should have regretted asking, but the question hadn't stopped weighing on him since he'd met eyes with the doctor in that flash of a second. Try as he might, he couldn't find any answers, but if Olivia could... "You always say 'it feels right,' " he tried to explain. She watched him like a disapproving, befuddled hawk. "Or 'it doesn't feel right.' This arrest, the doctor...how does that feel?"

"Ugh," Olivia groaned. "I don't know. Why bother? It doesn't matter what I think. The people in charge of all of this have their heads shoved so far up their damned arseholes that every single Tarl could put a pistol to their temples and beg them to cooperate, and the idiots would happily let us all slaughter ourselves."

"I just—I just didn't get the feeling the doctor was like that," Chris said, and he admitted to himself he'd been planning to accept Livingstone's offer as soon as this case had been over. Even with everything he'd have to give up, the chance to just leave it all behind had been so tempting when offered by a man he couldn't help but trust. To take Rosemary away, yes, but to *be* away...

"And why do you care what the doctor was or wasn't like?"

"I wanted to trust him," Chris murmured. He realized Olivia was watching, her nose twitching as she snuffled out the truth from his words, but for some reason, he just didn't want to stop talking. "I wanted—"

All three hells broke loose.

A deafening roar of sound erupted from somewhere off to his right, accompanied by a rush of blistering heat. At the very same moment, the carriage pitched to one side, sliding them both along the seats so they hit the far door bodily. Chris barely put his hands out in time to shield his head from knocking hard against the wall; Olivia wasn't so lucky. The sound of her head *crack*ing against the metal curtain rod was as sickening as the lurch in Chris's stomach and as terrifying as the sound of screaming outside.

"*Gods*," he gasped, tearing at the curtain. "What's *happening* out there?" Out the window, he saw spooked horses tearing off, carriages tottering behind on one wheel, and people shrieking and running as fast as they could in the opposite direction from where they were headed. Where they'd *been* headed, he realized; the carriage had stopped and it moved shakily from side to side, back and forth, as their cabbie tried to get the horses under control.

The skin on his arms felt tender from the blast of heat, and he realized, with growing panic, that the temperature was still rising.

"No," he breathed. "Oh, Gods, no."

Olivia blinked. She furrowed her brow, raising a hand to her head and wincing against the light from the window, a light that was tinged with orange and flickered across her pale skin. "What's going on?" she asked dazedly, and gasped when he reached out and seized her by the wrist.

The fingers of his other hand shook and trembled as he fumbled with the latch to the door. "We have to get out of here," he gasped out through his panic. His hand felt like it was made up of five thumbs attached to a raw steak, but he threw the latch, and then, when the door didn't open, threw it again, and again, and again, as if the result would change. His gorge rose in his throat, and, in a moment of blind, terrified panic, he threw himself bodily against the door, which shuddered, but didn't move.

A second roar of sound and blast of heat rocked the carriage from side to side. Their cabbie shouted something, their car *lurched* forward, and then the fleeing people outside the window were passing in a blur. "No, no, *no*." Chris's voice rose to a roar. "*No!* You're going the wrong way!" He pounded on the ceiling. "Dammit, you're going the wrong *way!*"

Olivia's eyes sharpened momentarily and then lost their focus again. "What's going on?" she repeated, her voice less fuzzy. The fingers of her hand curled around his wrist. "What's happening?"

The heat was growing more intense, and Chris could hear the sound of crackling flames. His heart thudded in his chest. He focused all his attention on Olivia. He *needed* her to be here with him. "We need to get out of here," he said. "Now."

Olivia's head bobbed like a wine cork in a sink. *Dammit*, Chris thought. *Dammit, come back, come back.* And then her eyes snapped as she *willed* her ringing, spinning brains into focus. She nodded at him and yanked him towards the other side of the carriage, throwing herself against the other door. The horses were pounding forward at a dead gallop, whinnying their fear even as they grew closer towards the object of it, and Chris could see the cobblestones beneath them passing as nothing but a beige blur, but anything was better than rushing closer and closer toward a heat that grew more and more intense.

Olivia pulled the latch and jostled the door, but it didn't move. She cursed quietly, yanked it, and then cursed *loudly*. She tugged and shook the door, a child's tantrum more than any actual attempt to free them. "I think..." She shook her head once more, focusing her wits. "I think the heat melted something. We need to—if we both throw all our weight at it at the same time—"

He understood and moved himself close to the door. He should let go of her hand, he thought, but he couldn't. Gods, he couldn't.

She looked at him with frightening intensity. "On three," she said. He nodded. She did, too.

"One," she said. The heat grew stronger.

"Two," she said, and her eyes were like chips of ice, the only cold things in the entire world.

"*Three*," she said, and Chris closed his eyes and *heaved* himself against the door as hard as he possibly could, feeling her move with him.

Something *snapped* and *cracked*, and Chris had to seize the splintered frame of the door in two hands when he stumbled forward and nearly fell headlong down into passing road. The carriage door hit the ground and was gone in instants as they raced past it. Orange light was everywhere and flames surrounded them. The horses were screaming madly, careening without any restraint right towards the fire. Chris's head hammered and his stomach twisted and lurched and groaned as he watched the road fly past. Suddenly, the flames didn't seem so bad, compared to splattering against the walk...

...until he remembered what was in them. What was causing them.

"We need to jump," Olivia said, apparently going through the same process as he had.

"On three?" he asked weakly.

"No time," Olivia said, and pulled him forward towards the door—

A riot of red and orange and yellow exploded right before their eyes, and mortar and brick flew towards them. Olivia yelped and hit the floor of the carriage in an instant, her truthsniffing giving her some prescience. Chris was not so lucky. The last thing he saw was the cracked piece of rubble speeding towards him, and then everything went black.

For a moment, he was spinning down a hole with no bottom, limbs flailing in the wind. He couldn't move, all the wind was knocked out of him, he was paralyzed, there was someone whispering at his ear *where is the list* and he was falling and falling and falling and—

He hit the far wall of the carriage, slumping onto the seat. Wetness ran down his face and into his eyes. He saw the entire world through a filter of broken glass. His stomach roiled and the stench of burning filled his nostrils. Burning rubber, burning fabric, burning meat. He was still moving. The carriage was moving. Not forward. The carriage was blowing backwards, it was *falling*—

Everything crashed to a halt. Olivia's body pitched against his hard enough to make him cough and sputter for breath. He lay against the wall of the carriage, looking up, looking *up* at the exit, the exit was *up*? And the door was a ring of fire leading to an amber sky, and smoke was drifting up like a chimney.

Oh.

Oh, the carriage was on fire.

Well. That made sense.

Olivia was slapping his face. "*Christopher!*" she screamed at him. He focused on her. Her features were blackened and her hands were touching his brow and temples, coming away covered in blood. He stared with horrified fascination at the red all over her fingers. Was that *his* blood? It was so red. She grabbed his cheeks in her bloody hands, her hands and his blood. "*Christopher!*" she repeated. "*Wake! Up!*"

Gods, he realized with a start, and panic coursed through him like water down a trench, the carriage was on *fire*.

She must had seen clarity strike him because she patted his cheek once, a pat that was more a slap. "Good," she said. "Good, stay with me." Their roles had shifted now. Her daze from before was completely gone, and now his head was bleeding. "We need to push the ceiling," she said. She spoke so quickly he could barely make out her words, climbing up to a crouch. "We need to unbalance the carriage and push it back on its side."

"No," he said, and coughed from somewhere deeper than he knew he had. The air was so hot and thick and it tasted like wood. His throat burned. "The floor weighs more. The seats. We should push—"

"*Do what I bloody tell you to!*" Olivia screeched into his face, and *that* moved him to obedience. He copied her stance, leaning his weight against the ceiling. "Rock it," she said, doing so, and he echoed her. "Yes," she said. "With me," she said. They rocked and the carriage rocked and Chris swallowed his coughs and held his breath. Tears streamed down his face and mingled with the blood. His eyes felt like they were going to pop, and they stung with grit. "Harder. With *me*." The carriage rocked more and more, and Chris could smell something like burned hair. He hoped it wasn't his. Gods, how was he going to look without his hair? "*Push.*"

The carriage screeched, the metal frame protesting their movements, and then it fell forward. They both crashed against the ceiling—the floor—and lay there panting, sucking in big breaths of poisonous smoke for just one moment before Olivia was seizing his wrist and pulling him towards the gaping hole of the open, burning doorway, out into the world.

They emerged from their tiny hell into a hell much greater. Everything was seen cracked and doubled, and with a curse, Chris reached up and pulled his shattered eyeglasses off his face, throwing them to one side. Useless. Flames were in all directions, and the gutted front of a building was before them. The horses looked like spitted pigs, and when Chris saw the body of the driver, his stomach lurched and he only kept it by reminding himself that any time he spent vomiting would not be spent breathing. He sucked in air, inhaling dust from the scorched ground he hovered over, and the heat was still intense enough to burn his mouth and throat and lungs, but there was no more smoke. That billowed up into the air, making a beacon to announce the inferno all around them to all of Darrington.

They couldn't stop, he realized, sucking in air and trying to steady his mind enough to lock onto one complete thought. The fire would spread and they were in the heart of the storm. He reached for Olivia and found her reaching back to him. "Stay low," she said, her voice hoarse. "The smoke will rise. Stay low."

They pulled one another along, stumbling over rubble and debris and soft, smoking, sweet-smelling humps that Chris refused to let himself think very hard about. He thought to look behind him, and when he squinted hard, he saw their carriage in the midst of the furnace. A chunk of debris almost as big as it leaned to one side, scorched and blackened, and Chris realized it had been pressing against the floor when he'd been telling Olivia it would be easier to turn the carriage that way.

How did she know?

He would ask her later.

The heat lessened and the smoke cleared as they made their way back toward a world that smelled of things other than burning, a place where there were colours aside from red and black and orange. Chris heard the sound of voices screaming and crying close at hand. There were other people left, people who weren't them or dead. His head pounded and his vision doubled and danced, but his heart yearned towards those voices, and allowed himself to think maybe, just maybe, they could get back to the world of the living...

Something creaked, and then, in a rush of air and heat, *crashed.* Pebbles went up, scoring the back of his legs as if thrown with a slingshot. Olivia shrieked in pain. His hand, which had been pulling her along behind him, suddenly came up empty as her fingers released their grip on his. He stumbled forward and hit the ground, and for a moment he simply stared without comprehending while Olivia sobbed a desperate, angry, defiant plea.

He stumbled onto his back, braced himself up with his elbows, and his heart twisted and dropped into his toes at what he saw.

Olivia's leg pinned beneath the fallen rubble was bad enough. Tears cascaded down her face as she screamed curses at the Three and Three. But that wasn't what turned his bowels to water.

A pulsing, glowing worm twisted and coiled around itself as it undulated lazily towards them in a haze of distorted phantom moisture. Its scales were jewelled in all the colours of the rainbow, but the crevices between them all pulsed a ruddy, baleful orange. It drifted over to them, slow but purposeful, and the temperature grew hotter and hotter the closer it came. The ground beneath it burned black in its passage.

It was nearly sated. It had wrecked its vengeance and it was full and sluggish and ready to return to the elemental plane, satisfied with its justice. But it had seen them, and thought it might have time for a little more fun, one last bit of vindication.

Olivia twisted about to look at him. "Are you a sodding *idiot?*" she screamed. "Get away!"

He scrabbled backwards like a crab, barely wincing as a sharp piece of rubble sliced down the palm of his hand. She was right. He should stand up and run as fast as he could, get safe. He would be able to outrun the sluggish salamander where she never could, pinned as she was. She was right.

He didn't move.

The salamander rose high into the air and hovered above Olivia. It took its time spinning around itself, lazily spiralling and twisting its way down. Pulsing orange-red light glowed from deep beneath its scales, stoking its own fire as it rubbed against itself. A darting forked tongue taunted her, and Chris watched his employer close her eyes tightly and howl in thwarted terror.

No! He gritted his teeth. *Leave her alone!*

He *projected* his rage, his *will* out at the rogue elemental. He flung the mental command with every bit of strength he had, feeling like a single man trying to hold back a deluge with only his outstretched arms. This was madness. He should be running. Spirits could be bound only by arcane song, and Chris didn't speak that language.

He wouldn't leave her.

Don't touch her!

And the salamander halted.

Its small, glowing red eyes broke away from Olivia and focused on him. They regarded him in confusion, puzzlement. His heart skipped a beat, his stomach fluttered oddly, and the man and elemental stared at each other, both watching to see what the other would do. Chris fumbled with his own mind, dazed and confused but unwilling to break whatever spell he had somehow cast. *Go away,* he commanded the serpent, but it only cocked its head slightly and narrowed its eyes at him. Its tongue flicked out at him, and orange light kindled deep beneath its scales. Heat blossomed like the seeking tendrils of a plant. Olivia cried out in pain.

No.

GO! AWAY! Chris *slammed* his entire self into the creature. It shuddered wildly and all the ruddy light went out at once. The chaotic life in its eyes fled, the tension left its sinuous body, and it fell, limp, vanishing in a puff of smoke and a roar like a spark finding tinder.

He shoved all his confusions and questions and amazement aside. What he'd just done had questioned every principle set down by Richard Lowry hundreds of years ago, but later, later. He crawled to Olivia, seizing the chunk of stone and mortar in both hands and attempting to push it off of her.

"Gods," Olivia said, and her voice was so hoarse it sounded like a whisper. "What…what just…I thought…"

He couldn't move the debris. He growled in frustration, braced himself, put *all* his strength behind it, every tiny last reserve he could muster. It didn't budge.

He laid his forehead against the stone, heaving deep breaths. The surface of it was warm to the touch, and when he raised his head, he saw with a sinking feeling in his gut the sheer devastation spreading around them. Three salamanders, if he'd counted the blasts right, and he'd only dismissed one. He skimmed that thought. Later. The other two were still torching and wreaking havoc at their leisure, and the fires were spreading. Already, the whole block was a conflagration, a riotous devouring inferno that swallowed everything in its path.

"We need to move this thing," Chris said, trying to sound calm. He blinked and raised his head to meet Olivia's eyes. "Olivia, we need to move this."

"I thought I was dead," she whispered. She shook herself and focused on the rock pinning her leg. It was smeared with blood from his head, and she seemed to remember all at once the pain it must be causing her. "That's bloody heavy," she said with a whimper. "Oh, fuck me, that's bloody huge."

"I can't move it," he said. "I'm not strong enough."

"Serves me right." She threw her head back and winced. Tears shone on her cheeks. "Hiring a handsome assistant instead of a tough one. You're bloody useless, Mister Buckley."

"You can call me Christopher," he said without thinking, and then flushed when she smiled through her tears. "For the moment," he amended. "If you bloody well help me move this damned thing so we can get out of here. Now."

She gritted her teeth as she placed her hands on the edge of the stone. He did the same on the other side. "Now…*heave*," he said, and they grunted simultaneously.

The rock shifted and Olivia's grunt became a howl of pain. "Olivia!" Chris cried, but as he pulled his attention from the stone to her, terror clutching at his chest, he caught a flash of movement out of the corner of his eye...

...and heard a familiar voice raised in song.

No, that was impossible. What would she be doing here? *How* would she be here? It wasn't *possible*. But he would know the voice anywhere, absolutely anywhere, and as he saw her walk into sight, calm as she was while striding through the wooded paths of White Clover Farms, his mouth went slack and his lips mouthed, *Rosemary*.

He'd never heard a song so complex or multilayered before. He heard her sing as if she were three different girls singing three different songs, but there was only one girl and somehow, only one song. An azure-skinned undine flew over their heads, and rain poured down in her passage, a deluge fanning out and spreading. A crystal dancer, a tiny fiaran, darted around Rosemary's head, frosting her glossy black ringlets with dainty little ice crystals, and sweet, blessedly cool air emanated forth from her, pouring forward like a wave.

One layer of the song commanded the undine. It was soaring and domineering and powerful. Another controlled the fiaran, and that song was musical and light and suggestive. The third and final layer, well, that was a searching song. It curled in through the burned out shells of buildings, snaked through the wisps of smoke left behind by the fires the undine's magical amphora quenched. It sought the rogue salamanders, exploring relentlessly. It was a binding song, the oldest and most common phrase in that arcane language.

Chris slumped against Olivia, unable to believe his eyes *or* his ears. It was his head injury, surely. He was hallucinating, seeing what he wanted to see, hearing what he wanted to hear. But when Rosemary walked past them, close enough to touch, she looked down and smiled, and her eyes twinkled, and Chris knew beyond any shadow of a doubt that this was really his sister, and somehow, she really had come to save him.

CHAPTER TWENTY-FOUR

The next thing he knew, he was blinking his eyes open to a sterile white room. There was a fat woman hovering over him with a caring face, and she was saying just loudly enough to disrupt from sleep, "Mister Buckley, you need to wake up, now."

Every muscle in his body tensed as he took in the three linked circles on the woman's white uniform above her heart and smelled the aggressively clean hospital scent. He sat up quickly—too quickly. The room spun wildly and his stomach lurched. Blight lights exploded before his eyes and the lifeknitter was taking him by the shoulder and forcing him back down onto the pillow. She was surprisingly strong for such a fleshy lady. "There, there," she said. "You can move about if you like, but do try to avoid sudden movements, dear, or we'll be pouring you back into bed."

"Rosemary," he said, and then, remembering what had happened more clearly, "Olivia."

"What day is it, dear?"

"What…"

"I need you tell me what day it is, please, dear."

He pulled his brows together and stared at her. Just what was she on about? "…Eadday," he answered.

She nodded and made a note on the board she had tucked under one arm. "And what is your given and family name and categorization?"

He shook his head in bewilderment. "Christopher Buckley. Wordweaver," he responded dutifully, and then, "What are you doing?"

She smiled at him. Despite her homely face and three chins, she had a radiant smile. "Don't worry, dear, you did just fine."

A familiar voice piped up from beyond Chris's field of vision. "You hit your head hard enough that your brains got rattled, Christopher." Olivia's tone was both sour and playful. "She's just being sure they all went back where they belonged, isn't that right?"

Her voice didn't sound like she was in terrible distress, but Chris still fought to slowly bring himself up to a sitting position and look about the room. Everything stayed still, this time, both outside of him and within. The lifeknitter gave him an encouraging smile.

Without his glasses, edges were blurry and undefined, but he could make out enough to see by. The room was white. They always were. He hated hospitals. There was a window, the light from which seemed too bright, and contained two beds. He lay in one, but the other, to his surprise, was unoccupied. Instead, Olivia sat in the chair beside it. Her leg was wrapped and wrapped and wrapped again in white bandaging, and a pair of wooden crutches was propped up against the wall beside her.

"Gods," he said, leaning back against the pillows again in relief. "You're all right."

There was a moment of silence during which the lifeknitter fluffed up the pillows behind his head so he could see Olivia better. When the fat woman moved out of the way and bustled for the door, there was a softness on Olivia's face of a sort he'd never seen before. "Somehow," she agreed.

He shook his head in disbelief. Had it all been real? The explosions, the debris, the fire, the salamander. He recalled in a blinding flash of memory how he had...*commanded* that elemental, and then shelved it. There still wasn't time to consider all the...the hundreds of dizzying implications that might have. Instead he sifted through all of it with surprising alacrity considering how "rattled" his brains had gotten, and honed his focus in on the last thing he remembered before it all went fuzzy, and then dark.

"Rosemary was there. She saved us..." he said, still not quite able to believe it.

Olivia rearranged herself in her chair. Her face tightened in a wince, one she tried valiantly to hide. "She's a beautiful girl," she said with lightness in her tone even Chris could tell was feigned. "She doesn't look a thing like you, aside from the eyes."

"Why was she *there*?" Try as he may, he couldn't wrap his mind around it. How had she known he was in trouble? *He* hadn't even known where he'd be, so how could she? And while he couldn't possibly say how long they'd been trapped in that hellish inferno, it couldn't have been *that* long...could it?

Whatever Olivia might have been about to say, Chris would never know. There was a flurry of activity near the entrance of the room, and moments later, Rachel Albany rushed in.

Chris couldn't have been more shocked at her appearance. His governess's plain grey dress was splattered with mud and her cheeks were heavily flushed. Her hair was only half held back by its usual prim bun, and the rest fluttered around her head in wild wisps. With his vision so blurred and the colours all running together, it made it appear she had a nimbus floating about her head, an angel's halo. Before he could really process her presence, she locked eyes with him and rushed to his side, dropping onto her knees beside his bed.

"*Christoph*—" The flush in her cheeks deepened even further as she visibly corrected herself. "Mister Buckley," she tried again, reaching out to grip one of his hands in both of hers. "Mother Deorwynn, thank all the Gods you're all right. When I heard—when I heard you and your employer had been on that block, I—" She cut herself off there, clearly overcome with emotion. Her big brown eyes scanned his face, and she released his hand to reach out and lightly brush her fingers across the puckered skin at his hairline. "Gods, this looks as if it hurts."

Chris found his own cheeks reddening at the gentleness of her touch. Awkwardly, he turned his face away from her, only to catch Olivia eyeing him with one eyebrow in her hairline. "Friend of yours, *Christopher?*" she asked mildly.

He regretted giving her permission to make use of his given name. "My governess," he said through clenched teeth, and sharpened his look into a glare when Olivia's second eyebrow climbed to meet the first. He pulled away from Miss Albany's prodding hands. "I'm quite fine, Miss Albany," he muttered. "There *really* isn't any need for such a display."

Her hands stilled, and then dropped to her side. "I…" Miss Albany said, and then cleared her throat. When she spoke again, her voice was as controlled and poised as ever. "I was very concerned, Mister Buckley, very concerned. All they told me on the mirror was that you were here, after having been on the block. Ever since that awful man arrived and took Rosemary with him, I—"

Chris snapped his gaze to his governess's. He narrowed his eyes. "What?"

One of Miss Albany's hands flew up to her throat. Her eyes widened. "You…you don't know?"

"*What* man?" he demanded.

"Avery Combs," she spat. "He appeared at the estate with five other men and took Rosemary. I *tried* to stop them, but I swear, it was as if…every single muscle in my body was *paralyzed*, Mister Buckley. I couldn't move an inch. When I called out after them, it was like they didn't hear a word I said. They said something about a tip that *'those reformists'* were going to sabotage some bindings, and then they were just gone."

His heart thumped in his head and his knuckles whitened where his fingers grabbed the bed sheets. "Where are they now?" he gritted out.

"*Here,*" she said. "In the front hall. They—"

Chris was out of bed before she could finish his sentence. The room spun sickeningly and colours blinked across his vision, but he grabbed the wall to steady himself and didn't stop to so much as catch his breath. He saw his clothes folded in a pile by his bedside, realized he wore nothing but a bed gown, but the thought of taking the time to dress seemed absurd. "Christopher!" Olivia called after him, and he heard Miss Albany hot on his heels. They were both in a different world.

He blocked out the starched white sheets, the bleached white walls, the lifeknitters in their white uniforms and three linked circles who watched him pass by. All hospitals were easy enough to navigate, and with his mind completely focused on getting to his sister as quickly as he could, it wasn't long at before he was in the foyer, which was locked in utter bedlam.

Miss Albany stopped beside him while his eyes scanned the room, trying to pierce the confusion to find what he was looking for. "I couldn't even get through to see her," Miss Albany spoke breathlessly. "Combs's men pushed me aside when I tried to get close. She should be—" She pointed, but Chris had already spotted the collection of bodies surrounding an unseen figure by the front window, and his heart sank even as he started moving.

Flashbulbs were going off and the entire area was bathed in flickering alp-light. Reporters shouted questions, all trying to be heard over one another, their assistants standing around weaving furiously onto their notebooks. Chris could barely hear his sister's high little voice, but he *could* see Avery Combs and the strong men who surrounded him, all with their thick arms crossing their barrel chests. The thought of those men manhandling Rosemary out the door of her home made his fists clench and his jaw tighten, and he pushed past the scurrying people who filled the room as if they were made of paper and twine. Silence seemed to fall behind him as the gathered people saw his face, and he began shouldering through the clump of reporters and photographers with only one thought in his mind.

Strong arms seized his elbows and grabbed him back, lifting him up. He growled and kicked out, twisting his head to one side. Flashing lights blinded his vision and a wave of sickening dizziness threatened to make him spew his breakfast onto the backs of the reporters in front of him. One of his flailing feet connected with and shoved a photographer hard. The man lost his grip on his camera, which shot forward and, despite his grasping hands and cry of alarm, hit the floor. The flashbulb shattered in a blinding burst of light. A spiral of black motes danced and swirled in the afterimage.

A collective gasp went up from the reporters, but before the alp could even fully materialize, Rosemary's sweet voice rose in song.

The press cleared a path between Chris and his sister. He watched her raise her hands and close her eyes, her face locked in that euphoria he only ever truly saw when she was binding. Before all the gathered press of Darrington, her perfectly pitched notes guided the half-formed outline of the alp, gently suggesting it might find better and more satisfying times on its own plane. Its image wavered only slightly—to which Rosemary raised her song's pitch just a single note—before collapsing in onto itself, vanishing in a tiny black pinprick and a flash of light that made many of the gathered members of the press to raise hands to shield their eyes.

After a moment of reverent silence, during which Rosemary's face was frozen in serene peace, the press *exploded* once again, even louder than before.

"Mother Deorwynn!"

"Miss Buckley, is it true your father taught you to—"

"—the history of your family and your impressive bloodline surely—"

"—six *Gods*, like it was *nothing*."

"When did you first 'bind? Was it always so *easy?*"

"After what she'd already—"

"*Enough!*" Chris roared, giving a sharp twist in the grip of the man who held him immobile. His voice simply seemed to drop into the cacophony of noise all around them, with only the closest members of the press noticing—and them turning only to give him a sharp and disapproving look. The man who held him tightened his grip and went to turn him away and propel him elsewhere…but then Rosemary's eyes opened and locked right onto his.

"Chris!" she said with relief and love plain in her voice, her first words since dismissing the alp. She pushed aside the closest reporter and rushed down the closing gap that had opened between them, throwing her arms around him and the man who held him, both. She buried her face in his stomach, rubbing herself against the fabric of his bed gown. "Oh, Chris, you're okay…"

Finally, the reporters quieted. The man holding Chris's arms slowly, reluctantly set him down on his own two feet, and then disentangled himself from Rosemary's embrace to step away. The only sound was the murmuring of questions from those not close enough to see, and the *pop pop pop* of flashbulbs as photographers from every paper in Darrington took front-page shots of Christopher Buckley in his nightshirt.

It wasn't exactly the social debut he'd always dreamed of, but at the moment, he couldn't bring himself to care.

"Rosemary," he murmured, leaning down to bury his face in her raven-black curls.

"I didn't know you'd be there," she said quietly. "When I saw you and Miss Faraday, I almost tripped up the song. They said you just hit your head and you'd be all right, but I was still worried. The lifeknitter said she could see a bruise on your brains." She raised her blue eyes to meet his, and scanned his features. She made a face, standing on her tiptoes and reaching up to touch the puckered place at his hairline. "I think you're going to have an ugly scar, big brother," she said, and though her voice had its familiar teasing tone, he could see how dull her eyes were, and the pinch between her brows. She'd drained herself again. "Your poor pretty face."

He smiled and chuckled quietly. "At least it'll be hidden in my hair," he said lightly.

She giggled and snuggled her cheek against him. "I'm so happy you're okay," she whispered, and he squeezed her tight.

Then he raised his head to the gathered reporters and photographers with their shuffling feet, muttered questions, and flashing cameras. He hardened his features, feeling his embrace go from warm to protective. Some of them exchanged glances, but they were as stubborn as the press ever were and needed to hear it for themselves. "My sister is thirteen years old," he said sharply. "A girl has a right to privacy."

Still, they didn't move. A few shuffled, glanced towards the door, the other occupants of the room. But not one of them took a step. Every camera still pointed their way, and there was a question hovering on every reporter's lips. Anger bubbled up in him as he wished he could somehow punch every single one of them in the gut. "Fine," he snarled. "Enjoy your story."

Seizing Rosemary's wrist in his hand and ignoring her cry of protest, he turned and pushed aside the big man who'd grabbed him, shouldering through the gathered crowd until he stood before Avery Combs. The man smiled down at him with all that easy, deceitful charisma. Chris couldn't tell the lights caused by the bruise on his brains from those caused by the popping of flashbulbs. He was dimly aware of Miss Albany coming up to stand at his side. "You had no right," he spat up at Combs.

Combs spread his hands innocently before him. He gave a disarming smile. "Mister Buckley," he said, "I know you must be very upset over what you've heard, but let me try and explain just what—"

"I'm contacting the police," Chris said firmly, tugging Rosemary and turning to leave the room.

"Chris!" Rosemary gasped.

"Ah—" Combs said, and Chris had a moment's satisfaction at the slightest hint of panic in the man's voice. But before he got more than a few steps, Combs had hurried ahead of him and stood to block his path. "*Mister* Buckley," he said again, and raised his hands once more, this time, in a gesture of warding. *Wait,* they said, *listen,* and despite his lack of will to do either, Chris pulled his sister close by his side, felt Miss Albany at his other, and narrowed his eyes, staring up at the tall, dark and handsome kidnapper.

He waited and listened.

"It was an emergency, Mister Buckley, and we didn't have long to try and find a binder available. I don't even think there is another one strong enough to handle the disaster we were warned the reformists would create. We knocked. We asked. Your sister agreed to come with us, and your governess said nothing at all in protest."

"*Liar,*" said Miss Albany, and, "It's *true!*" said Rosemary, and "What did you do to her?" said Chris, all at once.

Combs looked back and forth between the three of them, eyes narrowing. "What are you talking about?" he asked. The reporters behind them were a beehive of hushed whispers and exclamations.

Chris saw Miss Albany step forward and lift her chin out of the corner of his eye. "I couldn't move," she said with quiet ferocity in her voice. "Every muscle was paralyzed and I could only sit and watch from the parlour while you all took Miss Buckley out of my hands. What did you do to me, Combs?"

Combs shook his head slightly, and then he chuckled. Quietly at first, and then louder and louder until he was laughing quite loudly. "Fantastic!" he crowed. "Bloody *fantastic.* That's how you'll play this, then? Rich, I must say. I wondered why you just let us walk out with her."

"I couldn't move!" she repeated. "You—"

"I thought I recognized you," Combs continued, his booming, well-projected voice trampling over Miss Albany's as though she had merely whispered. "Your face seemed so familiar from somewhere. I know who you are, now. *Rachel*, yes, Rachel *Albany*. How convenient for the reformists that you somehow ended up as Miss Buckley's caretaker." He peered at her plain face, shaking his head. "How did you *know* about her?" He turned back to the reporters and called to them leisurely. "This woman is a reformist agent. She's responsible for the tragedy on Grapevine Street, today."

"My brother's politics have nothing to do with me. I am not a reformist," Miss Albany snapped. A flashbulb went off, and then another, and another.

"Indeed, you're very well known for never doing anything Garrett says," Combs purred, quietly enough that the press wouldn't have heard.

Chris's eyes darted over to Miss Albany's face. The governess's face was flushed with both shame and anger, her eyes flashing, but not meeting Combs's.

Rosemary tugged, murmuring, "*Chris*, you're *hurting* me."

He shot her an apologetic look and loosened his grip, but only slightly. He was terrified that if he let her go, the chaos on all sides might lean in close, swoop down, and carry her away.

When Combs spoke again, his voice was louder and had that courtly, polished quality Chris had seen when the man had first come to his estate to steal Rosemary away. "Did we drug you, Miss Albany?" he asked. "Is that what you claim? Well—" He spread his arms wide and indicated the room in which they stood, all the people gathered there, who had gone very quiet. "We're in a hospital. There are lifeknitters everywhere. Surely one could peer into your blood and see if there's anything unfortunate coursing through your veins. Then when your employer is good to his word and takes me to the police, he'll actually have some evidence instead of some ludicrous claims."

"You *bastard*. I know very well you wouldn't have given me anything that could be so easily detected!" Miss Albany was quivering with rage. Chris couldn't help but take a step closer to her side, pulling his sister along with them.

He instantly regretted it when he saw the way Combs's eyes flickered between them. "Oh," the man whispered, a small, ugly smile curling onto his lips. "Is that how it is, then? If *that* was what Livingstone had in mind, you'd think he'd have sent a prettier spy."

Rachel Albany spat in his face.

Spittle struck the handsome young traditionalist on the cheek and began oozing down towards the ugly curve of his lips. "Doctor Livingston would *never* have done what you're all accusing him of!" Miss Albany snarled, and the press *exploded* into a flurry of questions and exclamations and flashing and *pop pop pop pop*.

Chris seized Miss Albany's wrist in his other hand and then turned away from the chaos, yanking both women behind him. Miss Albany gasped in shock, and Rosemary protested with a squealed, "*Chris*, stop it!"

"Mister Buckley!" Combs called after them, louder than the press, his voice a perfectly composed facade of concern and confusion. "Mister Buckley, your own life was saved by the fact that we *did* bring your sister to Grapevine Street! Many more deaths and much more destruction were prevented! We are at a critical time in our history as a nation! Surely your sister's *privacy* is not nearly so important as the lives, the *futures* she could be saving!" Rosemary struggled to break away from his grip, loudly trying to agree with everything Combs was saying, but Chris ignored her and pulled her on.

He reached the exit at the same time as Olivia Faraday.

She stared at him, leaning heavily on her crutches. She glanced at the two women he held gripped in either hand, peered over his shoulder at the shouting press, popping flashes, and scheming traditionalist. "Problem, Christopher?" she asked.

So many, he went to reply, but then, of course, another surfaced.

A new burst of activity behind him caught Olivia's attention. Her eyes flickered away from his, and then widened. Readjusting her grip on her crutches, she shouldered her way between Miss Albany and him, breaking his grip on her wrist, and headed out into the foyer. "Wh—" Chris asked, turning about to watch her pass, but at the same time, she cried, "*Maris?*" and he saw a group of frantic lifeknitters and grim-faced police officers rushing through the foyer with a stretcher held between them, a stretcher covered in stained red sheets and holding a quivering and twitching body.

He pulled Rosemary back out of their way by instinct. Miss Albany followed. Olivia fell into hobbling step beside Officer Maris Dawson, whose orange curls bobbed up and down as she marched with purpose. "What happened?" Olivia demanded.

"One of the servants found her in the gardens and mirrored us," Officer Dawson replied briskly.

"Has she *said* anything?"

"Not a damn word. She's in shock."

Olivia locked eyes with Chris. For a moment, her gaze was sympathetic, but then that soft emotion dived beneath the surface, and his employer motioned with her head, indicating he should come with her.

No, no, why now? Why bloody now? He knew, he just knew, who was on that stretcher, but when it passed before him and into the stark white halls of the hospital, and he saw Duchess Evelyn val Daren's white face and staring eyes, he still had to lean against something lest he fall to the ground.

"Chris," Rosemary said, her voice suddenly trembling in fear. "Chris, that lady, she…she was…"

That something he leaned on was Rachel Albany. She supported his weight for only a moment before pushing him in the direction the stretcher had gone. "You have to," she said. "It's your job."

CHAPTER TWENTY-FIVE

She was right.

Dammit, she was right.

Chris turned to her and grasped her shoulders in his hands. He looked into her eyes and decided, once again, to trust her. "Go home," he commanded, and she nodded. "Mirror Fernand. Tell him to come and stay with you. Tell him to—that—tell him everything that happened, tell him Rosemary needs to be *protected*." She continued nodding, and when he pushed her a step back and released Rosemary's hand, she instantly took his sister into her care and turned to lead her towards the door.

"Come along, Miss Rosemary," she said, her voice steady and professional. Flashbulbs continued to pop, but Miss Albany walked as though she didn't notice them.

Rosemary turned back to meet Chris's eyes, her own filled with fear. "Chris," she said. "Is that lady going to be okay? Is she…"

He gave her an encouraging smile. "We're going to do everything we can," he called. "Now, go with Miss Albany and do what she says. *Don't* go anywhere with anyone, please. Trust me."

Rosemary bit her lip and nodded, turning away from him to follow after her governess. Chris watched them go until they vanished out the door and into the city, and then he had to put his faith in Rachel Albany and leave it to her. He turned and hurried down the hall at a near-run, after the clump of lifeknitters, police officers, and Olivia Faraday.

Olivia was stumbling along with her crutches and dragging her crushed leg, *somehow* still managing to position herself by the Duchess's gasping face. "*Duchess*," she said, her voice a sharp, heartless command. "Listen to me. *Focus on me.* Who did this to you? You need to tell me!" The Duchess said nothing in response, only blinked and sputtered up at the Deathsniffer. Chris couldn't see how she was hurt, only that there was blood everywhere, and a distinct too-sweet smell like cooked meat. He'd smelled enough of that today.

When Olivia reached out a hand to try and grab the Duchess's shoulder, she tripped over her crutches and pitched forward. She was stopped from hitting the ground only by the quick reaction of one of the lifeknitters, who hauled her to her feet and immediately pushed her harshly backwards. Anyone but Olivia would have fallen and been left behind. "We're trying to *save* this woman," the lifeknitter snapped, and hurried on after the stretcher and his peers while Olivia made a frustrated hissing noise and fell back beside Officer Dawson and Chris.

"What happened?" Olivia asked again, never so much as taking her eyes from the red bath of the Duchess's stretcher. She swung her crutches like she'd been born with three legs instead of two.

"I don't know anything you don't," Officer Dawson replied sharply, her own eyes locked on the Duchess's shivering body just as Olivia's were.

"Bollocks. Where was she found? How is she injured?"

"Shot in the shoulder," Officer Dawson ground out. "Standard issue firepistol from what I could tell, but they wouldn't let *me* close, either. Lacerations, too. Deep ones, all over her. It might have been a windpistol, but I doubt it. Not a knife, though. Too many cuts too quickly for a knife. They found her in her gardens at the estate. Flew her into town by the val Daren winged carriage. And *that's* everything I know."

"Caldwell?"

Officer Dawson hissed in frustration. "Just reached the station before I responded to *this* bullshit," she spat. "Five good coppers swearing on their stripes she was shacked to the seats in the back of a police car when this happened."

"I knew it," Olivia muttered, and then seemed to notice Chris. She shot him a hard glare. "Why aren't you writing anything down? Where's your notebook?" she snapped.

He gaped at her. "In the back of a *burnt out taxi?*" he responded incredulously.

She blinked and looked quickly away, but not before he actually saw something like shame bloom deep in her eyes. She focused her attention back on the stretcher and Chris *heard* her teeth grind and her jaw creak as she saw all the answers she might ever find leaking out with the Duchess's lifeblood. "*Shit,*" she cursed loudly, and then they all turned into a room.

The lifeknitters expertly moved the Duchess from the stretcher she was carried in on onto a white bed. Those fresh sheets soaked through with blood in an instant. Olivia moved up to her side again, and none of the lifeknitters protested her presence, but flowed around her like a river around a stone.

"*Duchess,*" Olivia said, reaching out to grip Duchess val Daren's closest shoulder in her hand. "*Duchess,* I need you to look at me."

The lifeknitter on the opposite side reached out to hover a hand over the Duchess's heart, closing her eyes and swaying slightly on her feet. "We need to stop the bleeding," she said quickly. "Her heartbeat is too fast. She can't take it."

"*Who* did this to you, Duchess? You need to tell me, you need to *tell* me so I can *fix* it."

A second lifeknitter joined the first. He turned up the Duchess's hand, laid two fingers against her wrist. His eyes half-lidded and the eyes beneath seemed to be staring at something only he could see. "I'm in the bloodstream," he said. "It's…it's too thin, we…there's too much blood gone and it's still…"

One more lifeknitter was there with a needle and thread held between her thumb and forefinger with the touch of an expert, but she wasn't closing any of the cuts, merely staring at the Duchess's body in confused, overwhelmed horror. "There's too *many*," she cried. "I can't—I don't even know where to—"

"*Who did this to you?*" Olivia *shook* the Duchess. The woman's head lolled from side to side and her mouth opened and closed like a fish drowning on a dock. "Just say a name. Just a fucking *name* and it'll be *over.*"

Yet another figure in white with three linked circles over their heart pulled down the sheet covering the Duchess's chest. Chris's eyes widened in horror. The burn covered her entire left shoulder; the hole punched directly through her upper chest. Somehow, it was more horrific than even the burned corpses on Grapevine Street had been, because of how clean and white the flesh around it was, how the Duchess still barely lived through it, staring up at the ceiling and gasping for air. Her breath rattled in her chest.

"Duchess." Olivia put her face right above the other woman's, so their noses were touching. She gripped her chin between her fingers and *shook* her head like a ragdoll's. "Duchess, look. Look at me. *Look* at me. *Who. Did. This?*"

The lifeknitter who'd been holding the Duchess's wrist released it and stepped back, shaking his head. "I don't know what we can do. I don't think there's…anything."

"Put some pressure on the damn lacerations! Do *something*. She's still breathing!" one of the others cried. "We don't *give up!*"

But the rest of the lifeknitters all stepped back, but for the one with her hand over the Duchess's heart. One by one, they raised their hands to the linked circles on their breasts, eyes closing in despair and defeat.

The Duchess's hand flew up. It wrapped around Olivia's wrist. Her eyes focused abruptly. "Deathsniffer," she said urgently.

"*Yes*," Olivia said breathlessly. "*Yes*, that's me. Duchess. That's me. Tell me, how did this to you? Just say a name. All you have to do is say a name. Who was it? Who was it?"

But the Duchess merely gasped for air, rattling like the bones of a long-dead corpse. The fingers gripping Olivia's wrist in a white-knuckled grasp loosened one by one, and then the hand fell onto the reddened sheets beneath her. "Ahh…" The Duchess breathed. "Ahh…"

"Duchess."

"James…"

"*Duchess.*"

"A…Ana…" The last sounded more like the Maiden's sigh than a name, but the horrific, creaking, hoarse breath that was drawn after it was like the opening of the gates of the third hell.

It was the last one.

The lifeknitter whose fingers had hovered, splayed, over the Duchess's heart slowly withdrew her hand. She shook her head slowly, and then raised it to lay against the linked circles on her heart. "May she sing with the Maiden," she murmured, and her words were echoed by all the other lifeknitters in the room, doctors, nurses, assistants and all. "May she sit with the Mother. May she be guided by the Crone."

"May she find peace," they all said in unison.

"*No*," Olivia cried, and, to Chris's utter shock and horror, she *pounded* on the dead woman's chest with a closed fist. "No, *no*, you stupid *bitch*, all you had to—all you had to *fucking* do was say a *fucking name!*"

And then Officer Dawson was there, gripping Olivia by her shoulders and *yanking* her away from the body. "*Faraday!*" she said the name as a command. Olivia fought her for a moment, twisting in her grip and reaching out with clawed fingers, and Chris feared they may come to genuine blows…but then Olivia went limp in the policewoman's arms, her crutches falling to the ground in a clatter.

Officer Dawson passed the lifeless Deathsniffer into the arms of a nearby lifeknitter, bending down to retrieve the crutches. "She should probably go back to her room. She was badly hurt and she's obviously worked herself up," the policewoman said, handing the crutches to a different lifeknitter, who nodded in agreement.

Olivia said nothing to Chris, and he didn't know what he was supposed to do. He knew, however, that he had no desire to remain in the hospital room with the dead-silent lifeknitters and the corpse. A thousand images from the night of the Floating Castle flashed through his head. After less than a second's hesitation, he trailed after the lifeknitters guiding Olivia. He tried not to be noticed, even though he was sure he was. They didn't appear to take offense to his presence, however, and after they finished laying Olivia back in her bed—and she stared at the wall with blank eyes and blank face—one of them turned to him and, without saying a word, prodded with strong fingers at his puckered stitches.

His skin tingled strangely where the man's fingertips pressed against him. The lifeknitter's features slackened. He knew the man had slipped beneath his skin and was seeing all the mysteries there—his skull, his brain—and shuddered at the thought. At least, he reminded himself, he hadn't been categorized as a lifeknitter. The abilities themselves were awful enough. The thought of spending his days locked in the white prison of a hospital, replaying memories of the worst night of his life over and over again...

The lifeknitter withdrew his fingertips. "What day is it?" he asked gently.

Chris managed a grim sort of smile. Or at least, a grimace. "Eadday," he said. "And my name is Christopher Buckley."

The lifeknitter flashed his white teeth in a smile through his beard. "I see you've already been given the test." He scanned his eyes over the stitches again and nodded once. "You can leave, I think. Come back in a week and we'll have those removed.

Otherwise, you're in remarkably good shape, considering what you've been through."

Chris couldn't help it. He slid his eyes to Olivia, whose blank gaze was as unnerving as the Duchess's horrible last breath had been. "What about her?" he asked quietly.

"She'll need to stay overnight. Don't worry. We'll keep a close eye on her."

"Ah," said Chris. He smiled politely at the lifeknitter, who smiled back and moved towards the door. The other one fluffed Olivia's pillows, examined her leg, arranged her crutches against the wall, and then smiled at Chris on her way out, as well. Olivia didn't stir the entire time, simply stared and stared at the wall, barely blinking. Barely breathing.

Chris studied her empty expression. His eyes clung to her lifelessly pale skin, the dull gleam in her eyes. Her fingers were limp where they laid at her side, and her body was barely curled. He licked his lips, considering saying something. To ask if she was all right, perhaps, or simply to excuse himself before turning to leave. He *had* to go home, after all. After a mad sort of day like today, after *everything* that had happened…he had never needed to go home so badly in his entire life.

He turned away from Olivia and took one step towards the door. Just one.

And then he turned back.

He walked to her bedside, unsure of what he was doing, exactly, but certain of his need to do it. He settled into the chair there, crossed his legs, and waited.

Olivia stirred after only a moment. She raised one of her limp hands to push hair away from her face, and for the first time, he noticed how scorched the ends were, how clumps were gone. How unlike him, not to notice something like that. She blinked slowly, and then rapidly, before settling her gaze on him and focusing her eyes onto his face. She grimaced and squinted. "Don't you have somewhere to go?" she asked, and neither her boundless, unnerving cheer, nor her snapping anger, nor her listless and strange sadness were in her voice. There was nothing there at all.

Chris cracked a smile, very small. "Yes," he said quietly. "But you don't."

She closed her eyes. "No," she murmured. "No, I don't."

They sat in silence for a long period of time. Olivia moved onto her back, wincing as she moved her leg. She breathed, now, her chest rising and falling. Her eyes remained closed, but a bit of life slowly returned to her features. Just a bit. But it was just enough. At first, Chris's thoughts were at home, with Rosemary, with Fernand, even with Miss Albany. He thought about all the things that had been said, Combs's claims that Miss Albany was some sort of reformist spy, Miss Albany's references to the exact strange phenomenon that he'd nearly forgotten experiencing the night before. He thought of Rosemary. Gods, Rosemary, caught up in all of this. What would he do for her? What *could* he do for her?

But the thoughts drifted away from him, pulled out to sea, and they left him thinking more clearly about the burning carriage, he and Olivia pushing it over together, how her quick thinking had saved his life. And thinking, too, about Duchess val Daren and Analaea and even the Duke. With the Duchess dead, was this even Olivia's investigation, anymore?

And he thought of Olivia. He tried, he really did try, to understand how she thought, why she was who she was, but he couldn't. He couldn't fathom her.

She spoke into the silence.

"I ruined that woman's life."

Chris held his tongue. He wasn't sure what to say.

Olivia pressed the palms of her hands against her eyes. "I did," she continued. "She came to me for help finding out who killed her husband, and I bloody terrorized her. She was right. It *was* my fault her daughter died thinking she was a villain. And right up until the very moment she breathed her last, I was there in her face having no gentleness of heart for her, wasn't I? In a way, I suppose it might be my fault she died at all. If I weren't so bloody convinced it was her all along, maybe I'd have found the bastard who really did it. Maybe could have saved the girl, too. I'm a right piece of work, aren't I?"

Chris found his tongue felt too big for his mouth. "It wasn't—" he tried, and then faltered. "You're not—" he tried again, but that seemed to go nowhere, as well.

"It was," Olivia sighed. "I am." She shook her head and let her hands fall to her sides. Her voice sounded limp and hopeless. Another moment of quiet, and then, "I don't feel badly," she said quietly. "That's bloody buggered, isn't it? I don't bloody feel badly at all. I tortured that woman. I convinced her daughter she was a murderer. I called her a killer when she was just a cunt, and I wouldn't even let her *die* in peace. I should hate myself. I should." She shook her head from side to side, slowly. "But I don't." She squeezed her eyelids tight. "I never do."

Chris knew the proper response.

What Olivia was admitting to was monstrous. With her saying the words, taking ownership of the feelings, it was impossible to believe she was just a misunderstood genius. What she'd done to the Duchess, the entire val Daren family...terrorized was right. Tortured was right. She confessed to it, and it rolled off her like rain. *I never do,* she said, as if she did this all the time.

And she did, Chris realized, and suddenly he knew with perfect clarity where the mysterious Constance had gone. She'd heard this very confession and she'd reacted the way any normal, sane human being would have. She'd recoiled in utter horror, stared at her employer with terrified distress in her eyes, and under the weight of the sort of judgement, Olivia had banished the poor girl from her sight. Chris wondered at how many other Deathsniffer's assistants there had been for Olivia, which model number he was. Five? Ten?

Twenty? However many there were, he knew with absolute certainty they had all reached this exact moment with O. Faraday, Deathsniffer, and they had all done what anyone would.

He'd never be able to say why he didn't.

"Olivia," he murmured quietly. And when she didn't react at all, he repeated himself, louder. "*Olivia.*"

Slowly, she opened her eyes. She turned her face to look at him, like a sickly flower to sunlight. She blinked at him slowly, a furrow appearing between her brows. "I should hate myself," she repeated, and when he said nothing, she took a deep breath. The very end of it trembled. "You should hate me," she said, quieter, and he knew that was what she *really* meant.

"I don't," he murmured.

Quickly, as if their eye contact had burned her, Olivia turned away from him. Chris thought he'd seen something glimmer in her icy blue eyes…but, of course, he'd lost his eyeglasses, and he couldn't be certain of what he was seeing at all.

"I almost died today," Olivia said.

"So did I," Chris said, and then, with a ghost of a smile touching his lips, added, "We didn't, though."

"No," Olivia replied. "I suppose, somehow, we didn't."

For a very long time after that, it was completely quiet.

Chris's thoughts should have been with his battered family and his uncertain future at the Buckley estate, but somehow, they weren't. It was as if he and Olivia were wrapped up in a soundshield. It shut out everything beyond the two of them and the hospital bed. Not even the stark white walls, the smell of starched sheets and hard lye soap, the distant sounds of lifeknitters moving through the halls could upset him. The night of the

Floating Castle was miles away, and so was everything else. Nothing existed but him and Olivia Faraday, not the past and not the future.

The light faded from the window. Sunset, twilight, and then darkness fell, and the time continued onwards. It seemed to pass like rushing water, there and then gone in an instant. Not a single word was exchanged. Nor did either of them sleep. Their silence was companionship, and into that silence, Chris poured the odd sort of understanding he had for his strange employer. Neither of them were heartreaders. She couldn't read his affection. He couldn't read her appreciation. But somehow, he knew they both felt it.

It must have been sometime past midnight when Olivia suddenly and abruptly sat up in bed.

Chris started, looking over and her, and was shocked at the transformation there. The drifting, listless expression she had worn for hours and hours was completely gone. He knew the Olivia he saw now. Her jaw was set, there was a manic little smile on her lips, and her eyes shone with pure determination. "Christopher," she said sharply, and focused her eyes completely on him, once again the businesslike employer who'd ask whatever she wanted from him. "I need paper. I need pens. I need *data.*"

He knew an order when he heard one. He climbed up from his chair and the room spun only a bit as he hurried out to the nearest nurse's station. He gathered up a sheaf of paper and a pen and an inkwell, hoping none of them would be missed, and hurried back to Olivia's room.

She was still sitting up when he entered, and brightened at the sight of him with his prizes. "Ooh!" she exclaimed, clapping her hands together in delight and then extending them greedily like Rosemary begging for a sweet. "Bring them here! Yes!" There was a tray behind the cupboard. Chris presumed it was for invalids to eat their meals in bed, but he decided to repurpose it. He set it before her and laid the supplies she'd requested before it, and she immediately dipped the pen in the inkwell and began scratching out onto the paper.

Viktor val Daren, she wrote in the middle, and then immediately crossed the name out. "He died first," she said. "In his office, with the door looked, with his willy out of his pants. Throat was slit. He was filled with shock and disgust." She tapped the pen against her chin, looked as though she was going to say more, and then seemed to decide against it. She dipped her pen and began scribbling once again.

She drew a line from the Duke's name outward, and then wrote at the tip of it *Evelyn val Daren.* "She didn't kill him, because she died, herself," Olivia said. "She died in her gardens, shot with a firepistol, and those lacerations…" She shook her head. "I'll need an autopsy. We'll come back."

Another line and another name. *Analaea val Daren.* She crossed it out. "*She* died in her bedroom. Messy. Blood absolutely everywhere. She was screaming as she died, do you remember? With Will? 'No, no, I don't understand,' she was saying while she got herself sliced up." Again, Olivia tapped the pen against her chin. She stared at the paper with a deeply searching expression, as if desperately hoping it would calmly offer up all the answers she was looking for. "Was it a staff member? Maybe."

Another line. *Staff,* she wrote. "None of them seemed suspicious. None of them *stood out.* That was a mistake. I need to—I'll go tomorrow. I'll sit down with each and every bloody one of them and hear their entire sodding life's stories until one seems even slightly possible. That's what I'll do." She nodded to herself, and circled the word.

She drew a line from the Duchess's name. *Traditionalists,* she wrote. "Interesting," she said. "But nothing to do with the murders." For the first time since he'd set her tools before her, she looked up at Christopher. "Do you disagree?"

He floundered. *No,* was his instinct, but he looked at it from all angles. The Duchess had been spending the Duke's money to fund the effort to imprison Doctor Livingston for sabotaging the Floating Castle. Maybe the Duke had found out. Maybe he'd demanded it stop. There were gaps everywhere in the theory, but…

"Maybe?" he said helplessly. "I—this isn't really my—it just seems as possible as anything, at this point."

"I agree," Olivia said, nodding. She circled the word *traditionalists*, and then, after seeming to think for a moment, pulled another piece of paper off the bottom of the sheaf and handed it to him. "Take notes," she said, and without waiting for response, immediately went back to what she'd been doing.

Rayner Kolston, she wrote after drawing another line out from the Duke's name. "Kolston was right," she said. "He definitely had Duke val Frenton killed back in the day, but he'd have to be some sort of legendary bloody idiot to kill Duke val Daren in the exact same way. He doesn't stand a sodding thing to gain from it. Sure, his clients might remember that case out of fear, but who else remembers it? Just reporters and police officers, that's who. The last people he'd want attention from. He'd need a bloody death wish." She tapped below the name. "Still, unlikely as he is, and he is *bloody* unlikely, I've seen nothing to completely rule him out. Maybe investigate his alibi more closely. Find something to completely eliminate him." She didn't circle *or* cross out his name, simply drew another line and wrote *Vanessa Caldwell.*

"This is where it gets interesting," she said, and then wrote *William Cartwright* in the far corner of the page. She didn't attach any lines to it at all. "We need to remember everything William saw, because him seeing Vanessa Caldwell at that crime scene when we *know* she isn't responsible makes *everything* he saw that day interesting." She began scribbling things down. "Caldwell's reflection in the magic mirror. The kitchen with the tomatoes. Ana dying—I wish he could have stayed with *that* longer. I'll bet there were some answers there." She twirled the pen in her fingers.

"What else? Help me, Christopher, you useless arse."

"Kissing the Duke," Chris said, feeling as odd as ever remembering that strange second-hand memory.

Olivia nodded, scribbling away. "Walking up the front path," she said. "The key—she had the key, didn't she? The antique key, she put it in the lock. I remember. The room." And her brow furrowed. "That room. You found a drop of blood outside the door. Maris' grunts found the key. And there was something else in there. " She tapped the pen furiously against the page, leaving inky black marks. "We took that room apart. We tore it down and put it back together. I remember Will seeing the room. There was a big hump of bloody clothes in the corner, wasn't there? The place was *plastered* with blood"—*Taptaptaptaptaptaptaptaptap*—"so *why* didn't we find anything?"

She went to cross off Vanessa Caldwell's name and frowned when no line came out of the pen. With a sour face, she moved to dip it once more. The edges of the inkwell *clink*ed as she moved her pen about in it. She withdrew the pen, not bothering to tap the ink off the end, and a giant blob of blackness fell onto the edge of her page and splattered in all directions.

Olivia froze.

Chris watched the change come over her face. It was like watching the day dawn, the sun come out from behind the clouds, a pegasus spread its wings and launch into flight. "Oh," she whispered. She breathed out, a *puff* of air, and then, reverently, she lowered her pen down to the page.

She drew a line from Analaea's name.

Ethan Grey, she wrote.

And then she drew a line from that name back down to the Duke's, thick and wide and purposeful.

"Yes," she said, looking down at her handiwork while Chris stared and tried to understand, tried not to breathe. "Oh, yes. Why didn't I see it? Why didn't I—"

Suddenly, she was a flurry of movement. She threw the tray to one side, sending ink and papers spraying in all directions. Blackness splattered all over the starched white sheets of her hospital bed, and the inkwell shattered when it hit the ground, creating a black stain like a smashed bug all across the white floor. Papers fluttered about like falling snow.

Olivia launched herself from the bed, pushing Chris to one side as though he was a pesky piece of furniture. While he stumbled and grabbed the cupboard to avoid falling, she seized her crutches and began swinging herself out of the room like a demon out of the hells.

By the time he gathered himself and chased after her, she was halfway down the hall. She was headed towards the foyer with a single-mindedness that rivalled that which Chris had sought out earlier, and even with her crushed leg and crutches, he was out of breath keeping up with her.

"Are you saying," he panted, "that—that Ethan Grey—"

"Oh, just *wait* until you see!" she crowed. "It's *elegant*, Christopher. It's bloody *elegant*."

There was a single woman in white at the front desk. The previously crowded and buzzing foyer was dark and empty. Olivia fairly threw herself against the desk, causing the girl to jump. Her white uniform didn't have the three linked circles above her heart, and Chris suspected she was a mere wordweaver, like himself.

"I need to use your bloody mirror," Olivia said breathlessly.

The girl shot a look behind her into the closed office, her lips parted in surprise and confusion. She turned back to Olivia and Chris with eyes wide, taking in their bed gowns, mussed hair, Olivia's crutches, and Chris's stitches. "I…" she said, flustered. She shook her head. "I don't think…we let patients…"

"*Now*," Olivia commanded, and the girl scurried down off her chair with a quiet *meep*. She opened the door to the office and Olivia followed after her, graceful as a deer with her three strange legs.

Immediately upon entering the room, Olivia moved to the

mirror and seized the mallet, striking the lowest note on the chimes over and over and over. Chris was struck with a sense of déjà vu, and he remembered doing this before, the day they'd idly thought of how little they knew about Mister Grey, what an unknown he was. Olivia had tried to contact an operator to get his frequency, to talk to him about the fight the three of them had had the night of the gallery...

He enjoys the company of other men, which apparently is a very big deal to some people, Olivia had said. Chris's heart skipped a beat. No...it couldn't be...

A man's face appeared in the mirror. "Hello," he said, his voice genial. "This is the Darrington City mirror operator, do you need assistance?"

"Ethan Grey," Olivia said, voice pregnant with breathless excitement. "*Seeshifter* categorization."

"One moment, please," the operator said, and the mirror clouded.

The last time, the operator had found nothing. Nothing at all. *There's no one matching that name and categorization in our records, miss,* the pleading operator had told them, cringing as if expecting a blow. They'd asked for a worldcatcher, an artist who could capture the spark of life and movement in his work, and there hadn't been any such a person in Darrington.

"Olivia," Chris said, heart pounding in his throat. "You don't think he's a—"

The mists cleared. "I have a frequency for that name and categorization," the man said with a smile, having no idea of what he'd just told them. "Wait just a moment, and I'll put you through."

Olivia turned to Chris, and her eyes glittered like sapphires or diamonds. "Ethan Grey is a bloody faceshifter," she said, and it all fell into place.

CHAPTER TWENTY-SIX

C ancel that connection, please, my good fellow."
Olivia had turned back to the mirror before Chris could
even react to the revelation she'd just throw before his
eyes. He spun with dizziness from more than his
bruised brains. Olivia was already dismissing the operator with the
usual cascade of chimes and before the mirror could even dim all
the way, she drummed out a frequency he didn't recognize.

"A faceshifter..." Chris murmured, raising a hand to his temple.
"Then...Miss Caldwell..."

"Darling Vanessa wasn't even there that night!" Olivia crowed.
"Gods, it all makes so much sense! The question has been
fluttering around in the back of my head all day! Why would a
backgammon player like Grey court a Duke's daughter as his
cover? It's madness! It puts him under more scrutiny than anyone
on the down-low would ever want! But it all makes sense, don't you
see? He chose Analaea for a reason! He *wanted* to be where he was.
Ethan Grey—" The picture of the mirror solidified and Maris
Dawson's handsome face appeared, her orange curls a snarled nest
and her stout little body wrapped in a dressing gown. Without
missing a beat, Olivia simply turned in the middle of her tirade,
eyes glittering wildly, "—was in love with the Duke!"

Officer Dawson's brow furrowed. "...Miss Caldwell was?" she
hazarded. "And do you have any idea what time it is? I thought you
were at the hospital overnight!"

"No, no, no," Olivia waved her off impatiently. "Miss Caldwell has nothing to do with any of this! Just like I suspected from the start! No, Maris, I'm talking about *Ethan Grey*!"

Officer Dawson's eyes went wide. She gasped and then sighed, surprise and then release. "Yes," she said, eyes sliding closed. "Oh, yes. That feels right. An artist. He would have moved in the right circles, known about val Daren's reputation, even met him."

"He'd never be accepted as one of the Duke's protégées. He patronized only beautiful young women! But he couldn't help it. He fell. He fell hard, and he fell right into a pit full of Sins of Passion."

Maris's eyes flew open again and a frowned marred the relief on her face. "But in the mirror—the seeing?"

"Oh, this is the best part, Maris, you are going to *love* this!" Olivia clapped her hands together and then leveraged herself on her crutches to lean forward conspiratorially. "He's a faceshifter! He's been masquerading as a worldcatcher this whole time, but the categorization records don't lie! He's registered as a seeshifter, and the only reason for a seeshifter to fake another proficiency is—"

"Mother Deorwynn and Father Calhoun." The policewoman in her dressing gown gasped. "He went to the Duke as Caldwell and then when the Duke realized the truth—" Her gaze sharpened. "Faraday. Can you walk?"

"I can walk, Maris." Olivia sighed, but Officer Dawson had barely stopped.

"Good. Call a hackney, get to the station, and bring your assistant. There's a faceshifter in Tarland and we need to get him in hand as soon as possible."

"Mister Ethan Grey, categorization seeshifter!" Officer Dawson shouted outside the locked door of the apartment building. "This is

Officer Maris Dawson of the Queen's Police. You have until the count of three to open this door."

Cowering against the far wall of the surprisingly upscale bookstore where Ethan Grey rented out the top floor, Chris glanced at Olivia, who stood on her crutches like a bundle of energy. She still wore her burned, grimy, and ruined gown, but her ice blue eyes were all but crackling. "Olivia," Chris murmured, feeling a chill go through him as Officer Dawson hit *two*. "Shouldn't he have answered by now? What if—?"

"Shush," Olivia commanded, and Officer Dawson counted *zero*.

The policewoman pulled her pistol, which glowed faintly silver in the dim light of the hall. "Clear the area!" she commanded, and aimed the gun at the doorknob. The shot was the sound of a glacier breaking in half. A blast of cold erupted from the barrel of the gun and turned the brass knob white. Officer Dawson wound up and planted a hard kick right beside the crystal-frosted latch.

The door burst inward without resistance, the knob and surrounding wood shattering like glass.

"Hang back!" Officer Dawson snapped, and, pistol held at the ready, stepped into the yawning hole left by the door.

The only light from inside came from the silver light of the icepistol. Officer Dawson might as well have been walking into a cave. It was black as ink outside, the sun still hours from rising, and no illumination shone from inside the apartment.

"Ethan Grey," the policewoman said evenly, her voice calm and clear and her finger on the trigger. "You are under arrest. Please come quietly and peacefully, and no force will be required."

Eerie silence followed Officer Dawson's statement. Chris heard the ticking of a clock from somewhere, Olivia breathing beside him, and little else.

Slowly, the barrel of her gun never wavering, the policewoman took a step farther into the room. She dropped one hand and fumbled around with something, and then her fingers tapped a light and awoke a slumbering salamander, who roared to life. The light was shockingly bright after the dark, and Chris saw the entry of a messy, lived-in sort of flat.

The Officer nodded at them just once, then jerked her head into the room. Olivia started forward, the *thumping* of her crutches unnaturally loud, and Chris started after her.

"Grey…" Officer Dawson's voice ushered them into the flat. "If you are present, you are officially in violation of law." The flat was indeed lived in, with waistcoats and shoes and hats scattered about everywhere. There was a thick blanket on the couch; it didn't look like Grey used his bed. And all around the room, leaned up on surfaces, nailed on walls, or even still resting in the cradle of their easels, there were paintings.

Chris was drawn to the closest one against his will. Three women, gowned and hatted in a style dated thirty years or more back, sat at a wrought iron, white painted table. Despite the fact that they were not the focus of the painting, he could see their ribbons, sleeves, and skirts all fluttering in the breeze. The focus of the painting was the garden. Flowers of all colours, a rainbow kaleidoscope, stretched out toward him, starting at the feet of those tea-drinking young ladies and ending so close he felt as if he could reach out and touch them. Each petal seemed to shiver on the promise of a wind, and Chris could swear he could faintly smell the blossoms.

"Well," Olivia said behind him, musingly, as Officer Dawson threw open doors. "He's quite good, isn't he?"

Chris reached out and ran his fingers along the surface of the painting. It seemed terribly wrong that his fingers stopped when they reached the oil and canvas of the surface. "He isn't even a worldcatcher," he murmured. "All this is done with illusions."

"Illusions and paint," Olivia agreed, picking up a discarded brush, stiff with unrinsed paint. "I don't think painter is one of the authorized professions for a seeshifter. It encourages them to get too creative. Start flirting with the idea of shifting people. He'd have to have done all of this on his spare time if he hadn't falsified his categorization."

Before Chris could reply, Officer Dawson appeared back in the main room. She looked as if she'd just smelled something foul and she holstered her pistol. "He isn't here," she said.

Olivia nodded. "I suspected when he didn't answer your first call. I didn't hear anything from inside, after all." She sighed. "Well, that begs the question. Has he fled, or is he just out?"

Chris turned away from the painting to gape. "It's long past midnight and it won't be dawn for hours," he said. "Where would he be?"

"Seeshifters tend to entertain a thriving nightlife," Officer Dawson grunted. "And their tricks are especially appreciated when they're off Lowry books."

"*Appreciated*," Olivia added, "is police euphemism for 'well-paid.' "

"So either he's gone to ground, or he's going to," Officer Dawson growled. "Eadwyr's sagging tits," she swore, making Chris jump and flush brightly. "We *cannot* have a faceshifter loose in Tarland. If the people find out about this, it's going to be chaos. We outlawed this for a reason!"

"And he could be anywhere if he's run…" Chris said. He felt a bit dizzy, considering it. A man who'd been able to do that to the Duke, and to Ana, who could wear any face he wished.

Officer Dawson turned to Olivia. "Faraday," she said, her voice low. "I know we're not supposed to just speculate, but please. You're a hundred times stronger than me. You never believed for a moment it was Caldwell, even when we saw her damn face in that mirror. Speculate."

"All right, speculation," Olivia agreed. She took exactly ten seconds to look around the room. "He hasn't been gone long. Look here." She three-legged hopped to a painting, one Chris hadn't seen before. When his eyes fell on it, his heart seized up in his chest. Analaea val Daren's beautiful, soulful brown eyes stared out of the canvas and her lips quirked into a small smile, which immediately vanished when he made eye contact with her. A few tendrils of her brown hair stirred around her ears as Olivia reached up and drew her fingers through the words painted there in bright red.

I M SO SORRY

Her fingertips came away sticky and scarlet. "So, there's that," she shrugged. "In addition, he's either left in a hurry, or intends to come back. These paintings obviously mean a lot to him, as they jolly well should. They're damn good. But he's left them all, every one."

"Then if he *has* run, he's still in Darrington," Officer Dawson murmured.

"But if he hasn't," Olivia said, wiping her crimson fingers off on her ruined dress, "you're going to spook him if you turn loose the hounds. He hasn't gotten by with falsified categorization for years without having a good ear to the ground for trouble."

Officer Dawson growled.

Chris's eyes were drawn once again to the painting of Ana. The words painted across the top. The tail of the "y" trailed all the way down the painting until it reached Ana's shoulder. That ghost of a smile crossed her lips once again as Chris met her eyes, and then faded back into the ethereal, strange sadness she'd always worn.

"Why Ana?" he heard himself murmuring. "She thought it was the Duchess. Why kill her?"

Both women turned to look at him. Olivia's face fell into thought and she leaned her weight on one of her crutches as she considered. "You know," she said, "that is a very good question. Ever since I saw her lying there, I've just had one of my feelings. That she was killed because she knew too much. But Christopher here says in their last conversation, all she talked about was how she suspected her mother and didn't respect her word any longer."

Suddenly, both women were looking at him. Chris blinked and then held up both hands. "I—don't look at me!" he protested. There were two truthsniffers in this room, and they were eyeing him as if he was the one full of insight.

"'I don't understand,'" Olivia quoted, and the vision of Analaea covered in blood and cuts, screaming those very words, flashed before him. "She didn't know why he was killing her. And in the end"—she indicated the painting—"he regretted it. You were the last one who talked to her, Christopher. Other than, presumably, him."

Ana *had* talked about Grey during that conversation, hadn't she? Chris struggled to remember what it was he'd heard her say. Grey had been in a mood. He'd barely spoken to Ana and then had stormed away to pull down his paintings. The night the two of them had fought, it had been about her mother's insistence that he was...

Chris gasped.

"She said—" His words tumbled out of his mouth. "She said she felt brave. She said she was finally going to talk to Mister Grey about her mother's accusations, because it wasn't about her anymore." He squeezed his eyes shut. Analaea val Daren had sparkled that morning, and now she was underground somewhere.

"Ahhh," Olivia breathed. When Chris opened his eyes, he saw a beatific look had come over her face. "She came to him. She said, 'Darling, I know all about your secret.' And he jumped right to the worst possible thing, panicking so hard he murdered the one person of influence who might have fought for his happiness."

Chris swallowed around the lump in his throat and he stared into Analaea's eyes. For a moment, he could swear he heard her voice—*Can I call you Christopher?*—but that was surely beyond even Grey's talents.

"Sad as that is, it's not really relevant right now." Maris's solemn, quiet voice belied her dismissive words, and she hung her head with a sigh. "This all might have gotten away from him, but he's a faceshifter, a killer, and we haven't learned anything by this—"

"Oh, no," Olivia interrupted. "Do you think I'd entertain my assistant's soft little heart if it wasn't for a reason? This is very relevant, and we've learned plenty." She indicated the painting behind her. I M SO SORRY. "We've learned Grey panics when he thinks he's threatened, even if he knows he'll be all right. He killed three people, threatened Chris's sister, and if that isn't enough to make someone lose it—"

"Ah," Officer Dawson said, light dawning over her face.

"Turn loose your hounds, Maris," Olivia said with a little smile. "This coney has gone underground, and it can change its stripes at will."

CHAPTER TWENTY-SEVEN

A s Christopher Buckley waited, he wished he was anywhere else.

Every police officer who passed by gave him a curious glance. He met their eyes and smiled politely, inclining his head in greeting at them. One by one they sized him up, dismissed him, and went on their way. Some greeted him in return. Most simply held his eyes curiously until they rounded a corner and were forced to look away. He constantly feared Officer Dawson passing by, seeing him there, demanding to know what he was doing, but wherever she was, today, she didn't appear.

It had been two days since Olivia had ordered the arrest on Ethan Grey for the murder of Viktor and Analaea val Daren, but no trace of him had been seen despite all of Officer Dawson's precautions. No papers reported on the faceshifting murderer lost in their midst. The police had insisted it be kept quiet until the man could be apprehended. After all, with two days passed, there was no guarantee he would be. He could be anywhere—any*one*. And to tell the people of Tarland someone had broken every law and every taboo of illusion and gone faceshifter would cause mass panic. Officer Dawson would rather hang the murders on Vanessa Caldwell than allow that, especially in these troubled times.

Instead, the papers had babbled nonstop about the genius wizardling Rosemary Buckley, the Grapevine Incident, and the accusations lobbed between Avery Combs and Rachel Albany, sister to the infamous reformist ringleader Garrett Albany. Chris had disallowed any of them into the estate, and kept Rosemary under lock and key. The last thing she needed as an appetite for fame.

He had to get her out of Darrington.

Over and over again, he'd tried to think of how to do it. He'd counted his coppers, he'd looked at train tickets, he'd opened an atlas and made a list of every town he could afford to take her. But in the end, there had been only one way available, and only one path that led there.

Another set of footsteps was headed his way. Chris fought down a surge of nervousness and raised his head to deliver yet another polite smile to the police officer who would walk past wearing a furrowed frown. Instead, the officer sat down beside him and crossed his arms across his slender chest.

Officer William Cartwright looked over at him. His long dark hair fell around his shoulders in gentle waves, and his pouty lips were pursed. "They're getting him ready, now," he said. "You won't have very long."

Chris smiled. "I won't need very long," he replied gratefully. He wasn't sure what had possessed him to contact the timeseer, but the thought had just come to him and refused to leave him alone. He was sure he hadn't imagined that strange, unspoken exchange that had passed between them the day of the seeing, and when he'd asked the operator to put his mirror-gnome through to William Cartwright the truthsniffer, the pretty young man had agreed rather readily to do what Chris asked.

"Should I ask what it is you need him for?" Officer Cartwright—*William*, Chris reminded himself, the boy had insisted upon William—asked, looking out over his peers at their work. The station was quiet today, a marked difference from the first time Chris had come here. William had to keep his voice hushed to avoid being overheard. "Are you going to cause trouble for me, Christopher?"

Chris had never given the boy permission to use his own first name, but it seemed magnificently rude to take offense when he'd been granted the same courtesy after only minutes of acquaintance, so he chose to simply accept it and move on. "I don't know," he responded honestly, feeling his cheeks flush. "I don't...I'm not entirely sure what *would* get you into trouble."

William sighed irritably. "I *suppose* I'll just have to risk it," he muttered sourly, and he shot Chris a dark look. "You'll owe me a favour."

"Of course," Chris replied easy, turning to quickly shoot the boy a friendly smile once again.

He caught something flicker deep in the boy's long-lashed eyes as he turned back away, and a bolt of unease went through his heart. Was it entirely wise to be trading favours with this young man when he didn't yet understand the strange connection he felt between them?

William sighed. His slender hands brushed imagined dirt from the smart lines of his police uniform, but he lost interest in it immediately. Chris saw him fold his hands into his lap, and watched him fidget a bit in his seat. Finally, his voice low, the young man spoke the words that had clearly been hovering at the edge of his tongue since he'd sat. "You really don't remember me," he said. "Do you?"

Chris blinked, then twisted in his seat to look at Officer Cartwright in surprise. Something dark lurked behind the glossiness of the beautiful young man's eyes, and his long lashes fluttered before his gaze dropped to his folded hands. "No," William said sadly. "I didn't think so, though I *had* hoped..."

"I don't understand," Chris said quietly. "Remember— remember you from where?"

William merely shook his head. "You've forgotten about it," he said dismissively. "And so should I." He stood, brushed his uniform out, and stiffly bowed his head to Chris. "I'm going to check on him. It shouldn't be long at all, now."

Chris had barely a moment alone with his confusion. Moments after William vanished back into the private depths of the station, he reappeared, indicated with a single crooked finger that Christopher should join him. Climbing to his feet, he did as he was bid, grabbing the door just before it shut and following the strange young man who apparently knew him—*somehow*—back into the private areas of the station.

He was led through a narrow hallway where William's sharp, polished boots echoed off the walls and ceiling with every step. The alp-lights flickered, and one appeared to have gone out entirely. Chris wondered how long it had been like that. He wondered if the alp had caused anyone blindness before it vanished. And he also wondered if Tarland might actually run out of 'binders to do everyday tasks like put alps in lights. What would they possibly do if they *did?* Alternate methods would have to be found, or else his countrymen would be wandering about in the dark.

It was a good state of mind to meet Doctor Francis Livingstone in.

William opened the door to a small room, and gestured for Chris to go inside. "Don't be long," he said. "If the wrong person asks where he is, this could end very quickly. I'm not a real police officer, you know." He gave Chris a gentle shove inwards, his girlish hands warm on the back of Chris's coat, and closed the door firmly behind them.

"Well," a voice said from behind him. "If it isn't Mister Buckley. I've...not been doing so well, since we last spoke, I'm afraid."

Chris turned.

The doctor didn't lie. His previously clean-shaven face was now covered in a rough, week-old beard. His hair looked shaggy and unkempt, his eyes the dull glaze of someone who hadn't slept well in many nights. His fine suit had been replaced by a tattered prisoner's issue, and the circles under his eyes and caverns in his cheeks made his face look hollow. The grey in his hair seemed greyer, the lines in his face deeper. Worst of all was the sick pull of what was definitely not a smile at his lips. Chris couldn't help the burst of pity that went through him. The warm, buttoned-down, honest man who'd come to his home and spoke glowingly of his granddaughter was gone, possibly for good.

He swallowed. "Doctor," he said, bobbing his head respectfully. "I…"

He was hoping the doctor would interrupt him, ask what he was doing here, and take the burden of introduction off his shoulders, but Doctor Livingstone merely sat with his thin hands folded on the table, bound by shackles, looking up at him. Waiting.

Chris sighed. He stepped forward, pulled out the chair on the opposite side of the table, and sat down. He knew what he'd come here to ask, and he knew what he hadn't, but the two things seemed to confuse and switch around in his head, and when he opened his mouth, the wrong question came out, like he knew it would. "Did you?" he asked, and he heard with shame the ache in his voice. He closed his eyes, not wanting to meet the doctor's. He didn't want to see whatever was displayed there.

A pause. The other seat creaked. "If you have to ask, I don't have an answer for you," the doctor said quietly.

"That's not fair," Chris said, opening his eyes. He placed both his hands on the table, palm down, and he *did* meet the doctor's eyes, then. "You don't have any right to be hurt. I barely know you. We spoke only once. And—"

"Did you come here only to throw more accusations I can't answer at me, Mister Buckley?" the doctor said. He didn't sound angry, or even defensive. He just sounded tired. Tired and sad. "I've had quite enough of that in the last week, let me tell you."

"I just…" Chris shook his head. "I just need to hear you *say* it."

The doctor rubbed his wrist where the shackles chafed him. Chris winced and had to look away when he saw how red and raw the skin had been rubbed. This was a man meant for laboratories and lecture halls, not chains and bars. "One thousand, five hundred and seventeen people died on the night of the Floating Castle," the doctor said quietly. "People always talk about the five hundred upper class invitees, but they never mention the three hundred on the serving and maintenance staff. And the building didn't fall into the ocean. There were thousands of people who—"

"I know," Chris said, sharper than intended. Gods, did he ever know.

The doctor shook his head sadly. He closed his eyes, and there was real pain on his face as he visibly considered all the bodies that night had left in its wake. "No," he said quietly. "I didn't, Mister Buckley. I wouldn't. I *couldn't.*"

Chris nodded, feeling the villain for having asked. He believed him. He couldn't not. Try as he may to maintain some suspicion, some healthy scepticism, he couldn't help but believe him. If nothing else, it felt good. The doctor's chains clanked and then they sat in silence with their hands on the table between them.

"I..." Chris said eventually. He threaded his fingers together, considering how to proceed, but no elegant solution presented himself, and he ended up spreading his hands helplessly. "I really need your help," he said, his voice a thin plea.

The doctor gave a tight smile. "I'm not really in a position to be helping anyone, Mister Buckley," he said.

"No, I know," Chris hurried to assure him. "I know. I—I just...my sister." He took a deep breath, trying to gather up his scattered thoughts. "You offered to help my sister, Doctor Livingstone, and I should have just agreed right there before it was all too late, but I see now, Gods, I see you were right. She can't stay here in Darrington. It won't get better. It will only get worse. When she's an *adult*, she can make a decision for herself, what to do with her abilities, but right *now*, she's—" He raised his hand to his face and pulled off his new eyeglasses, throwing them down on the table. He pinched the bridge of his nose. He so badly wanted the doctor to interrupt and provide him with some help so he could just stop *begging*, but no assistance came and he had to continue in a thoroughly pathetic, plaintive little voice. "I've tried going to the police for help, but they're understaffed and they say I don't have a case. My sister is in danger, Doctor. It's my job to protect her, and I can't, and I *need* you to help me," he pleaded.

Ringing silence, then, "Mister Buckley…" the doctor said quietly. When Chris opened his eyes, the doctor was regarding him sadly. "Mister Buckley," he repeated, and spread his wrists as far wide as they could go. His shackles clattered. "My hands are quite literally tied."

"There has to be someone," Chris pressed, misery settling onto his shoulders. This wasn't how it was supposed to be… "Someone else in your movement. If you could just give me a name and a categorization, or even an address, I could go and find them and I'm sure…"

But the doctor was shaking his head. When Chris trailed off, the doctor filled the silence, his voice low and slow. "I've only barely been in control of *my movement* for years, Mister Buckley," he said. "Many years. There are so many facets and fragments and differences of ideal and opinion. The 'reformist agenda' is as varied as a fishwife's grocery list. It's been all I've been able to do for a very long time now to keep everyone under the same banner, because once we split off into our splinter groups, we've been divided, and then…" There was cavernously deep regret in the doctor's eyes. He sighed. "I've been gone for almost four days now, Mister Buckley, and while it shames me to admit it, I couldn't vouch for what side a single person with the sort of clout you need is on."

"Miss Albany said…" Chris murmured.

"Rachel is not a reformist. She doesn't understand the politics of the movement. She shares the views but she is not a part of the group. And her brother is the *last* person you should trust to take care of your sister. I'd put her in the hands of Hector Combs himself before I'd let Garrett Albany touch her." The ferocity in the doctor's voice at the last sent a shiver down Chris's spine even as what was being said put despair into his heart.

"So what do I *do*?" he asked, and then flushed at how high his voice climbed. He buried his face in his hands. "The family fortune is bloody *gone*. It's *gone*. I don't—I can't—I *need* to—" He cut himself off completely, biting back the sob of frustration that would make his humiliation complete.

"I don't know what you need to do, Mister Buckley," the doctor said, in a voice that was not unsympathetic. "And I *am* sorry I can't provide the help I told you I would be able to. But you must understand…right now, I have more important things to worry about."

"Will they get you?" Chris asked, clinging to the last shred of hope, that this charge would just blow over the doctor would be out and able to assist in days.

But, no. "Probably," the doctor said sadly. "All the traditionalists have ever needed is me out of the picture. I don't know what they have on me, but they've got the strongest and best of every categorization in Tarland working tirelessly for their goals. Whatever they've conjured up, I doubt a truthsniffer in the world will be able to tell it stinks."

The door behind them opened. Chris didn't need to turn to look to know it was William, especially when he recognized his pinched, sweet alto voice. "I'm sorry," he said, quickly and quietly, "But you need to finish up. Hannah is sniffing about, wondering why I've been using her clearance. She won't like this, not one bit."

The doctor stood from his seat. "There's no need to draw this out," he said kindly. "I think we're mostly done here, wouldn't you agree, Mister Buckley?"

Chris took a deep breath, and then nodded. Carefully, as quickly as he was able, he slipped all the spilled pieces back into their cupboards and closed the doors firmly behind them. He slid his specs back up his nose, and he took another breath, and then one more, steadying and anchoring himself. When he climbed to his feet, he had his most polite smile on his face, and he reached out to grip the doctor's outstretched hand in courteous familiarity. "Thank you very much for your time, Doctor Livingstone," he said. They shook hands like old business partners. "I appreciate your efforts."

"And I'm sorry I couldn't help you more, Mister Buckley," said the doctor with a sad, sad smile. "I truly am."

When the doctor reached the far door, two officers escorted him out of the room. Chris watched him go with a pit in his stomach, not moving until William tugged at his arm, pulling him towards the door they had entered from. "It would be best if you're not here when Hannah finds out I had him out," he said. "I know she seems very sweet, but you *don't* want to see her angry."

"No, of course not," Chris replied, allowing himself to be pulled out the door. William released his arm when they got to the hallway, and they hurried back down the long, narrow corridor until they reached the front room where he'd spent the morning sitting and waiting.

William didn't stop there. He strode to the front doors with a confident stride, holding one open and indicating Chris should pass through ahead of him as if he was a gentleman and Chris were the lady on his arm. He continued to walk and not stop until they reached the corner near the station, where carriages pulled by palfreys, unicorns, and wing-clipped hippogryphs passed by and the roar of Darrington was all around them. Then and only then did William turn and gave him a look that was, shockingly, quite sympathetic. "He didn't give you the answer you were hoping for," he said.

Chris shoved his hands into his pockets. "No," he said, not quite wanting to meet the timeseer's eyes. "No, he didn't."

"That's unfortunate," William said. They stood awkwardly for a moment. William reached into his uniform pocket, pulled out a pocket watch, and studied its face. He winced and snapped it shut, dropping it back into his pocket. "I have work," he said abruptly. "And bloody Hannah will want an explanation for what I was doing with our most impressive prisoner."

"What will you tell her?" Chris asked, genuinely worried he might get the young man into trouble. After all, he'd taken this risk for his sake, and asked for nothing in return.

But William cracked a sour-looking smile and shrugged one slender shoulder. His face looked bored more than concerned. "I'll tell her it was a grand whim of mine. I'm known for those, and they always give me what I want in the end. I'm too important to make angry. We have a system, they and I. They keep me on their tight little leash, and I make it difficult for them." He peered up into Chris's face for a moment, and then sighed and patted the pocket where he'd dropped the watch. "I really do have to go," he said, and brushed past Chris, starting back towards the station.

"Wait," Chris cried after him, half-turning. He fumbled for words to express his feelings of guilt. "I—if you'd just tell me where you think you know me from," he said haltingly. "Then maybe..."

William shook his head and sighed irritably. "That would defeat the sodding purpose," he muttered, and then, in a softer voice, he continued. "I'd like to see you again, Christopher. I'd like..." he turned his head to look back and beneath his thick, long lashes, there was something childishly vulnerable in those dark, luminous eyes. "I would like to see you again," he repeated, and all the languid, pouting bitterness was gone from his voice, leaving behind only hope.

Well, it wasn't as though Chris would be leaving Darrington. He pushed down a rush of bitterness of his own at the thought and fumbled up a courteous smile. It was all he could give. "I can see no harm in that," he said, and William sighed and turned and walked away, leaving him on the corner with the city pouring past him in all directions.

Taking only a moment to orient himself, Chris started off for home. It would be a bit of a hike, but he couldn't justify spending the royals on a taxicab. Olivia had been very generous, letting him have these days during the fruitless hunt for the missing faceshifter to attend to business with his sister, but not generous enough to pay him full wages. And even if she had been, if he was *ever* going to do something about Rosemary…

He smiled and nodded to another passerby, letting all his engrained courtesies do the work while his mind wandered. He thought back to what Fernand had said only a week before, which seemed quite impossible, for surely it had been an age. No more money, he'd said. Just make due until Rosemary came of age. It had seemed difficult, but reasonable, at the time. Now…

Now, everything had changed. Ever since White Clover and the observation wheel and the cloudlings, *everything* had changed. There would be no waiting until Rosemary came of age. Jackals prowled around her on all sides, and nothing he could do seemed enough to hold them at bay. Even Rosemary herself seemed to barely grasp the situation, the *danger*. They'd argued and argued and argued again since he'd come home from the hospital on Healfday morning, and he never seemed to win the arguments by anything but angrily telling her he was her legal guardian and she'd do what he said. She's saved lives, she'd said. She'd *agreed* to accompany Combs. If she could stop elementals from ruining society, why should she wait until she was nineteen?

She made so much sense when she threw those things in his face that he completely lost his own sense of reality. She was too much like his damned father, in the end. Right now, he knew he was right. Right now, he knew even if she could feasibly prop the current order up for the rest of history, the issue wasn't so simple. They would use her up and throw her away. They would abuse her. They would break her. They would ruin her bloody life. But one she began talking to him, so articulate and well-spoken and *so* much like his father...

At least Miss Albany made him feel sane again, afterward.

It would get worse, he told himself again, waiting for a break in traffic so he could dash across the street. It would get worse before it got better. Rosemary would grow more and more willful as she grew older and older, and Chris would lose more battles than he won. He'd become the enemy. Combs would make himself into Rosemary's saviour. While Chris could do nothing but watch, his sweet sister would be turned inside out and poured into a dying dream, and then—

Gods, he didn't even want to think about what happened then. His mind couldn't go that far, and couldn't take the pain of trying.

He needed a solution, but solutions just weren't bloody coming.

When he felt the first drop of rain on the end of his nose, it seemed only logical. With a sigh, he pulled the brim of his trilby hat down further over his face, resigning himself to the deluge that followed. At least, in one of the Three and Three's few mercies, it wasn't a cold rain.

By the time he reached the estate, he was soaked to the bone and had come to one conclusion, that being he had to get Rosemary out of Darrington. Somehow, he'd make it happen. He'd have to. It was that simple.

It was an obvious resolution. It solved absolutely nothing. And yet, he still felt as if a weight had lifted from his shoulders when he passed through the soundshield and felt it stirring the few dry hairs that curled behind his ears, protected from the rain by the brim of his hat. The conviction was a start, at least. Work upwards from there.

He expected Rosemary's voice, either excited to see him, or gunning for a new battle, when he opened and closed the front door, but silence greeted him. A flash of panic went through him, as it had every time he'd woken up the last two days and didn't immediately see evidence of her presence, until he looked up and saw Miss Albany standing at the banister at the top of the staircase, her hands clutching it. She smiled down at him in her prim way, grey skirts and sensible shoes and carefully arranged bun as fantastically drab and out of fashion as ever. He smiled back up at her, making a face as he pulled off his drenched hat and settled it on the rack. "It didn't go very well," he said, trying to inject false cheer into his voice. "But the doctor seems...very well."

"I'm glad to hear it," Miss Albany said. She hitched her skirts and started down the stairs. Chris could see her ankles and averted his eyes quickly, clearing his throat. Heat touched his face as he pulled off his soggy topcoat with disgust.

"Bloody chucking it down out there," he murmured awkwardly. He used his toes to pull off his shoes. They were soaked, too. He sighed as he took a moment to study them. He'd been spending an inordinate amount of time walking through puddles, of late. "Where's Rosemary?"

"Your adviser came and took her out not long after you left," Miss Albany said. "Iced cream, I believe he said."

Well, so long as Fernand was paying, that was just fine. Rosemary was easier to manage when she was being spoiled by someone, and it certainly wasn't him, of late. He sighed. This entire period of time would have been so much easier if she'd burned herself out again, but the lifeknitter who'd seen to her, Doctor Jameson, had been shocked at how quickly she'd adapted to the new stresses she was juggling into her established 'binding abilities. *She's a savant,* he'd said, shaking her head. *I've never seen anything like her.*

"If you don't mind, Mister Buckley," Miss Albany said, and Chris finally found the courage to raise his eyes to her once more. She stood at the foot of the stairs, her hands folded before her. She looked…nice, he reflected. The soft edges he sometimes saw in her where in full force, today, and she seemed to be holding herself differently. More confidently, but less stiffly, somehow. He dragged his eyes to her face, trying not to embarrass himself any more than he already had. She smiled encouragingly at him. "There's something I'd very much like to discuss with you. Would you come with me?"

Without waiting for a response, she turned and climbed back up the stairs. After a moment's consideration, he shrugged off his waistcoat as well, and loosened his tie. Perhaps it was inappropriate to be clad in only his shirt and trousers in the company of a lady, but this was his home, and as far as he was concerned, there was very little worse than being fully dressed in clothing that was soaked through.

He followed after Miss Albany to the second floor. To his surprise, she walked past the solar there, and past the little parlour tucked into the corner of the hallway. In fact, she kept walking all the way to the end of the hall, and stopped, turning back to look at him with her hands folded neatly before her, in front of the door to the master bedroom. *His* bedroom.

His feet stopped walking before he reached her. She was only six paces from him, but the hall seemed to distort the distance between them, growing longer and then shorter, and he put a hand to the wall to steady himself as a wave of dizziness overtook him. "Miss Albany," he said, with his most polite voice, but the words seemed to be coming from somewhere far away. "Miss Albany, as we are unchaperoned, I think I would feel more comfortable—for your sake—if we spoke in the solar." He indicated a vague location somewhat behind him, and he smiled. He could always find it in him to smile.

She smiled, as well, though hers was considerably less measured and courtly. "Mister Buckley," she said softly. "You needed concern yourself with my honour. There is something I feel I should show you in your bedroom." Her eyes fluttered down from his, then, and he watched her fist her hands into her skirts. "And really," she said. "You might call me Rachel."

"That would be unprofessional, Miss Albany," he said. It came out as little more than a whisper. He thought of how she had looked with her hair all around her shoulders in the darkness of the front parlour, the way her womanly curves had looked so soft and appealing in the dim, soft light there. She looked a bit like that, now, he thought, unable to help himself from running his eyes over her. Did her lips look puffier than usual? Did her breasts look slightly larger? Was there something in her eyes, something...something...

Inviting was the word, and he shook his head, taking a step away from it. "That would be very unprofessional," he repeated, more firmly. "And I would be remiss to take advantage of..." He didn't know how to finish. Of whatever madness had overtaken her, some mystery of womanhood that none of his very limited experiences with the breed had prepared him for. He smiled, instead.

Her eyes fell and two spots of colour bloomed high in her cheeks. "Yes..." she said smally, and nodded. "Yes, of course, sir. I only thought..."

"I don't—" he growled in frustration. She sounded so wounded, looked so rebuffed. No, that wasn't how this was supposed to be. He was behaving the gentleman, and she should react with gratitude. Shouldn't she? In a bizarre, dizzyingly out of body moment, he caught a glimpse of the situation from her perspective. She was plain, sparrowish, tightly wound and apparently in possession of a nightmarish brother who certainly would make all her attempts at courting a hell. And he, why...he was handsome. Very much so, everyone agreed. And kind to her. And *fond* of her, which she would *feel* from him and certainly interpret in whatever way she wanted to. Wasn't that what women did? Gods, he didn't know.

"Miss…" he faltered. "Miss Albany, I just—"

She was moving, he realized, walking towards him at quite a brisk pace. Her skirts swirled about her ankles and he saw determination in her eyes and the set of her jaw. He barely had time to take a step back and babble out a confused protest, and then she was throwing her arms around him, closing her eyes, tilting her face upwards, and for *some* reason, Chris's body just did what felt natural.

The kiss stole his breath away. His heart stopped beating entirely, and then started again, thumping like a mad drum in his ears. His blood rushed and pulsed, and he gasped into her mouth, wrapping his arms tightly around the firm lines of her body, pulling her closer against him so she…

No. *Something is wrong*, he realized with the clarity of a pealing bell, and every muscle in his body stiffened—

—a *moment* before he felt the press of cool steel against his temple.

"I don't understand normal men," said a familiar voice that did *not* belong to Rachel Albany. "What must it be like, living in a world where it's all so *easy* as that?" And then, sharply. "Put your hands above your head or I bloody swear I'll melt your brains."

Chris did as he was told, and then let his eyelids flicker open. Before him, dressed in a grey wool gown ten years out of style, stood Ethan Grey, and his face was illuminated by the soft orange glow of the firepistol he held to Chris's head.

CHAPTER TWENTY-EIGHT

The barrel was pressing up against Chris's forehead. The metal was cool, and Chris could see the orange nimbus that buzzed around it from the corner of his eye. His heart thumped in his chest like a marching band.

The dress. Oh, Gods, the dress. "Where is she?" Chris asked breathlessly, unable to help himself. And then, following the thought to its logical conclusion, he moaned and felt as though a sack of bricks had hit him in the chest. "Mother Deorwynn," he gasped. "Where's Rosemary?"

Ethan Grey's soulful, artist's eyes were flashing with anger, now. "I warned you," he said tightly. "I thought I made it perfectly bloody clear what was going to happen if you kept asking questions."

No. Oh, no. Gods, no. "I'm sorry." Chris swayed on his feet. His stomach shrivelled into a tiny little ball that sent waves of pain all through his body, radiating from his middle. "I'm sorry, I'm—"

"He's sorry! Well, lovely. That certainly does something about the coppers all swarming my flat, the streamviewers at every bloody intersection looking for anyone casting an illusion. It *certainly* bloody well helps me get my arse out of Darrington!"

Do you want me to feel sorry for you? Chris wanted to scream. *You killed three people! You're a bloody faceshifter! There's nothing worse than that, nothing!* But every surge of his blood through his veins was singing *Rosemary, Rosemary, Rosemary,* and all that came out from his lips was a tiny whimper. "Please," he said, his vision blurring. "Oh Gods, please say you didn't hurt her, I, Gods, please..."

Grey gave a growl of disgust. He took a step back from Chris, gripped the pistol in both hands, pointed the barrel down, right between Chris's eyes. Chris could see his finger stroking the trigger. "She's fine," he said.

Chris gasped and moaned as a wave of relief threatened to knock him off his feet. Tears fell from his eyes and slid down his cheeks. "Oh, Gods," he breathed. "Oh, thank all the Gods."

"The governess, too." Grey squirmed uncomfortably in the grey dress, looking down at it with disgust. It was Miss Albany's dress, it had to be. Gods, had he hurt her to get it for his sick illusion? "For *now*, and *only* for now. If you want them to be breathing when the sun sets tonight, you'll do what you're told."

"Anything," Chris gasped. "Anything you say. Just don't hurt them."

Grey looked him up and down, more slowly this time. One corner of his mouth crooked as though something had occurred to him. A chill touched Chris's spine. He remembered the feeling of the Duke's whiskers rough against his cheeks. *No*, he reminded himself, that had been Ethan Grey standing in that room, holding that knife, not him. Ethan Grey, coming to the Duke as his mistress. "Do..." Chris hesitated. He swallowed. "Do you..."

Grey's lips firmed into a thin line. "You're all the same," he said. "Do you really think anyone is stupid enough to—*no*." He shook his head. "No. I want *money*."

Chris's heart skipped a beat. He stared down the barrel of the firepistol. "Oh..." he said weakly.

"I can't get into a bank, or a store, or even bloody take a purse off a lady in the street with how the coppers have their eyes out for me," Grey continued. "But I've seen all the papers. They won't stop talking about you, your amazing little sister. You have this big house, this important father. And I thought to myself...well. I've been to that place. I know the way in there. *That's* one way to get myself some royals."

But he didn't have royals. He didn't have a dime and nickel to rub together. There was a wad of ten notes in his pocket, an envelope with forty in his study, and that was the extent of the Buckley family fortune. Chris licked his lips and swallowed again. His throat was so dry it was painful. His fingers trembled and he hoped Grey didn't notice. "I..." He gave a tremulous smile. "I have jewels," he said. His mother's jewels, and the thought of giving them to this faceshifting pervert hurt his heart, but nothing was more important than Rosemary's safety. "Expensive pieces, very valuable. I can—"

"*No,*" Grey said, tightening his grip on the firepistol. The nimbus *flashed* as the salamander responded to his anger. "Do you think I'm an idiot? I'll take those into a shop and find coppers waiting for me there, too. No. Nothing that can be traced. I want *notes*. I want *royals*."

Gods, he didn't *have* royals. He could say that, admit it, but it wasn't the answer Grey was looking for. There was a wildness in those eyes, a terrifying desperation. He didn't know what this man would do, but the answer that came to him when he asked the question was *"anything."* "I..." Chris took a deep, shuddering breath. What was he going to do? Gods, what the three hells was he going to *do?* "There..." The lie leapt onto his lips. "There's a vault," he said. "My father kept money in a vault in his study. It's on the third floor. There's a combination lock." He held his breath, hoping against hope.

"What's the—" Grey cut himself off with a jerk of his head. "No," he said, and Chris's heart sank to his toes. "No, none of that. You'll come with me and you'll do the combination, yourself."

"I won't—" Chris began.

"Shut up," Grey said, and twitched the barrel of the gun. "Keep your hands over your head and don't make *any* sudden movements.

I swear to Eadwyr and Healfdene, I'll blow your head off if you make me." Chris swallowed all the empty promises he'd been about to offer, closing his eyes and taking trembling, deep breaths. "Turn around," Grey said, and Chris obeyed. "Good. Now move."

Somehow, his feet moved. One in front of the other, he started back down the hallway.

What am I going to do?

Because he had to do something. There were no vault, no combination, and no royals. His plan lasted only until Grey realized that, and then he was back to the same inevitable conclusion. He breathed deeply, turning his brain inside out, desperately searching for an answer. He was aware of the gun pointed to the back of his head like he could see it. So, too, was he aware of how Grey was built similarly to himself, but a good head taller. If it came to it, he wouldn't be able to overpower the man, not even with the element of surprise.

"I'm not a monster, you know." Grey's voice suddenly cut through his tormented thoughts.

It caught him so off guard he blurted his next words without thinking, "You're a bloody faceshifter!"

"You have no *idea* what it's like," Grey shot back in defiance. "No one has any fucking *idea* what it's like, being the way I am. All the things you have to hide, how if you don't, your whole *sodding* life is ruined! It's just a—a *spiral*. You start out with one little illusion to cover something up, but it really *wasn't* that big of a deal, so you do it again. But then people are asking questions, and when they know you're a seeshifter, they suspect. So then you tell them you're a worldcatcher. Why not? I'm a better painter than an illusionist, anyway, and I can mimic worldcatching good enough. But the more and more lies you keep throwing onto the pile, the more you—hands *up!*"

Chris thrust his hands all the way into the air, heart leaping into his throat. "I wasn't doing anything," he said quickly.

"They're just tired."

"You think I'm something evil," Grey said. "I don't *want* to be here, you know. I just want this all to be over."

Chris held his tongue, simply putting one foot in front of the other. They weren't far from the narrow staircase to the third floor, now. He didn't know what the hells he was going to do when they reached the top of it.

He stumbled and caught himself before he fell when the barrel of the gun jabbed *hard* into the back of his head. His wound from Grapevine Street pulled and he yelped in pain. "*Say* it," Grey commanded. "I know what you're thinking. *Say* it."

Chris gritted his teeth. "You killed those people," he ground out.

"It wasn't supposed to be that way."

"You took a knife into the Duke's estate."

"I didn't—I didn't know how he'd react, when he realized it was me. I thought, if he attacked me, I should be able to defend myself. I didn't think anything would come of it." A pause, and then, more forcefully. "I *didn't*."

"I didn't say a word," Chris murmured.

"It was never all meant to happen like this, dammit. I *loved* Viktor. It was never—you wouldn't understand. Nobody would ever bloody understand."

He didn't want to understand. He didn't want to think about any of this, not when Rosemary was in danger. He ran through possible courses of action in his mind. He could fall backwards down the stairs into the faceshifter, knocking him off his feet. No, that would never work. He could point to a place on the wall, say it was the illusive vault, hope against hope Grey would cross to see it for himself. No, that was idiotic. He could simply break into a run and hope his luck was stronger than Grey's aim. Certainly, if he wanted the back of his head cooked. He felt dizzy.

"I never wanted him dead. It was the *last* thing I *ever* wanted. It was just…after he *rejected* me, I just—"

"The stairs are here," Chris interrupted, not wanting to hear anything the man had to say. It wasn't the Duke's body he was seeing in his mind's eye, but Ana's. She'd bled to death, holding her guts in, trying to understand why the man she'd so loved was doing this to her. Ethan Grey could lie to himself all he wanted, but that alone made him a monster. "We need to go up."

Grey pressed the barrel of the gun between Chris's shoulder blades and pushed him towards the narrow staircase. Chris stumbled forward a step and mounted the first step, hands still held above his head. He wondered where his sister and her governess were. Were they terrified? Were they hurt? What had Grey done when he took Miss Albany's dress? *No*, he reminded himself, *focus on now. You need to do something. Find something and do it.*

An image flashed before his eyes. The salamander's scales all going dark, its sinuous body becoming limp. The way it had just fallen.

He froze for a second. The barrel of the gun bumped against his back. "Keep moving," Grey growled.

They were nearly to top of the stairs. Chris did as he was told, taking another step, and then another. He still didn't know what had happened, that day. There hadn't been *time* to consider it, to wonder.

They reached the top. Chris's heart thumped in his throat. He knew he had about half a second during which it would be worth the risk, and even then, the case might be that nothing happened at all. But he had to take the risk, the chance. He rounded down the hallway, and Grey was still on the last step. There was no line of sight between his back and the barrel of the gun. He closed his eyes tightly. He took a deep breath. He gathered his will.

And he *pushed*.

DROP IT, he projected, *smashing* every bit of conscious resolve against the faceshifter. He *forced* his concentrated willpower down Grey's throat, feeling it all rush out of him in a desperate wave. He heard a gasp like he'd crashed into the man and knocked his wind out, and it would have to have been enough.

He said a prayer and ran.

He dashed madly down the hall, pumping his arms and puffing out his breath. He heard a vile curse being spat, but there was no telltale sound of the pistol hitting the steps. His heart jumped in his mouth. No. "*Stop*," Grey roared, and Chris ran. He ran like devils were chasing after him. Where was he even *going*, he wondered, but he knew before his eyes even locked on the door.

"*Wrong choice*, Mister Buckley," Grey called, his voice no longer muffled by the narrow confines of the staircase, and Chris threw himself against the wall by instinct. He hit too hard, his head rolled along the plaster and smashed against a doorframe and stars erupted before his eyes, pain centered on the healing stitches along his hairline, but his movement had been wise. The *crack* and the *roar* of a discharging firepistol burned up the hallway behind him, and the tennis ball sized sphere of molten flame singed the hairs on the back of his neck as it sped past, punching through the plaster of the far wall. He stumbled back into motion, hand on the wall to keep from tripping and falling. He could see blue sky through the hole.

He *threw* himself against the doorway, fumbling with the latch. He couldn't stay still, it was *death* to stay still. He threw the door open and then himself inside of it. The door *shuddered* wildly in his hands and blackened splinters burst outwards, but the strong oak held against the fireball where the plaster hadn't. "I swear to Elder and Crone, Buckley, if you don't stop right *fucking* now—" Grey growled, his steps *thumping* up the hallway.

Chris stumbled over his old train set, knocked over his painted rocking horse. One of the carved handles that were its splendid ears snapped off when it hit the ground.

The window was still open from that night almost a week before when Ethan Grey had stood over his sister's bed wearing Chris's face and left a note and a knife. The sound of the rain was a pounding rush, its wetness a spray across Chris's face. He swung his weight up against it, his ribs crying out in bruised pain as they smashed against the windowsill. He reached up and out, gripping the shingles in this hands, and pulled himself up faster than he'd ever managed even as an eager child using the toy box as a boost. Squirming his body along the shingles, scratching and scraping until he was completely out on the roof, he pulled himself up tight into a ball and pressed his back against the overhang, shivering in the cool night air.

What now?

He heard the door to his childhood bedroom creak slowly open. "Mister Buckley," Grey's voice was dangerously quiet. Chris could barely hear it over the sound of the pouring rain. He closed his eyes and held his breath. "Mister Buckley, how exactly do you think this ends?" Grey continued. The floorboards creaked as he slowly made his way around the room. "If I find you, I put this gun against your head and pull the trigger. If I don't...well, your little sister and the brown shrew who watches her can pay for it, instead. Is that what you want, Mister Buckley?"

He couldn't stay where he was, shivering in the rain and hoping it would end. There was nothing Chris wanted more than to simply curl up and wait until the danger passed, but it wouldn't happen. It wouldn't. He forced his eyes open, turned his head in all directions, searching for his next move. When he craned his neck all the way around, and warm rain fell on his upturned face, his eyes fell on the wrought-iron trimmings cresting the overhang...and then the roofing not far above it...

As quietly as he could, Chris climbed to his feet and turned around.

"Gods, come *on*," Grey cried suddenly. Chris's hands froze on the iron trimmings they clung to, heart in his throat. But there was a tortured sort of desperation in Grey's voice as he continued. "I don't want to hurt anyone. I bloody *don't*. Just come on out and give me the royals and I'll go. I'll be *gone*." The iron was slick with rain. Chris's hands slipped as he pulled himself up. He tightened his grip and clung desperately to his weak purchase, hanging against the wall, fighting back terrified sobs. "If I *wanted* to hurt you or your sister, I'd have done it the first night I followed you home! Just come *out*."

Pulling himself up onto the overhang, Chris scrabbled with his socked feet to get purchase on the edge, and then perched there like a gargoyle, panting as softly as he could. Below, he could hear Grey begin to grow frustrated, tossing his boyhood wardrobe doors open, throwing his old things about, dumping over the toy box. Chris took a trembling breath and continued climbing, pulling himself up to the steeped roof hanging over the window he'd come out from. All it took was a glance down at the landing below to see how much higher this was than he'd anticipated. His head swam.

"It's just all gotten so out of *hand…*" Grey pleaded. "After Viktor, I thought it couldn't get any worse, but then Ana was there, telling me she knew what I was, what I'd done, and it just keeps *spiralling*, and, and…"

Chris remembered the knife slick and sticky in his hand, weaving in and out. Ana's voice howling, *I don't understand, I don't understand.* The way her blood had splattered the walls, the ceiling, and the frilly pastel room. No, he resolved, setting his jaw. No, he wouldn't feel pity for this man.

A rough, wild wind whipped his hair against his face, splattering his eyeglasses with large drops of water, and, he realized with a tremble in his heart, sending the blue curtains dancing in the room below him.

His fingers clutched the iron spikes cresting the edge of the roof in both hands. Warm rain poured down his face and dripped off his chin. "Ah," said Ethan Grey. "I see."

Chris breathed heavily, and trembled, and waited.

He saw Grey's head poke out from the room. Then his neck, and his shoulders, and finally, his back. The gun was gripping in his left hand, glowing orange and pulsing, but for the moment, he needed all the power of his arms to pull himself up.

Chris jumped down.

He landed on Grey's back just as the faceshifter was climbing to his feet. "*Oof*," he gasped in a rush of surprised air, dropping like a sack. The gun clattered against the slippery shingles, skipping to a halt just by the roof's edge, dancing from side to side with its grip in the rushing gutter. They rolled.

Chris tried to keep his arms wrapped around the taller man, but their skin was clammy and slippery from the rain. Grey struggled mightily against his grip. Chris wrapped his legs around him, gasping as Grey stumbled to his feet. He *heaved* his weight forward, unbalancing the taller man, forcing him back to his knees. When Grey went to bend forward and use his hands to brace his weight against the roof, he found himself scrabbling at empty air.

Chris's heart went into his throat. He saw the ground so far below, so far it could have been on the other side of the country. His head spun and his stomach shot up into his throat. In a panic, he threw himself back off Grey, hitting the roof's surface hard enough to jar every bone in his body. He shook soaking hair out of his eyes. Gods, he couldn't *see*.

He tore his specs off his face and threw them back into the window behind him, and when he looked back, Grey was standing above him. He had only a moment to process this before the taller man was *on* him, planting knees on either side of him, face close to his, and arms wrapping around his throat.

Chris had only enough time to *gasp* in one final breath before the faceshifter's thumbs pressed hard against his Adam's apple. "You should have just given me the sodding money," Grey hissed. His hot, moist breath was like a kiss of death against Chris's face.

He struggled to draw in a breath, just one sweet breath of air, but there was a dam in the way. He raised his hands, clawing his nails against Grey's wrists. He kicked his heels against the shingles.

His eyes went wide. His heart thumped blackly in his sinuses. *No air,* his body told him urgently. *No air. Need air.*

"You just *had* to keep asking her your *questions,*" Grey spat. "The only person who had all the pieces, and you kept pushing her to put it all together. It could have ended with Viktor! It didn't *need* to get bloody worse! The Deathsniffer herself left well enough alone! Why did *you* have to keep asking Ana your bloody *questions?*"

There were black spots appearing before his vision. They swam about, popped, and reappeared elsewhere, bigger and flashing blue and yellow and white. Chris's kicks were growing weaker, his thoughts losing their definition. The edges of everything blurred. He stared up into Ethan's grey eyes, mouthing words he couldn't form. Thoughts spiralled down into the blackness beneath thought like birds with broken wings. *No,* he tried to project against Grey. *Let me go. No.* But he couldn't find the will in him, and Grey's only reaction was the slight furrowing between his brows.

His face was wet.

Rosemary, Chris thought as everything dimmed, and then, *Mother...*

It seemed only fitting, somehow, that he died here. In a way, this was where he'd been born, coming into the world as if for the first time to the sound of screeching metal and shattering glass and the taste of vomit in his mouth.

From far away, a lifetime away, he heard someone begin to sing.

He could breathe. He gasped in air, coughing and sputtering. Grey's knee was against his chest, and he was kneeling, his head craned somewhere far away, listening. "What the bloody...?" he murmured, and Chris knew he had only one chance to live instead of die. And he had to live. He had to. Who else would protect Rosemary?

He gathered his will. *MURDERER,* he projected at Grey, *throwing* himself hard to one side at the same time.

"No," Grey gasped. He fell to one side, raising to clutch his chest as if his heart had burst. Chris rolled away. "I loved him. I'd have done *anything* for him to have *noticed* me like he did the *girls.*"

He was too weak, too clumsy, too woozy to spring to his feet, and so he pulled himself up with effort. Grey clutched his head in his hands. "I never meant to—I *never*—" He raised it then, glaring at Chris with the ferocity of a wounded animal, his body tensing. "You could *never understand!*"

Chris glanced for the gun and found it gone. It must have fallen, it must have been carried away by the rainfall rushing through the gutters. He didn't have time to think of a better plan. He threw himself at Grey.

They met in a clash of limbs. Grey's superiour weight bore them forward, stumbling towards the edge. One of Chris's socked feet went up to his ankle in water, and the gutter groaned and creaked beneath him. Grey's teeth were locked together in a terrifying, determined grimace, his jaw clenched, his eyes wild. He forced Chris back, back. They teetered on the edge, high enough for a fall to splatter a head like a burst melon, and he was so much stronger, so much heavier, so much *clumsier...*

Yes.

Chris made his body go limp. Grey's eyes went wide. They overbalanced, shot forward, and Chris dropped to his knees at the last second. Water splashed all around him; the gutter shrieked. Grey's arms flailed. His feet tangled in the lines of Miss Albany's grey skirts. He pitched forward, and as he fell, he screamed, and he screamed, and he screamed, until he—

The gutter snapped.

Chris's limbs flailed, his hands grasped wildly for purchase, and his heart slammed up against the roof of his mouth. He fell for what seemed like forever and then his fingers barely managed to lock against the edge of the roof. He hung there, suspended in the rain. Grey had fallen to his death and it had been his fault. Water poured from the broken gutter into his upturned face, tasting of mould and dead leaves. He coughed and sputtered but the only other option was to look down. His feet flailed, searching on instinct for somewhere to stand, some solid ground. If he looked down, he'd see Ethan Grey, or whatever remained of him. Did murdering a murderer cancel itself out? He was hanging. His fingers were slipping. The water rushed over him and he was drowning in it.

He wondered if it might be better to simply fall and die and have it done with. He was getting tired of nearly dying.

No, The warm thought coursed through him like a cloudling's spark, one moment of perfect clarity in a sea of confusion and chaos. *You need to live. Fight. Live. Help is coming.*

And then, moments later, he heard her sweet voice. *"Chris!"*

Her water song was the greatest of them all. It was an ancient song, a binding song, none of its words recognizable anymore as anything but an incantation. Rosemary's voice was girlish and innocent, and as she sang, a flurry of frothing bubbles and a throaty woman's chuckle erupted near his ear.

Rosemary's song guided the turquoise undine with her waving indigo hair. The elemental swirled to the gutter, adding the water from her eternally pouring amphora to the deluge springing forth from the drain. Even as Chris watched, the water took on a life of its own, moving, *thickening.* It formed a translucent, shimmering rope. It looped around his wrist, looping and looping all the way up to his elbow, and then it lifted him.

He found himself on his hands and knees, gasping and trembling, warm rain falling all around him. Two tiny hands touched his cheeks and he opened his eyes to see the undine cradling his face in her fingers, staring into his eyes with her head tilted to one side. Her azure skin glowed faintly and her lips curved in a fey little smile, but the curiosity in her swirling eyes was like nothing human, and Chris felt as though he stared into the depths of a great maelstrom from which there was no escape.

He recoiled as though he'd been burned, and then Rosemary's song reached its crescendo and the undine popped like a bubble, erased from any sort of existence he understood.

And then his sister was wrapping her arms around his neck, burying her face into the curve of his collarbone. "*Chris*," she sobbed. "Did he hurt you? Are you okay? Where is he?"

For a moment, he could only *be*, resting there on his hands and knees, breathing and *living*, stunned at both. And then he crashed back into himself, and he realized who was here with him. He gathered her up into his arms, burying his face into her limp curls, holding her so tightly she protested and squirmed, but he couldn't bear to let her go. He couldn't bear to let her go.

"Rosemary," he choked out. "Oh, Rosemary. I swear I'll never let you fall into danger ever again."

That was all that mattered.

Chapter Twenty-Nine

M iss Albany clutched a heavy blanket around her body to hide her state of undress from all the police officers, reporters, and photographers scurrying about, but Chris couldn't help but feel embarrassed on her behalf, seeing how uncomfortable she clearly was. And how miserable. He didn't think he'd ever seen anyone look more terrible wet. Her stringy hair clung to her forehead and cheeks and neck like the grasping fingers of a drowned woman, and everything about her seemed to droop like a doused flower.

Still, despite her obvious discomfort and the spots of colour that refused to leave her cheeks, she comported herself with professional calm and clarity as she nodded to Officer Dawson's pressing questions. "Yes," she said. "He was wearing the face of Fernand Spencer and separated me from Miss Buckley before subduing and binding me, and then—then removing my gown and wearing it." Her chin raised slightly in stubborn pride. He had to admire that. His own state of undress was considerably less extensive, and he felt thoroughly naked. "I believe it must have been too difficult for him to shift his face and clothing at the same time."

"That's consistent with our records on the breed," Officer Dawson said, making a face in clear disgust. "He bought Miss Buckley in after that?"

Miss Albany nodded. "We're very fortunate Mister Buckley managed to somehow overpower him," she said, and her voice lost a bit of its flintiness. "If he hadn't thought so quickly…" She glanced over at him, and when she met his eyes, he looked away from her, his *own* cheeks burning. He recalled with a strange flutter and twist at his insides how he'd wrapped his arms around her and kissed her so readily when he'd thought she'd offered herself for it.

Another police officer, one he didn't recognize, was talking to a manic Rosemary. His sister alternated between what seemed like restless excitement and skittish terror as she reviewed the details of their ordeal. "Miss Albany helped me spit out my gag, and then I could sing! If I was as loud as I could be, I *knew* I could reach the gnome in the mirror and ask him to find you! I called another gnome to come and untie our ropes, and then I had to go and help my brother, even if it was dangerous!"

"You were a very brave girl," the police officer said with a flash of teeth through his dark bristly beard. He reached up and gave her a respectful tip of his hat. "I'd say you about rescued him."

Rosemary shot him a mischievous smile. "I'd say," she agreed, her blue eyes sparkling. Chris returned her grin with one of his own. It wasn't easy to find a smile for her, but it was the least he could do, after she'd saved his life for the second time in less than a week. Of the two states she was fluctuating between, he preferred the slightly unnerving cheer.

The rain had ceased, though the clouds had yet to clear, and people were stopping in the street to watch all the bustle milling around in the front of the Buckley estate. It had been years since there had been any activity there at all, aside from rapidly growing weeds and grass that never seemed to be cut often enough. They couldn't hear anything from beyond the soundshield, but they could tell something of interest was going on, and it was human nature to pause and peer and wonder at it. No press had been allowed inside the soundshield, either, but that didn't stop the photographers from taking their pictures for the papers. Chris couldn't even imagine what the headlines were going to assume for tomorrow's paper.

"Christopher?" the uniformed officer standing before him asked.

Chris blinked and shook his head, directing his attention back to William Cartwright. "I'm sorry," he said with his best apologetic smile. "Could you repeat the question?"

William sighed irritably, giving him a flat look. "Did you *push* him?"

"No," Chris said quickly. "He fell." In truth, the series of events that had passed on the rainy rooftop were a strange, adrenaline-fuelled and distorted blur in his memory. Already, the edges were all indistinct and runny and fuzzed, like the world without his eyeglasses. He couldn't say with certainty whether or not he had pushed Ethan Grey to his death, but in the version of events he'd already begun to build around in his mind, he hadn't.

He had enough trauma on that rooftop.

William made an unconvinced sound in the back of his throat, scribbling something down in his notebook with a pen that looked nearly out of ink. It seemed to create more scratches than writing. "Did he confess to the crimes he's been accused of, and would you testify accordingly before a magistrate of the Queen's peace?"

"Yes, he did. And yes, of course I would, if I were called on."

Chris watched him write in silence for a moment, but after a quick glance around to see who might be listening in, leaned forward. "I thought you weren't a real police officer," he murmured, his curiosity having grown to overshadow his polite restraint.

The timeseer flicked him a nonplussed look and snapped the notebook closed. "I'm not," he said. "But there aren't nearly enough of them, like anything else these days. And I have a uniform." He rolled his eyes. "Besides, despite all the fuss made about truthsniffing, it's really not bloody difficult. Anyone could do it." He tucked the notebook into the breast pocket of his uniform, and reached up to settle his hat more firmly on his head. His full lips pursed. "When I said I'd like to see you again, an hour in the future wasn't exactly what I had in mind."

"Ah," Chris said, flushing. He lowered his gaze. "Neither did I."

A beat of silence, and then William folded his hands before him. "You don't seem well," he said.

Chris snapped his eyes back to the other young man's. "I just fought for my life." His voice was sharp. "I don't *feel* well."

"You pity yourself," William said, not seeming to notice the warning in Chris's tone. He tucked his long, shining hair behind his ears. "Instead of just doing things, you fret needlessly about them." He gave Chris a long look, one that seemed especially prying because of Chris's state of undress. Chris wrapped his arms around his middle and gave the young man a look he hoped was sour and threatening, but it didn't seem to be heeded. William simply turned about with that confident peckishness he displayed in all things. "Just do them and stop feeling sorry for yourself. It's unappealing. No one likes that." And he walked off, ignoring Chris's attempt to call after him and have it out.

Now he stood alone in the hurricane of movement around him. One of the reporters beyond the soundshield caught his eye, and he waved him over enthusiastically with a wide smile, but Chris turned away in disgust. The vultures seemed to follow his family about everywhere, of late, and fate seemed inclined to simply bred more corpses for them to come down and feast on.

He found himself walking without really intending to. He laid his hand on Rosemary's shoulder as he passed her, and smiled awkwardly at Miss Albany without fully meeting her eyes, but he didn't stop at either of them. Though he never sat and decided his destination, he'd had one in mind from the moment he started moving. *Instead of doing things, you fret needlessly about them.* Well, perhaps he did. Perhaps, wherever he knew him from, William Cartwright knew him better than he knew himself.

Olivia Faraday stood with her chin between her fingers,

examining the splattered corpse of Ethan Grey like it were a collapsed cake: disappointing and unpleasant, but perhaps there would be better luck with the next one. Grateful to not be taking notes, for once, Chris didn't let himself look very hard at the body. Instead, he looked very hard at Olivia. The look of mild, scholarly interest on her face, the pull at her lips that could have been either a smile or a grimace, the studious depth to her icy blue eyes. She was wearing a bustled red gown with black trimmings, black lace gloves, and her curled hair was piled up and covered by a hat garnished in stuffed male hummingbirds, all the very height of fashion. Her crutches and bandaged leg did a great deal to spoil the illusion of an elegant and average socialite, however. As did the way she stared down at the corpse he'd caused, as if judging whether or not it was still suitable to eat.

He tried to remember her as he'd seen her that night in the hospital, but that Olivia seemed very far away, and this one seemed so close.

"Olivia," he said, and she snapped to attention like she'd been shocked.

"Christopher!" she exclaimed with a manic grin.

"I—" he began before being cut off.

She reached out and seized both of his hands in hers. "You are a *genius*!" she crowed. Before he could react to either of these things with more than a confused gape, her face darted forward and she pressed a kiss to each of his cheeks before wrapping her arms about his middle and pulling him tight. "An absolute *genius!*"

"Oh," he said faintly. He put his hand to her shoulder and went to push her away, but couldn't bring himself to do so. His stiff body hung in her arms like frozen meat. She didn't seem to notice.

"Do you know what Constance would have done if a killer had come into her house and threatened her? Or Herbert? Or Margaret? Or Timothy?"

"I...can't imagine."

"They would have bloody gotten *killed* is what they would have done!" Olivia giggled madly. "Every single one of them! Useless! *They* would have been the ones on the ground, here, looking like someone dropped a bloody watermelon. But you! Not you! Not Christopher Buckley!" Her laugh could be described only as a cackle. Chris was sure if she'd been hale and hearty, she'd have picked him up by his middle and swung him around. She gripped the collar of his shirt in both her hands, not even seeming to notice he was half-dressed. "You are perfect!"

"...thank you," Chris said. He didn't know what else *to* say. He wished she was angry at him for spoiling her resolution. Or sympathetic he'd been put under such distress. Or *anything* but what she *was*. Anything else, anything at all, would have made this easier.

She kissed him once more, a lusty peck on the mouth, before turning back to survey her new corpse once again. "Bloody fantastic," she breathed. There were two spots of colour high on her cheeks, and she breathed like she'd run a marathon. "Bloody fucking fantastic," she said again, and he felt *his* cheeks begin to burn. "Did he say anything?" she asked. "Was I right? Was it jealousy that made him kill the Duke?"

"Something like that," Chris said. "From what I gathered, he'd hoped the Duke would...I don't know. Suddenly find it all a brilliant idea, if he came to him as Vanessa and then changed his face to his own. Obviously, it didn't work out, and being rejected was..."

"He didn't handle it well, no, of course not," Olivia said, and for a moment, a bit of her glee faded. "Who likes being rejected? Especially someone like him. His whole bloody life was probably some form of rejection or another, hmm? I almost feel sorry for him."

Chris choked on those words. "He was a murderer."

Olivia tsked. "Of course he was! We determined that. But nobody is only just *one* thing. Mister Grey was a killer. And a brilliant artist! And a handsome charmer! And he was also a man who'd been taught to hate himself. Hating yourself that much for that long could make anyone snap." For a tiny flash of a moment, he saw the Olivia from the hospital. But she hadn't hated herself, and her single moment of softness passed as she clapped her hands before her and continued, voice bubbling. "And snap he did! And the daughter! Were we right? An innocent question and then panic?" She shot him a look like a little girl on her birthday, eyes twinkling. "Tell me we got it!"

Chris nodded.

"Naturally! And the Duchess…" Olivia chewed at her lip, and then shot him a questioning look.

"He didn't mention the Duchess," Chris admitted. "Or if he did, I don't remember it."

"Hmm," Olivia mused. "That's odd, isn't it? He admits to everything else, but not that? Why? Obvious enough it was him, I'd think." She looked over the body, and a small furrow appeared between her brows. "Obvious enough…" A dark cloud seemed to pass beneath her features, but in an instant, it was gone. When she turned back to him, the sun had come out, and she was bright-eyed and grinning. "I say, Christopher, I think we should—"

"Miss Faraday," he said, forcing the words out and finding them more painful than he'd ever anticipated. "I regret to inform you I need to resign my position in your employment."

Olivia blinked. The twinkle went out of her eyes. Her smile fell off her face and died between them. "What?"

"I'm leaving Darrington," he hurried to explain. "I don't know exactly when, yet"—*or how, or where I'll be going*—"but it will be as soon as I possibly can, and I think it would be best if I tendered my resignation now, rather than later."

"I don't understand," Olivia said. Her eyes scanned his face, as though searching for a sign he was lying to her, telling some grand joke. As if he would.

He pushed himself onwards, knowing if he looked back for a moment, he'd lose his nerve. "I'll continue doing any work you wish of me while I prepare to leave, until you're able to find a new assistant. I'd prefer to make the transition as smooth as possible for the both of us. If you could—"

She slapped him.

His head *snapped* to one side. His thoughts scattered in all directions like a flock of disturbed ducks. He tasted blood, and raised a hand to his lip to see if it came away bloody. It didn't.

He shook his head, trying to gather his wits back together. He readjusted his spectacles. When he blinked down at the face of Olivia Faraday, she stared up at him with a face that was *not*, as he'd expected, furious, but rather deeply and immeasurably wounded. He waited for her to fling accusations at his face, but they didn't come.

They stared at one another for a long time. He saw something that might have been tears glimmering in Olivia's eyes, and might have simply been glittering resolve. Her lip trembled, but the hand she'd raised to strike him never fell, never even moved. As for himself, he felt...he just felt...

"Oh, thank all the Gods! Christopher!"

He'd never been so grateful to hear someone call his name in his life. He blinked and turned away from Olivia, towards the voice he'd heard. He broke into a smile at seeing Fernand push his way past disgruntled police officers, his face a mixture of relief and concern, and it was very easy, very *welcome* to find the excuse leave Olivia's side and hurry to Fernand's.

He went to clasp hands with the old man, but, to his surprise, Fernand spread his arms wide and folded him into a tight embrace instead. He thumped on Chris's back with the pommel of his cane, making Chris gasp as the wind in his lungs protested. But then he laughed and accepted it, returning the gesture. He tried not to think of Olivia, standing somewhere behind him. He tried not to think of how inexplicably devastated she had been. "You, young master," Fernand wheezed into his ear, "need to stop getting into these life-threatening situations! Gods, it seems every time I have someone on the mirror, lately, they're telling me how you nearly lost your sorry life!"

"Mother Deorwynn, Fernand, believe me, I know," Chris laughed. He pulled away and looked up at the old man, who even stooped was taller than he was. "If I said I was sorry, would you forgive me for it?"

"Bah!" Fernand scoffed, clapping him on the back one last time. "There's no point in saying you're sorry if you're just going to keep doing it."

"Well, I'm certainly intending to stop. I just…" Chris blinked. Suddenly, it was as though a brilliantly illuminated path was spread out before him. He saw exactly what he had to do to leave Darrington, to help Rosemary. All he had to do was ask. "Fernand," he said. "I…" He shook his head, amazed at how obvious it was. "Could I speak to you inside?"

Fernand frowned, but nodded readily. The police officers let them go inside without any complaint, and though some of them milled about in the foyer and on the second floor landing, when Chris brought Fernand into the dining room and they sat the head of the table, they might as well have been in their own little world.

The sumfinder's lined face was a picture of concern as he laid his cane across his legs and leaned towards Chris. "What is it, young master?" he asked gently. "Is there something I can do to help you?"

"*Yes*," Chris said, and it was easier than he'd expected. He gave a weary smile and folded his hands in front of him on the table. He sighed. "Fernand…you know I hate asking for anything more from you than you willingly give. I still don't even understand why it is that you *have* given so much. We haven't been able to pay you since I was sixteen, and—"

"Even if you could have, I wouldn't have taken it," Fernand cut in. He laid a wrinkled hand across Chris's folded pair, and when

Chris met his eyes, there were full of a gentle sort of fondness. No—not fondness. Something deeper. "You and little Rosemary are more than just children of a favourite client, Christopher," he said kindly. "You're family to me. You're more family to me than the family I actually have."

Chris closed his eyes and let out a deep breath. Well, it was time to test that. "I need your *help*, Fernand," he breathed. "Doctor Livingstone was completely right. Rosemary can't stay in Darrington. She can't. It's a cesspit and it'll ruin her. But the doctor is gone and there's no one to fulfill his promise, and I don't even have the money to board up the estate, much less to move us anywhere." He opened his eyes and focused deeply on Fernand's, trying to pour the depths of his pleading into his eyes, hoping his oldest and truest friend would see it, there. "Can you help us?" he asked. "Please? We don't need much, just enough to—"

Fernand was chuckling. Gently, he squeezed Chris's hand and shook his head. "Young master," he said with a smile. "Oh, young master."

"What?" Chris asked. "What's—what's so funny?"

Fernand shook his head, still chuckling. "Yesterday, I mirrored my useless prat of a nephew, and I told him he won't be inheriting my estate in Summergrove even if he were the last upstart in Tarland." His smile widened when he saw the look on Chris's face, and he squeezed again. "You see, Christopher? We're family. I knew what you needed before you even asked for it, and I'm more than willing to give it. Summergrove is a beautiful little country town. Far nicer than Cooperton is, or anywhere else you could take Rosemary. She'll be safe there. She'll be happy there. *You'll* be happy there."

Chris felt a prickling in the back of his eyes. *No, I can't accept this,* was the courteous, proper response. Certainly, he could never condone a man writing a blood relative out of his last will and testament, just to pass everything onto a pair of impoverished siblings who were technically employers. A gentleman would decline the offer, graciously, and ask with great humility for a loan with interest, instead.

He clasped Fernand's hand in both of his. "I can't thank you enough for this, Fernand," he said. There was ferocity in his voice. He squeezed his eyes tight, trying to shut away the tears of thanks. "I *will* pay you back for this, not because I think I owe it to you, but because I *want* to."

When he opened his eyes, it was to the sight of Fernand using his free hand to wipe tears from his wrinkled old cheeks. He caught Chris's eye and nodded gravely, and then held one another's gaze until Chris broke into a smile and pulled his hands away, settling them back down into his lap.

Fernand found a bit of his usual composure, then, straightening and fixing his tie and giving a firm nod as though to himself. "Well," he said, and it came out very hoarse. He cleared his throat and tried again. "Well, then, Christopher," he said. His voice was gruff, but staid. "I'd like you to come by tomorrow, late in the evening, and we'll have some papers drawn up. I'll mirror my solicitor in the afternoon, give him a few extra royals to put a rush on it, and we can have it all dealt with and finalized by Godsday at the latest, hmm?"

And then something passed beneath his gaze, something Chris couldn't place. Fernand swallowed hard, blinked and furrowed his brow, and then continued speaking, his voice even gruffer than before. "And…and there's something else, young master," he said. "Something…something your father left behind." He shook his head. "He meant for it to be for Rosemary. He told me you weren't strong enough for it, you never would be strong enough for it. But your father…your father was wrong about a great many things, Chris. And I always thought he was the most wrong about you. Michael saw only one sort of strength, but he was a short-sighted blighter to the very end. Aye, you're strong enough for it, my boy. You're as strong now as Rosemary will ever be."

Chris had never heard words that had made him so happy. "What is it?" he asked.

He didn't know what to expect. He certainly didn't think the next words would chill him down to his core and make all the lights in the room dim. "A list," Fernand said quietly. "A very important list."

That night, after the corpse had been taken away, the reporters had been given their damned interviews, and the police officers had finally been satisfied with all of their answers, Chris sank into a fitful, restless sleep.

Fever dreams ripped through his mind, vivid and vibrant and seething with motion and colour. He dreamed of voices speaking next to his ear while he couldn't move a muscle, of being held down against his bed by Duke val Daren's kiss, of a ring of fire floating above his head and Olivia slapping him with her face blackened and slapping him with her face pale. He dreamed of Analaea's insides on the outside, Duchess val Daren's death rattle, the Duke's penis covered in blood and tucked back into his trousers to spare the family embarrassment. He raised a firepistol and pulled the trigger against Ethan Grey's temple, and the vilest sort of deceiver burned like kindling, screaming for mercy. *Nobody could understand*, he shrieked. *Nobody could understand.* And the worst part of it was that, for just one moment, Chris thought that he could.

He dreamed of Rosemary's voice raised in eerie, skin-crawlingly wrong music, binding a host of elementals to her command, but she couldn't keep them under her control, and they turned on her, burning and drowning and cutting and freezing.

He grabbed Rachel Albany and kissed her deeply, but she pulled away, her hair rolling around her shoulders, whispering *my brother will see us.* Francis Livingstone smiled a sad smile and waved goodbye to him with a black face, hanging from a noose. William Cartwright snapped a pocket watch shut, made an angry sound, but when he raised his face, his cheeks were wet with tears. *You didn't remember,* he accused. *You said you'd always remember.*

He dreamed of sitting on the roof and watching the Floating Castle fall just when he wished it would.

When his eyelids flickered open to morning light streaming through his window, and he saw the drawn, pale face of Olivia Faraday standing over his bed, he thought for a long moment it was just another nightmare.

Certainly, it must have been just another nightmare.

Her mouth tightened. He squinted against the sunlight, throwing up his arm against it. He closed his eyes, and then opened them, and she was still there. Sun picked out the golden highlights in her white-blonde hair, brought colour to her pale eyes. The morning light didn't dissolve her like a ghost.

"Mister Buckley," she said quietly, her voice humming. "I need you to come with me."

"What?" he asked, not understanding any of it. "Why?"

"I need you to come with me," she repeated. "Now." There was no command or anything resembling a sharp edge in her manner. Her eyes were soft, and her mouth was sad, and something was very wrong.

Their hackney stopped in a part of town he knew very well.

Despite having known Fernand Spencer since he was old enough to know anyone, Chris had been to his home less than twenty times. When he'd been a child, he and his parents and eventually little Rosemary would go visit for dinner on

Midwintersfest. They'd stuff themselves with roast wild geese, apple cider, and blackcurrant pies. After the Floating Castle, they'd maintained that tradition, and it had always seemed wrong to the lot of them to go there on any day but the shortest. Chris barely recognized the place without snow.

In a trance, he followed Olivia into the manor. It was small, compared to the Buckley estate, but Chris had always thought it was cozy and warm and comforting. Even without the candles and ribbons, the fir boughs and pinecones, the holly sprigs and mistletoe, it was a place that meant *peace* and *love* and *family*, more so than even his own estate ever had.

Olivia lead him up a flight of stairs, and then stopped before a door. She turned to Chris, her face grave. "His housekeeper found him this morning," she said quietly. "She mirrored the station. The station put the file on Maris's desk, and she took a quick look and then assigned it to me. She didn't read the name. She didn't know the connection at all. No one did. It was just a coincidence. Just one of those things."

He nodded.

Olivia nodded, too. "The doors were locked from the inside," she said. "The windows, too. All latched. I've been over it all five times. According to all the evidence, there's only one explanation."

Chris nodded again.

And Olivia did, too. "All right," she said, and opened the door.

He stepped inside the modestly furnished water closet, sweeping his eyes around his surroundings. He felt curiously numb. He'd been in here before, many times. He'd come up to take a piss after having too much mulled and spiced cider, the only day of the year he ever indulged. He'd look out the window at the falling snow while he made his water, and then he'd let the bound undine take it away somewhere else. He'd admire the massive, claw-footed ceramic washtub on his way out and wish he could replace the old one at his own home for one like this.

403

How curious, that he'd find his oldest and only friend in that tub. How curious.

The bathwater was scarlet and the old man's face was white. His eyes were open, staring grotesquely at nothing, and his features were locked into an expression of deep sadness and pain. One of his hands was in the bathwater, still, and hidden by the thick red mess it had become. The other splayed out of the tub, hanging over the floor, and the wrist was slashed down to the bone. Blood had rushed out of it, gushing all over the tiled floor, a red waterfall. A knife had fallen onto the floor beside the tub.

Fernand's poor face. His staring eyes bored into Chris's soul. He crossed the floor, uncaring of what he did to Olivia's precious crime scene, and drew the old man's eyes closed. It was more difficult than he'd anticipated, and he had no choice but to use force, and rather than an act of respect, a granting of peace, it felt like a desecration.

And then he stood there, hands fists at his side, until the first sob came, wracking through his body. And then the next. And then the next. He fell to his knees, his trousers pressing into the sticky, congealed blood. He clung to the side of the tub like it was his lifeline.

Olivia was mercifully silent. Chris was barely aware of her existence as he sat there, pathetically weeping out his soul. He seized Fernand's limp, cold hand, sticky with blood, and he pulled it to his chest, gripping it tightly, threaded his living fingers with those dead, lifeless ones. The madness swept down on him like a tide, and he let it carry him away. This grief. This mad, blind grief that blotted out anything else. He let it pick him up and take him somewhere a million miles away, a cold dark place without hope or sense or future, and nothing mattered, nothing bloody mattered at all.

It felt like years had passed when he went to draw more tears from the well and found it completely dry. He heaved and sputtered without them for a time, but they quieted, as well, in time, and when he sat back on his heels in the dead silence that fell, and cracked his puffy eyes open, his eyes fell on a paper.

A paper covered in familiar handwriting.

"That's what I brought you here to see," Olivia's voice said quietly. "After I take it off the floor, it gets put into evidence. And then even I can't touch it, once I rule on the case. Which I assume I'll have to do, once William runs a seeing on that knife. Like I said, there's only one explanation."

With shaking hands, Chris reached out and peeled the paper up from the floor. Three quarters of it were soaked completely through with Fernand's lifeblood. Whatever writing had once been there was gone for good. But the first quarter of the page was still readable, though droplets dotted it here and there, and Chris's heart pounded in his throat as he scanned it.

My dear sweet Rosemary,

If you're reading this, I'm not there with you any longer. I have left you in some way that did not seem entirely natural or lacking in suspicion. I do not know whether this will happen, but there is the chance it will, and the chance is great enough for me to write this letter. I am leaving it with Mister Spencer, along with instructions that it be given to you once you are officially categorized. I hope, by the time you are reading this, you've had time to heal from my departure from your life.

It is important that the contents of this letter never reach your sweet mother or your dear brother. They are cut from the same cloth, just as you and I are, and neither of them have the strength you and I share, my darling. Your mother is a fragile creature, and your brother a delicate one. Neither would ever be able to attend to this task I have left behind for you, and you must exercise caution to hide this from them. The last thing you would want is to incite one of Christopher's jealous fits, correct?

Enclosed, I have left a list I have spent the last five years compiling. I realize it is not as helpful as it might be, but you must understand just how difficult it has been to track down even this information. It is imperative that—

The red tide enveloped the writing there. Chris peeled back the page, and, sure enough, there was another beneath it.

Katie, it read, *sumfinder*.

He furrowed his brow, running down the items—or were they names—that hadn't been rendered indecipherable by the blood that had soaked even higher up this page than the last.

Maiden, spiritbinder.

Boathouse, truthsniffer (?).

Wil IV, lifeknitter.

?????, lifeknitter.

Dorothy, ??????

??????, heartreader(?) (needs more investigation)

Panther, spiritbinder.

The final name was underlined and circled multiple times. And all beneath it were impossible to make out.

"You should probably make a copy," Olivia suggested, and Chris nodded.

"You…" his voice scraped painfully through his throat. He coughed. "You might bring me something to weave on," he said, and heard her turn and walk away, leaving him alone with the letter from his father and the body of his friend. "Oh, Fernand," he whispered into the quiet. "Oh, Fernand, *why?*"

And as it turned out, he had tears left to cry, after all.

The pantry smelled of spices and preserves and the sweet scent of old rotten apples. Christopher barely moved when he heard the door open behind him, and then close. He stared blankly at the leg of the table he sat at, blinking slowly in the tirelessly cheerful light streaming in from the single high window. When the blanket was wrapped around his shoulders, he reached a hand out to pull it closer around him, and when her graceful, long-fingered hand slid a mug of hot apple cider onto the table before him, it was all he could do from picking it up and hurling it at a wall.

Olivia settled into the other chair at the table. She leaned her crutches against the wall and propped her injured leg up on a big old jar of raspberry preserves. He couldn't help but notice she didn't even try to make eye contact, not even when he refocused his gaze to try and make it with her. He didn't know if that was for his benefit, or her own.

"Thank you," he murmured very quietly. Contrary to what he *wanted* to do, he took the cup into his hands, surrounding its body with his grip. The warmth soaked through the cup and into his skin. He breathed deep the scent. He didn't drink, though. He didn't want to drink.

Olivia ran her pinkie finger along the edge of the table. When he bothered to care, he noted how she'd cut her hair considerably shorter since their night at the hospital together. It fell only to her shoulders, now. The burns, he suspected, were the cause of the change. He doubted she would have gone to a barber if she'd had the choice. He wondered if it had already been done the day before, when they had spoken over Ethan Grey's broken body. When she had slapped him. He hadn't noticed. That was odd. He always noticed that sort of thing.

She didn't say anything, and so he did. "I don't understand," he said. "I spoke to him yesterday. He was fine. He was bloody fine."

"I don't understand, either," Olivia said quietly. "I never understand."

They weren't talking about the same thing, he knew, but it didn't seem to matter. "Why would he—why? Yesterday, he was..." He shook his head. "It doesn't make sense. It doesn't bloody make sense."

"He had an appointment with his solicitor today," Olivia said. He flinched at the prying tone of her question. He could even *see* her attempting, as she never did, to blunt her edges, and still it made him want to stand and walk out of the room to see her treat Fernand's suicide like just more death to stick her nose in. "Do you...know anything about that?"

He could have laughed. Yes, he knew plenty about that. He knew that, in addition to having lost his only friend in the entire world, the one single thing left in his life that had been there for as long as he had...he'd lost his road out of Darrington, too. He hadn't signed anything. Fernand hadn't even met with the solicitor. The only people who knew anything about Fernand's intentions were himself and the nephew, who would certainly not be advocating any changes to the inheritance. "I don't think it's related," was all he said, miserably.

Olivia nodded. He could see her burning to ask more questions. She wanted to pick his brain to find out everything she knew in relation to Fernand, to why he would have done such a thing. It wasn't enough to have a solution, not for Olivia Faraday. She needed an answer, as well.

She didn't ask, though. He had to credit her for that, even in his ravaged emotional state. She didn't ask. He thought of how she'd looked the day before, the strange and genuine devastation on her face when he'd told her he no longer intended to be her assistant. For some reason, he doubted she'd made that face when Constance had resigned.

It was as if she heard his thoughts. "Why did you leave?" she asked. Her voice was very small, as if she feared his answer.

He sighed. He considered taking a sip from his cup, but he still didn't want to. Not without a stomach full of goose. Not without Fernand. "I told you. I'm leaving Darrington." And he closed his eyes, shaking his head. "I *was* leaving Darrington, at least. Now I don't bloody well know *what* I'm doing."

"*Why?*"

"Because of *Rosemary*," he said, snapping his eyes open and glaring at her. "*Obviously*. Haven't you understood *any* of what I've been experiencing, these weeks I've worked with you? None of this was ever—it wasn't supposed to *be* this way. It was supposed to be *simple*, at least until she was categorized. Not easy, but bloody *simple*. But then that *rubbish* with the cloudlings at White Clover changed *everything*, and ever since then, try as I may, I can't bloody *protect* her!" He slammed the cup down on the table. Olivia looked up at him with wide eyes, and he realized he'd climbed to his feet, he'd raised his voice, and somehow, once again, tears were streaming down his cheeks.

Angrily, he swiped at them, continuing before she could interject. "I can't. Not here, at least," he said, sinking back into his chair. "Not in this city. Not so long as every eye is on her face. The only way out is out of Darrington, and Fernand—" He choked and gasped and swallowed. "Fernand was going to help us. He was going to send us to Summergrove. Everything was finally—Gods, how am I going to protect her *now?*"

A bubble of pure rage rose in his throat, rose into his mouth and then popped. Madness overtook him and, in the most childish display he'd exhibited since he was nine years old, he knocked the cup across the table as though it had personally offended him. Cider flew everywhere, a torrent of hot spicy liquid, and Olivia gasped and leaned away from the trajectory of the cup as it bounced off the table, hit the solid stone floor, and burst into a hundred pieces.

Immediately, he felt ashamed, slumping back in his chair. Breaking Fernand's cup and spraying apple all over Fernand's pantry was *not* going to bring Fernand back. Nothing would do that, not a bloody thing. He was only making a fool of himself. He choked back a sob, raising a fist to press it tight against his forehead. It pulled the skin of his healing gash.

"I'm sorry," Olivia said gently.

He knew it was a stretch for her. All of this. But he couldn't bring himself to care, so he merely shrugged one shoulder in surly acceptance of the empty comfort, not wanting to look at her.

He'd thought that would be it, but he saw her hesitate out of the corner of his eye, and then continue speaking. "It wasn't...me, then?" she asked.

"Gods, Olivia," he spat quietly. "Not every sodding thing is about you."

The strangest thing happened then. She smiled. Not her manic, eerie, rictus sort of smile, or her mocking playful cruel smile. There was a genuine smile somewhere in the expression he saw Olivia make, and it was so strange and fascinating to him that he turned his head back to look at it fully. She brushed hair back from her face and squared her shoulders. "I can help you, Christopher," she said.

He frowned. "What?"

"I can help you," she said. She spread her hands on the table before her. "Summergrove. That's a lovely little town. Very peaceful. Very quiet. Very...nice." She turned her hands up so her palms were exposed, and then closed them into fists. "I know," she said, "because I grew up there."

"That's—"

"Quite the coincidence, I know. And, to continue the coincidence, my mother still lives there. Elouise Faraday. We have a large, well-established orchard. A full staff and a whole crew of pickers and planters. It's safe, and quite lovely."

He peered at her, certain she'd finally gone quite mad. "What are you offering, Olivia?"

She cocked her head, and her smile took on a bit of its usual character, playful and teasing, but not mocking. "Exactly what it sounds like I'm offering, ninny. My mother is a woman of excellent character. You could send your sister to stay with her. She'd take very good care of her. The staff are all old faithfuls, so new faces trying to work their way in would be treated suspiciously. Whoever tried to come after your sister, they'd find it a right bloody task."

"I—" Chris shook his head, trying to get his bearing. He ran a hand through his hair. "I can't pay you."

"I'm not asking you to pay me."

"I don't understand. You would send my sister and me to your girlhood home, to live with your *mother*, and not ask for anything in return?"

Ah, but there Olivia shook her head, folding her lips together and dropping her eyes from his. "I didn't say you," she said quietly. "And I didn't say for nothing in return."

He opened his mouth to ask what she was thinking about...but he realized he already knew. He closed his mouth. Shook his head. "Why?" he asked, and he found, as he did so, that he really, truly wanted to know. "Why does it have to be me? Why does it matter? I'm completely bloody replaceable, Olivia. You have to know that. How many assistants have you gone through? Why do you *care*?"

Olivia took a deep breath. She folded her hands and turned up her chin. "You're good at it," she said.

"I'm not."

"You're a fast weaver. Fastest I've seen."

"Does that matter so much to you as this?"

"You're quick-witted."

"And yet you're always ahead of me."

"You have a strong stomach."

"You're a bloody buggering *liar*, Olivia Faraday. I'm a sodding *mess* when you put me with a—*Gods*." The image of Fernand's ashen face flashed up before his eyes, and Chris staggered with the force of it. "Gods," he repeated, quieter. He put his face in his hands for only seconds before raising his head to stare at Olivia right in the eyes. She flinched from his gaze, moved as if she'd look away, but then didn't. "I want to know why you want me so badly," Christopher said. "I want to know why it matters to you enough you'd do something like *this* just to keep me?"

And Olivia Faraday's eyes flickered down to where her hands curled together on the table. Her mouth moved, but no sound came out. She took a deep breath, and when she let it out, it trembled, just a little. "Because, Mister Buckley," she said quietly, "you're the only one, the *only* one, who looks at me and doesn't see a monster."

Chris pressed his hand to his forehead. He felt hot. He felt cold. He felt…drowned. There were too many things scattered around his head, too many things that were too large and too unwieldy to go into their cupboards. "I want to be with my sister," he said pleadingly. "I need to be there with her, guiding her. Helping her. *Being* with her. Don't you see that? Don't you *understand* that? She's everything to me."

But Olivia's vulnerability folded back under the surface. Her hands fisted and her eyes went cold. "The terms aren't negotiable," she said, jutting her chin forward.

"If you want me not to think of you as a monster," Chris snapped, "you won't act like one."

Olivia Faraday stood up. Despite her crushed leg, she moved with the grace of an Old Blood Duchess while she reached for her crutches and arranged herself. She looked down her nose at him, and regardless of her size, she seemed a thousand feet tall. "Make your choice, Mister Buckley," she said simply. "I'm sure you'll actually find it quite an easy one." And with that, she hobbled from the room, shutting the door behind her.

Chris pressed his forehead against the wood of the table. He would have screamed his frustration, stood up and tore apart the room, if it would have done any good. He'd never been one for grand gestures of rage, not even with his father, not even the night of the Floating Castle.

He thought back to that night, now. Not the events that had spiralling outwards like an impossible whirlwind after he'd seen the Castle give its first shudder, but to the night before. For once, he didn't think of his father, but of his mother. He remembered Julia brushing hair back from his forehead, leaning down to kiss him gently. She'd sang to him a little song before she'd left, and told him to remember that no matter how he blustered and raged, his father loved him very much. She'd waved at him from the doorway while Michael had called from the first floor, his powerful voice booming all the way up. Julia Buckley had been his rock, his anchor, his lighthouse in a storm and the very centre of his universe. And somehow, the morning after the Castle fell and she was gone forever, life had managed to continue without her. *He* had managed to continue without her.

How had he done that, he wondered?

But he knew the answer even as he asked the question, just as he'd known what he'd do about Olivia's proposal from the moment she'd made it.

He'd adapted, of course. Because things either adapted and survived, or they didn't and blew away on the wind.

EPILOGUE

Olivia Faraday spun her parasol as she watched.

Her assistant embraced his little sister fiercely, holding her to him as if somehow, he could stop her from getting on the train and smokestacking away into the distance. She buried her face into his neck, eyes tightly closed, and he threaded his fingers through her dark ringlets, turning his face in towards her. They spoke to one another, probably quite loudly, but the salamanders and cloudlings that made the trains run were *not* the quietest of beasts, and Olivia had made herself keep something resembling a respectful distance, and couldn't hear a word of it. Unfortunately.

She cocked her head, curiously trying to decide what it would like, loving someone that much. Mister Buckley had made it fairly clear his choice to return to her employ would not have been made if she hadn't dangled this ultimatum before his eyes, and she couldn't help but try and bend her ideals to the idea that someone could be important enough to give away. It was like watching a play in a foreign language.

"Last call," the conductor's voice boomed across the platform. "Last call for Gilton, Cardinalia, Summergrove, and Northshire! Last call!"

Christopher Buckley straightened. He gave one last, very professional farewell to his governess, who clasped his head and nodded her prim little head as though she were a sparrow indeed before gathering up her charge's things and taking hold of the girl, steering her towards their boarding platform. Mister Buckley did not, as Olivia might have, turn about and walk away, but rather, he waited, standing there with one hand clasped against his mouth, and he waited, and he waited, and he waited, long past when the girl and her caretaker could no longer be seen, long past when the train chugged off, long past, even, when the platform emptied and the caboose had long been gone.

Olivia, not given to sentimentality, was impatient enough to actually consider turning and leaving on her own, but she chose not to press her fortune with any particularly grand gestures of disdain. In fact, she did nothing, neither moving nor speaking, until Mister Buckley slowly and finally turned himself about and dragged himself over to her.

She could see from his face he was in some distress, but she chose not to say anything, unsure of whether or not anything was appropriate. While her instinct was usually to speak rather than hold her tongue, this...arrangement was delicate, still, and for once, she cared if she offended someone. So she simply dragged on her lace gloves and straightened her feathered hat, and waited, once again, for him to make the first move.

"They're gone," he said finally, eyes still staring out where they had last seen the train vanish.

"Yes," Olivia agreed.

"Rosemary...she..."

Olivia did not sigh or roll her eyes or make a joke, though all of those seemed like the most appealing courses of action. Rather, she smiled gently and laid a hand on Christopher's shoulder, and wondered how long she'd feel obligated to behave this way, and when she could go back to normal, instead. "She's going to have a lovely time in the country, I swear it. She'll just love my mother." And perhaps Elouise would love her back. There was a first time for everything.

Mister Buckley sighed. He closed his eyes. He was very melancholy in every way, but he did nod, and then they stood there, Olivia's hand resting awkwardly on his shoulder, for so long she wondered if the exchange had really been worth it after all.

And then he raised his head and met her eyes. "Well," he said, and smiled. It was a tight smile, a forced smile, a faked smile. But it was a smile. And that was a start. "What do we do now, Miss Faraday?"

"Now," she said, and looped her arm through his, turning away from the platform. "We wait for more murder."

ACKNOWLEDGEMENTS

When you've always been writing and never been published, you come up with all sorts of things you plan to say in your first set of acknowledgements. And then you go to actually write them and find you don't even know where to start. The strange thing about writing thanks for your first book is that you want to write thanks for everyone who's put you on the path to it. So I've done that.

The person I have to thank most is Elzie, who is the only reason anyone ever took a second look at this book. Without her constant support and love, it wouldn't exist, and without her heartlessly hilarious criticism, it wouldn't be any good.

Thanks to my beta readers who helped me immeasurably to get a sense of what I had when it was out of my head and on paper: Elzie, Dots, Mum, Will, and Meg.

All the folks on the business side who helped me get here definitely need mention, too: my amazing, wonderful, perfect agent, Caitlin McDonald, who was the first stranger to believe in this thing; Vicki Keire at Curiosity Quills, who loved it enough to bring me into the family; my talented and helpful editor, Chrystal Schleyer; my production guy and helping hand, Andrew Buckley; and Lisa, Nikki, and everyone else at CQ.

Thanks have to go to all my close friends who have been around every single day to listen to me chatter about the planning process, the writing process, the submission process, and the publishing process: Dots, Willfor, Elzie, Meg, Sara, Mike, Frozen, and Zap.

There's my family, of course. Thanks to Daddy, who's been reading to me since I was born. To Mum, who's read this book cover to cover more than anyone else, including me. To my sister, Erin, who was always the captive audience to my crazy stories and encouraged me since we were babies together, and my brother-in-law, Danny, who's learned quick to cheer when Kate calls with good news.

And the miscellaneous people: Doctor Dan, who I couldn't live without, Mrs. Artichuk, who taught me what I was capable of, Margaret Hanson-Clarke, who was my invaluable writing buddy all through my teenage years, the curators of numerous tumblr blogs filled with Edwardian fashion plates, who will never know just what a godsend they've been, and my favourite barista at the local Starbucks, who occasionally sneaks me a second refresher when I've been sitting at the same table for hours with my laptop.

ABOUT THE AUTHOR

Kate McIntyre was born and raised in the frigid white north, having spent her entire life in Moncton, New Brunswick. She learned to appreciate the quintesstial Canadian things: endless winters, self-deprecating jokes, the untamed wilderness, and excessive politeness. Somehow it was the latter that she chose to write about.

She has been writing since she was five years old and nothing has ever stopped her for long. Her first novel was about a lady mouse detective saving her turtle janitor boyfriend from kidnappers, so it's nice to know she always loved lady detectives. She is the proud author of sixteen embarrassing hidden novels and one publishable one.

Kate loves crochet, video games, board games, reading, and listening to bad pop music very loudly. She spends several months of the year in Illinois, and the rest of the time lives in a big country home with two cats who refuse to stay on diets and the world's friendliest dog.

THANK YOU FOR READING

Please visit http://curiosityquills.com/reader-survey
to share your reading experience with the author of
this book!

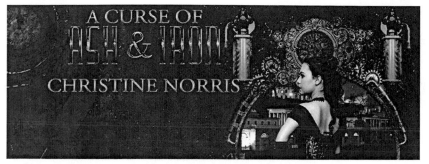

A Curse of Ash & Iron, by Christine Norris

Eleanor Banneker is under a spell, bewitched and enslaved by her evil stepmother. Her long-lost childhood friend, Benjamin Grimm, is the only person immune to the magic that binds her. Even if he doesn't believe in real magic, he cannot abandon her to her fate and must find a way to breach the spell - but time is running short. If he doesn't succeed before the clock strikes midnight on New Year's Eve, Ellie will be bound forever…

The Curse Merchant, by J.P. Sloan

Baltimore socialite Dorian Lake makes his living crafting hexes and charms, manipulating karma for those the system has failed. His business has been poached lately by corrupt soul monger Neil Osterhaus, who wouldn't be such a problem were it not for Carmen, Dorian's captivating ex-lover. She has sold her soul to Osterhaus, and needs Dorian's help to find a new soul to take her place. Hoping to win back her affections, Dorian must navigate Baltimore's occult underworld and decide how low he is willing to stoop in order to save Carmen from eternal damnation.

Nefertiti's Heart (The Artifact Hunters #1), by A.W. Exley

Cara Devon has always suffered curiosity and impetuousness, but tangling with a serial killer might cure that. Permanently. After the death of her father, Cara searches for his collection of priceless artifacts. Meanwhile a killer stalks among the nobility. Cara crosses paths with the murderer, both of them in pursuit of Nefertiti's Heart, a fabled mechanical diamond said to hold the key to immortality.

Shadows of Asphodel, by Karen Kincy

Ardis knows better than to save a man on the battlefield. Even if he manages to be a charming bastard while bleeding out in the snow. When she rescues Wendel, it isn't because he's devilishly handsome, but because he's a necromancer. His touch can revive the dead, and Ardis worries he will return from the grave to hunt her down.

Wendel pledges his undying loyalty to Ardis. She resists falling for him, no matter how hot the tension smolders between them. Especially when she discovers Wendel's scars run much deeper than his skin, and it might be too late to truly save him from himself.

CPSIA information can be obtained at www.ICGtesting.com
Printed in the USA
BVOW02s1438230715

410083BV00003B/126/P